THE COASTAL CRUISER

By Tony Gibbs

PRACTICAL SAILING
PILOT'S WORK BOOK/PILOT'S LOG BOOK
POWERBOATING
SAILING: A FIRST BOOK
BACKPACKING
NAVIGATION
ADVANCED SAILING

THE COASTAL CRUISER

A Complete Guide to the Design, Selection, Purchase, and Outfitting of Auxiliary Sailboats under 30 Feet–with a Portfolio of Successful Designs

by Tony Gibbs

W. W. NORTON & COMPANY
NEW YORK LONDON

Published simultaneously in Canada by George J. McLeod Limited, Toronto.
PRINTED IN THE UNITED STATES OF AMERICA

FIRST EDITION

Library of Congress Cataloging in Publication Data
Gibbs, Tony.
The coastal cruiser.
Bibliography: p.
Includes index.
1. Motor sailers. I. Title.
VM331.G48 1981 623.8'231 81-9620
ISBN 0-393-03267-1 AACR2

W. W. Norton & Company, Inc. 500 Fifth Avenue, New York, N.Y. 10110
W. W. Norton & Company Ltd. 37 Great Russell Street, London WC1B 3NU

1 2 3 4

for Elaine and Bill and Eric

•

Contents

Introduction

The Advantages and Drawbacks of Small Sailing Cruisers

The first question, of course, is "How small?" For this book, I've arbitrarily set an upper length limit of 30 feet overall. This is no magic number, nor even a scientifically selected one. Thirty-footers can be impossibly cramped or immensely capacious, but it has seemed to me for some time that the 30-foot barrier more often than not divides the larger small cruiser from the smaller large one. Or to put it more coherently, it separates the yacht where size is perhaps the first consideration in planning from the one where it is less important than some other characteristic.

Most cruising authorities seem to have done their recent voyaging in relatively large boats, 40 feet being almost a minimum. And for crossing oceans, anything much smaller will probably be prohibitively uncomfortable if not necessarily dangerous. My own cruising background (for the record) includes ownership of five quite different cruising sailboats less than 30 feet long—a 24′9″ sloop, a 29′7″ ketch, a 23′ catamaran sloop, a 17′ catboat, and a 21′ one-design racer-overnighter. I have also owned, or been possessed by, a 37′ 25,000-pound ketch, an experience that really requires another book—preferably illustrated by Charles Addams—to do it justice.

In addition, as an editor of *Motor Boating & Sailing* and later of *Yachting*, I've had a chance to cruise and sail aboard a wide variety of yachts, both American and foreign. Some of them are described in detail in Chapter III.

But this doesn't address the question of why someone should be cruising in a small yacht in the first place. For many people, to be sure, there's no choice: It's a small boat or none. For others, unconvinced that a larger yacht is necessary or desirable, it's a conscious decision. For many, even most, the under-30-footer is either a first cruising boat or—in an increasing number of cases—a first sailboat.

This book speaks, I hope, to all three groups, but it does presuppose that the reader knows how to sail. If you're one of the large number of people who buy cruising-size boats with the idea of teaching themselves to sail, my suggestion is to spend a week and a few bucks in a formal sailing school or, if you are lucky, find a skilled friend to break you in. While a small cruising yacht will seem very tiny indeed out on the open water, it can appear positively bargelike when maneuvering in constricted spaces.

What can an owner expect from the kind of boat we're talking about? In theory, a small cruiser should be capable of just about anything a large one can do, but in fact, it's a bit different. The average small cruising yacht can accommodate two to four people for up to a week without either complete replenishing or the probability of mutiny. For practical purposes, this kind of boat is ideal for weekending, being relatively simple to get under way, but not as easy to set up as a daysailer. Its range is anywhere from twenty-five to forty miles in a sailing day, but it can significantly expand that range if it's one of the many trailable yachts with a beam of eight feet or less.

In terms of performance, the smaller cruiser can be a sparkling, nimble sailer, but the more emphasis that's placed on accommodation, as we shall see, the more lumpish the boat is likely to become. This nearly inescapable fact derives from what makes up the true size of a boat. It's not just length overall, nor is it any other single measurement, but rather a combination of dimensions (the yacht's *cubic,* in boating shorthand), weight, and the disposition of space.

What should the prospective owner of an under-30-footer have a right to expect in his yacht? Some time ago, in the throes of a rare fit of efficiency, I set down a list of criteria for my next cruiser, which was to be a vessel of twenty-five to thirty feet. All the attributes I listed were possible in this size range, and while the reader's requirements may differ from mine, the following list suggests what can easily be found these days.

Basically, I was looking for fast, comfortable cruising for a regular crew of four (two adults and two others), plus the possibility of an occasional and hardy overnight guest or two. Good speed—by which I meant the ability to attain hull speed (see Chapter II) with relative ease—under working sail and/or engine was a must, as was decent performance on all points of sailing.

The boat had to be easy to handle under working sail (by which, these days, I meant main and #2 genoa), and should perform really well under light sails. She had to be capable of being single-handed (which is only partly a function of size), and had to have the directional stability that makes self-steering worth the money, without sacrificing too much nimbleness.

In terms of design, the hull had to be safe and comfortable under way, and reasonably quiet down below when the boat was under power. I wanted shallow draft—this being one of the things that is increasingly important in today's crowded anchorages—but I did not demand trailability. Others might, and it is worth searching out, though not, I think, an absolute requirement for most people in this size boat.

Under sail, I wanted the boat to be stiff rather than tender; that is, I was willing to settle for a somewhat abrupt and demanding return to uprightness, as opposed to the tendency to heel and then take off. I wanted low maintenance, which generally means little or no exterior wood, a bare minimum of complex hardware, and a simple rig. I prefer a big, uncluttered cockpit, recognizing the offshore dangers of it, but I also wanted no exterior vents into the hull, which suggested either a very small diesel or an outboard.

Down below, I demanded full, standing headroom, which I construe to mean my height plus two inches, in the main cabin at least. Because it means so much to so many, a separate head compartment was vital, preferably (but not necessarily) with its own washbasin. At that time, the great toilet controversy was at its height, and my feeling was that a portable toilet was the best compromise (see Chapter IX).

Beyond privacy in the head, I wanted separate fore and main cabins, even if the forecabin was nothing but a double berth. There had to be adequate stowage that was both dry and ventilated. In fact, the whole accommodation had to be capable of being ventilated, as there is no faster way to make a small cabin seem coffinlike than to cut off the flow of fresh air.

Finally, in the area of accommodation, the galley had to be adequate to the boat's mission: That meant an icebox that could keep a week's chilled provisions cold without immersing half of them, a two-burner, gimbaled stove; a sink into which it was possible to insert a decent-size pot; and a flat working surface separate from the companionway ladder, where no one was likely to put either his foot or his seat. There also had to be stowage for utensils and dry and canned food.

Because I feel strongly that a sailing cruiser—especially a small one—should be at least as much sailing machine as home afloat, I wanted a lot from the rig. Sharing with a number of the new breed of cruising-yacht architects the feeling that a boat should carry more sail area rather than less in her working rig (you can always take some off), I wanted my all-around performance criterion to be available with the minimum number of sails. Stowage of bulky items like sails is very restricted on a small cruiser, so I aimed for a sloop rig—hard to aim for much else in a boat under 30 feet—with roller-furling genoa. That meant only two more sails, small jib and spinnaker, were necessary for the basics of a first-class sail wardrobe. There are, of course, a number of other possibilities, discussed at length in Chapter IV.

Because the deck and cockpit of a small cruiser are necessarily quite small, there isn't the room for a brigade of deck apes to move about, yet many small cruisers' work areas are laid out as scaled-down versions of larger craft. I wanted a cruiser whose cockpit had been designed to be worked by one or two people, a vessel where going forward would be minimized, not because of danger but because of the bad effects of weight in the nose of the boat.

What surprised me, once I began trying to convert this list into a single yacht, was how many boats currently available came close to fitting my ideal profile. Since that time, only a few years back, more and more designs have appeared on the market with the qualities of imagination and forethought. This book is intended to help the reader organize, order, and recognize his own priorities in a small cruiser. That done, the remainder of the text will attempt to show how to purchase, rig, and equip such a boat.

Most people who've done even a small amount of serious boat investigation are aware that every boat is a compromise. It has been said that there are three basic aims of sailing yacht design—top performance, excellent accommodation, and low cost—and that a good designer can work any two of these three into a boat, but never all of them. Although somewhat overstated, there's a lot of truth in this provocative remark.

In a small cruiser, one has already made a decision toward low cost (relative to larger boats) and away from superior accommodation (again, relative to boats with more area to work in). What this means in terms of our three-part equation is that trying to rejigger the factors of cost and accommodation is even harder than usual: You spend a disproportionate amount of money to increase the interior luxury perceptibly. On the other hand, the amount of usable space and the level of creature comfort available today are light-years ahead of what designers offered at the turn of the century or even a few years ago, when boats were built of fiberglass, but designed by men who were still thinking in wood.

What's more, today's small yachts outperform their predecessors of the same size. It is fashionable in some cruising circles to extol the performance of ancient designs, what's generally summed up as "the Colin Archer school." Under certain conditions, virtually any boat will find her legs and take off, but for day-to-day sailing, week in and out through the season, the older designs just don't stack up. I hasten to add that this need not be a crippling disability: I once bought a gaff-rigged catboat at least partly because I liked the way a gaff rigger looks—and why not? I subsequently found the handsome looks weren't an adequate substitute for the ability to beat to windward efficiently, at least in my mind, but for two years the decision was in favor of character, whatever that is, over performance.

It seems to me important for a writer opening a book like this to lay as many of his prejudices as he's aware of before his audience. After twenty years of cruising, I've accumulated a fair bundle of them. Of course they all seem perfectly reasonable to me, but some—a few—may be questionable.

First, I have come to feel strongly that the first job of any sailing boat is to sail well, not only because good performance is in itself what being on the water under sail is about, but also because bad performance is often dangerous: A boat that winds up in irons when sloppily tacked, a boat that can't fight through a steep chop to get off a lee shore, a boat that doesn't handle reasonably well—that's a boat that will sooner or later get her skipper and crew into trouble.

Second, over the past few years it seems to me that the authorities have turned a legitimate search for safety afloat at least partly into a bureaucratic employment bureau. A few of the practices recommended in this book will be billed by some as "dangerous"; some may even skirt legality (and I'll identify them). These procedures are ones that, in my opinion, have stood the test of reality, even if they haven't matched the arbitrary standards set up by various government groups. My point here is not anarchy, but the firm conviction that the skipper has the duty and the privilege of making certain decisions afloat that no organization can take away.

Third, in many situations there may be several courses of action that are equally correct—or equally poor compromises. Books like this are too often prone to present "the answer." It seems to me that anyone who plans to take a boat to sea ought to be aware that in some crises there is no answer, or six answers. At the same time, it is usually the case that any plan is better than none at all, and I am a strong advocate of making one's action decisions beforehand, and then not second-guessing them in the heat of emergency.

Finally, I am not by temperament of experience a do-it-myselfer. This is a purely personal attitude, not meant to suggest that there's anything wrong with doing one's own work. Far from it. But because so many of my own experiences in this area have been disastrous, I tend to shy away from recommending that you should embark on major construction projects in your boat—unless, of course, you're more interested in building than in sailing.

THE COASTAL CRUISER

I

Design Parameters of the Small Cruiser

One of the greatest problems facing most boat designers is the contradiction between the need for a fast, handy hull on the one hand and a load-carrier on the other. These opposing demands are especially hard to reconcile in a small cruising yacht, in part at least because so much of the boat's contents are related to human dimensions, from headroom to appetite, which remain much the same regardless of boat size. So while it is a temptation for a designer to create a small cruiser by scaling down a larger one, this procedure is often a mistake. The proper small cruising sailboat is an independent creation.

It is, therefore, important for the prospective buyer to differentiate between a boat that is actually a shrunken version of a larger model in the same builder's fleet, and a small cruiser that has merely a family resemblance to a larger one. One of the most complete lines of cruiser-racers in the world, that of Canada's C&C Yachts, well illustrates this point: To the reasonably knowledgable, C&C boats of all sizes share a common, rakishly attractive appearance. Yet inside there are vast differences from size to size, as the accompanying illustrations of three of their boats demonstrate.

Accommodations

In the contest between performance and accommodation, let's first consider the latter, in its broadest sense.

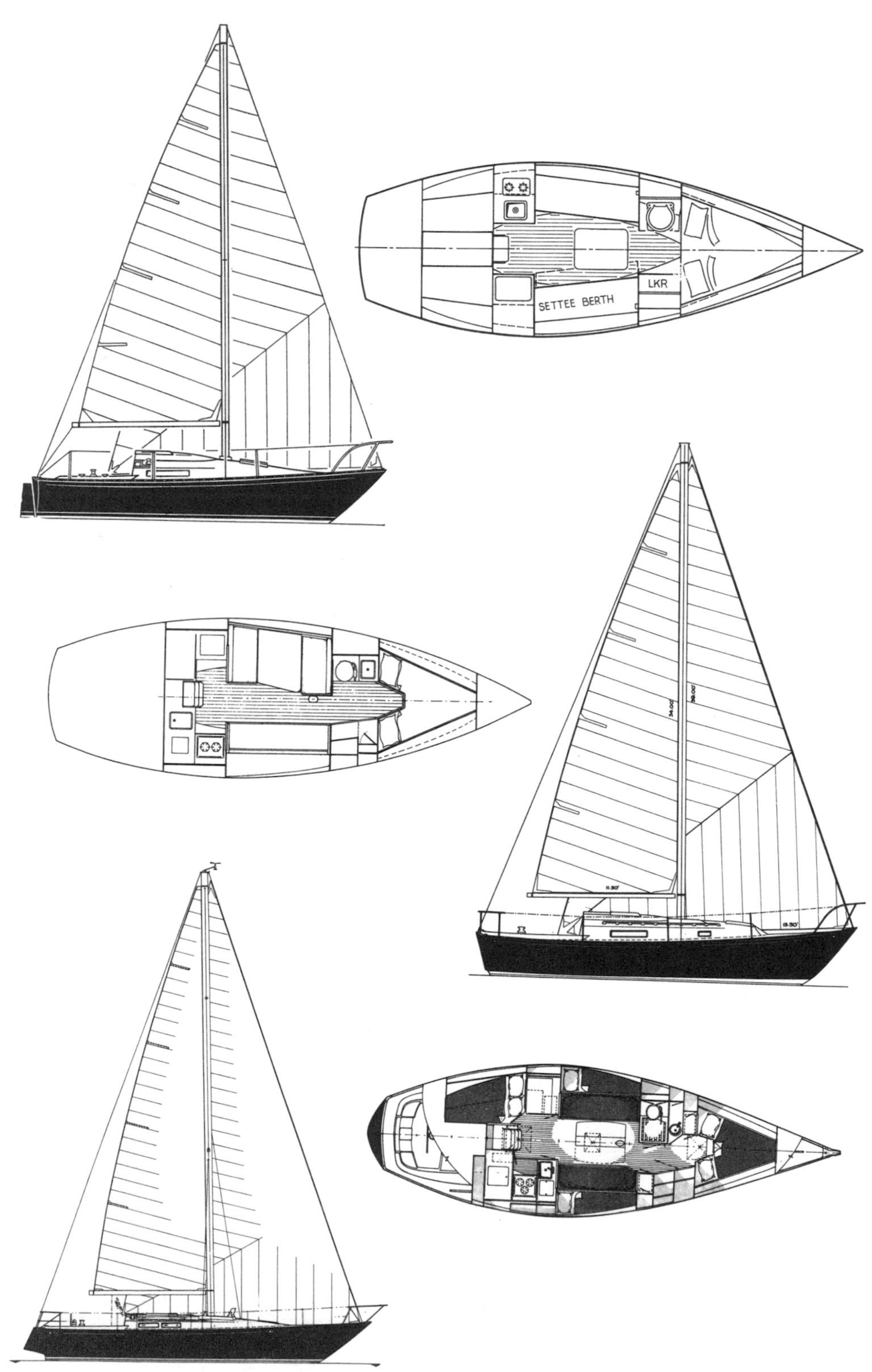

C&C 25, 30, and 38 illustrate the way accommodations jump as size increases.

The classic sailboat hull of the 1920s and '30s, with narrow beam, low freeboard, and long overhangs, is a terrible load-carrier. Only after World War II when yachting, and especially cruising, became a mass-market activity was there a commercial impetus to build small cruisers with decent performance and outstanding carrying capacity.

To get some idea of how far accommodation has come in the last thirty years it's only necessary to compare the three C&C yachts illustrated above with a wood-hulled yacht of the late 1940s, and then with a fiberglass cruiser of the 1960s, when designers were still groping to see what fiberglass as a material implied.

Loads in the hull

In calculating the optimum shape—and all shapes are compromises—of a given boat, the designer has to consider where the major loads will normally fall, and what kind of hull form will support them while not impeding the boat too much. For a small cruiser, with a normal crew of two to four, there are two big fixed loads and two movable ones.

Fixed loads consist of the engine and battery, which combined can average 100 to 500 pounds, and the fuel and water tanks, which may total 80 to 100 gallons—between 300 and 400 pounds. The movable weights are of course the crew—say anywhere between 300 and 750 pounds—and the gear, which can include sails, lines, ground tackle, electronics, tools—500 pounds doesn't seem too much to estimate. For a 30-footer, then, these weights can come close to a ton, probably a tenth or more of the vessel's total displacement, and thus are a force to be reckoned with.

Under way, which is the primary mode the architect has to worry about, one can normally assume that human weight will be concentrated aft, especially in a cruiser where the skipper cannot disperse his crew to trim the boat properly without risking revolt. In an inboard yacht, the engine and battery will normally live toward the stern, often under the forward end of the cockpit. The reasons are practical enough: Space directly beneath the cockpit sole in a small cruiser is waste area for most applications where one needs access from all sides. By placing the engine near its controls and propeller, one can reduce the chances of mechanical problems. Sealing off the engine in this relatively out-of-the-way spot keeps smell and noise to a minimum—although "minimum" may not be the word that leaps to the mind of a person who has been in a small boat's cabin when the auxiliary engine was running.

Outboards are a different situation. Aboard many small outboard-equipped racers, the engine is struck below as a matter of course, but in most cruising yachts the outboard lives (and sometimes dies) clamped to the extreme after end of the boat, while its 6-gallon tanks and 12-volt starting battery occupy

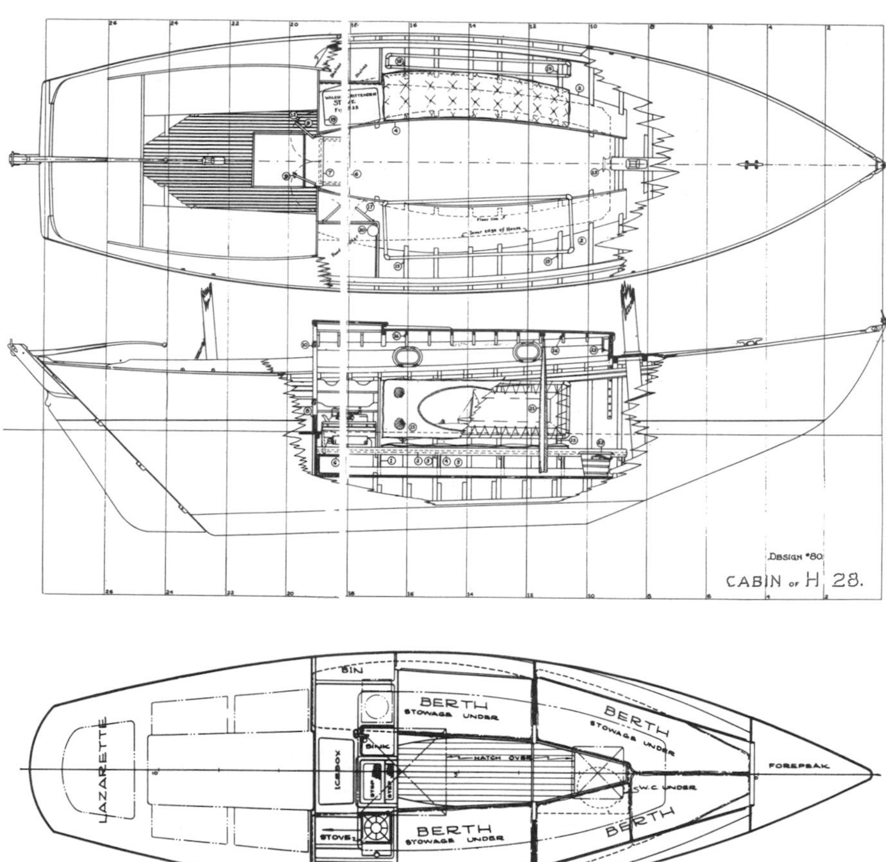

Interior arrangement of the H-28 ketch, designed by L. Francis Herreshoff for construction in wood. She featured two fold-down berths, a bucket head and a primitive galley. Seafarer's Meridian, a 24′9″ sloop designed by Philip L. Rhodes, had four berths, two of them extending under the galley counter. But there was no separate head and the icebox was under the bridge deck.

space somewhere in the cockpit. An electric-start outboard of 10 or 15 hp. weighs at least 75 pounds, and placing this weight at the very stern means that extended overhangs are quite out of the question: There must be something below the engine to support its weight and vibration, and some contact aft between hull and water. As a general rule, fuel and water tanks are best located in the middle of the yacht, for several good reasons. To begin with, the engine, the head and the galley are all likely to be within the central half of the boat's overall length, so that the required fuel and water lines can be that much shorter with tanks amidships. In addition, the boat is likely to be widest and

C&C 24 sailing with a small Mercury on the transom bracket. To be out of the water when the boat is well heeled on starboard tack, the motor must be capable of a high tilt.

deepest slightly aft of her longitudinal midpoint, allowing more space for tankage.

A popular spot for at least one major tank is right on top of the ballast keel, below the floorboards. Not only does this keep weight low in the boat, magnifying the effect of the ballast, but it is also a location that's moderately accessible for cleaning, and a damp area not much good for anything else in a weekender. Other likely spots are below the pair of berths that normally flank the main cabin sole. This is a less ideal place, simply because underberth tankage is measurably higher than keel-top tankage, and also because it uses up dry, accessible space that is more conveniently employed for clothing, bedding, tools, and other materiel used all the time.

In older boats especially, fuel tanks are frequently located under the cockpit sole, adjacent to the engine. Often the fuel fill is a screw cap in the sole itself, which has always seemed a questionable practice to me, an invitation to water in the fuel. And in some boats, the main or alternate water tanks are placed forward of the customary bow V-berths. When a boat has relatively full, buoyant bows this may be acceptable, but a major tank all the way forward can make a considerable difference in a small cruiser's trim—although the space forward of the V-berth join is difficult to utilize for day-to-day stowage.

The classic recipe for carrying weights in a boat is to keep them centralized and low down. Placing weight low is a fairly obvious precaution: The more weight below the waterline, the less ballast (for a given hull and rig shape) is required to keep the vessel upright. The argument for centralizing weights is a bit more complicated, and has mainly to do with lessening a boat's tendency to pitch.

Controlling pitching

A boat pitches when her bow rises to meet an oncoming sea and then crashes down as that sea passes. Except for submarines, all vessels pitch to a greater or lesser degree, but there are ways of minimizing the problem—and problem it is, for when a boat's pitching becomes synchronized with the approaching seas so that a rhythmic up-and-down motion develops, it can stop her in her tracks.

The first and basic step in preventing uncontrollable pitching is in the design of the boat herself. A boat with full, buoyant bows and a narrow stern—the classic "cod's head and mackerel stern" shape—is least resistant to savage pitching: When her bow is lifted by the seas, this boat's stern, with minimal buoyancy, drops easily. In short, steep seas, such a boat can be truly miserable (although in flat waters she may perform well).

Conversely, a vessel with a narrow, fine bow and a relatively wide stern will resist pitching: Not only will the bow not lift as readily as a fuller forebody, but the buoyant stern will damp whatever pitching begins. As in all things, of course, there is a price to be paid. The finer bow will not support so much load forward, either permanent stowage or working crew, and if the fine bow does not lift over waves, it is likely to go right on through them, which makes for a wet boat.

Design aside, the disposition of a boat's cargo (be it human or inanimate) will also affect her tendency to pitch. By concentrating loads amidships, one leaves the ends of the boat light, increasing their buoyancy. The boat will rise quickly and subside quickly, and the only problem will be preventing her from getting into a hobby-horsing rhythm when the wave period matches the boat's waterline length. In this situation, one fast remedy is to change heading slightly, which will have the effect of lengthening or shortening the waves relative to the boat's length.

Carrying substantial weights in the bow and stern will effectively slow the boat's response to the seas, and will also make that response easier and less

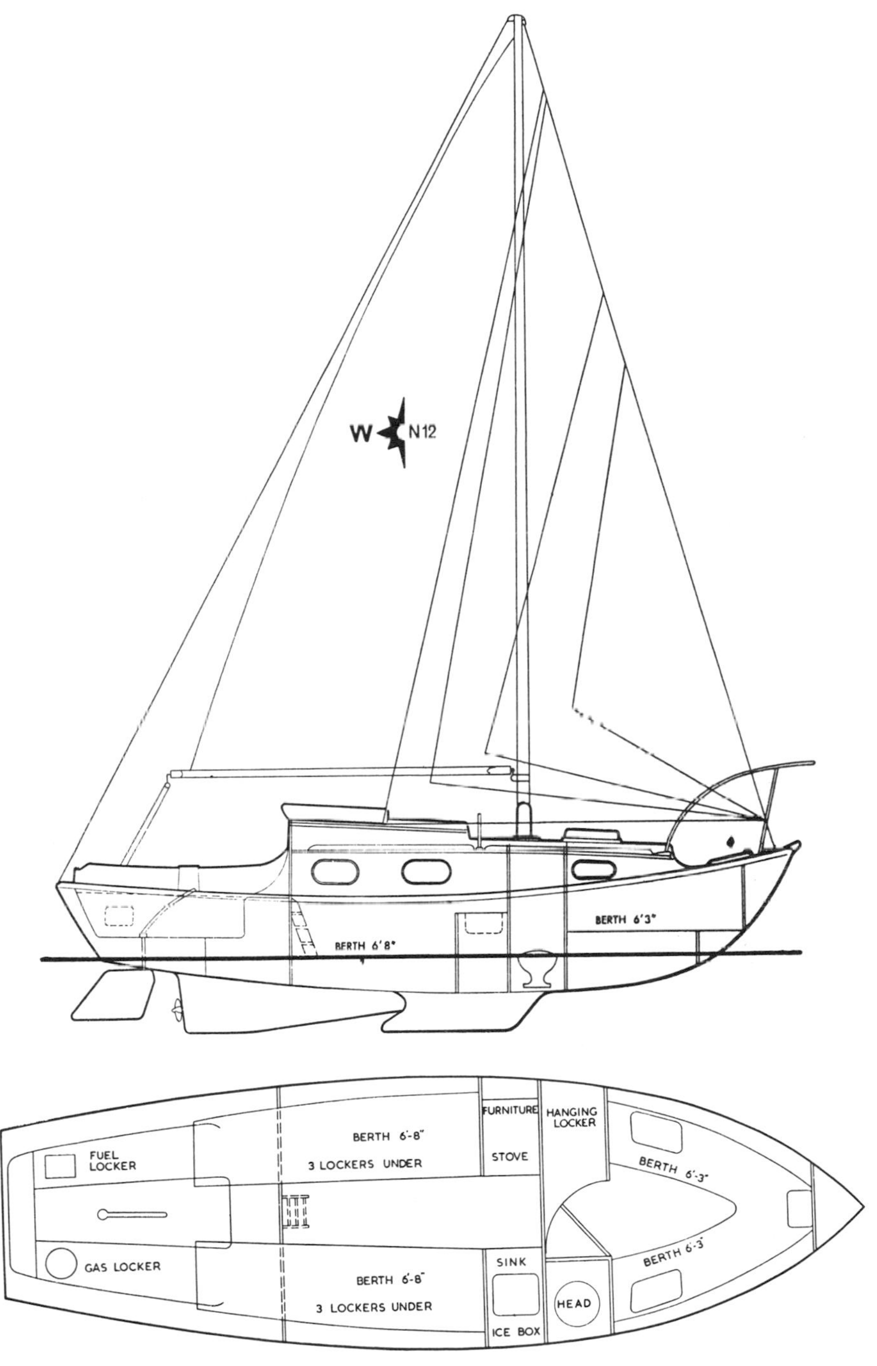

Westerly Nomad twin-keeler: A classic example of the cod's-head–mackerel-stern hull shape.

abrupt. In seas of a certain size, however, a bow- and stern-heavy boat can begin a nearly uncontrollable pitching reinforced by the weights fore and aft.

The concept of hull speed

The average cruising boat works within the flexible limitations of the speed: length ratio. In order to have some idea of how fast a given boat is able to go (quite different from how fast she usually *does* sail), it may help to examine the attributes of the speed:length ratio.

Most people who have examined yacht design even slightly have encountered the term *hull speed.* This is a useful, if overworked, term that describes the maximum potential speed through the water of a cruising yacht. Unlike some formulas connected with boating, the calculation for hull speed is not an absolute, but before looking more closely at it, let's examine why there is such a thing as a maximum potential speed at all.

Reasonably enough, the water displaced by a hull moving through water has to go somewhere, and in so doing, it forms waves—not the familiar V-shaped wake one associates with moving boats, but a wave train, or group, moving along with the boat and at the same speed. These waves can be seen, looking astern of a boat, as a series of following swells at right angles to the yacht's centerline. The speed of waves is directly related to the distance between crests: The slower the wave, the closer together are the crests, and at low speeds, a boat's wave train, starting at the first or bow wave, may comprise four or five small waves along the length of the waterline.

As the boat, and its associated waves, gather speed, the crests move farther apart, until at some point there is one crest at the bow and another at the stern, with the boat more or less suspended between them. The boat cannot, without a great increase in power, climb over the bow wave and escape its own wave train. And this maximum speed, at which the boat more or less falls into a hole of its own creation, is hull speed.

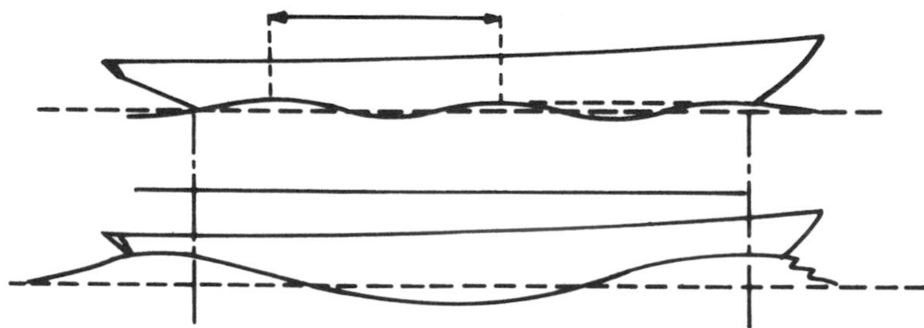

As a boat approaches hull speed, the wave system extends and deepens until she is traveling between two crests.

The vast majority of sailing cruisers cannot get out except when surfing, caught up in the momentary express-train ride on a wave from an outside source—a wind-driven sea or another boat's wake.

Hull speed is directly related to a boat's waterline length (LWL). Most authorities feel that a boat can achieve a maximum speed in knots somewhere between 1.25 and 1.5 times the square root of its waterline length in feet, or 1.25 $\sqrt{LWL}$ to 1.5 $\sqrt{LWL}$. In terms of the real world, take as an instance the Cape Dory 28, a boat with a waterline length of 22′2½″. The square root of this waterline is 4.7: multiply it by 1.25, and the result is 5.9 knots; multiply by 1.5, and you have a shade over 7 knots.

Two additional factors make the calculation of hull speed less than straightforward. To begin with, a boat's length overall (LOA) is always greater than its waterline, and as a boat heels, it increases its effective waterline. A boat going hell-for-leather at nearly hull speed is likely to have a somewhat extended waterline and thus a greater potential maximum speed.

Consider our example again: The Cape Dory 28 has an LOA of 28′1¼″. Say that as it nears hull speed, laid over on a screaming reach, the waterline extends to 25 feet. This gives us a new hull speed of 6.25–7.5 knots (and incidentally accounts for at least some of the tall stories told by skippers).

The second factor affecting hull speed is the displacement of the boat. Lengths being equal, a heavier, beamier boat makes a bigger wave train than a lighter one does. And a more substantial wave system restricts the boat's ability to get up to the high end of the hull speed range.

Speed:length ratio

In fact, however, the attainment of hull speed is a sometime thing, which brings us back to the speed:length ratio: This term merely expresses the ratio between a boat's speed in knots *at the moment of description* and her waterline length in feet. Thus, any boat has an infinite number of speed:length ratios, from 0 up to hull speed (or beyond).

Alas, the average cruiser does not get up to hull speed more than a couple of times in a sailing year, if that, and the experience is often so strenuous that the crew wants no more of it. In terms of hard reality, achieving a speed:length ratio of 1.0—5 knots for a boat with a 25-foot waterline—is good going. Averaging 0.7 to 0.9 is more likely over a long voyage where one will encounter a number of different points of sailing. Going to windward, which is hardest on the crew if not on the boat, normally results in a speed:length ratio of around 0.6—and that, bear in mind, is speed through the water, not necessarily speed over the bottom or speed directly toward one's objective.

If the target of one's cruise is directly to windward, the distance actually sailed is going to be something like two-fifths more than the straight-line distance; *and* at a speed of perhaps half the boat's potential. Since most people think of covering distance in automobile terms, the distance a sailing yacht can cover is likely to appear pathetic by comparison. The modern sailing cruiser can, without converting one's family into foredeck apes, aim at speeds measurably higher over the day's run than older boats could achieve. Part of this is simply progress in yacht design per se. Part of it is recognition that most pleasure sailing is done when winds and seas are mild, and thus a boat need not be built and rigged to cope with survival storms while traversing Chesapeake Bay or the Thames Estuary.

But the factors that make for good light-air performance are quite different from those conducive to heavy-weather speed. Nor is speed the only element of performance, at least as far as a cruiser is concerned. The principal attribute of a lightweight boat with lots of sail is that it takes relatively little breeze to get her going, and because she does not create as deep or pronounced a wave system, she can edge up more easily toward her maximum hull speed than can a heavy yacht of the same waterline. At the same time, a lightweight boat loses momentum as fast as she gains it, and she is likely to stall out between puffs unless she is nimble as well as light.

Forces that slow the boat

The question obviously arises: What is a light or a heavy boat? It is, of course, largely relative, and once again we come up against the difficulty of approximating a complicated description with a relatively simple formula. The one that's used here is called the displacement:length ratio (often abbreviated D:L), and is arrived at through the formula $\frac{D}{(.01\ LWL)^3}$, where D equals the yacht's displacement in long tons of 2,240 pounds each, and LWL is the yacht's waterline length in feet. Thus, a boat 20 feet on the waterline with a displacement of 5,000 pounds would have a D:L of 279 (2.23 divided by .008).

Fashions in weight change with time, and we are in a generally lightweight phase at this point, for two good reasons. First is the repeatedly demonstrated fact that lightweight boats are snappier performers by and large than heavyweights. Second is that (thanks to fiberglass) it no longer requires exquisite craftsmanship to build a seaworthy lightweight, and weight equals materials, which equal money.

It is hard to draw absolute dividing lines, but a D:L of 325 seems a reasonable border between medium and heavy displacement boats. One of the best of the heavy-displacement designers, for example, is Carl Alberg, whose solidly built Cape Dory designs consistently come in with D:Ls over 350. Perhaps the highest D:L in standard stock designs is that of the 13,500-pound Westsail 28, which equals 464. The Fairways Fisher 30, although quite heavy, has a D:L of 416, thanks to her long waterline.

At the other end of the spectrum are the ultralight racers and racer-cruisers.

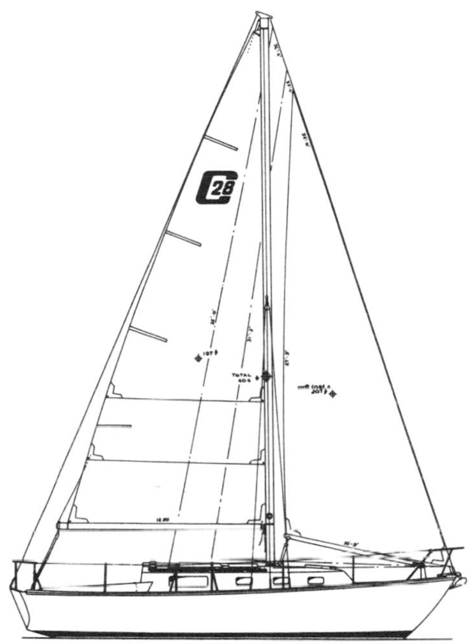

Alberg-designed Cape Dory 28, with a displacement:length ratio of 358, is typical of heavy-displacement craft.

An excellent example is the Bill Lee–designed Santa Cruz 27; with her LWL of 24 and her displacement of 3,000 pounds, she comes in with a D:L of 97. For most purposes, anything with a D:L of 150 or less, such as the Dockrell 22 (139), is extremely light. One hundred and fifty to 200 (Paceship 23, Ranger 23, Westerly GK 29, O'Day 22) is light for a racer and very light for a cruiser.

Two hundred to 250 used to be considered a moderate ratio for a racer and light for a cruiser. Now it's more like medium for both. In this D:L slot fall such standards as the twin-keel Vivacity 24, Westerly GK 24, Paceship 26, Albin 79, O'Day 30, Nicholson 27, Pearson 26, and Islander 26. Moderately heavy racers and cruisers run between 250 and 325, and include the C&C 29, Nor'Sea 27, Marshall 22 catboat, and Morgan Out Island 30.

But displacement:length ratio isn't the whole story. All it suggests is that a boat is heavy or light for her effective length, and that she will (or won't) require a good press of sail to move her along speedily. Another way of judging potential in a design is the sail area:displacement ratio, a useful second step to apply to a boat whose D:L you know.

The math here is rather more complex, and requires a scientific calculator to work out. But since such machines are increasingly common, here's the formula: $\frac{\text{SA}}{(\text{disp. cu. ft.})^{2/3}}$. In English, you divide the measured sail area in square feet by the yacht's displacement in cubic feet to the two-thirds power:

To find this latter figure, divide the boat's displacement by 64.05 (the weight of a cubic foot of salt water) to obtain displacement in cubic feet. Then square that figure, and take the cube root of the result.

It sounds more complex than it is—with the proper machinery, anyway. Take an older but still popular cruiser-racer, the Tartan 27, a fairly hefty boat with a displacement of 6,875 pounds and a sail area of 372 sq. ft. Her SA:Disp. ratio is 16.5. And what is the significance of that?

Well, it puts the boat fairly in among the racers: SA:Disp. ratios of 8 to 14 may be considered motorsailers, or at least rather lightly canvased for their displacement; cruising boats generally run between 14 and 16, and racers are 16 to 17.5.

One final piece of shorthand, or maybe sleight-of-hand. This is the so-called Bruce number, and is sometimes useful as a simplified way of appraising sail area and displacement. Simply divide the square root of the sail area (in square feet) by the cube root of the displacement in pounds: $\frac{\sqrt{SA}}{\sqrt[3]{Disp.}}$. A Bruce number of 1.0 is often considered the dividing line between fast and slow boats. Our Tartan 27, with a long record of racing successes, has a Bruce number of 1.01 (and in this calculation, the second place after the decimal is meaningful). Bear in mind that all three of these convenient formulas—D:L, SA:Disp., and Bruce number—are only indicators. Their validity can be compromised by a good or bad hull shape or sail plan, or simply by poor sailing.

Aside from displacement, length, and sail area, there are different forces that act to hold back a boat going at an S:L of 0.6 as opposed to one going at an

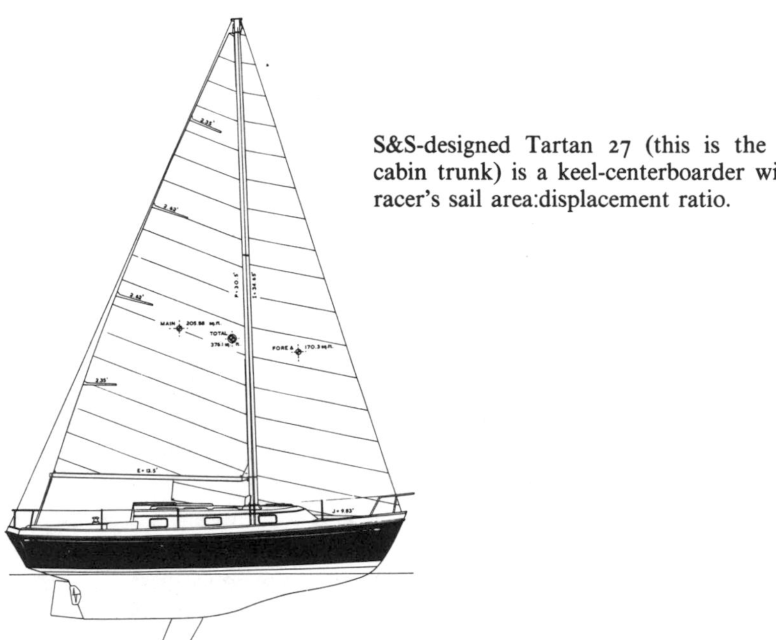

S&S-designed Tartan 27 (this is the new cabin trunk) is a keel-centerboarder with a racer's sail area:displacement ratio.

S:L of 1.2. The hull is the part of the yacht restricting speed, and the factors contributing to slowness go by the collective name of *resistance.*

While there are several such factors, two stand out. One is wave-making, discussed above. Tests suggest that for medium- and heavy-displacement yachts, wave-making becomes an important factor at S:Ls of 0.9 or so and above. Below those speeds, surface friction of water on the hull accounts for most of the resistance. In an ultralight racer-cruiser, the British authority Douglas Phillips-Birt calculated that skin friction constitutes 75 percent of the boat's total resistance at an S:L of 0.8; 70 percent at 0.9; 65 percent at 1.0; 51 percent at 1.1; and 37 percent at 1.2. For a heavier displacement yacht, skin friction may be something less of a factor—75 percent of the total resistance at an S:L of 0.4, and only 50 percent at an S:L of 0.9. It should be borne in mind, however, that the entire amount of resistance is climbing as boat speed increases; it's just that skin friction increases less rapidly than wave resistance, beyond a certain point.

The factors involved in skin friction are fairly obvious if one stops to think about them for a minute: Besides boat speed, they comprise the amount of wetted surface, smoothness of surface, and length of surface. As we shall see a bit further on, designers have been whittling away at wetted surface over the past few decades until, in some boats, they have reached what appears to be an irreducible minimum. Some have said that certain designs go too far to eliminate drag in this respect, and do not leave enough boat in the water for proper balance and stability under sail.

At the same time, designers have no choice but to accept the increases in

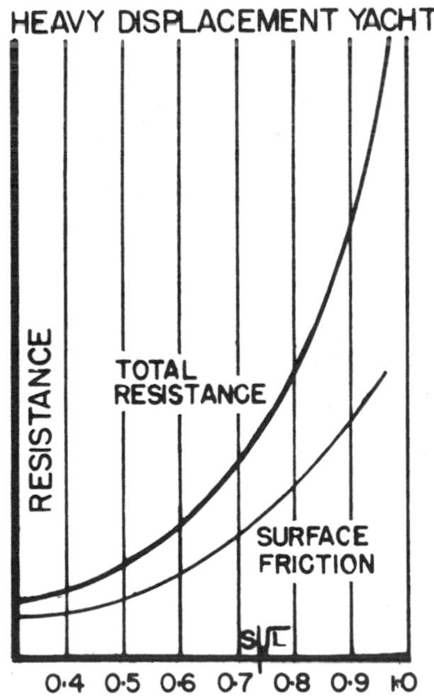

Skin friction as a component of total resistance, at various speed:length ratios.

skin friction that go along with increased speed and waterline length (although it may be comforting to owners of larger boats to know that a longer hull's resistance is not proportionally greater than a short one's).

Most owners, especially racers, concentrate on hull smoothness in their attempts to reduce skin friction. As far as cruising skippers are concerned, a hull that is smooth to the touch, with no adhering slime or unnecessary projections, seems the best that can reasonably be hoped for. The reasons have to do with the nature of skin friction on boat hulls. As a boat moves through the water, it does not simply cut through, as a knife blade cuts through a solid. Instead, a hull carries along with it a thin film of water—the boundary layer—moving at varying speeds. The British designer Maurice Griffiths has estimated that the water layer alongside the boat, a few thousandths of an inch in thickness, is moving at very nearly the same speed as the hull itself. The entire boundary layer that is moving in the same direction as the boat will

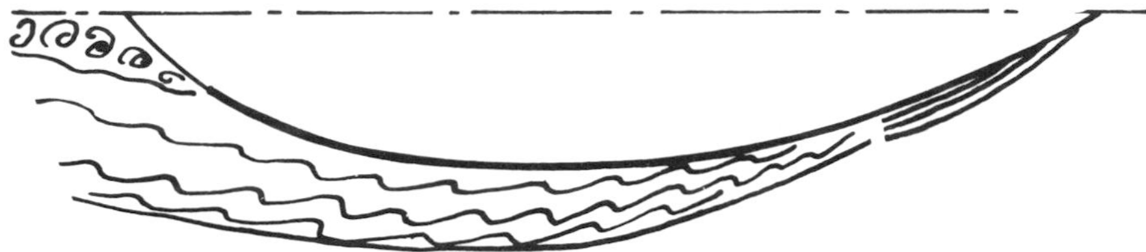

Laminar flow, a condition in which the boundary layer of water is undisturbed by friction-created turbulence, may be achieved over the forward part of the hull.

increase in thickness moving from bow to stern, and reaches a maximum width of perhaps five inches.

There is a direct connection between the amount of turbulence created by a hull's passage through the water and that hull's surface smoothness (not to mention its shape—abrupt humps and lumps cause a turbulence of their own). A boat with a very smooth and well-designed hull, moving at normal displacement speeds, may achieve a condition over the forward part of the underbody called *laminar flow.* What this means is that the boundary layer is undisturbed by friction-created turbulence and divides into unmixing, parallel layers, each one from the hull outward moving at a slightly reduced speed. The frictional resistance that remains derives from shearing between the layers and produces only a sixth as much drag (according to Griffiths) as ordinary turbulent flow.

Besides the forward part of the hull, laminar flow now seems achievable over most of a fin keel and centerboard. Without a major breakthrough—and one does not seem likely in the foreseeable future—it seems unlikely that much more can be done to reduce skin friction, and most skippers will be content to live with it.

Weatherliness and draft

One area in which cruising sailors frequently yield something for nothing —or very nearly—is in the search for shallow draft. It has become an article of faith with many yachtsmen that shoal draft is automatically an asset of great value.

But for boats in the size range we're talking about here, draft is just one factor, and not necessarily the most important. Besides, design advances over the last decade and a half have made it possible to have monohull centerboard yachts of startlingly shoal draft—see the Paceship 26 in Chapter III, for instance—and of course shallow draft, with or without boards, has long been a mark of multihulls.

Other things being equal, a relatively deep, finely shaped fin is the most efficient appendage for good windward performance. A centerboard is probably next best, with a shoal keel and twin keels following in that order. In a production 30-footer these days, a keel boat's draft is likely to be on the order of 4′6″ or less, with slightly deeper draft on racing hulls and very traditional types. At the same time, more and more production builders are providing both keel and centerboard versions of the same hull, or shoal and deep keels with perhaps a foot of draft difference between them.

So if you live in an area where four and a half feet is not a problem, then a keel boat will probably give you best sailing performance. If your area has large patches of water five feet deep and less, then a centerboard, stub keel, or multihull will probably give you most peace of mind. Before deciding, though, it's worth taking the time to check your area by investing in the local small craft or harbor chart and looking for yourself. It may also help to take an informal census of popular boat types in your area, especially those types that have been popular for more than a season or two: Today's hot boat may be great, but for long-term value the classes that have a large number of representatives and relatively few entries in the for-sale columns at local brokerages are the best bets.

Of course if you plan to trailer your yacht, then a centerboard or swing keel is simply a must. For more detail on the requirements of trailering, see Chapter XI.

Underwater hull shape

Cruising yachts evolved in part from fishing craft and in part from assorted other small boats, most notably the fast and seaworthy pilot schooners that had to keep the sea in all seasons and weathers.

It was known that deep-draft vessels had less tendency to slide off to leeward than did shoal-draft ones, but eventually it was discovered that one could cut away the underbody substantially without compromising a boat's windward ability. Indeed, the increase in speed caused by the decrease of wetted surface made for far faster craft and a hull form that is still seen today in such classics as the Folkboat.

Cutting away the hull forward loses a little buoyancy at the bows, but very little usable interior space, and the gain in performance is more than enough to make up for any loss in carrying power. A similar hull with somewhat less draft and less wetted surface is the keel-centerboard hull, where the board is entirely contained in a slot in the keel and thus does not protrude above the cabin floorboards.

The next stage in hull design goes to a pure fin for the keel, often with a spade rudder aft at the end of the waterline. The remainder of the underbody is cut away as much as possible, with increased beam providing the buoyancy lost as the hull's depth is reduced. A fin keel or a centerboard that forms a retractable fin, plus a spade-type rudder, makes for a very maneuverable boat that will pivot fast and recover quickly. In certain high-wind conditions, the rudder will emerge as the boat heels, causing a loss of steering control, runaways, and even broaches when too much sail is carried too long. By and large, however, the "big dinghy" type of hull, with wide beam and high freeboard, has proved itself as a versatile cruiser-racer, especially in the size range where cubic inches of accommodation count as much as performance.

A variant hull type mentioned above is the swing keel, which really exists as an offshoot of the trailerable sailboat boom. Boats of this type have a long, fin-shaped ballast keel pivoted at its forward end. It retracts into the accommodation or into a stub keel. It is unlike the centerboard, which it otherwise resembles, in that it is heavily weighted—providing ballast between 25 and 30 percent of the total displacement—and locked either all the way up or all the way down.

Swing keelers are often shaped like big dinghies and can sail, if properly tuned and rigged, like good daysailers. Because they're designed for trailering, they're limited to an eight-foot beam by the U.S. laws regarding highway trailering without special permits. They often have kickup rudders, and their underbodies are shaped to be launched and recovered with reasonable ease. Anyone considering such a boat would be well advised to make sure he or she has the appropriate trailer and access to hard-surface ramps. A trial launch and recovery is also a good idea. The drop-keel or daggerboard cruiser-racer (like the AMF 2100) is much the same kind of boat, although its ballast may be molded into the hull.

About the only other hull type seen in monohulls is the twin-keel cruiser. This vessel usually has an orthodox hull, rather heavily constructed, with a protective skeg for the rudder. But its most salient attribute is the pair of fin or bilge keels, angled at about 30 degrees to each other, that allow the boat to sit on the bottom (or "take the ground," as the British say). Twin-keel

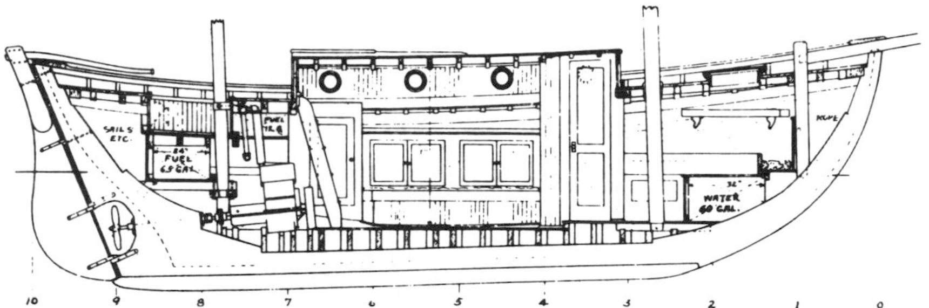

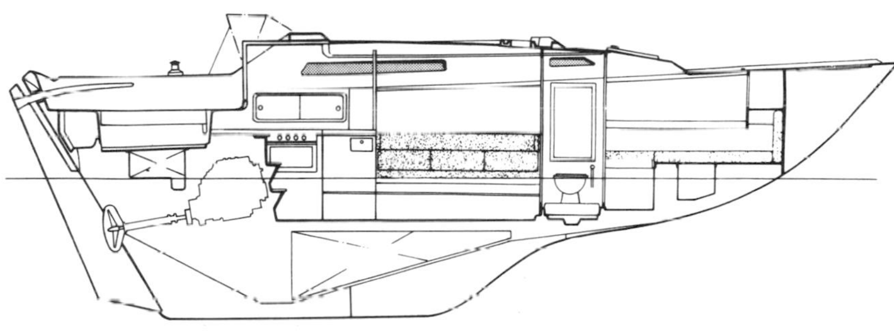

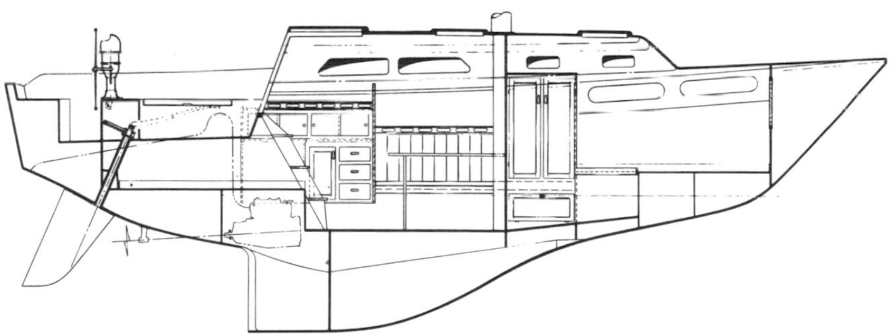

Transition of the hull profile: Earliest yachts were derived from load-carrying workboats, as was the Tahiti ketch. Later, it was found that some lateral plane could be sacrificed by cutting away forefoot area, as in the Nicholson 31. Semifin keel with spade rudder eliminates even more underwater surface, shown here in the Bruce King–designed Ericson 29.

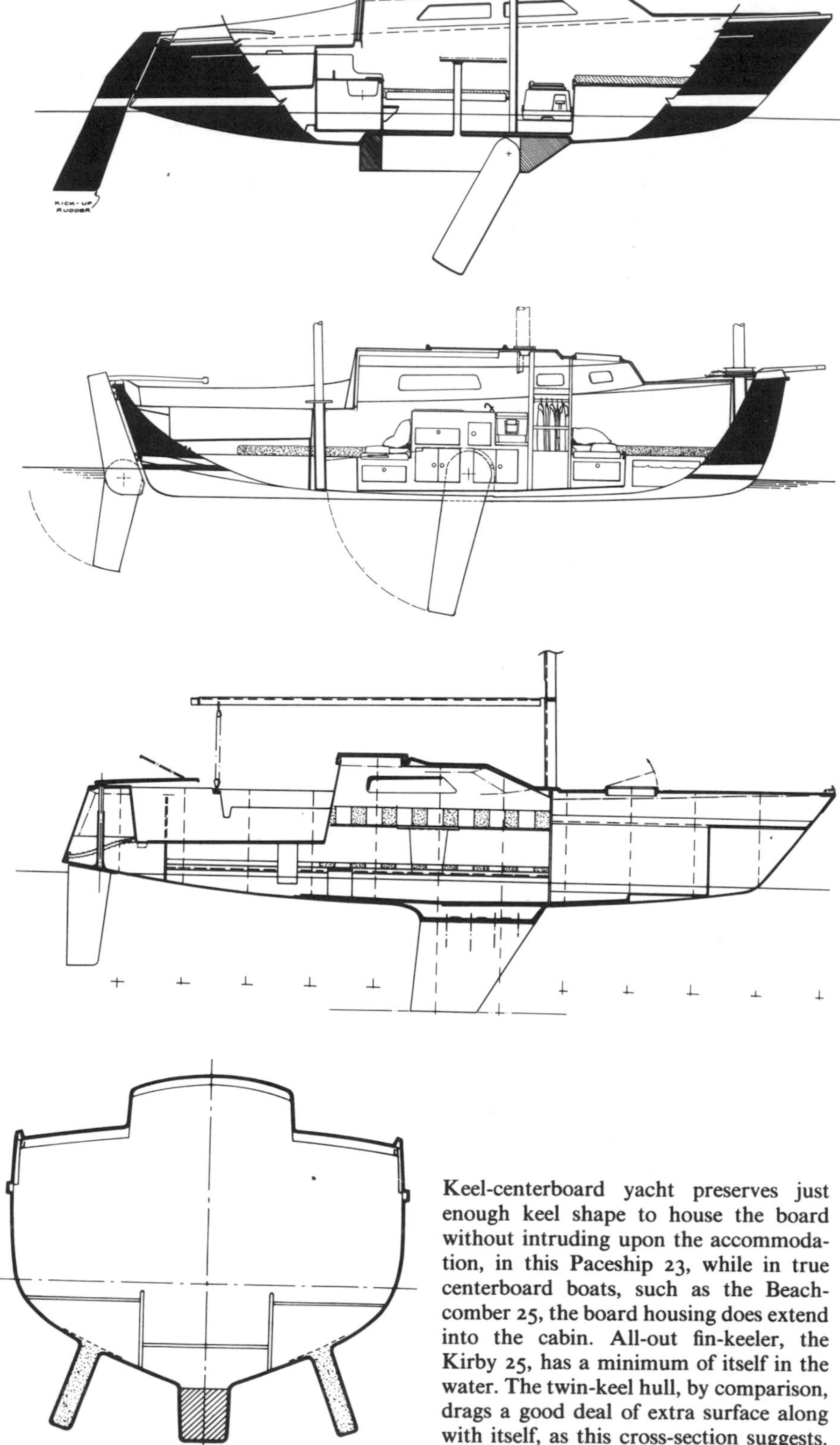

Keel-centerboard yacht preserves just enough keel shape to house the board without intruding upon the accommodation, in this Paceship 23, while in true centerboard boats, such as the Beachcomber 25, the board housing does extend into the cabin. All-out fin-keeler, the Kirby 25, has a minimum of itself in the water. The twin-keel hull, by comparison, drags a good deal of extra surface along with itself, as this cross-section suggests.

adherents maintain that such a design has better stability than a single keel and equal performance off the wind, without too much reduction in windward ability, as well as possessing markedly reduced draft. This seems to me largely wishful thinking because a twin-keel makes a lot of leeway when close-hauled but does open up a lot of shallow cruising grounds. The twin-keel hull is pulling a significantly greater amount of underbody through the water, and the three separate protrusions—keels and skeg—create a considerable turbulence.

What about the multihull?

To a considerable extent, multihulls break the rules. They are not constrained by normal speed:length ratios, they perform quite differently from monohulls, they cannot yet be handicapped effectively in the same fleet as monohulls and—perhaps most tellingly—they are not sailed by the same kind of people who form the sailing establishment.

Basically, there are two kinds of multihulls that concern us here, catamarans and trimarans. In the under-30-foot lengths, trimarans have not really reached their accommodation potential, and even catamarans are somewhat more limited than monohulls of this size.

The reason has to do with the usable space in a multihull. A catamaran has two equal-size hulls each of which is about half the beam of a monohull of the same length. In small cruisers, this is a very narrow hull indeed, yet in cats under about 35 feet (with some salient exceptions) the hulls are where the standing headroom is: The bridge deck, normally used to house the main cabin, is usually limited to about five feet of headroom in a 30-footer.

The constriction is even more severe in a small tri, where the side hulls are really only balancing floats, incapable of carrying much in the way of gear and no accommodation whatever. The load is thus placed entirely in the main hull, which is typically a little more than half as beamy as a monohull of the same length.

Then there is the question of loading. A 30-foot monohull can carry a couple of thousand pounds of weight, properly distributed, with little or no problem. The load is perhaps a fifth of her displacement, and the buoyancy of the hull shouldn't be compromised. A 30-foot catamaran, on the other hand, will only weigh 5,000 pounds or so, and a load proportionately half again as much, imposed on two very narrow hulls, can severely impede her performance.

My 23-foot Hirondelle cruising catamaran (see Chapter III), an amazingly spacious little boat, was very weight-sensitive, and would lose as much as a knot of speed when my two sons, whose combined weight was well under a hundred pounds, went forward to stand at the bow pulpits.

On the other hand, the 30-foot Iroquois, probably the most popular production cruising multihull yet built, can carry a substantial amount of cargo and

Prout-designed Quest catamaran is representative of modern multihull cruisers, although its extreme cutter rig is unusual.

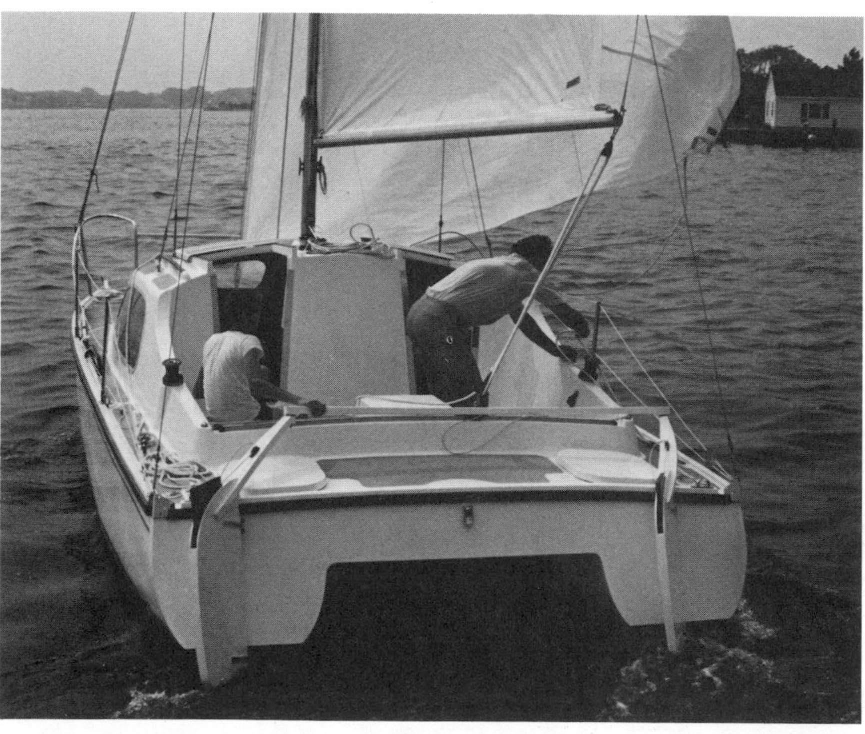

Well-designed cats, like this Hirondelle, can tack very fast indeed, but they also lose way quickly because of their high sides and light weight.

crew without sacrificing too much in the way of performance, and has a remarkable amount of space, if one doesn't mind the low headroom in the main saloon. She also has a sparkling turn of speed, caused by a large sail area, light weight, and the fact that cats and tris are capable of breaking out of the S:L ratio trap and planing. Not that they do so as a regular thing: In the two seasons I owned her, my Hirondelle achieved 10 knots only once—which was one time more than any cruising monohull of that size was likely to.

The biggest bugaboo of multihulls is, of course, the possibility of capsize, especially in catamarans. In coastal waters, a tri will seldom encounter the winds and wave shapes that would dangerously depress the leeward hull and cause it to trip, pitchpoling the boat. A cat, by contrast, can be flipped by wind alone, once the windward hull is unglued. My Hirondelle never exceeded 10 degrees of heel in two years, and was mostly sailed with a 180 percent genoa, but according to the builders, a little over 20 degrees and the windward hull would become unstuck, following which stability would decrease dramatically.

II

Sailing Cruiser Rigs

The rig for a small sailing cruiser is limited only by economics and imagination: If you want a three-masted square rigger under 30 feet, you can have one (and it has been done, at least once). Most of us, with flabby egos and pinched wallets, have settled for the done thing, or minor variants thereof. In cruising sailboats 30 feet and less, the sloop is the overwhelming choice because it's simple, effective, efficient and—most of all—familiar. Just because something is popular with the great majority doesn't mean there's anything wrong with it, but it's worth a few minutes' thought to examine the alternatives.

In doing so, it helps to begin by considering what the full range of possibilities is. First examine what the rig is intended to do.

Cruising people are prone to dismiss weatherliness in a boat, apparently clinging to the turn-of-the-century fisherman's dictum that only fools and racers beat to windward. While this may indeed be true, it's also my opinion that a boat unable to work to weather efficiently is basically unsatisfactory in one very important performance area, and will eventually be a disappointment to owner and crew. Let us say, for sake of argument, that the wind in your cruising area blows equally often from every point of the compass, and that the directions in which you are likely to go are equally divided. (This is obviously unlikely, but go along with the situation for a moment.)

There will, then, be about 5 percent of the time that you'll be running dead downwind or nearly so. You will be on a reach of one sort or another about two-thirds of the time, and you'll be close-hauled about 28 percent of the time —or will you?

Bearing in mind that a course dead to windward of you requires the boat to sail a total distance nearly 40 percent longer than a straight-line course, and considering that a boat can probably make significantly lower speeds close-hauled than reaching, then the total number of hours you're likely to spend on the wind approaches half.

That puts rather a different value on windward ability. Unless one plans on a lot of motoring as a matter of course, or a great deal of flexibility in selecting destinations, then windward ability is really very important, perhaps the most important single performance characteristic there is.

In going to windward, a boat's rig becomes an airfoil, behaving more or less like an aircraft's wing. It has not yet been conclusively demonstrated that there is no such thing as an accelerating slot effect between main and jib, but it does seem to be the case that a long, taut jib luff is one of the most effective agents in producing good windward performance.

Many feel a fairly slender mast in a marconi-rigged catboat can do quite well, offering the advantage of simplicity and lower cost, but in today's small cruisers, most catboats are gaff riggers, with treelike masts, and consequently poor windward performance. One new development is the Nonsuch 30, which is discussed in Chapter III.

The sloop rig

The standard sloop remains, for reasons of cost and sailing efficiency, the rig of choice in nearly all cruisers under 30 feet. In describing the standard sloop, it's easiest to use the shorthand developed by racers, but one must bear in mind that the terms employed are not directly concerned with objective reality, but rather with handicap formulas.

Even allowing for the fact that a real mainsail is somewhat larger than its measured equivalent, mainsails by and large have been considerably smaller than foretriangles in recent years. In most modern masthead-rig boats, jib is the primary source of drive, going to windward and off the wind except on a broad reach or a run. As we shall see later on (see Chapter IV), most cruisers carry a headsail larger than the main (or reefed main) right down to storm canvas, and many handle better under just the jib than under the mainsail alone.

The problem is that no single jib is adequate for a broad spectrum of conditions, and the smaller the cruiser, the narrower the band of winds that a given sail can cope with. Thanks to the advent of reefing genoas, it's now possible to reduce the number of headsails needed to assure safe and satisfying cruising to three, spinnaker aside. One can easily get by weekend after weekend with just a reefing #2 genoa, but sooner or later something bigger or smaller will be necessary, and that means money, stowage space, and (not necessarily least) someone going forward to change sails.

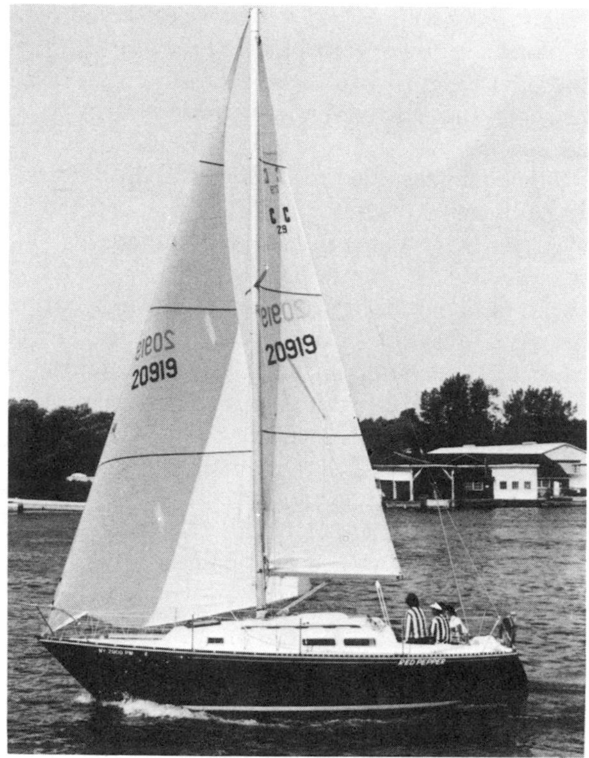

Modern racer-cruisers normally carry a genoa considerably larger than the main. On this C&C 29, black lines help crew judge curvature of the sails.

The new crop of fractional-rig cruiser-racers (see the Ericson 30+, in Chapter III) are returning to the large-mainsail form, but mostly in order to achieve racing goals. Their very tall mainsails are designed for light-air windward work, with an early first reef that makes them, in effect, masthead-rig sloops once that first reef goes in.

If you're buying a sloop-rigged monohull cruiser in the under-30-foot range and if you value performance, you should probably go for a sail area:displacement ratio of 15 or better, a Bruce number approaching 1.0, and a foretriangle that's significantly bigger than the rated area of the mainsail, or a racer's ⅞ bendy rig. You get no guarantee, but with these three factors working for you, the odds are in your favor.

Variant rigs

What about other rigs than the sloop? Technically, there are five serious possibilities, beginning with the catboat. The classic, gaff-rigged catboat ap-

A classic gaff-rigged catboat like this 24-footer may well have a higher sail area:displacement ratio than a racing sloop, but her performance, except on a reach, will be unequal to the modern rig.

pears to be the simplest rig, with one mast and one sail, but it's not necessarily so. A gaff-rigged cat of cruising size will require two halyards to raise the gaff and the single great quadrilateral of sail, as much as 275 sq. ft. in one lump.

One person can certainly handle both halyards at once on a 17- or 18-footer, as I've done myself. But I can also recall that it was no airy task. Once under sail, of course, there are no decisions to be made about which headsail to choose. But to make up for that, there's the ever-present question of reefing. The average catboat has a sail area:displacement ratio rather higher than that of a racer, but a cat is designed to ghost along in a puff and be reefed down early.

With a classic Cape Cod cat, reefing is accomplished prayerfully, and the last couple of points are tied in while standing on the barn-door rudder. In the two years I sailed a 17-foot cruising cat, I found that reefing was advisable if not vital in winds over about 10 knots—beyond that, weather helm became savage and the boat tended to overpower the helmsman.

The vast majority of catboats, picturesque as they are with their great sails, are inefficient sailing boats to windward, but can make up for it off the wind. They are great fun to single-hand, or to day-sail with a cockpit full of people, as tacking amounts to nothing more than putting the tiller over, and an emergency reef is always possible by simply casting off the peak halyard and allowing the upper third of the sail to fall behind the rest of it.

There are Marconi-rigged catboats of cruising size, but not many: People who go for a catboat in the first place generally find the whole image appealing, and that includes the gaff rig. A Marconi cat has a taller spar than the gaff-rigged equivalent, and slightly less sail area. It also will normally have a forestay like the gaff-rigger, and a couple of shrouds as well. It will be somewhat more efficient to windward, but not as weatherly as a sloop.

Until the handicap rule was changed about a decade ago, the small yawl had considerable popularity among racing-cruising people. The reason had nothing to do with the rig's absolute efficiency and everything to do with the fact that a yawl's mizzen and mizzen staysail were virtually uncounted in the boat's handicap. Thus, while the small yawl's mizzen is a truly laughable sail, to a racer it was better than nothing.

Now that this particular rule has been altered, the yawl as a rig has virtually died, except in secondhand boats. Stock yawls under 30 feet were variants of the same boat rigged as a sloop. The mainsail would lose a little area at the clew, where it could easily be afforded, and the mizzen was a tiny afterthought. A yawl is essentially a sloop, after all, with a small balancing sail dead aft. The usefulness of the yawl's mizzen sail is dubious, except for heaving-to, and the mast itself is really only a site for the mizzen staysail, which can amount to a considerable area off the wind, even in a yawl. The mizzen staysail can be useful indeed to a cruiser whose sailing territory affords a good deal of close and beam reaching, but for the skipper facing large dollops of windward work, the mizzen is no asset and may even be an overall liability: On the wind, the mizzen sail cannot draw, and so one is merely pulling an extra amount of windage about, not to mention the extra money involved in a mizzen and the extra sail stowage required (although a mizzen staysail in boats under 30 feet overall can be packed pretty small).

Whereas a yawl is essentially a single-masted boat with a small balancing sail aft, a ketch is a genuine two-sticker in which the mizzen carries a significant fraction of the total working sail area. The classical recipe for a ketch's sail distribution used to be that the combined area of mizzen and foretriangle equaled the area of the mainsail, the idea being that this arrangement gave one the most variable assortment of balanced rigs—three lowers, jib and mizzen, or main alone would each sail the boat, at least in theory.

In practice, however, having a large sail at the aft end of the yacht tended to give her a substantial weather helm as the wind piped up. Most ketch skippers have found that the first sail reduction, when the wind is anywhere forward of the beam, is to reef or strike the mizzen. This will usually bring a ketch back on her feet until the next reduction, which may involve reefing the main and/or shifting to a smaller jib. Only when one is on a reach in a really brisk wind does the hoary combination of jib and mizzen prove much. And, when the wind is really too strong, however, both ketch and yawl can usually (depending on the length of the keel) heave to easily under mizzen alone.

But having a large mizzen, and having it forward of the rudder post, means two things: First, the mizzen is spang in the middle of the cockpit, where it's

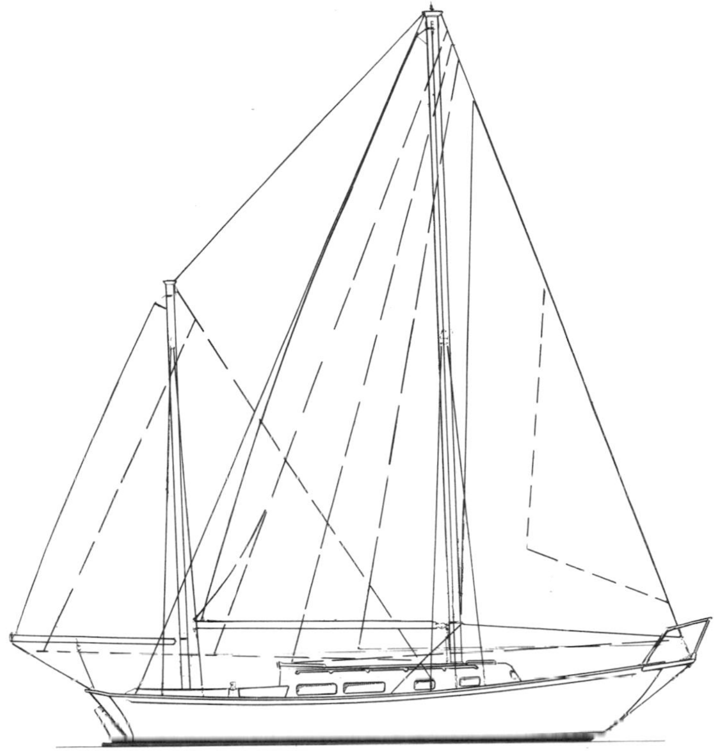

The Seawind ketch, said to be the first stock fiberglass boat to make a circumnavigation.

certain to be in the way a good deal of the time. Second, it means the rest of the rig is moved forward, and what suffers of course is the foretriangle area, the part of the rig that moves a boat to windward. Many ketch owners have found that to get decent balance in a good breeze they are well advised to add a short bowsprit to the original rig—or face the necessity for striking the mizzen and sailing undercanvased.

The whole rationale for a ketch is to spread out the sail area longitudinally in three manageable chunks. In a boat of 35 feet or so, this begins to make some sense. But in a 30-footer, it means running against logic. There's usually no need for a split rig in a boat this size, and several sound arguments, both financial and in terms of sailing efficiency, against it.

And if this is true for a yawl and a ketch, it's even more applicable to a schooner. Whether gaff or staysail, a schooner carries her largest working sail aft, where the mainmast can be relied upon to skewer the accommodation. The advantage is that the main can be worked from the cockpit fairly easily. The disadvantages in terms of weather helm and inability to point are like the ketch's, only more so. Where a schooner excels is on a reach, when she can put up, in addition to her working sails, a small but potent spinnaker and an

A small schooner, with gaff foresail and Marconi main. The peak of the gaff is vanged to the main masthead to keep it from sagging off, but she will still not be as weatherly even as a ketch.

immense gollywobbler—a staysail that sets between the two mastheads.

The final alternative to the sloop, and one that abruptly became fashionable again after a long hiatus, is the cutter. The ancient prescription for a cutter rig called for a single mast at least 40 percent of the LOA aft of the bow, and two or more headsails. The modern cutter is nothing more exotic than a sloop with a double-headsail rig. The small staysail is usually self-tending on a club or boom, while the high-cut yankee is roller furling—a convenient combination, since the staysail requires a high-cut sail ahead of it, and roller furling also requires a cutaway foot to work properly.

Unfortunately, the same arguments that apply against a twin-stick rig can be made, in a different degree, against the cutter. In a small boat, the slots between yankee and staysail, and staysail and main, are tight, and the amount of trimming necessary to get all the sails to pull well can be tedious on most points of sailing. In addition, the presence of an inner forestay makes short-tacking a true pain in the neck. And finally, the extra complication means

Two cutters; the gaff-rigged Cornish Crabber is a fiberglass replica of a classic design, while the Bayfeld 29 is a more modern rendering of the same theme. Both boats have loose-footed staysails, which is fairly unusual among cutters.

Variant attachments for staysail booms. The bronze pedestal employed by Cape Dory is a traditional design that allows the sail to assume a full shape when running. The stay-mounted fitting requires less deck hardware but it must necessarily chafe the stay.

extra expense—to what advantage? In boats of 30 feet and less, there really is no point in two sails forward of the mast, at least not most of the time.

This spoil-sport attitude sounds discouraging as realism so often does. It's important to add that realism isn't everything: If a ketch (or yawl, schooner, or cutter) makes your blood run faster and generally provides you with the joy that sailing ought to be all about, why then get one by all means. My only concern here is to suggest that you know what you're paying that extra money for—and it's not performance.

Spars

In the vast majority of small cruising boats today, one may choose any type of spar as long as it's aluminum. There are a few holdovers that still carry bright-finished wood masts and booms, and a few trailbreakers whose vessels already sport carbon-graphite or other exotic materials, but the present advantages of aluminum are so great that it seems likely to be the material of choice for some time to come, if not forever.

Aluminum has several things going for it as a spar material, and relatively few drawbacks. Compared with previous materials, it has a high strength: weight ratio, and present-day anodized spars require very little maintenance aside from an annual cleaning (for which there are special compounds) and waxing. Neither wood spars nor aluminum ones are very practical when it comes to major repairs—it will usually be cheaper and safer to strip the old unit of its fittings and start anew.

Attaching fittings, indeed, can pose something of a problem for the skipper new to aluminum but, with care and the proper tools, it is probably easier to attach almost any fitting to aluminum than to hang the same gadget on a wood spar. In either case, it is important to plan ahead, as unnecessary holes will weaken the main fabric. In the case of aluminum, there is—sometimes—one added complication: Because aluminum is fairly high on the galvanic table, metal fittings that are *not* aluminum should be insulated from contact with the spar by a plastic barrier, which can be an ultrathin pad precut to shape.

Most aluminum spars are simple tubular or oval shapes, called extrusions, that are the same diameter and wall thickness from one end to the other. These are simple to fabricate and, as marine materials go, pretty cheap. To save weight or enhance appearance (or both), some spars are tapered, usually from a wide base to a narrow head. The normal procedure for accomplishing the taper is to cut out a narrow, long V, with its wide end at the masthead, and then close up the wound. Properly done, this creates no additional weakness beyond the increased narrowness, but it is questionable whether much is accomplished: The weight saved is minimal, and will not have much effect on the average cruiser's balance. One place where a tapered mast can make a difference, however, is in a small cruising catboat or other craft with extralarge unstayed masts. The removal of a very few pounds, when they're carried high up and well forward in a fine-bowed hull, can make a perceptible difference, and it certainly does look more attractive.

In former times, when boats and their fittings were far weaker than they are today, masts were almost universally stepped on the keel and braced at deck level, in addition to being stayed. In today's smaller cruiser, however, most masts are stepped either on deck or on the cabin top. This has three obvious advantages—and, as in all things, a couple of corresponding drawbacks. First, by not carrying the spar down through the accommodation, there's a significant space saving. The compression load of the spar, which may be compared to a bow and arrow with the bow fully drawn, is often transferred to the keel by a compression strut, which is either a heavy pole or, in many cases, a piece of wood that also serves as a doorpost. In some cases the primary load is taken to the hull by one or two U-shaped overhead beams, which can be integrated into the accommodation as bracing for the main thwartships bulkhead. Either way, when inches count it pays to keep the mast out of the main cabin or the head, where it would normally go.

. . . And into which it would normally leak. For while a proper mast coat can prevent most moisture from running down alongside a spar, a mast has a number of openings—for halyards and fittings—through which water can enter its interior. A keel-stepped mast inevitably brings that water down below. Barring a leak in the mast step, a deck-stepped spar cannot.

Finally, a keel-stepped mast is normally a professional rigging job requiring a crane and several yard workers. A deck-stepped mast need not be, if it is designed to be raised and lowered by the crew. This can be a tricky and demanding job, as the mast from the normal 25-footer is just about all an average adult can carry, and far more than an individual can raise without organization and the proper deck fittings.

The standard deck or cabin-top fitting for a do-it-yourself spar is called a tabernacle. In essence it is a large hinge on its side, and it may allow the spar to tilt either forward or aft, depending on how the raising procedure is to be accomplished. On very small trailerable cruisers, under 22 or 23 feet, the spar normally inclines aft. It's raised by one crewmember walking forward from the cockpit and lifting to the limit of his or her reach, while the other pulls on a line tied to the forestay, with his pulling power perhaps amplified by a winch. As a rule, the upper shrouds, backstay, and/or aft lowers are made fast to give the spar some support in the thwartships plane.

Beyond about 25 feet LOA, few boats are rigged for mast stepping and unstepping by the owner. These yachts use a simple plate on the cabin top to accept the heel of the spar, sometimes with a pin arrangement to add a little security. Any deck-stepped spar should have a drain hole at its base, to prevent water filling it to the first through-the-skin aperture, which may be a couple of feet above the deck. The interior wiring, which can supply one or two lights as well as instruments, will normally lead to plugs on deck, from which the wires run inside the cabin roof ceiling to the circuit board back aft. Too many manufacturers are excessively generous with the wire coming out of the spar,

Tabernacle-mounted mast on this 26-footer raises from forward aft and makes use of the mainsheet tackle for mechanical advantage.

creating a potentially messy coil that can snag a foot or a pole. The whole thing can either be shortened and the end fittings respliced, or the skipper can use waterproof tape to secure the spare length to the base of the spar.

In any case, it's an easier matter to deal with than what happens to the wires in many keel-stepped spars, where the wiring exits the mast near the base and is often forgotten when unstepping the spar, until a rending tear suggests that there will be no lights aloft for a while.

Surveyors and others whose primary consideration is safety tend to prefer keel-stepped spars, although no one I've met would make that an absolute requirement. I've had boats with both deck- and keel-stepped masts, and I will admit to a slight preference for the security of a keel-stepped rig in a boat of 25 feet or more. One not-uncommon hazard of the swaged fittings that secure most rigging terminals is that they can let go without warning. With a keel-stepped mast one normally has enough extra support to keep the stick up until one can take the stress off the mast. When the mast ends at the deck, the loss of an upper shroud or stay usually signals the ditching of the rig.

The counterargument to keel-stepped masts is that if the spar ever does break in such a boat, its demise will often tear a large hole in the cabin roof. Maybe. In point of fact, few spars are lost from cruising yachts of the size we're discussing, when operating in the coastal waters where they have any business being. Perhaps the best argument for keel-stepped masts I can adduce from my own experience is that, while they are a little more difficult to insert, they are more forgiving while attaching and detaching the rigging. In sum, I'd vote for deck-stepping if the rest of the rig were so designed that I could raise and lower the spar myself, or with the aid of one or two friends. If the rig were too heavy for that, I'd opt—were there a choice—for a keel-stepped mast.

In properly engineered masts, the internal wiring is run in a plastic tube that's secured, usually with pop rivets, to the inside of the spar. This not only keeps the wiring from chafe but it also minimizes slapping, which can be absolutely maddening at anchor. Even with the wiring encased in tubing, an aluminum mast can be a noisy companion, thanks to the amplified whanging of halyards and lifts, whether internal or otherwise. If your cruising plans include overnights at anchor, it will be a good investment to pay extra for a sound-deadened spar, assuming it's not standard with your boat.

Halyards

The question of halyards has been reopened in the last couple of years, thanks to the advent of genuinely low-stretch polyester and Kevlar line. Normally referred to as *prestretched,* this material makes a practical halyard that's cheaper and easier to deal with than the former favorite, half rope/half wire, spliced in the middle. This latter kind of halyard, if properly measured in the

Sliding gooseneck is a good fitting that's seldom seen anymore. With a 2-1 or 3-1 tackle to a fitting at the base of the mast, it makes a main halyard winch unnecessary.

first place (and not all were), was so calculated that when the sail was fully hoisted the wire halyard ran down the spar with just enough to spare for three or preferably four turns around the halyard winch. Thus the loaded sail was supported by the low-stretch part of the halyard, while the rope tail served for hand hauling to the point where the winch took over.

With all-rope halyards the sail-raising procedure is the same, except that there is of course no need to worry about precisely where the halyard hits the winch drum. Even with the best prestretch polyester, however, there is enough give in the halyard so that about fifteen minutes after getting under way—especially if the first course is a brisk beat—the sail's luff has become truly scalloped. It's a relatively simple matter to head up and send a hand forward to take the slack out of the halyard, but my own preference is to use a sliding gooseneck to provide loading at both ends of the luff.

One simply raises the sail until it's two-blocked to the halyard sheave, then socks down on the sliding gooseneck downhaul (which should have a 3:1 or even 4:1 purchase). Under normal conditions this will take virtually all the stretch out of a mainsail luff, and it's usually unnecessary to sweat out the slack later. Unfortunately, it's more expensive to install a sliding gooseneck, so most of them are fixed today.

Most of today's boats, whatever their rig, depend heavily on a masthead genoa. To get a sail like that to work at its best, a taut luff is absolutely vital. It's possible to achieve that happy state with an all-rope halyard, but an extralarge halyard winch will be necessary to do it.

For low-loading sails like those in a gaff rig, or sails like spinnakers where a taut luff isn't required, the halyards might as well be all rope. The standard sloop will require, for my money, three and a half halyards: a jib halyard, mainsail halyard, spinnaker halyard and a main boom topping lift that can serve as an emergency halyard. For gaff rigs, the mainsail requires two halyards—a throat halyard that raises the inner end of the gaff, and a peak halyard connected to a wire span at the balance point of the gaff.

Modern rope is fantastically strong, compared with the manila line of a generation or two ago, but it's a mistake to buy too-light line for any function where you'll have to be hauling on a good deal of it for an extended period. In my experience, an average adult male's hand becomes cramped after hauling on line less than about three eighths of an inch (1″ circ) for more than fifty feet or so. People with large hands will find half-inch (1½″ circ) line much easier to use. But for a topping lift, which will be nothing but windage 90 percent of the time underway, I'd contradict myself, and make a compromise in favor of quarter-inch or even three sixteenths of an inch diameter (¾″ circ) polyester. Just remember, you may have to ride a bosun's chair to the top of the mast, suspended by that line, so pay strong heed to the working strength tables in Chapter V.

To serve as a halyard, a topping lift must obviously be rigged to a block at the masthead (for a mainsail and most jibs). If it's possible to work the topping lift through one of the masthead sheaves, so it runs down both the forward and aft sides of the mast, that's the best arrangement, as you can then employ it as an emergency halyard for main or jib. If not, the spinnaker halyard can double as emergency jib halyard, and the topping lift can use a cheek block at the masthead, even though the lead won't be very good.

Too many boats today come with a topping lift that's fixed at the masthead and runs to a block at the outer end of the boom, thence to a cleat on the boom itself. While this is an adequate rig for easing and tightening the sail's leech, and it's cheaper for the boatbuilder, it's not nearly as satisfactory for a cruising skipper, who wants if possible to have backups for every system aboard.

A cutter or other double-head rig will normally not have a winch for the staysail halyard, on the grounds that it's impossible to get a really taut luff anyway: Socking up on the staysail stay merely pulls the mast out of column in most small boats, as there is seldom a corresponding pair of aft lowers to match the pull. My feeling is that when you really want a staysail, in heavy weather, you want a taut luff on it, and you may do well to pay the price, which means running backstays (see below) and a staysail halyard winch.

The relatively tiny mizzen on a 30-footer hardly requires a halyard winch, but it should have a downhaul. You will seldom be using the mizzen going to windward, since it accomplishes nothing or less, but on a close reach it'll pay to be able to get a taut luff. On even a small ketch, the mizzen staysail can be a powerful piece of cloth, as big as the main or bigger, and it can impose a correspondingly heavy load on the mast. One of the best ways to counteract this without additional staying is to rig the mizzen staysail halyard so that its fall (the loose end) can be lead aft to a block at the yacht's quarter and thence forward to the windward sheet winch, or simply to a cleat.

I've mentioned downhauls for sliding goosenecks earlier in this section, but there are other uses for this versatile and seldom seen tackle. On smaller racers especially, a downhaul to the jib tack isn't unusual; it's usually a multipart purchase made fast to the tack eye with the fall led aft, and is an excellent way to increase jib luff tension or, with a three-quarter rig, put a bend in the mast to flatten the mainsail.

Many of today's cruisers lead halyards back to the cockpit, via sheaves inset into the mast base for each halyard. The lines run aft, often through a bull's-eye fairlead, to a winch at the after end of the cabin house, with a cam cleat or stopper ahead of the winch. Mounted singly or in a cluster ahead of the winch, the stopper is a lever-actuated cam cleat. It allows you to raise a sail, set it up taut with the winch, then stop it and cast the line off the winch drum to make place for another. It's possible to have two or three halyards led aft to the same winch, for a saving in cash and complexity that is well worth contemplating, as long as you also allow for some abrasion of the line.

On the face of it, you would assume that casting off a halyard, whether from the cockpit or the mast, would cause the sail to which it was attached to drop to the deck. As any experienced sailor knows, a jib or staysail will seldom drop more than halfway down its stay, because of the friction of the snaps on the wire. If these sails are to lower, there must be a positive downward force to encourage them.

This force can be supplied by a light line downhaul made fast to the head

Four cam-action stoppers ahead of a single winch allow any one of the halyards to be tensioned on the winch, then stopped and released from the drum.

of the sail and led through a block at the tack and thence aft. My own opinion is that this rig is better than no downhaul at all on a small boat with a dangerous foredeck, but that a roller genoa and even staysail are much better. In any case, it seems to me that for a shorthanded boat, some way of furling the headsails without going forward is a major asset, and one to strive for.

Spar fittings

The most obvious fitting on any spar is the track or tracks in which the mainsail (and mizzen) luff or foot runs. On wood spars, of course, the track is almost always exterior, screwed at intervals to the wood. Aluminum spars have both external, attached track and internal grooves that accept slugs or bolt rope luffs. There seems to me little functional difference between the two, except that the currently popular nylon sail slugs seem prone to jamming in internal grooves, while with a bolt rope, the entire luff comes free from the spar as the sail drops. Most important to the skipper is the gate fitting toward the base of the mast, into which the slugs or slides fit and by which they are restrained from escape. In my opinion, the gate should have a positive locking action so that, when the sail is lowered, the bottom slides don't get off the track.

In addition, if one has a sliding gooseneck, it will usually run on a short section of reinforced T-track screwed to the mast. This track is about twelve or eighteen inches long and should have a positive stop at the top as well as at the bottom, to keep the boom from escaping when the sail is fully hoisted. The upper stop must, however, be removable so the boom can be unshipped when necessary, as when the mast is unstepped. A mainsail with bolt rope along the foot, running in a boom groove, is good aerodynamically, but it will not accept a vang or preventer strap between the boom and the sail's foot. A fitting on the underside of the boom will be necessary for attachment of the vang tackle.

The next most obvious mast fittings are of course the halyard winches, assuming they're not located on the cabin top. The table on this page gives the suggested sizes for various makes of winch in terms of the size sail they will have to raise. In even a small boat it will pay to have at least one halyard winch capable of raising a crewmember to the masthead. I vividly recall going aloft in a 25-footer I owned and having the halyard winch simply disintegrate as I reached the masthead, from the excess strain put upon it. Fortunately the crewmember holding the other end of the halyard was heavier than I and had quick reflexes.

Winches should be high enough off the deck so that the person grinding them is working approximately at waist height. Be sure that all the halyard winches are the standard drum type, and not the old-fashioned temperamental reel version sometimes used for mainsail halyards.

Table of winch sizes

<table>
<tr><td>Boat length (ft.)
Genoa size (sq. ft.)
Mainsail size (sq. ft.)</td><td>20–23
200
130</td><td>24–26
300
160</td><td>27–30
350
180</td></tr>
<tr><td>Genoa sheet</td><td>Barient 10
Lewmar 7
Barlow 16</td><td>Barient 18 or 19ST*
Lewmar 16, 16 ST or 24
Barlow 19</td><td>Barient 21, 24 or 23ST
Lewmar 30 or 42ST
Barlow 25 or 25ST</td></tr>
<tr><td>Spinnaker sheet</td><td colspan="2">Barient 10
Lewmar 7
Barlow 16</td><td>Barient 18 or 19ST
Lewmar 16, 24 or 24ST
Barlow 25 or 25ST</td></tr>
<tr><td>Halyard</td><td colspan="2">Barient 10
Lewmar 7
Barlow 16</td><td></td></tr>
</table>

*self-tailing

Reel halyard winch for an all-wire halyard. Although gussied up with modern design, this type of winch is still dangerous to use and offers no great advantage.

About a foot below the halyard winch is the halyard cleat—again assuming a mast-mounted winch. This cleat should not be straight up and down, perpendicular to the winch drum, but should be canted so that the first turn of line around the cleat's base allows the crewman to put a friction-created brake on the halyard. Normally, the cleat's horn should be tilted toward the direction from which the line comes off the winch drum. Since U.S. (and most other) winches turn clockwise, this means that if a vertical line is drawn through the center of the winch and the cleat, the cleat's axis should be about 30 degrees to the left of that vertical.

When installing aluminum cleats on an aluminum spar, the best practice is to drill and tap the required holes for machine screws, rather than using self-tapping sheet-metal screws. In a smaller cruiser, however, it's not really important. What is critical is to size the cleat according to the diameter of the line it will handle. As the wire rope of a combination halyard should not reach as far as the cleat all you have to take into account is the line diameter. The following table, from *Skene's Elements of Yacht Design,* is based on a suggested cleat length of one inch for each one-sixteenth inch of rope diameter:

Line dia	circ	Cleat
1/4″	3/4″	4″
5/16″	1″	5″
3/8″	1 1/4″	6″
7/16″	1 3/8″	7″
1/2″	1 1/2″	8″

(These are the largest lines a halyard cleat on a 30-footer will have to handle, but it's worth bearing in mind that a boat's mooring cleats should be big enough to handle some of the great, barnacle encrusted hawsers used on yacht club guest moorings: A twelve-inch cleat forward and ten-inch cleats aft are not too large.)

Two different, equally proper cleats leading from the same winch. Note how the Clamcleat is shimmed up so line comes into it at the same height it leaves the winch drum. Note also angle of standard cleat to drum—line winds clockwise around winch, exits at the "R" of Lewmar.

Mast wiring

Running and anchor lights are currently in a state of legal flux as far as U.S. waters are concerned, and the problem of what kinds of lights to carry may not be settled by regulation for several years. The possibilities are shown in the accompanying table of running-light configurations. For my money, the new, International Rule tricolor masthead light, showing red, green, and white over the same port, starboard, and aft arcs as have traditionally been covered by two or three separate lights is a vast improvement over the previous arrangements.

Running Lights

(*Note:* Until the end of 1981, quite different running-light patterns were allowable in international and in U.S. territorial waters. With the passage of a law homogenizing inland and offshore rules of the road, lights of the International Rule will appear on all new and nearly all older sailing craft, according to the following table.)

VESSELS UNDER SAIL ALONE*

Side lights: Separate or combination light showing red to port and green to starboard 112.5 degrees each side of centerline, visible one mile.

Stern light: white light aft showing 67.5 degrees each side of centerline (135 degrees total), visible two miles.

Optional masthead tricolor: In place of the foregoing, a tricolor light at the masthead, showing red 112.5 degrees from centerline aft to port, green 112.5 degrees from centerline aft to starboard, and white for the remaining 135 degrees aft; visible two miles.

Optional all-around lights: *In addition to* the individual side and stern lights specified above, a vessel under sail may also carry, near the masthead, a red light over a green light, each showing through 360 degrees and visible for two miles.

VESSELS UNDER POWER ALONE, OR UNDER POWER AND SAIL**

Side lights: As above.

Stern light: As above. (*Note:* Tricolor and all-around red and green lights may not be employed under power or under power and sail combined.)

"Masthead" or bow: At least three feet above the side lights, a white light on the centerline showing 112.5 degrees from the vessel's centerline aft on each side, 225 degrees in all; visible two miles.

VESSELS AT ANCHOR

All-around light: A white light, visible for two miles, showing 360 degrees around the horizon.

*A vessel under 23 feet in length may show a hand-held white light if it is not possible for her to carry fixed running lights.

**A vessel under 23 feet in length may, in lieu of the above, display only a white, all-around light, if she is capable of a maximum speed of seven knots or less.

Not only does the tricolor light employ one bulb instead of three, with a correspondingly lower power drain, but it also shows at the one point of a sailboat—the masthead—that's most visible to large commercial craft, and it cannot be screened by a sail. The tricolor's only drawback, it seems to me, is that a wholly different set of red, green, and white lights have to be rigged lower down, so it will be possible to show a 20-point steaming light above them when under power.

The legalistically inclined skipper might consider the following lighting recommendation:

For operating under sail alone, the International Rule tricolor masthead light.

For operating under power, or under sail and power, a combination red-and-green bow light mounted on the pulpit, a 20-point white light two-thirds of the way up the mast (this can often be combined with a deck light shining downward from the same fitting) and a 10-point white stern light aft.

For anchoring, an all-around white light with its own independent battery to be hung from the forestay.

Whatever one's choice, it should be remembered that electricity on a small boat is a mixed blessing. Most often when a running light won't light the trouble is simply in the bulb socket—not so easy to remedy when the problem is twenty feet above the deck. Top-quality light fixtures are a good investment on a boat. In some cases, it may be impossible to see whether the masthead

Good planning can keep the masthead relatively uncluttered. Combination wind-direction vane and anemometer cups are on forward side of spar, with VHF-FM antenna behind and to starboard.

light is on or off unless you fly a burgee above it. One way to cope with this mystery is to wire a low-power bulb into the masthead circuit down at the base of the spar. If one light works, then the other does too, and the lower bulb can be a handy reminder to turn off the masthead light when the dawn comes. This is, by the way, a good reason for the self-powered anchor light: You may run its 12-volt battery flat, but you'll still be able to start your inboard engine.

While the selection of instruments for the small cruiser will be covered later, a few points about their antennae may be worth bringing up here. If at all possible, try to set up your masthead electronics at the time the boat is first commissioned. You should have no trouble getting three sets of wiring—lights, wind speed/direction, and VHF-FM coaxial cable—into the mast tube. It doesn't seem to hurt VHF-FM reception at all to run the antenna lead down the inside of an aluminum mast, and since this type of radio's range is directly related to the antenna's height, the masthead is really the only sensible place for it.

When wiring a mast with electrical connections other than the built-in lights, make sure that the connectors are both reasonably water resistant and at the same time easy to undo when the mast is pulled. Taping the standard double-socket connectors immediately the connection is made seems to be the best way to keep moisture out.

Boom hardware and reefing gear

Most mainsail and staysail booms are fairly simple constructions. The most important single fitting is probably the gooseneck, which should be engineered to attach the mainsail tack perfectly in line with the sail's foot. The gooseneck may also contain the cranking attachment for roller reefing in older boats, or the hooks for jiffy reefing in newer ones, as discussed more fully below. It's a good idea, when you acquire your new boat, to measure the clevis pins that secure both tack and clew to gooseneck and outhaul, and procure some spares for your ditty bag.

On a small cruiser, the outhaul fitting frequently suffers from the spar-maker's economy. Indeed, on small, inexpensive vessels I've run across, it consists of nothing more than a fixed eye at the outer end of the boom. Considering that foot tension is fairly important to effective sailing and to the life of your sail, it seems to me that you deserve better. A sliding car with a block built in to achieve a 2:1 purchase is adequate for most people, with the clew line led through a cheek block on the boom and thence forward to a cleat on the same spar. For 30-footers an interior tackle setup for the outhaul is probably excessive, but do make sure that you can tension and ease the mainsail foot without swinging from the end of the boom.

I'm a relatively recent convert to jiffy reefing, having sailed in boats with point reefing and roller reefing first. Standard point reefing, which is effective and good-looking when properly done, is simply slower than an emergency procedure has any right to be. Roller reefing in theory allows for an infinite adjustment of sail area, so you can retain perfect balance in the sail plan. In practice, however, that kind of precision is like keeping a scalpel to slice bread, and most roller reefing requires two people to accomplish properly—one to crank and the other to haul aft the sail's foot to keep it from bunching—while jiffy reefing is truly a one-person operation.

Jiffy-reefing gear for the small cruiser is marvelously simple. At the forward end of the boom, one or two stainless-steel pigtail hooks are bolted or welded to the gooseneck to secure the reef tack cringle or cringles (if you have two sets of reefs). On the aft end of the boom are one or two cheek blocks with beckets and, forward, a cleat. The reefing line leads from the becket pin around and under the boom, up along the sail and through the reefing clew cringle, thence back down to the block and forward to the cleat. A second reef requires a similar arrangement.

To tie in a jiffy reef, one lowers the mainsail until it's possible to hook a pigtail into the tack reef cringle, then raises the sail again and tensions the luff. Now raise the aft end of the boom with the topping lift until it's parallel to the water. Pull on the clew reefing line until the clew reef cringle is as far down and aft as it will go and cleat the reefing line. Ease off the topping lift and you're in business. It's as easy to do as it is to describe. Although the procedure leaves an untidy bunt of sail fabric, it really doesn't matter as long as the reefed "foot" of the sail is stretched taut; some neat skippers have a set of grommets in the sail and reeve a light line to wrap up the extra fabric.

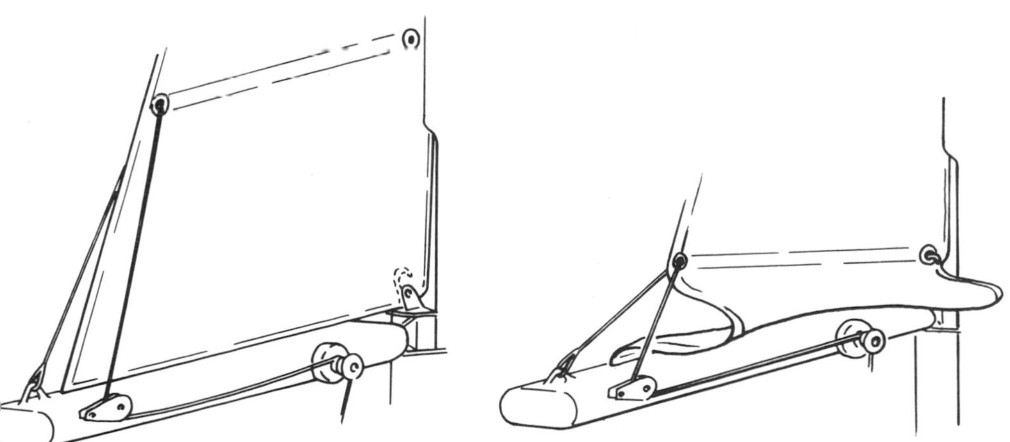

Jiffy reefing simplified. After lowering sail and hooking tack reef grommet on fixed hook at gooseneck, bring clew reef grommet down and out to stretch foot taut. Placement of cheek block and hook are critical.

There is a wrinkle in jiffy reefing that seems worth examining: Instead of having a separate cheek block and cleat for each reef, the reefing block is mounted on a short length of track screwed to the boom. The block can be moved and secured to any one of several spots along the track, and by releading the reefing line, you can tie in as deep a reef as is built into the sail, without duplication of gear. Whichever system you adopt, the important thing to remember is that the clew reefing block must be so mounted that the pull from the clew reef cringle is both down and aft, to stretch the sail's foot.

Many cruising people still seem to feel that a main boom vang is something of interest exclusively to racers, and that's a shame because a proper vang can make up for a lot of shortcomings in a rig. This is especially important when the mainsheet is secured to one or two fixed points and, to make matters worse, runs from the outer end of the boom.

This kind of mainsheet rig is simple and cheap, and requires a minimum amount of engineering. It's also the least effective, because (without a vang) you can only flatten the mainsail by pulling the boom down and toward the centerline—and the boom will never be better than nearly over the centerline, because when the sheet is eased, even a little, the boom rises upward almost as much as it swings outward, bellying the sail and putting twist into it. If you have a midboom sheet track, of course, it's possible to have the mainsheet pulling almost straight downward even when the boom is out over the boat's quarter and you're close reaching.

But to exert downward pressure on the boom when you're beam or broad reaching, a vang is usually indispensable. There are two basic types that do much the same job. First is the built-in vang, which in some craft is a permanent part of the rigging and is called a kicking strap in Britain. It runs from a fitting on the underside of the boom to another fitting in the deck just abaft the mast. Even though the boom may swing right out to the shrouds, this vang is still doing its job. It doesn't need to be slacked and reset when the boat tacks, because it pivots with the boom.

If you have such a piece of equipment on your boat, or if it's available as an option on a boat you're considering, it's a worthwhile choice. But it's a dangerous item to try and install yourself, especially when the downward pressure is exerted by a multipart tackle that may have more pull than the boom has give. Check with the builder or designer of the boat. It may be safer to attach some kind of reinforcing strap to the boom before fitting a permanent vang.

In this case, you're probably better off rigging a temporary vang, consisting of a reinforced fabric strap that slides between the boom and the foot of the sail. Through the rings at the ends of the strap you clip one end of a handy-billy tackle—usually a four-part purchase with snap shackles—and clip the other end of the tackle to a stanchion base or a car on the genoa track. This vang can also function as a preventer (to *prevent* unwanted jibes), and the handy billy can serve a number of other purposes in and around the boat.

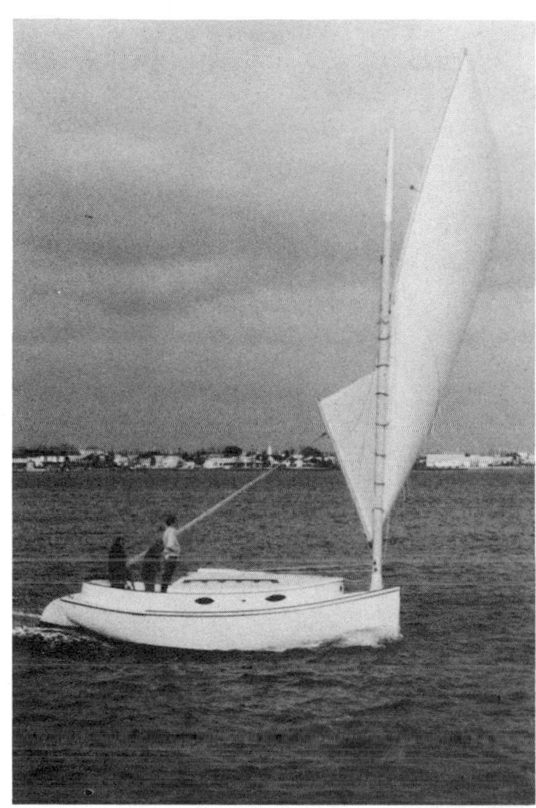

Without a vang, this catboat's mainsail twists badly on a run, and could wind up in a goose-wing jibe, with gaff on one side of mast and boom on the other. In equally heavy winds, a vang keeps the boom of this sloop relatively level.

If your boat has roller reefing, you won't, of course, be able to fit this kind of vang once the first reef has been rolled in. A substitute is a claw, a three-quarter ring of metal or heavy plastic with rubber feet at each end of the partial ring. These feet bear against the boom or reefed mainsail without damaging either, and the vanging tackle snaps into the bottom part of the ring, below the boom. It looks like a makeshift, and to a certain extent it is, but it works quite well. You may also roll a length of synthetic webbing in with the reef, to give an eye when the roll is complete.

Sail hardware

Sheet tracks are the best way of sheeting a boomed sail. A standard arrangement includes a length of track, a car to slide along it (to which the mainsheet is made fast), and movable stops that allow one to position the sliding car at any point along the track. In terms of hardware, the whole system must be strong enough to absorb some pretty abrupt stops, as in uncontrolled jibes; one must also be able to force the car back and forth when the whole arrangement is under tension. For my money, one should look for the following when checking out a mainsheet track: First, the track itself should be substantial, through-bolted along its length with large washers and a backup plate or plank

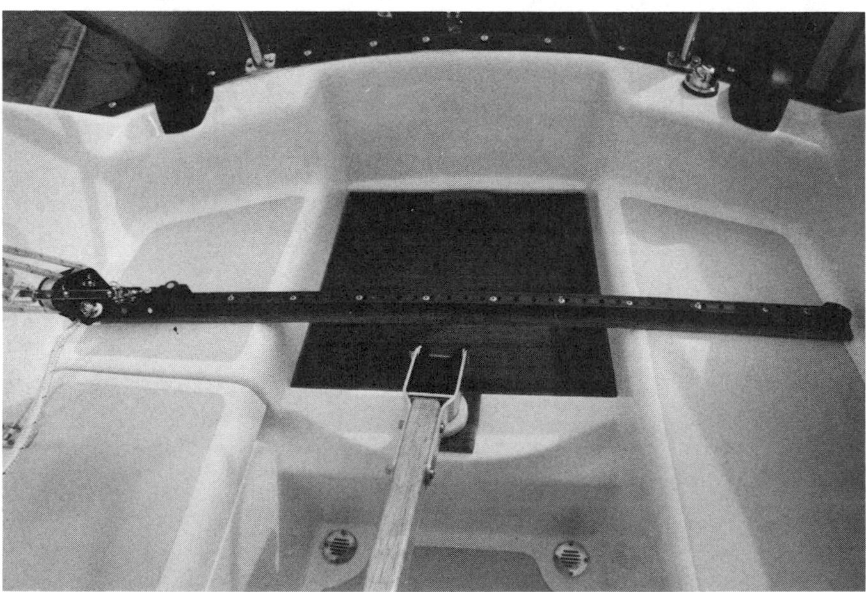

Mainsheet track at aft end of cockpit; it will be difficult for the helmsman to trim the sheet with his free hand, and the lazarette locker is partially blocked by the track—which is at least reinforced on its underside to prevent upward bending.

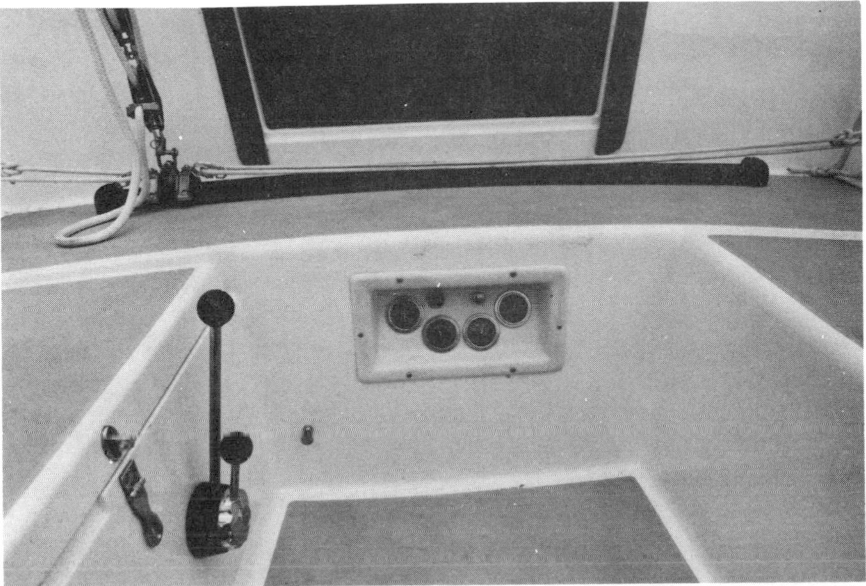

A sound bridge deck installation. Trimming lines to either side of the cockpit allow the car to be moved from side to side easily. Note also the good placement of engine gauges, and the throttle and gearshift levers waiting to snag the sheet.

to spread the loads. A car on roller bearings isn't absolutely vital, but it can certainly make the sail a great deal easier to trim when one is hard on the wind in a smart breeze. On more and more boats, there are block systems on the traveler car and at either end of the track to give the crew mechanical advantage when moving the car under load. This kind of tackle can be rigged to incorporate a jam cleat, thus making unnecessary the use of movable stops on the track itself.

End stops and intermediate stops (if any) must be strong enough to absorb the crash of the traveler hitting them at full tilt, at the end of an uncontrolled jibe. Many good stops have a piece of rubber built in to take at least some of the shock, but the main defense is simply hefty construction. At the same time, at least one end stop should be readily accessible, so the car can be removed for repair, replacement, or winter storage.

The question arises, How much mechanical advantage should a mainsheet have? This depends, of course, on the size of the mainsail and the strength of the crew. Few if any boats in the size range we're considering should require a mainsheet winch, and in my opinion a four-part tackle on the sheet is a good starting point most of the time. For those who have managed to forget schoolroom physics, a small refresher on block and tackle may be in order. Without going into the whys of the subject, suffice it to say that one calculates the mechanical advantage of a given tackle by counting the number of strands pulling on the moving end of the system.

Old-fashioned mainsheet system. Although it has plenty of power, it cannot get the main boom amidships or to windward, and the boom bails are wrongly aligned.

In the case of a mainsheet, the boom is obviously the moving end of the tackle system. If one has, say, a double block on the boom and a double block with a becket down on the track, the lead off the block on the track gives one mechanical advantage of 4:1: the line goes from becket up to the first sheave on the double block—one—back to the first sheave on the lower block—two—back up to the second sheave on the boom block—three—down again to the lower block—four—and out the sheave to the cleat.

This means that a 25 pound pull on the sheet will result in a force of nearly a hundred pounds on the boom—the slight loss being caused by friction. If one reverses the rig so that the double block with becket hangs from the boom, the mechanical advantage is five, but the final lead, off the boom block, will probably be inconvenient to deal with.

At first glance it would seem that the more mechanical advantage one has, the better; but this isn't the case. The more parts a tackle system contains, the more line one has to pull to achieve the same amount of change in the position of the boom. Line costs money, and in terms of trim, it costs time as well. A whole lot of extra line makes the cockpit into a spaghetti factory, so the best compromise for most skippers is to rig a mainsheet tackle that the weakest member of the crew can handle—albeit just barely—when the wind pressure on the sail is the most one might expect before reefing.

This sounds like an esoteric calculation, and to a degree it is. Some thoughts to ponder, when trying to work it out, are these:

According to sailmaker Wallace Ross, a man can pull horizontally, when standing with feet braced, about 75 pounds using both hands or 50 pounds with one hand. One time-tested formula for the pressure of wind on a sail is as follows:

WIND SPEED IN STATUTE MPH.	PRESSURE IN LB. PER SQ. FT. OF SAIL
15	1
20	1.5
25	2.5
30	3.5
40	5

Allow about 10 percent for friction, and work it out for yourself. Chances are your boat's architect is way ahead of you, and your sheet system is quite adequate. It may, however, be more than adequate for light-air conditions. If this is the case, there's nothing to stop you from simply abolishing one or two parts of the mainsheet, either by reversing it or unreeving a part. One other way to save sheeting time and money is to insert a small wire span between the boom and the upper mainsheet block. This significantly reduces the amount of line that's required for the remaining part of the system, and makes for less stretch in the sheet when the boat's close-hauled.

Except for the old-fashioned, nearly all mainsheets today incorporate a cam cleat in the lower block of the rig. Although this kind of cleat does chew up line a bit (as do self-tailing winches and sheet jammers), the increase in speed and ease of use more than makes up for wear and tear on the lines.

Given a track-mounted mainsheet, the next question is where to place the track. There are at the moment three popular locations. First and simplest—for the builder, anyway—is to run it across the aft end of the cockpit coaming,

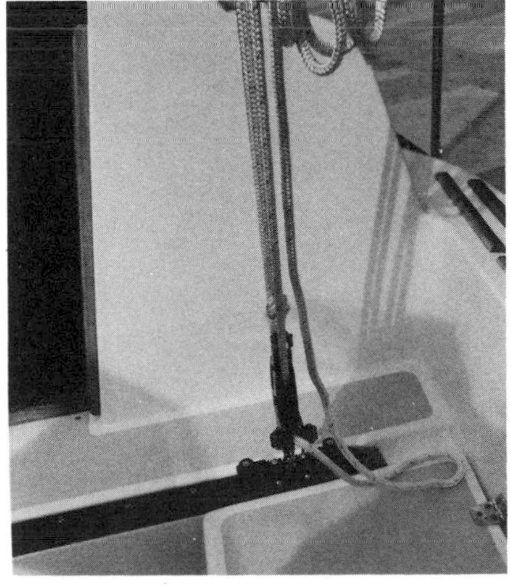

Recessed mainsheet track is easier on the crew.

presumably secured through the top of the molding. This provides a track that's out of the way of the crew, has a decent run from side to side, and is directly accessible to the helmsman. In boats where the main boom is long enough so that its end is directly over the track, it's an acceptable system. But in most newer yachts, the boom is short enough so that there is an awkward lead aft, interfering with the person at the wheel or tiller and producing a savage stress along the mainsail leech.

A better location, from the point of view of sail trim, is created by a mainsheet track that runs across the forward end of the cockpit. For a track the same length as one across the aft end of the cockpit, a midcockpit arrangement allows for a vertical downward stress on the sheet with the mainsail farther out to leeward. It also distributes the stress on the sail somewhat more evenly. It is easier for a crewmember to handle the trim of the main if it's forward in the cockpit than if it's behind the helmsman—although for shorthanded sailors it's correspondingly harder for a lone skipper to get at, and it cancels out some of the utility of the bridge deck seat; it may even pose something of a hazard for small children's hands.

The best spot for a mainsheet track is mounted atop the deckhouse, on a reinforced metal bracket over the fiberglass trunk into which the companionway hatch slides. This location allows the widest boom angle combined with direct downward trim, keeps the moving parts away from the hands and seats of the crew, and distributes the stress as well as any other system. More and more so-called performance cruisers are adopting this arrangement, which has only one point against it that I can see—the creation of a tripping point on top of the doghouse. Still, with jiffy reefing there's no reason for someone to be on the doghouse except when furling sail.

Other spars

One of the most useful spars on a small cruising yacht, and one of the most neglected, is the whisker pole. Many people use the spinnaker pole, which is a lot better than nothing, and some others use a boathook, which may not be better than nothing. A proper whisker pole is neither of these, but a spar with different fittings at each end, designed to extend the clew of the largest jib out as far as it can reasonably go when the boat is running.

This means that at full stretch a whisker pole is probably longer than a spinnaker pole. But in order to pole out smaller jibs (if you carry them), such a pole may be too long. A good compromise is the pole of adjustable length, composed of two pieces of alloy tubing, one sleeved inside the other. A twist-lock adjustment allows the crewmember to set the pole at whatever length is called for. The weakness of the twist lock, for saltwater sailors, is corrosion: If the pole is chocked on deck, as most are, it's bound to absorb seepage from

A good cabin-top mainsheet rig. The individual blocks help spread the load on the boom.

spray, and this can ruin the twist-lock's ability to lock, which depends on the friction of a rubber eccentric against the inside of the pole wall. If possible, it pays to chock the pole either vertically in the rigging or up the forward side of the mast, or carry it down below.

The inner end of a whisker pole is a conventional, spring-loaded jaw, like that of a spinnaker pole. It fits into a fixed eye on the mast, either a single fitting in smaller cruisers with smaller jibs or matching eyes on either side of the mast for bigger boats. The eye should be attached so that when the sail is winged out the whisker pole is parallel with the water. The normal fitting on the pole's outer end is a prong with a rounded end that fits into the sail's clew cringle and stays there when the jib sheet is hauled aft. A whisker pole is much lighter than a spinnker pole for a boat of the same size, and it shouldn't require a topping lift under normal circumstances.

On a boat under 30 feet, rigging a whisker pole is very simple: Set the boat on a broad reach or a run with the sail about halfway out; stab the pole's outer fitting through the clew cringle, and snap the inner jaw in place. Take up on the jib sheet until there's no danger of the sail leaping free of the pole, and then cleat the line. If your pole is long enough, the sail should be almost fully extended at right angles to the boat, making a very effective running rig that's also easy to control. To figure out the approximate length of a whisker pole for your boat, you first need to know the LP—*luff perpendicular*—of the largest genoa you own. In sailmakers' language, most genoas are described in

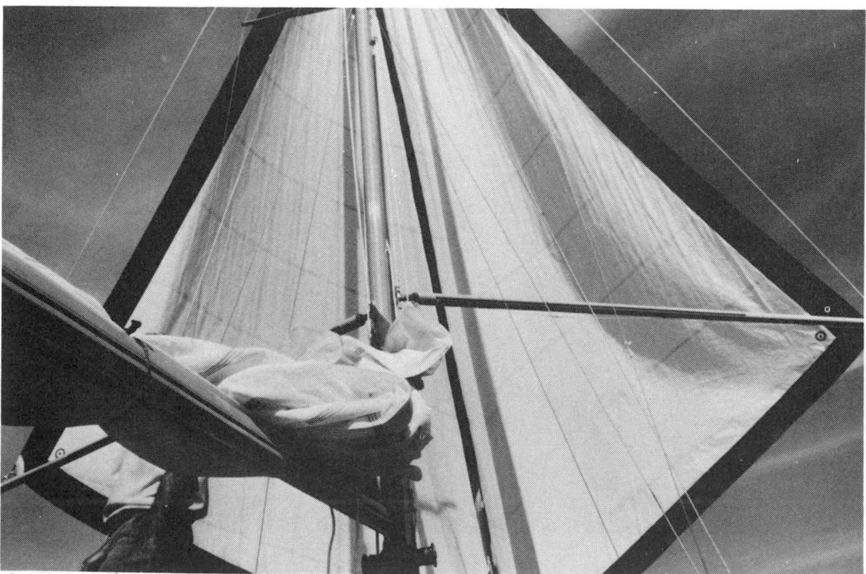

Twin-headsail rig in operation. Each of two roller-furling genoas has its own pole with topping lift. The poles stow along the shrouds when not in use, but remain clipped to the mast track.

terms of their LP—130 percent, 150 percent, 170 percent and occasionally 180 percent. The length of the LP of a given jib is simply the boat's J measurement multiplied by the percentage of LP. Thus, if your boat measures 10 feet from the forward side of the base of the mast to the tack fitting, she has a J of 10. The LP of her 130 percent genoa is 130 percent of 10, or 13 feet.

Spinnaker poles, with few exceptions, equal in length the boat's J measurement, which is why they're usually too short to boom out a genoa of more than 130 percent, the minimum size in normal use. A proper whisker pole should probably be about 85 percent of the LP for a given jib. On a boat with a 10-foot J measurement, then, the 150 percent will have an LP of 15 feet, and the whisker pole should be around 12½ feet. The same boat with a 180 percent jib would need a whisker pole over 15 feet long, hence the utility of adjustable poles.

A recent fad in downwind cruising rigs calls for twin whisker poles set to twin genoa jibs, or two genoas that are at least almost equal in size, for use when running down wind for long periods. The hardware is quite sophisticated, consisting of two poles that ride cars up and down a track on the forward side of the mast. When not in use, the poles stow up the mast, at the farthest reach of the track, with the outer end of each pole chocked at the gunwale against the toe rail. Heavier than normal poles, these can be used one at a time or both at once, and they do possess topping lifts. When the downwind twins are set, they replace both the staysail and mainsail, which only interfere with them. On boats with a tiller, the twins can be rigged for downwind self-steering.

The drawbacks to this rig are cost, which can equal or exceed that required for spinnaker hardware, complexity, and weight aloft when the poles aren't rigged. My own feeling is that unless one's normal sailing involves a lot of courses dead downwind in good breezes, with few course changes, this is a needlessly complicated setup. For most weekend cruisers, its only advantage over the spinnaker is the avoidance of one superlarge headsail that's set flying. My own inclination would be to get a good chute and learn how to handle it.

Spinnaker gear

A spinnaker is nearly always a boat's largest sail by far, about twice the square footage of the foretriangle, and thus substantially larger than the biggest genoa. But probably half the fear of spinnakers can be laid to the spinnaker pole, a brute of a spar that can run amok and lay waste an entire foredeck. Virtually all small-cruiser spinnaker poles today are light alloy tubes with identical spring-loaded jaw fittings at either end, capable of being opened by pull cords reaching the length of the pole. The jaw fits in an eye that can be adjusted vertically for height along the forward side of the mast—the aim usually being to raise or lower the inner end of the pole to keep it horizontal to the surface of the water. In a boat of the size we're dealing with, the car carrying the eye normally has a spring-loaded pin that drops into holes drilled into the vertical track on which it rides, providing a large but not infinite number of adjustments. For the cruising skipper, this is quite sophisticated enough.

There is also a bridle attached at each end of the pole, with a ring at its center point to which one snaps the spinnaker pole topping lift (called the pole lift by most sailors). Finally, the pole has another bridle with a central ring to which one snaps the end of the spinnaker pole foreguy (sometimes called the pole downhaul). This line leads from the ring on the bridle through a block on the foredeck and thence back to the cockpit. Between them, the pole lift and the foreguy control the vertical and horizontal movement of the pole, and the foreguy does most of the work, preventing the pole's outer end from being lifted skyward by the spinnaker.

Chainplates

Chainplates are a cause of some controversy today in terms of their size and the way they're attached to the fabric of the hull. The chainplate's function is simply to spread the load of the rig as widely over the hull as possible, and it's not unknown to have a chainplate strap run right down the hull to the keel. Unless the hull is superlight, however, this shouldn't be necessary.

Secure, if old-fashioned, set of chainplates on a Nor'Sea 27. Uppers and double lowers bolted through the hull.

In times gone by, the chainplate was through-bolted to a considerable expanse of the topside planking, with the plate itself visible on the outside of the hull. Most fiberglass boats have the chainplate running on the inside of the hull, preferably glassed into place and through-bolted. The bolt heads are seldom visible, being glassed over. The advantages of this system of chainplate attachment (or of attaching the plates to the hull exterior) are that one spreads the load to the maximum extent, over what is presumably a strong, well braced part of the hull surface, and that the shroud lead is at the maximum angle to the mast, making for the least load on wire and fittings.

The problem is that as boats become wider amidships, it is increasingly difficult to lead the overlapping genoa jib past a hull-mounted chainplate. The accepted position for jib sheet leads is something like 12 degrees off the centerline of the boat, and while the sail itself obviously trims in a flattened curve even when close-hauled, that 12-degree figure gives some idea of how flat the arc has to be. The way it's achieved, on more and more boats, is to move the chainplates inboard, so the genoa can set outside them: While it's possible to get a genoa inside or even between shrouds, it's not easy and it does lead to excessive chafe.

Inboard chainplates cannot, obviously, be bolted direct to the hull. If they're reasonably close, they can be led through the deck to a reinforced piece of fiberglass which is itself glassed to the hull. Mostly, however, today's chainplates are bolted to bulkheads, which is one reason why so many small cruisers have the head compartments amidships, facing hanging lockers of considerable fore-and-aft dimensions: Such a layout provides a good excuse for a couple of bulkheads, to which the chainplates may be made fast.

Properly done, there is nothing wrong with this setup. The bulkheads must of course be strength members themselves, not merely sheets of quarter-inch plywood, and they must be properly butted and glassed against the sides and cabin top of the boat. In nearly all yachts of 25 feet and less, there are single pairs of lower and upper shrouds, led to one chainplate a side. Since few of these rigs go down in the course of a season, they pass the primary test. For boats above 25 feet, however, the single pair of lowers seems to me less justifiable. At 28 to 30 feet, with a tall rig, one is not getting a great deal of support for the lower half of the mast with this arrangement. The classic setup calls for forward and after lowers as well as uppers—three chainplates a side. For a cruising boat, the extra weight aloft and the extra cost would seem to me to be well balanced by the extra security.

A slightly less strong, but still acceptable, rig has a single pair of after lowers acting against an intermediate, centerline forestay, which does the work of the two forward lowers. As long as the intermediate forestay is firmly fixed to a well-secured chainplate, itself secured through the deck to a bulkhead, this is probably quite adequate from the point of view of strength, although it does make for extra abrasion of the jib and sheets when tacking, and on this size boat the inner stay is usually too short and too close to the mast to allow setting another sail.

Somewhat more usual rig on a Columbia 7.6: Note uppers and single lowers, led to one chainplate a side. Interior view shows solid bolting of chainplate to main cabin bulkhead.

Frances 26 sloop (see Chapter III) has traditional double lower and single upper shrouds. Note jiffy-reefing lines set up for three mainsail reefs.

Standing rigging

Stays and shrouds are units, top to bottom, collectively forming a system. On modern boats there aren't too many such, and it may be worthwhile taking a look at each entity.

The forestay is in most modern small cruisers a masthead wire, balanced by the standing backstay. The forestay holds up the spar as well as the headsails, except when a boat carries a roller-furling jib on an inner stay. Normally, the forestay is retained even with a roller jib, as a safety factor, although a cutter-rigged yacht or one with certain types of roller furling may avoid the extra weight and windage and take its chances.

When rerigging a boat to accept a roller-furling jib inside the previous forestay, the most common mistake is to place the roller tack fitting too close behind the original tack plate. This is a perfectly natural thing, for one is only trying to preserve as much foretriangle as possible, but it's important to drop back about a foot in order to allow the roller jib to avoid entangling the standing forestay, especially when the jib is being furled without the proper amount of tension. If you're putting a roller jib on a boat whose J measurement is marginal to begin with, the best course of action is either to get a roller system that doesn't require an extra stay (see Chapter IV) or to consider a stub bowsprit for the standing headstay.

The backstay has become somewhat more complicated than the jibstay because it's no longer simply a part of the standing rigging but has, in many modern designs, gone halfway to becoming a piece of running rigging as well. The simplest backstay is a single piece of wire running from the masthead to a transom chainplate on or near the centerline. Although moving the backstay *slightly* off the centerline of the hull will put a small wringing stress on the rig, it really doesn't seem to matter a great deal. On some boats with transom-mounted rudders and tillers that come over the transom, the lower element of the backstay is shaped like an inverted Y. This is also the case in some ketches and yawls, and it does seem cause for a little extra difficulty in tuning the rig precisely. Other yachts have twin backstays all the way from the masthead to the corners of the transom. There's nothing wrong with such a rig, and if anything, it's easier to tune than a Y backstay. It certainly adds an extra element of safety to an important part of the rig, although it can interfere with the setting of some ancillary sails on a ketch or yawl.

As a result of racing experience in day-sailing one-designs, more and more cruising-size yachts are now arriving with backstay tensioners. For boats of the size we're discussing, hydraulics are not really a factor, and so any tensioning is likely to be done with a multipart tackle. The principle is quite simple: By adding tension to the backstay of a three-quarter or seven-eighths rig, the masthead is bent aft, the mast bends slightly forward at midheight, and the mainsail is correspondingly flattened all along its luff. Ease the tension, and the sail becomes fuller. It's a lot quicker and probably more effective than

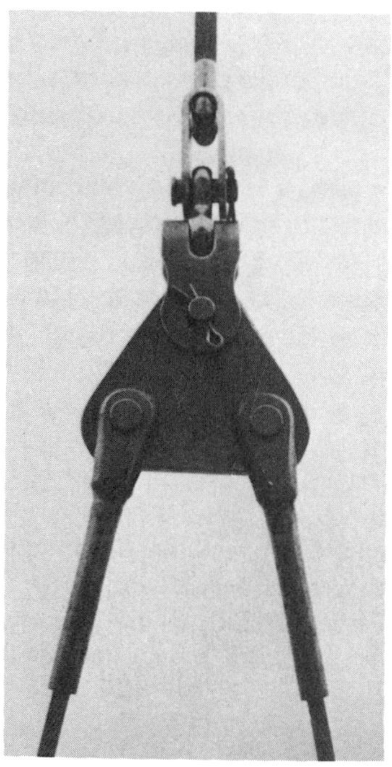

Standard attachment for inverted-Y backstay. Note toggle fitting at top.

fiddling with outhauls and halyards, and it also works, if less dramatically, with masthead rigs.

As shown in the illustration, the tensioner is a pair of blocks riding the twin backstays, made fast to a central ring. Also attached to the ring is the tackle, with a built-in jam cleat, made fast to a reinforcement on the transom or afterdeck.

The standard upper and lower shrouds are simple enough so they need no further discussion here, but if a staysail stay is employed, it deserves some extra thought. By staysail stay, I *don't* mean the small inner forestay mentioned above, but a regular stay from which a sail is set. I have my suspicions about the utility of the cutter rig in boats under 30 feet—or under 40, for that matter—but if you do have this kind of arrangement, it is probably worth while to rig it with a quick-release fitting at the lower end of the staysail stay. This is a variety of pelican hook, capable of being set up reasonably taut by its own leverage, yet able to be released easily and quickly to allow the setting (and tacking) of a really large headsail in light weather, or spinnaker pole to be dipped through the foretriangle. The released stay is normally made fast against the forward side of the mast until needed again.

Since the staysail on a small cruising cutter is really a heavy-weather sail, it can impose quite a load on the mast. Accordingly, it should be balanced off

Backstay tensioner rigged on a small cruiser.

with running backstays, unless the mast is of exceptionally heavy section. Running backstays are a classic pain in the neck, and for my money should be integrated into the rig for heavy-weather use only. When not required, they should be strapped against the lower shrouds out of the way. When they are needed, however, there must be some way of setting them up quickly and releasing them even more quickly. The accepted methods are either deck-mounted levers, which are fastest, or a tackle led back to the cockpit sheet winches, which requires less machinery on the boat.

On small ketches and yawls, the mizzen backstays are doubled, led back to a compromise position that affords neither good strength nor a complete lack of interference with the mizzen boom when running. Unfortunately, there isn't a great deal of choice. With a small ketch, however, it's possible to provide a second set of deck plates all the way aft to which the weather mizzen backstay may be shifted when running in storm conditions or when carrying the mizzen staysail in unusually heavy weather. If this stay is not worked into a tackle, an extra toggle or span will be necessary to lengthen it when it's moved aft, but such a provision is definitely a safety factor, especially if one habitually carries a large mizzen staysail in all weathers.

III

Coastal Cruisers–A Design Portfolio

In theoretical terms there are literally hundreds of designs available for cruising yachts of 30 feet and less, but from a practical viewpoint there are, thankfully, limitations to the list. One is constrained by price, geographical proximity, design suitability, and a number of other factors. Even so, a careful searcher without too many crippling prejudices is likely to find that his shortest serious list of possibles numbers a half dozen at least.

This critical portfolio is not intended as anything like a complete listing of types, never mind models. Nor does it pretend to claim that each of the boats discussed is the very best of its kind. What I have done, however, is compile a fleet conscientiously selected because they are good, small cruisers in a broad spectrum of types, and because in many cases I am personally familiar with them. More inclusive lists exist. Perhaps the most nearly complete listing of boats currently in production is the *Yachting* annual, *Boat Buyers Guide,* which provides dimensional data and occasionally prices for most U.S.–built production yachts. More complete information on a narrower spectrum of vessels appears in another annual, *Sail* magazine's *Sailboat & Equipment Directory,* while *Practical Boat Owner* in the U.K. publishes a good survey from time to time. A photo, plan, and brief blurb (written by the builder) describes a good cross-section of current yachts, but by no means all of them. In recent years a critical summary, *The Independent Yacht Survey,* has attempted to provide generic evaluations of production yachts. Because of its high price and limited distribution, its future is cloudy, but even an old copy —if you can find one—will make thought-provoking reading.

Every boat is a compromise, and a small cruiser involves more give-and-take than perhaps any other type of yacht design. The boats listed below seem to me to have survived the compromising process successfully in both looks and function. They are also all available to the determined purchaser, even though some are no longer in series production and others never were. I have grouped them in what appears to me a rational fashion, though there are certainly other ways of doing it, notably by length.

Reading accommodation plans

When you are looking at the accommodation plans of new boats, it's important to realize just how much of the space the boat apparently contains is really usable and how much, while existent, is just air space.

There are two main problems facing the neophyte trying to figure out a boat's accommodation from its plans. First is the fact that plans represent a three-dimensional shape—and a complicated one—on a flat surface. A complete set of lines makes it easier to see what the real cubic area of a boat may be but, unless one has access to such normally restricted information, it's hard to get a true picture from the overhead view manufacturers normally provide.

The second difficulty is in trying to relate a scaled set of plans to the realities of the human shape. Here, at least, there is an answer, and we'll get to it in a little while.

Back to plans. An accommodation plan of a boat will almost always show the outline of the craft at its outermost edge, giving the impression that it's

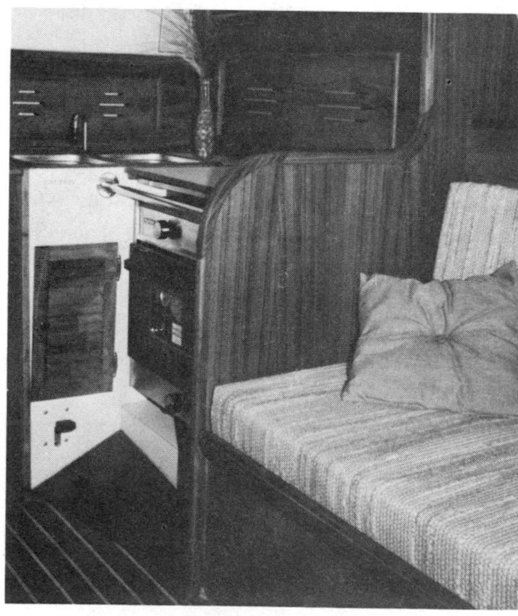

Note how hull curves up at stove. This would probably not be apparent on plans.

a good deal larger than it is. In the case of an old-fashioned wood yacht of carvel construction, there can be a significant difference between the dimensions on the exterior of the planking and the usable space within the ceiling. Even with a fiberglass boat, where the distance from gelcoat surface to inside of the headliner is a couple of inches at most, the accommodation plan can still be a deception.

The reason, of course, is that nearly all hulls slope inward from deck to waterline, and what you see at deck level isn't what you're getting down around your ankles, or even your hips. Perhaps the best and most cold-blooded way to assess the real space inside a boat, based on the accommodation view alone, is to look at the cabin sole or floorboards. These are usually indicated, and they give a murderously accurate idea of how wide the boat is at that point, normally just above the turn of the keel. Where there are no floorboards, there's no level surface on which to stand—a problem most in evidence in the corners of galleys.

Another question is headroom. Once one gets up to about 30 feet overall, there's decent headroom in all but the raciest monohull boats. Below that length, however, one is subjected to partial, or "almost," headroom. Most authorities agree that having an overhead half an inch less than your height in deck shoes is far more annoying than having it six inches less.

So bear in mind that when a manufacturer quotes a headroom figure, it will probably be genuine for some part of the boat. But it may well be inflated by a couple of inches at least for most of the main cabin and head; and the forward

Low overhead in this sitting-headroom cabin is more apparent in a photo than in plans.

cabin, in the size boat we're talking about, will seldom have anything like genuine headroom for the average American or European.

Many experienced cruising people who like to travel in small, flush-decked yachts feel that sitting headroom is all one really needs below. This is not a judgment anyone can make on your behalf. But if you decide that sitting headroom meets your needs, be sure you've got it over those areas in the boat where you'll be sitting. Sometimes the side decks come in far enough over the saloon bunks so you have to lean forward to straighten—more or less—upright. Sometimes there's sitting headroom in the main cabin but not forward. Sometimes there's vertical headroom but not, in a normal sitting area, shoulder, hip, or leg room.

Which brings me to "standard" man and how to use him. Standard man is a useful fiction created by engineers who need to have a shorthand way of figuring out how much space is needed for someone to sit, stand, lie, and work. The problem with the kind of calculations involved is that once they're made, they tend to be frozen, while the human race continues to grow. One standard man still in common use is 5′9″, and while that is certainly an ideal size—my own, in fact—it's nevertheless true that an increasing number of people are bigger. The adjoining table gives useful dimensions for people who are 5′9″ through 6′2″, but it's also handy to know that, for the majority of mankind, there are some standards we have grown used to, even though we may not fit them ourselves. For instance, most of us will find a stand-up work surface feels natural about 36 inches off the deck, while a sitting surface is usually 18 inches high, and the table at which one sits is about 30 inches. Risers on a stair or ladder are uncomfortable for most people if they're more than a foot apart, and in any case, all the steps in a ladder should be the same distance apart vertically. According to Frank Kinney, author of *Skene's Elements of Yacht Design,* a compartment door's minimum width is 21 inches, and an escape hatch should not be less than 18 inches square, though Roger Marshall, in *Designed to Win,* suggests that a doorway can be 18 inches wide.

Tables of sizes

For a person 5′9″ high:
arm's length = 2′6″
normal vertical reach = 6′3″
Shoulder width = 1′6″
Hip width = 1′2″
Feet side by side = 8″
Foot length = 12″
Sitting height = 4′5″
Leg clearance when sitting = 2′0″
Width of seat = 1′3″
Elbow room, per person = 2′3″
For people 5′10″ high, multiply by 1.015; for 6′0″, multiply by 1.043; for 6′2″, multiply by 1.07; for 6′4″, by 1.1.

Fiberglass classics

TRITON

Designer: Carl Alberg
Builder: Pearson Yachts, West Shore Rd., Portsmouth, Rhode Island 02873
LOA . . . 28′6″
LWL . . . 20′6″
Beam . . . 8′3″
Draft (keel) . . . 4′0″
Displacement . . . 6,930 lb.
Ballast . . . 3,019 lb.
Sail area (sloop) . . . 371 sq. ft.
(yawl) . . . 382.5 sq. ft.

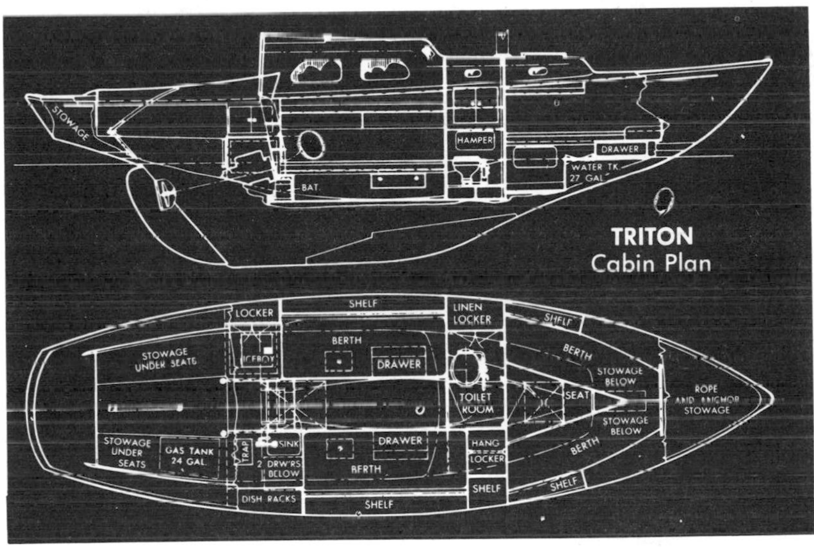

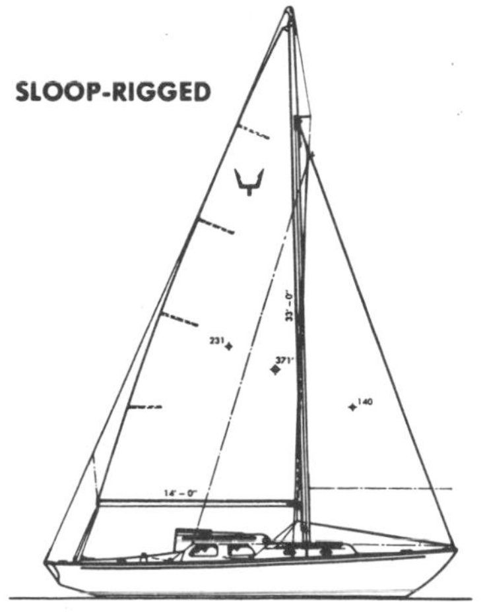

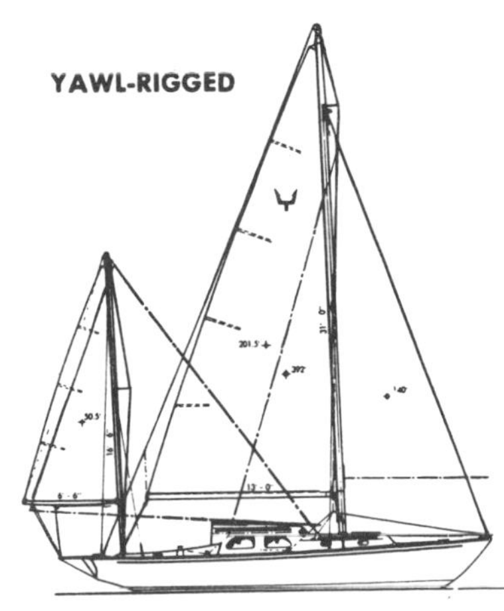

If one boat can be said to underlie the so-called fiberglass revolution in yacht building, the Triton has a fair claim to that distinction. In its day—the early 1960s—it was far and away the most popular cruising sailboat available, and even today an active class association exists to keep competition active and resale value high.

Even by the standards of twenty years later, the Triton is an imaginative and attractive boat, and her fractional rig is just coming back into style after a hiatus of many years. The optional yawl rig, however, seems unlikely to return in numbers, having existed only because of a loophole in the rating rule. The Triton's appearance is typical of Alberg designs, with a rather flat sheer and well-rounded superstructure; while the full underbody is also typical of Alberg yachts, the Triton is perhaps less heavy than most. Her layout below is both imaginative and practical, with a pair of berths in the main and forward cabins, plus the option of two more stretcher-type berths in the saloon. The head and hanging locker are lobby-style, running the width of the boat, while the galley is aft by the companionway, split in two by the ladder. The icebox loads through an opening in the bridge deck, with access through a vertical door below; I have lived with this arrangement in another boat and find it entirely satisfactory.

With shelves, cubbyholes, and drawers, the Triton has considerably more well-conceived stowage than most of the early fiberglass cruisers, and in many cases careful owners have improved upon her rather antiseptic appearance below decks. The standard engine was a Universal Atomic-4, and in most of the fleet it will have been replaced by now, or it will be due for replacement. The Triton has a reputation as a fast and able boat, and the only trouble for which she is widely known is a tendency for the jumper struts to come adrift occasionally. If not already fitted, a mainsheet traveler would be an improvement over the original sheeting arrangement.

Tritons have held their value well and show no signs of coming to the end of the road. A well-maintained vessel in this class can be an excellent used-boat bargain, although a careful survey is indicated.

TARTAN 27

Designer: Sparkman & Stephens
Builder: Douglass & McLeod, Inc.,
later Tartan Marine Co.,
320 River St., Grand River,
Ohio 44045
LOA . . . 27′0″
LWL . . . 21′5″
Beam . . . 8′7½″
Draft . . . 3′2″ (board up), 6′4″
Displacement . . . 6,875 lb. (new model: 7,400 lb.)
Ballast . . . 2,400 lb.
Sail area (sloop) . . . 376 sq. ft.
(yawl) . . . 394 sq. ft.

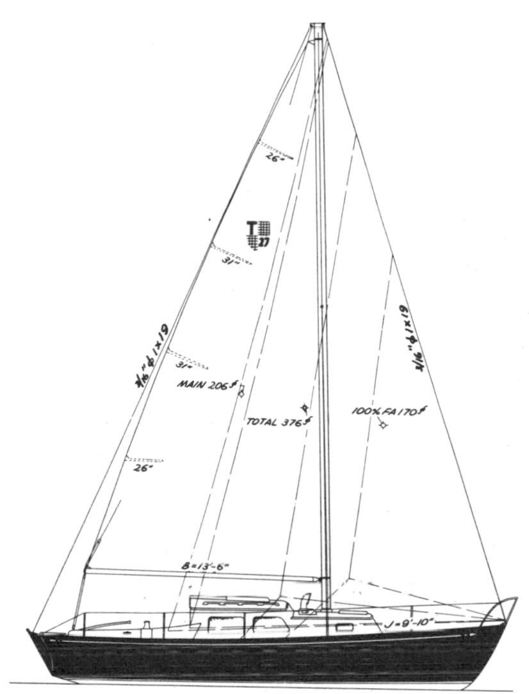
26"
31"
31"
MAIN 206
TOTAL 376
100% FA 170
26"
B=13'-6"
J=9'-10"

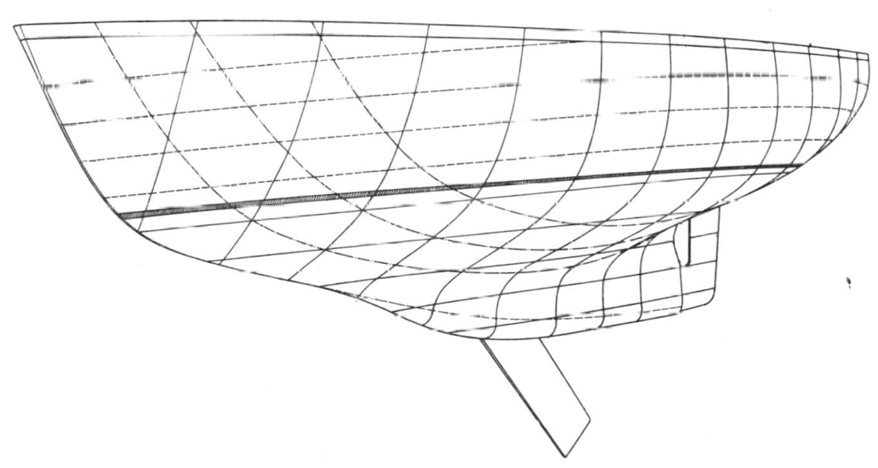

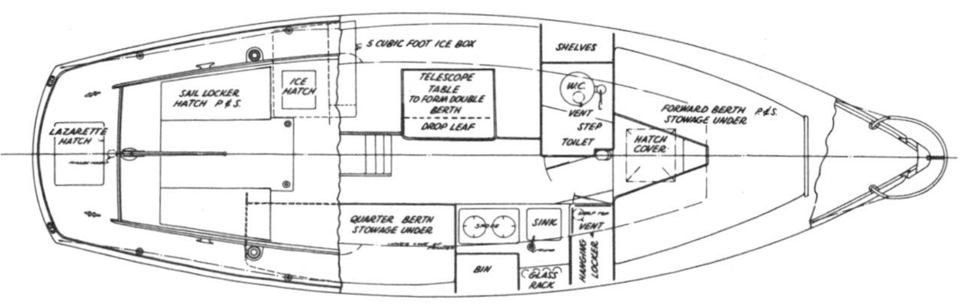
5 CUBIC FOOT ICE BOX
SHELVES
SAIL LOCKER HATCH P & S.
ICE HATCH
TELESCOPE TABLE TO FORM DOUBLE BERTH
DROP LEAF
W.C.
VENT
STEP
TOILET
FORWARD BERTH P & S. STOWAGE UNDER
HATCH COVER
LAZARETTE HATCH
QUARTER BERTH STOWAGE UNDER
SINK
VENT
HANGING LOCKER
BIN
GLASS RACK

Well over six hundred hulls of the original doghouse Tartan 27 were built, testimony to the success of this pocket cruiser-racer. She is perhaps a perfect example of a miniaturized yacht, a fact that becomes apparent when one is below. In most cases, shrinking the several elements of a boat doesn't succeed, because one cannot shrink the crew as well. In the Tartan's case, it will work for most people, because the design has been carefully done. Like the Triton, the 27 has a deck-loading icebox, but in this vessel the ice is diagonally across the saloon from the rest of the galley, and there is a pronounced shortage of work space for the cook, remedied in some boats by the owner's addition of a folding shelf to the half bulkhead at the aft end of the galley. The drop-leaf table and settee form a berth, but it will only be a double for very friendly or skinny folk.

The head compartment is just about the minimum size possible for real people, and the boat has only one genuine sea berth—which is enhanced, however, by the provision for a sea rail. Power is a Universal Atomic-4, and in most cases this engine is probably approaching the end of its useful life, if it has not done so already.

In 1979 Tartan Marine, the successors to Douglass & McLeod, brought out a revised Tartan 27, with a wholly new deck-cabin mold and interior layout, but similar in specifications to the first design. While the new interior is considerably more open than the old, with a chart table and a lobby-style head, there are many people who feel the original boat had a charm that has been lost in transition. One less-mourned loss is the gasoline inboard, which has been replaced by a 12-hp. Farymann diesel.

Despite the new version, the old Tartan 27s continue to hold their value very well, having been top-quality boats from the start. A salt-water sailor who is thinking of a Tartan 27 would do well to investigate brokerage listings on the Great Lakes, where the boat had a wide distribution. Lake-sailed Tartans are likely also to be in better shape, by virtue of having avoided salt water all their lives. But any Tartan 27, given adequate care over the years, will be a sturdy and attractive yacht and, well-sailed, a reasonable PHRF competitor in her sloop rig.

ARPÈGE

Designer: Michel Dufour
Builder: Michel Dufour S.A.
Importer: Dufour Inc., Seven River Rd., Cos Cob, Connecticut 06807
LOA . . . 29′6″
LWL . . . 22′0″
Beam . . . 9′11″
Draft (keel) . . . 4′5″
Displacement . . . 6,720 lb.
Ballast . . . 2,650 lb.
Sail area (approx.) . . . 400 sq. ft.

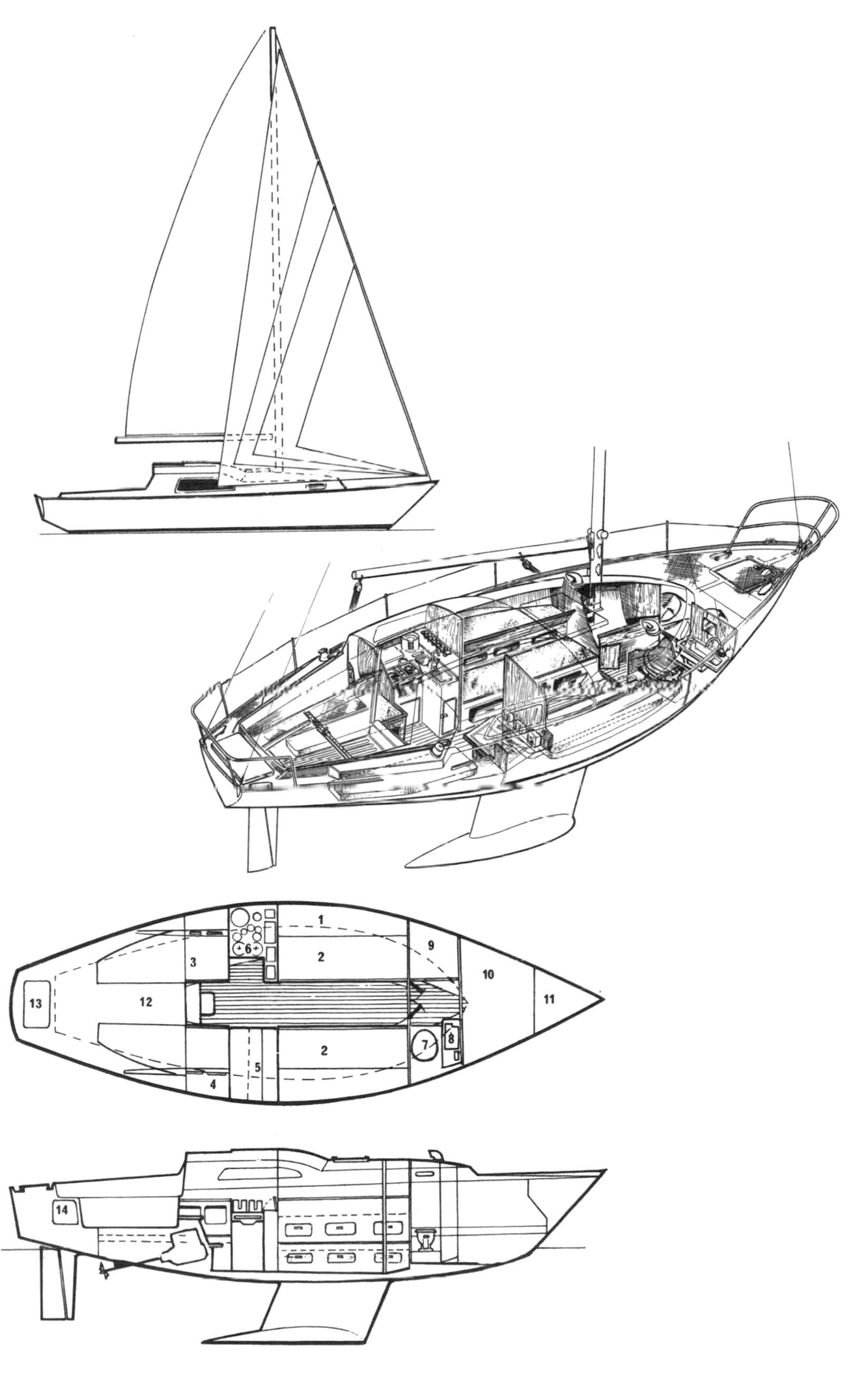

1
2
3
4
5
6
7
8
9
10
11
12
13
14

Although she never achieved in this country the stunning success that was hers in Europe, the Arpège cruiser-racer was widely admired here as well. She won the Half Ton Cup at La Rochelle in France and also stood at the top of her class in the rally for cruising yachts held by *Yachting World,* the British monthly. She remains to my eyes one of the handsomest boats Michel Dufour has ever designed, despite the fact that her aspect ratio has begun to look a bit stubby in recent years.

Arpège's layout carries French logic to a sensible limit, but produces a cruiser whose interior is quite different from any other boat I've seen. She has two large quarter berths flanking the companionway, and forward of them the galley to port and chart table to starboard. The galley is a marvel of ingenuity, with molded-in recesses for every conceivable utensil, and across from it the chart table provides badly needed work surface for the cook (assuming he or she can wrestle the use of it away from the navigator). Although early Arpèges had a tilted chart table surface, later ones had a level top that was a good deal more efficient in multiple applications.

The saloon is separated from the working part of the cabin by sole-to-overhead bulkheads, and can be completely closed off by a curtain. There are two narrow but usable pilot berths and two settees in the main cabin, making four sea berths in all. In an unusual feature, the head and a large hanging locker were way forward, with a sail bin forward of that. It was a setup that was somewhat more logical for racing than cruising, but it would certainly serve well for any offshore work.

The Arpège had one of the first molded-in foredeck anchor wells to be seen on this side of the Atlantic and, despite the obvious utility of the arrangement, it was nearly a decade before this feature was regularly seen in American boats. The inboard may be a 7-hp. diesel or 10-hp. gasoline model.

There are not too many Arpèges on the used-boat market, and because of the high initial price of Dufour yachts, the used models aren't cheap. Because they are so unusual, one is likely to fall passionately in love with them or detest them. I think they are splendid.

Catboats

NONSUCH OFFSHORE CATBOAT
Designer: Mark Ellis
Builder: Hinterhoeller Yachts, Ltd.
8 Keefer Rd., St. Catharines,
Ontario LZM 7N9
LOA . . . 30′0″
LWL . . . 28′9″
Beam . . . 11′10″
Draft (keel) . . . 5′0″
Displacement . . . 10,500 lb.
Ballast . . . 4,500 lb.
Sail area . . . 540 sq. ft.

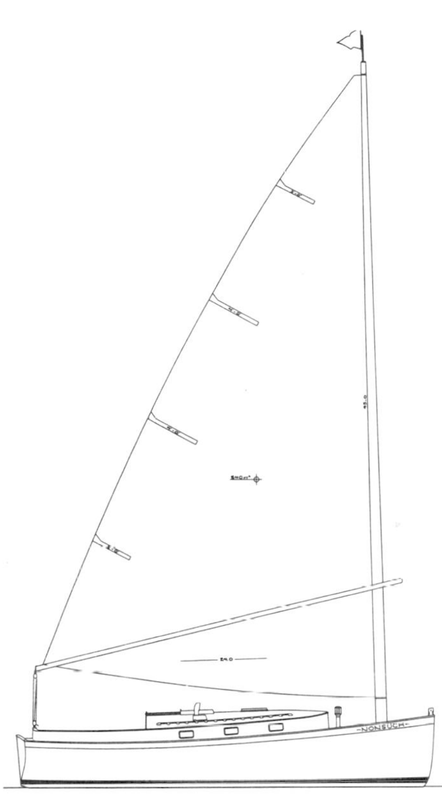

24.0
-NONSUCH-

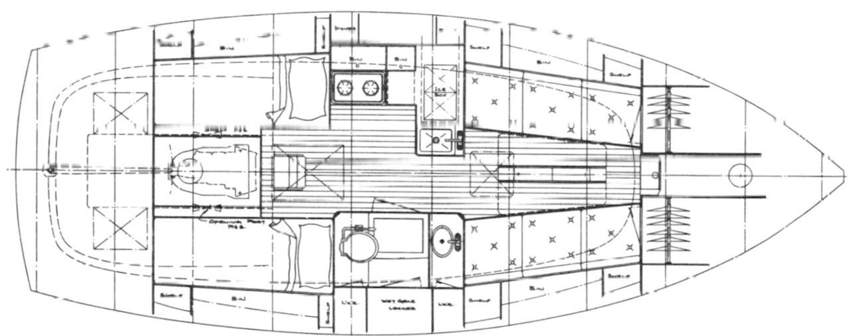

BIN
SHELF
ICE BOX
OPENING PORT
WET GEAR LOCKER

It would be hard to find a less classic catboat than the Nonsuch, a Canadian yacht designed to race as a class boat, while providing the comfort and ease of handling associated with larger catboats. In point of fact, the Nonsuch is far easier to handle than a classic, gaff-rigged cat or any other rig I've yet encountered. Her underwater hull form is rather like that of a big dinghy, with the exception of the fin keel and spade rudder, which give her impressive quickness in handling. Her beam is considerable, although less than would be called for in a cat of classic proportions, and it helps to keep her stiff.

But the Nonsuch's greatest asset, in my opinion, is her rig. Unlike the sleeved wishbone sails associated with Garry Hoyt's Freedom designs, the Nonsuch main has a luff made fast to a conventional track. The wishbone has a net beneath it, and to reef the main one simply eases off the halyard in a variant of standard jiffy reefing. When I sailed the boat, tying in a reef took about thirty seconds, and the control lines were led in such a way that it was unnecessary to leave the cockpit.

The boat appears to be quite fast both off and on the wind, and she is said to point about five degrees lower than a conventionally rigged masthead sloop. If there should be a complaint about her handling it's that the unstayed wishbone is almost too easy—once the sail is up, there is very little left to do.

Nonsuch's cockpit is not so large, relatively speaking, as that of a smaller catboat, but that may be just as well, as it is bigger than cockpits found in much larger monohulls. The extra space goes to accommodation, which in this vessel is princely, as long as one admires the open plan. The boat is laid out to handle four people in considerable comfort, with two extralarge quarter berths aft and a pair of settee berths flanking the drop-leaf table in the saloon part of the cabin. Both the galley and head compartment gain in space from being amidships, at the widest point in the hull, and both areas are functionally planned. The head contains a good-sized oilskin locker, but the main hanging lockers are forward in the eyes of the boat, flanking the Dutch fireplace that makes the cabin remarkably homey. Auxiliary power is from a 23-hp. Volvo diesel hooked to a saildrive lower unit.

Although a traditionalist will find the Nonsuch's appearance a bit hard to swallow, especially in drawings where her unusual aspects seem to be most obtrusive, anyone will have to admit that she is about as practical as a boat can get, once one has come to terms with the compromises inherent in the cat rig and open layout.

ATLANTIC CITY CATBOAT

Designer: David P. Martin
Distributor: Navesink Yacht Sales
1410 Ocean Ave.,
Sea Bright, New
Jersey 07760
LOA . . . 24'0"
LWL . . . 22'0"

Beam . . . 11′0″
Draft . . . 2′0″ (board up)
Displacement . . . 8,800 lb.
Ballast . . . 2,500 lb.
Sail area 450 sq. ft.

Dave Martin, who was for some years the house designer for the Pacemaker power cruiser firm, grew up in southern New Jersey where shallow, semi-protected waters opening on the Atlantic through narrow inlets encouraged the development of large, sophisticated catboats. Dave is also a very large man, and one of his obsessions as a designer has always been to create boats in which he could stand up. It's not an easy thing to do in a 24-footer, but this Cape Cod–type cat manages to offer 6′3″ headroom beneath the deckhouse roof. Her hull is a bit deeper than is customary in cats, and her cabin a bit higher, but on the whole she carries her extra headroom very gracefully.

She is something of a wonder in other respects as well, having the capability for sleeping six close friends. The dinette converts to a double, with the occupants' feet under the galley counter, the quarterberth handles two more, while the settee to starboard makes into an upper and lower. There is also reasonable headroom in the head compartment forward, and the galley is entirely adequate for weekending, with a two-burner gimbaled stove, a sink, and a portable ice chest in a fitted space (a far better idea, in my opinion, than the standard, too-small icebox so often seen on boat this size).

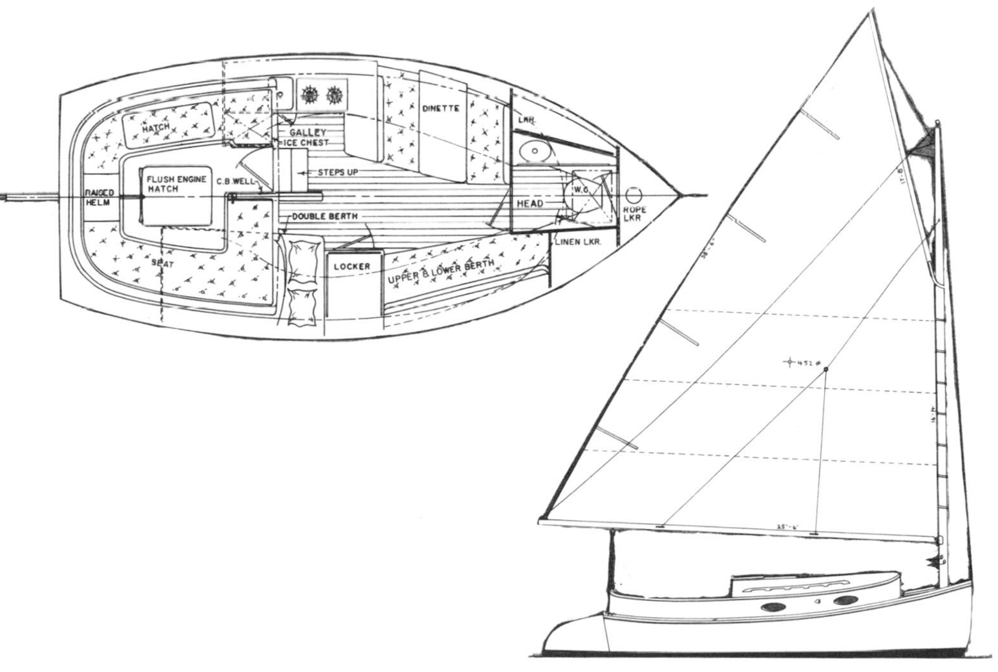

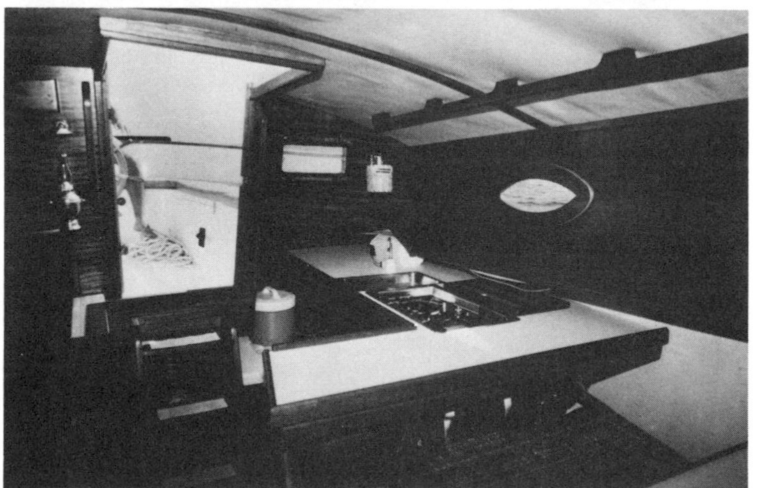

Two people could probably sleep under the stars in the 7½′ × 8½′ cockpit, and the 12-hp. BMW diesel is accessible through a flush hatch in the cockpit sole. She has tankage for 20 gallons of diesel and 38 of fresh water. A good deal of the room down below was created by moving the engine well aft in order to keep the centerboard out of the cabin as much as possible, and it only protrudes slightly.

While a boat this size with so much sail in a single chunk can easily be a handful, the Atlantic City cat distills the assets of the type, namely, utter simplicity, classic appearance, and a vast amount of room for her length. With the sails handled from the cockpit (this is an instance where lazyjacks might well be indicated) and a hatch just abaft the mast from which to handle ground tackle, she is a relatively easy boat to cope with under most conditions, provided one has not left reefing until too late. All in all, she seems to me a splendid improvement, thanks to fiberglass construction and Dave Martin's skill, on a classic concept.

Multihulls

HIRONDELLE

Designer: Chris Hammond
Importer: Symons-Sailing, Inc.
Box 415, Amityville
New York 11701
LOA . . . 22′8″
LWL . . . 20′0″
Beam . . . 10′0″
Draft . . . 1′3″ (boards up), 4′0″
Displacement . . . 2,700 lb.
Sail area . . . 250 sq. ft. (approx.)

I owned one of these engaging little cruising catamarans for two years, so I am not unprejudiced about her. She was designed and is built in Great Britain, the home of a number of excellent cruising multihulls, but has achieved popularity (in multihull terms) in the United States as well.

It would be a mistake to expect truly sizzling performance from this type of multihull, which her builders carefully characterize as a coastal cruiser. Rather, she offers sailing at speeds comparable to those of a well-designed monohull cruiser perhaps five feet longer, and quite remarkable interior accommodation for her length, with a couple of drawbacks typical of multihulls.

Hirondelle has a very high aspect ratio sloop rig and will handle reasonably well under any headsail alone, but is virtually helpless under her main without a headsail, as it is so small and so far aft that it serves more or less as a weathervane unless associated with a jib. Because of the vast working area forward, sail changes are easy, but the boat is also extremely sensitive to weight

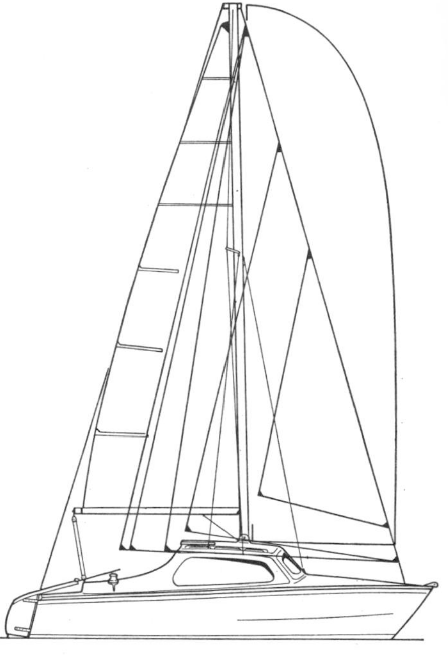

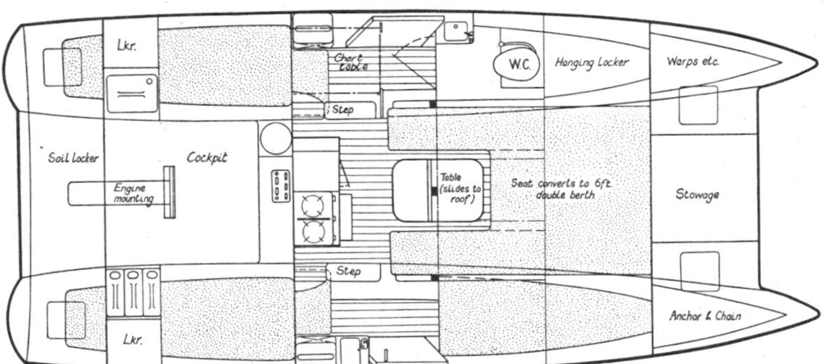

in the bows and can drop a knot of speed when an average adult stands at the forward pulpit. She has a pronounced knuckle in the hull forward that deflects spray and keeps her from nosing her fine bows under, but she is intended to carry weight well aft, where the hulls provide enough buoyancy.

Halyards, sheets, daggerboard tackles, and tiller bar are all accessible to the helmsman, so there is seldom need to go forward except to laze or change sail. A tiller extender is handy, but one must remember to keep it out of the way of the mainsheet slide when tacking or jibing. By virtue of having four adjustable narrow fins under her shallow hulls, Hirondelle can be made extremely nimble. By the same token, when motoring or when sailing downwind in light airs, both daggerboards and one rudder may be completely retracted, and the other rudder lowered just enough to provide steerage. The reduced wetted surface can give her almost an extra knot of speed.

Like all cats, Hirondelle jibes with magnificent ease. She tacks very quickly but must usually be put about rather abruptly, which cuts her forward speed noticeably. Because of her high freeboard and light weight, she needs to be sailed right up to piers and moorings before her sails are allowed to luff, and this can be somewhat nervewracking for novice crews. Although she never flew a hull in the two years I owned her, my Hirondelle felt sensitive enough so that I did not feel really secure when cruising unless I had another experienced multihull sailor available to handle the helm, and since I enjoyed single-handing, this was one of the reasons I finally parted with her.

My Hirondelle was powered by a 9.9-hp. Johnson long-shaft outboard with electric start, which lived in a well at the aft end of the cockpit. By a curious design coincidence, as the boat approached hull speed, the wave formation between the hulls was such that it caused near cavitation of the engine, which could be annoying in a choppy sea when one wanted to punch to windward quickly. Like nearly all multihulls, she was best sailed fast and free.

In terms of accommodation, Hirondelle was perhaps the most extraordinary boat I've yet owned. Her living and stowage spaces were simply immense, but one could easily be lured into taking all one's gear aboard, in which case the weight would cripple her performance. I normally carried two light anchors and rode, plus a couple of large fenders, in the cavernous bow lockers port and starboard. In the equally large lazarette that ran nearly ten feet across the transom we stowed dock lines, boarding ladder, barbecue, wind vane, and seat cushions. The bridge deck had three small lockers—one for the battery, one for the cooking gas bottle, and one that served as the British idea of an icebox. The only good thing about it was that it drained overboard between the hulls. Aside from that, it managed to melt ice more quickly than anything short of a blast furnace. We used a large cooler, just big enough to fit through one of the twin companionways; it lived on the starboard quarterberth, adjacent to the sink counter that ran along the inside of the starboard hull. Standing at the sink—there was just standing headroom (5′9″) for me in the hulls—one could make a half turn and reach the rest of the galley, disposed across the aft end of the deckhouse between the companionways. Because the boat never heeled more than ten degrees, it wasn't necessary to gimbal the British stove, which had two burners above and a grill—a small broiler—below. There was plenty of stowage for food and utensils in a large locker above the stove and in other spaces nearby.

There was a second full-length berth, with a stowage shelf over its foot, forward in the starboard hull, and a separate head compartment in the equivalent space to port. Forward of the actual head—we used a portable unit that we carried ashore to empty—was sufficient space to stow two genoas, the spinnaker, working and storm jibs, all of which slowly absorbed a certain amount of the cut-rate cathouse odor of the head deodorant. Aft in the port hull was a second huge quarterberth, with a second rubber watertank beneath it.

The main part of the deckhouse was taken up by a huge, U-shaped settee around a table that could be dropped down to form an exceptionally wide but rather short double, where one's feet stuck forward beneath the middle section of the foredeck. My two small boys, in their mole phase, would alternate entombing themselves in the recesses of the quarterberths and under the foredeck. They loved the boat for these hiding spaces, and also because they could leave their toys and games on the low railed table with no fear of anything's coming adrift.

In a shoal-water area with reasonably good but not excessively strong winds (say a dependable 10–15 knots), it would be hard to find a more sprightly and entertaining little family cruiser. And on rainy days, one has the option of sitting around the deckhouse table and watching the world go by—an asset common to multihulls and virtually unknown in monohull sailboats.

STILETTO

Designer: Bill Higgins
Builder: Force Engineering,
5329 Ashton Court,
Sarasota, Florida 33583
LOA . . . 26′10″
LWL . . . 24′0″
Beam . . . 13′10″
Draft . . . 9″ (board up), 4′0″
Displacement . . . 875 lb.
Sail area . . . 240 sq. ft.

The Florida-built Stiletto is as unusual and successful in her way as Hirondelle is in hers—and aside from their both having twin hulls, it would be hard to find two more different boats. Hirondelle is very much a cruising yacht that happens to have two hulls, while Stiletto is a high-performance cat that happens to have fairly primitive accommodations; she is first and last a boat for people who enjoy sailing, and sailing fast.

Stiletto's extremely light weight is partly a result of careful engineering and partly derives from her construction material, a laminate formed of fiberglass cloth over a hollow honeycomb stiffener that gives the boat exceptional strength as well as lightness. She has a single centerboard and two kickup rudders, and handles well under power with a 5-hp. outboard. She has the standard sail plan for a fast cat, consisting of a huge, fully battened main and a small jib set from a bridle. A genoa, drifter, and spinnaker are also available, but the latter does not really seem to the point, as a boat like Stiletto can almost always do better tacking downwind from reach to reach than she can running.

In terms of accommodations, Stiletto requires a few revisions in normal cruiser thinking. She has cabins in each hull, but they are compact, with stretcherlike berths forward port and starboard, a head aft in one hull and a

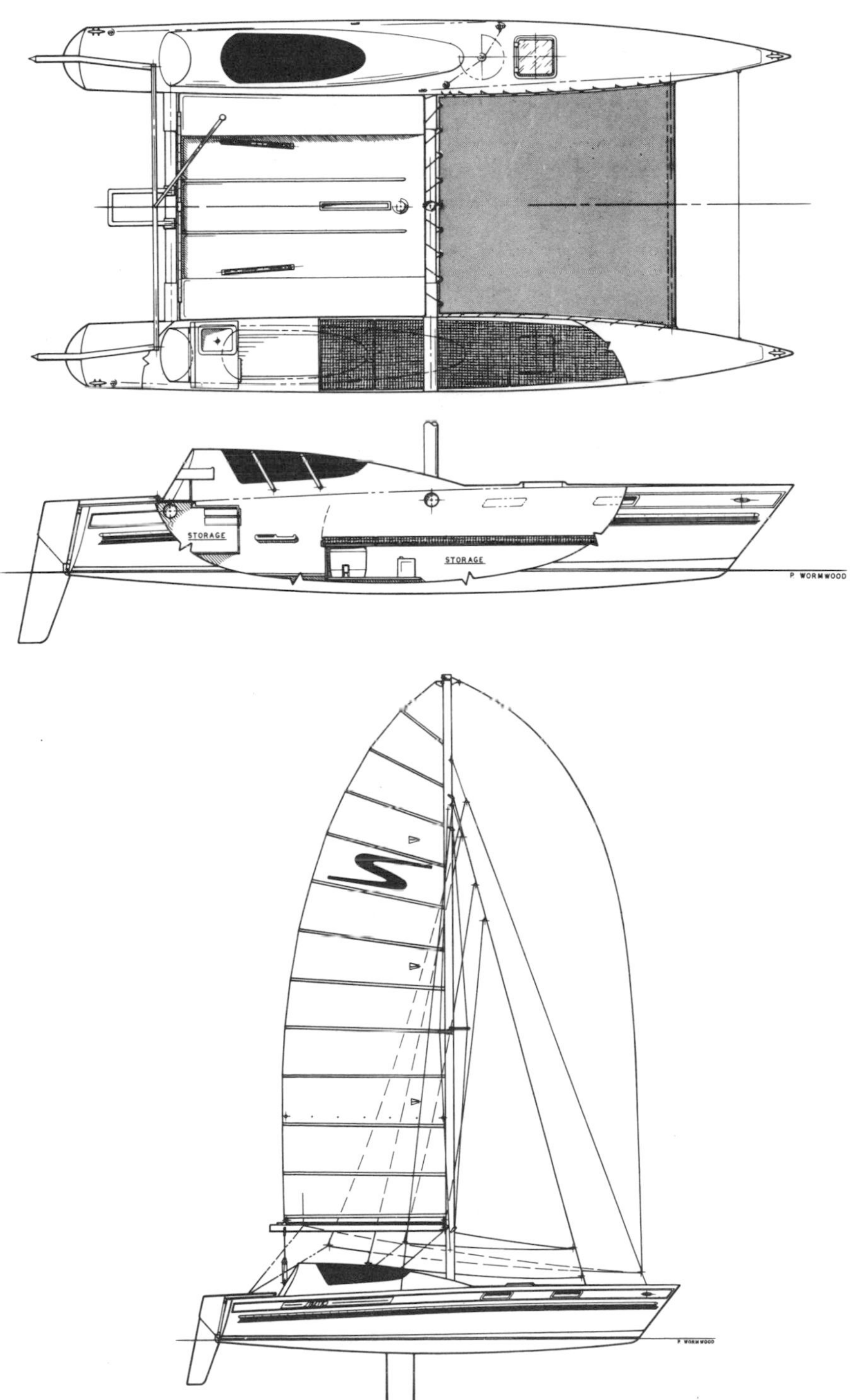
STORAGE
STORAGE
P. WORMWOOD
P. WORMWOOD

spartan galley in the other. Topsides, she has a rigid cockpit from about amidships aft nearly to her transoms, and an optional trampoline forward between the hulls. This space, which makes a marvelous double in good weather, can also accommodate a special tent for less-than-perfect conditions.

Stiletto can get up over 20 knots on a reach, and her performance is consistently exciting except perhaps dead downwind, a heading that should be avoided in nearly all multihulls and most fast monohulls. She can be folded down to trailerable width—a shade under eight feet—and pulled by a sports car on the highway. From park to launch takes a couple of reasonably experienced people about forty-five minutes, and more workers can appreciably shorten the preparation time.

Like the smallest cruisers, Stiletto is primarily a sailing boat, with a breathtaking turn of speed, and her living accommodations take a definite back seat. For people who truly enjoy sailing fast, and who are willing to put up with camping out afloat, Stiletto is a very real possibility. She is, however, a total contrast with Hirondelle, and it's foolish to conceive of cruising her in a nippy New England October—unless one is young or well padded.

Minimal cruising weekenders

AMF 2100
Designer: Ted Hood
Builder: AMF, Inc.,

Box 1345, Waterbury,
Connecticut 06720
LOA . . . 21′1″
LWL . . . 17′7″
Beam . . . 8′0″
Draft . . . 1′0″ (board up), 4′0″
Displacement . . . 2,200 lb.
Ballast . . . 850 lb.
Sail area . . . 209¼ sq. ft.

This one-design and MORC cruiser-racer was first conceived as an entry in the trendy Mini-ton class, but the rapid changes in class rules and measurements (something that has plagued all IOR-derived classes) made Hood and AMF revise their thinking. At about the same time, the J/24 leaped off on its sensational rise to popularity, and that success plus AMF's track record with one-design administration (Sunfish and Sailfish, among others) pointed toward a company-run one-design with MORC and PHRF fringe benefits, and the capacity for limited weekending and overnighting.

It is, of course, one thing to decide to go for all these elements of the market and quite another to produce a boat capable of satisfying them. It seems to me that Hood and AMF have largely succeeded—so much so that I bought 2100 number 73 for myself, and you must read what follows in light of that decision.

Because of the requirements of working on a boat magazine, I spend a lot of time sailing, but relatively little of it on my own boat. This has the effect of making me supercritical of performance (being exposed to so many other craft) and doubly eager to have a boat that is simple and inexpensive, to make the most use of my personal sailing time. In addition, I want to sail with my family, and need a boat big enough for four, preferably with the capability for overnighting occasionally and for racing casually. I have neither the money nor the inclination to join the IOR version of the arms race, so a strict one-design with strong equipment limitations attracted me.

After an extended search among many boats, my wife and I stumbled on the AMF 2100 when we went up to Marblehead, Mass., to sail and photograph one for a magazine story. She looked handsome to us, and an afternoon's sail with designer Ted Hood convinced us that she had the kind of sprightly performance we wanted—not only the ability to win a MORC or JOG race if we were up to it, but also the handiness to sail into and out of slips if necessary. We got the standard sail wardrobe—main, working jib, 150 percent genoa and spinnaker—and bought a 3.5-hp. Suzuki outboard to push her. This is small for a 21-footer, but as I've said elsewhere in this book, I think an auxiliary engine ought to be truly auxiliary, and since the 2100 can sail well in any wind at all, the only thing an engine is for is getting her home when there is no wind. In addition, the Suzuki has a number of good options—small alternator, plug-in tank to supplement the integral unit, and forward/neutral shift.

The 2100 has a large cockpit that seemed to me excellently organized for either serious sailing or just hacking around. All the sail controls except the

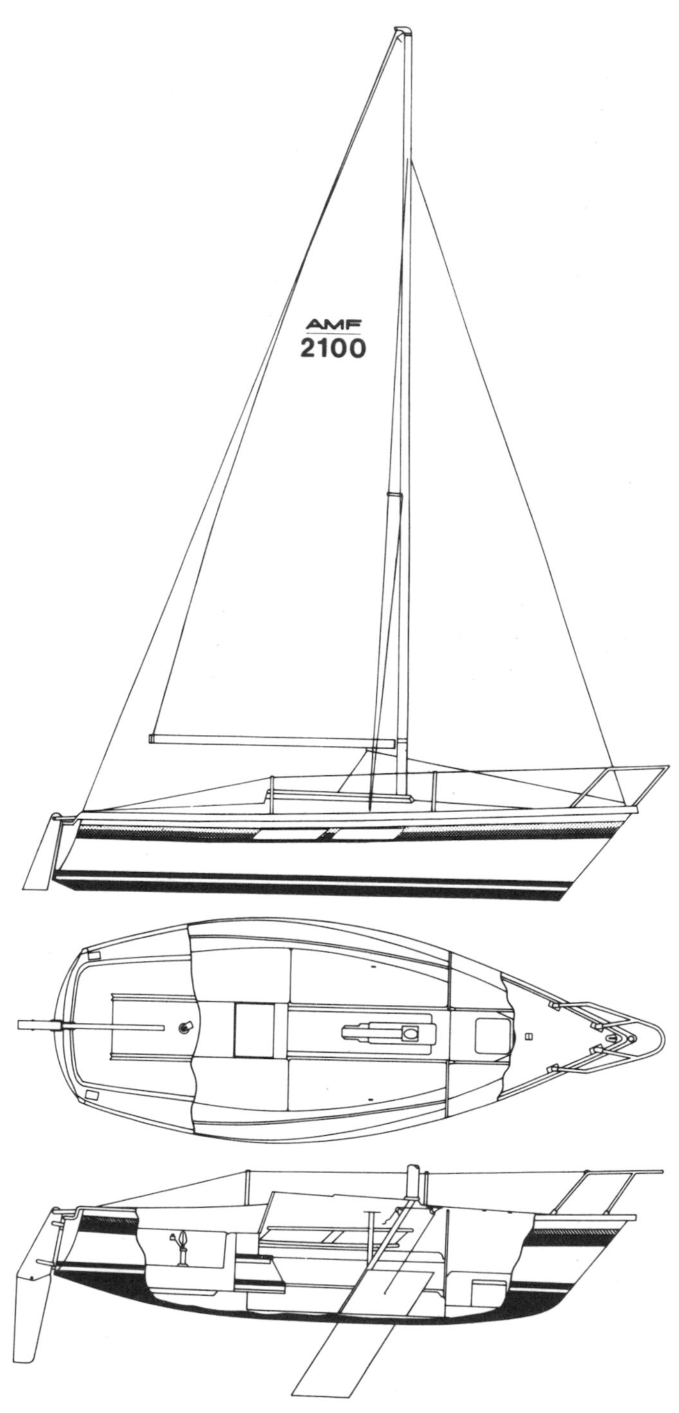
AMF
2100

backstay tensioner and mainsheet lead to a console arrangement placed around the companionway: Eight control lines come back off the mast to stoppers, and four of them can be taken to one or the other of the two Barient #10 winches that also serve the jib sheets. The original controls are main, jib, and spinnaker halyards, spinnaker pole lift, cunningham, boom vang and foreguy, to which we have added a jiffy-reef tack line. The mainsheet is located on a barney post in midcockpit, a decision by AMF that may want rethinking, and there is an optional backstay adjuster for the inverted-Y main backstay.

Down below there is an exceptional amount of space, created by the raised-deck shape of the boat. All the way forward is a surprisingly large sail-stowage and head compartment with a portable chemical john. The main cabin has sitting headroom throughout, and consists simply of a settee and a quarter-berth on each side with a fiddled shelf outboard. A one-burner propane swing stove is secured to a bulkhead, a 25-quart cooler lives under one of the companion steps, and a plastic combination sink/water tank fits beneath the other. It could hardly be more basic.

The daggerboard trunk dominates the cabin, with the block and tackle permanently rigged to raise the big board. While it would be possible to sail with the board raised, the designer's intent is to have it fully lowered at all times, a fact reflected in the class rules. There is a shortage of stowage space that's made more acute by the fact that the space beneath the berths is filled with enough foam flotation to support the boat and two or three times her normal crew. This is a compromise, of course, but since we are interested in performance first and cruising accommodation second, it seemed a reasonable one.

Under sail, the 2100 is a delight. The relatively small size of the three-quarter foretriangle means more easily managed headsails and a controllable but still exciting spinnaker. The only problem we encountered was the boat's sensitivity to weights forward, something that was accentuated in our trial voyage by the fact that Ted Hood himself, a large and powerful man, was acting as foredeck hand. We have one photo of Ted kneeling at the very bow, doing something to the tack fitting, and me sitting on the transom, which is entirely clear of the water. But there's no reason for anyone to spend much time on the foredeck, and the assets of the fine bow—a resistance to pounding or hobbyhorsing—outweigh the drawback.

Although we've done a good deal of cruising in a number of boats of assorted sizes, the 2100 offered us what we wanted at one stage in our voyaging lives. My suspicion is that a lot of beginning cruisers could get a better introduction to the sport by starting with a manageable, affordable, and delightful little boat like the 2100—or the Alberg Sea Sprite—before acquiring a larger and more demanding craft.

ALBERG SEA SPRITE
Designer: Carl Alberg
Builder: C. E. Ryder Corp.
47 Gooding Ave.,
Bristol, Rhode Island
02809
LOA . . . 22′6″
LWL . . . 16′3″
Beam . . . 7′0″
Draft (keel) . . . 3′0″
Displacement . . . 3,350 lb.
Ballast . . . 1,400 lb.
Sail area . . . 247 sq. ft.

Carl Alberg has designed a considerable number of successful yachts in his long career, of which the Triton, described earlier, is perhaps the best known. The little Sea Sprite is, however, just as representative of Alberg at his best and has been popular in the breezy waters of southern New England for over twenty years. In that time she has undergone several modifications as she has changed builders, including the addition of an outboard motor well and a fuel tank locker.

Although she is a very different boat, the Sea Sprite has many of the same essential aims as the AMF 2100, being primarily a roomy daysailer designed for family-class racing, with additional capabilities as an overnighter and minimum four-berth weekender. Accommodations are much the same in each

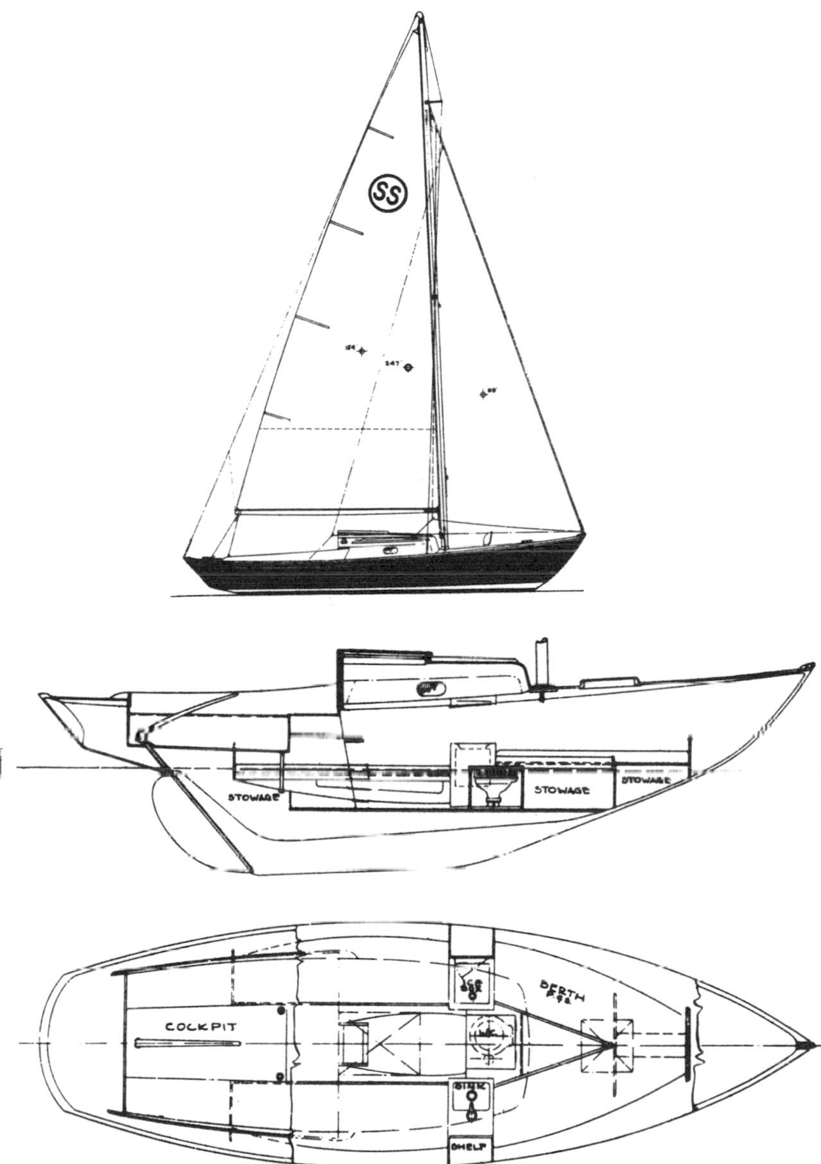

boat—four adequate berths, head, and galley consisting of icebox and sink. With stowage instead of flotation under all four berths, the Sea Sprite can handle somewhat more loose gear than can the 2100, but underberth stowage in a small boat is an illusory thing in many cases, being both oddly shaped and prone to soaking down every time the boat heels.

In terms of design, the 2100 and the Sea Sprite make an interesting comparison. Mr. Alberg's boat is about a thousand pounds heavier than Mr. Hood's, and more than half of that additional weight is in her cast lead keel. She carries about 40 sq. ft. more sail in a traditional three-quarter rig, with jumpers to counteract the forestay tension, as contrasted to the backward-angled spreaders used on the 2100. The Sea Sprite's rig, despite its apparent similarity, is more mainsail-oriented than is the 2100's. For instance, the latter boat has sail areas of 108 and 101 for main and foretriangle respectively, while the Sea Sprite has 154 to 93 for the same sails. The Sea Sprite would probably be a more comfortable boat in heavy weather than the 2100, but the numbers at least suggest that she would not be as fast—the shorter boat overall has more than a foot advantage in waterline length, and has a sail area: displacement ratio of 19.8 compared to the Sea Sprite's 17.7. Perhaps more informative are the respective displacement:length ratios—180 for the 2100, which suggests a light racer or a very light cruiser, as opposed to 348 for the Sea Sprite, which would qualify her as a moderately heavy cruising yacht.

It is as well not to try to attach absolute identities to these ratios, which are meaningless except in relation to the broad spectrum of yachts. If one were to attempt a judgment concerning these two boats, it would have to take into account such variables as the usefulness of a lifting keel (and thus the enhanced trailerability it represents), the desire for an up-to-date, racing-oriented boat as opposed to a simpler, more traditional style, and the present or predicted number of similar boats in one's cruising area.

Small offshore yachts

FRANCES 26

Designer: C.W. Paine
Builders: Thomas D.C. Morris
Box 58, Southwest
Harbor, Maine 04679
Birchwood Boats, Ltd.,
Vespasian Rd.,
Bitterue Manor,
Southampton 502 4AY
LOA . . . 26′0″
LWL . . . 21′3″
Beam . . . 8′2″
Draft . . . 3′10″
Displacement . . . 6,800 lb.
Ballast (keel) . . . 3,500 lb.
Sail area . . . 337 sq. ft. (sloop), 345 (cutter), 360 (gaff sloop)

Chuck Paine is a young designer resident in Maine whose fast cruising boats represent to me a consistently successful blend of the modern and the traditional. Of the boats he has done thus far, his Frances 26-footer is probably the most popular. Like all Paine's yachts, she has a shippy and traditional appear-

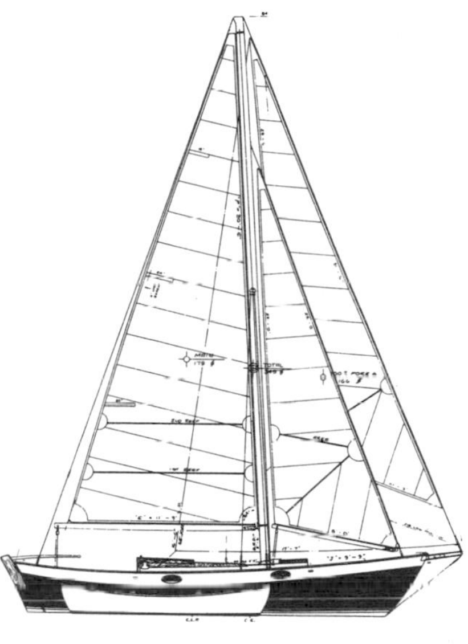

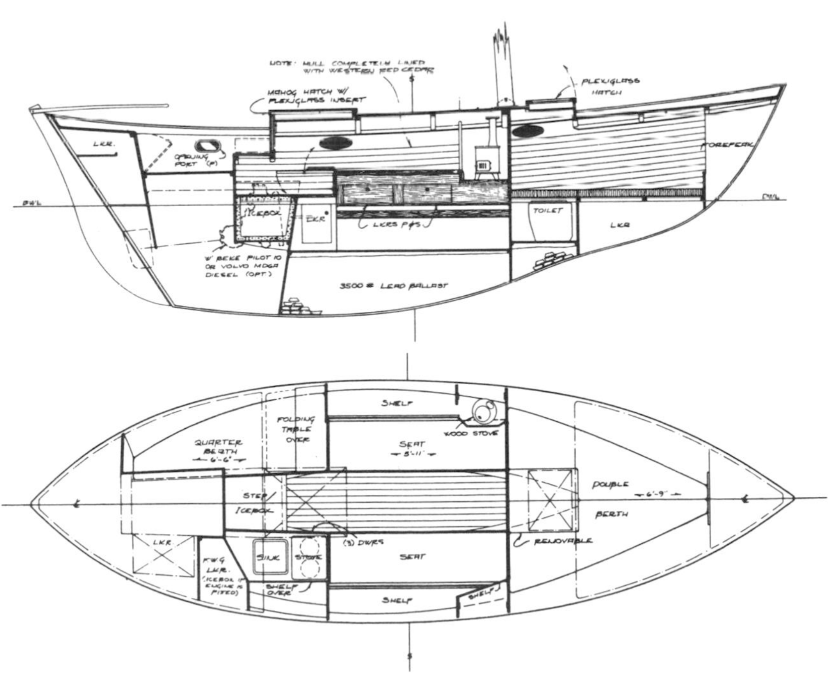
NOTE: HULL COMPLETELY LINED WITH WESTERN RED CEDAR
MAHOG HATCH W/ PLEXIGLASS INSERT
PLEXIGLASS HATCH
LKR.
OPENING PORT (P)
FOREPEAK
DWL
ICEBOX
BKR
LKRS P&S
TOILET
LKR
W/ BUKH PILOT 10 OR VOLVO MD6A DIESEL (OPT.)
3500 # LEAD BALLAST
SHELF
FOLDING TABLE OVER
WOOD STOVE
QUARTER BERTH 6'-6"
SEAT 5'-11"
DOUBLE 6'-9" BERTH
STEP/ ICEBOX
(3) DWRS
REMOVABLE
LKR.
F.W.G. LKR. (ICEBOX IF ENGINE IS FITTED)
SINK
STOVE
SEAT
SHELF OVER
SHELF
SHELF

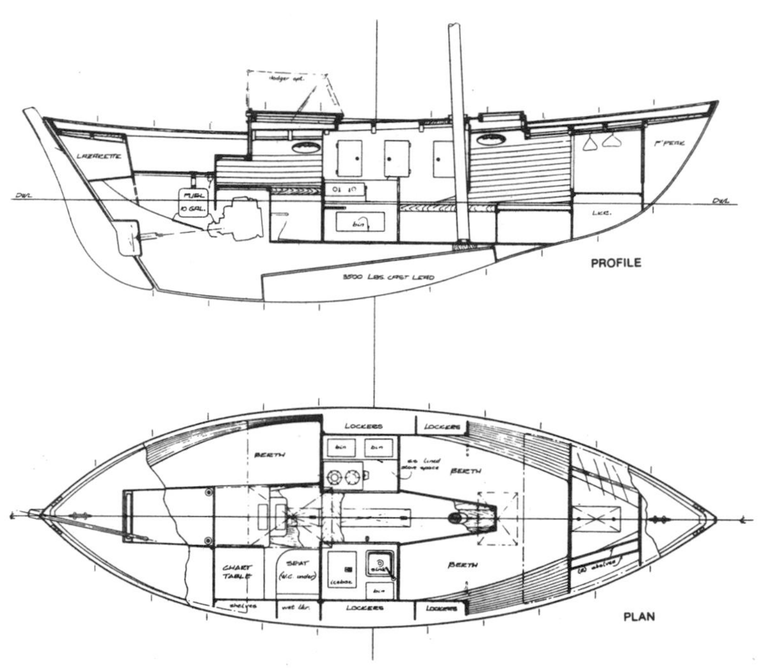

dodger opt.
LAZARETTE
FUEL
10 GAL.
F'PEAK
DWL
DWL
LKR.
bin
3500 LBS CAST LEAD
PROFILE
LOCKERS
LOCKERS
BERTH
bin
bin
ss lined stove space
BERTH
BERTH
CHART TABLE
SEAT (W.C. under)
icebox
sink
bin
(2) shelves
shelves
wet lkr.
LOCKERS
LOCKERS
PLAN

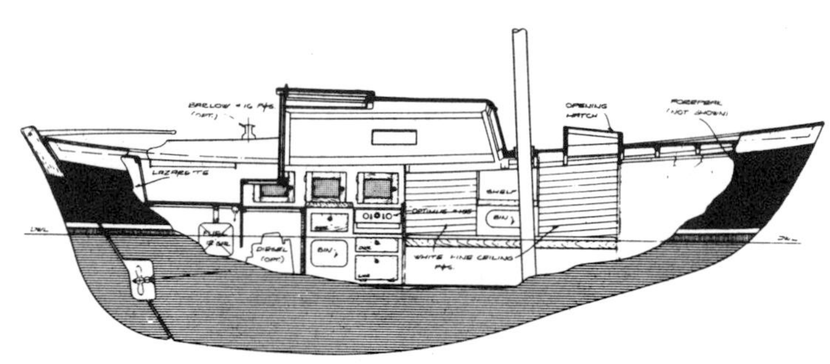

BARLOW #16 P/S (OPT.)
OPENING HATCH
FOREPEAK (NOT SHOWN)
LAZARETTE
SHELF
BIN
DWL
DWL
DIESEL (OPT)
BIN
WHITE PINE CEILING P/S.

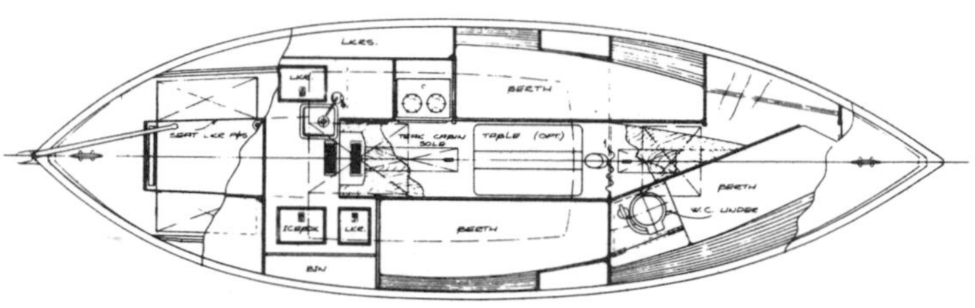

LKRS.
LKR
BERTH
SEAT LKR P/S
TEAK CABIN SOLE
TABLE (OPT)
BERTH
W.C. UNDER
ICEBOX
LKR
BERTH
BIN

ance, whether viewed in or out of the water, and regardless of which rig one is looking at. With a displacement:length ratio of 316, she is no lightweight, and her sloop rig's sail area:displacement ratio of 14.6 is not high, nor is that of her cutter arrangement, which gives a ratio of 15.4.

But Chuck Paine draws what used to be called a slippery hull, one that moves easily through the water, and the Frances is capable of beating the numbers, especially when in the hands of a really skillful sailor. I met one such owner who had his Frances rigged out to his own special requirements, which included a pair of ash sweeps (one rowed standing up in the cockpit, facing forward), wire jacklines along the side decks, and solar panels to generate the small amount of electricity his engineless vessel required.

In the United States, Frances is built by Tom Morris, who runs a small yard right across from the massive Hinckley operation in Southwest Harbor, Maine. Tom exploits the virtues of smallness, which are flexibility and attention to individual owners' desires, and they are exemplified in the thoroughly Protean Frances. Her standard arrangement is that of a flush-decked sloop with a self-tending jib on her seven-eighths rig. Below, she can sleep up to five, if two of them are smaller than 5′11″. Paine would probably be the first to denounce this cramming of people into what is really a rather small yacht, and he offers two three-berth plans, both of which are reproduced here, and a four-berth arrangement as well. For the record, I prefer the three-berth arrangement, with quarterberth and chart table aft and large hanging and stowage area forward, but each of the setups will speak to someone's requirements.

The flush-deck versions of the Frances give about 4′8″ of headroom throughout the cabin, which means in practice that it's relatively easy to move about down below, and one avoids the nearly full headroom problem of bruised skulls when one inevitably forgets. People who enjoy cooking might find one of the plans that place the galley by the companionway a good choice, as it allows the cook to straighten up under an open hatch and dodger. Tom Morris also offers a trunk cabin model with six-foot headroom, and while it's not as attractive to my eye as the clean sweep of the flush deck, there is a lot to be said for being able to stand up someplace down below.

It takes only a glance to spot the Frances's derivation from the Colin Archer root, but she is neither a slavish copy nor a cosmetic imitation. She has, it seems to me, the desirable attributes of the Archer dream—an easy ride, an exceptionally seaworthy rig above decks and below, and good if not record-breaking performance shorthanded and in any weather. Chuck Paine writes that he designed her for himself, for offshore passages up to and including a circumnavigation. Everything about her says that he succeeded, and perhaps she loses something in the way of fair-weather, weekending abilities because of her sturdiness and the necessary limits of a go-anywhere design. Still, it seems to me that the coastal cruiser who enjoys having a boat that can take any weather, who revels in being able to beat off a lee shore no matter what, and who may cherish (as which of us does not?) a tiny, circumnavigational dream—that kind of skipper could find a lot to love in this design.

VANCOUVER 27

Designer: Robert Harris
Sales agent: Simon Thomas Yacht Sales,
The Yacht Harbour,
Newhaven, Sussex BN9 9BY
LOA . . . 27′0″
LWL . . . 22′11″
Beam . . . 8′8″
Draft . . . 4′0″
Displacement . . . 8,700 lb.
Balast (keel) . . . 3,500 lb.
Sail area . . . 379 sq. ft.

Bob Harris has had a rather compartmented career as a designer, starting as one of the many who learned their trade at Sparkman & Stephens and then going off to make a considerable reputation for himself in the rarified and not terribly enriching field of multihull design. In recent years, however, he has returned to monohulls, boats that are very different indeed from the lightweight flyers he turned out in his multihull period. The Vancouver 27, which appeared in the early 1970s as an ocean-cruising sloop for two people, was originally designed for amateur construction in cored fiberglass, using either balsa or PVC foam. Later she was produced by a small yard in Canada, and she is now built in England as well. In the meantime, Harris has designed three other yachts bearing the Vancouver family name, all considerably larger than this initial venture, but all emphasizing sturdy, offshore capability at the

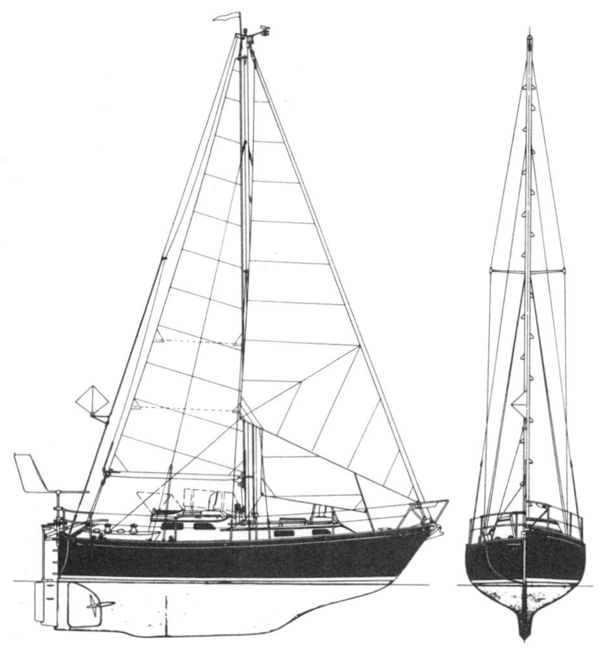

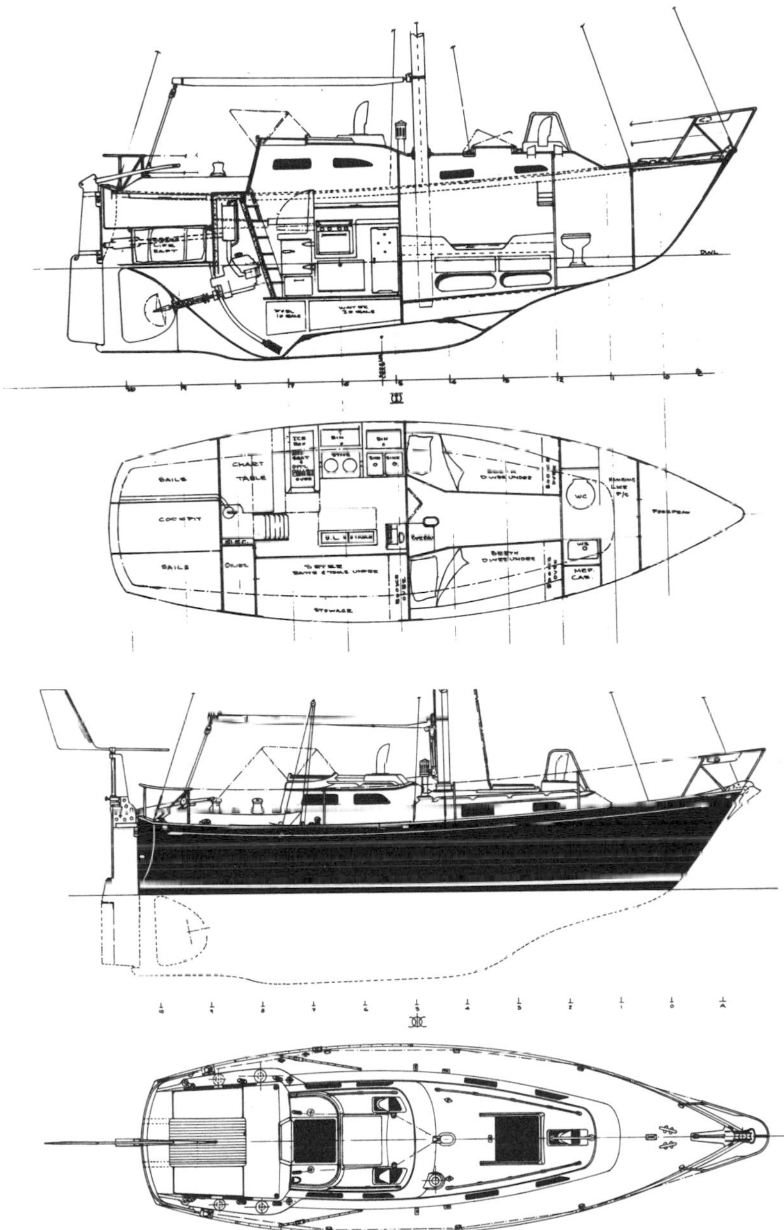

sacrifice of vast accommodation and some light-air performance. One Vancouver 27 owner, the novelist Donald Hamilton, has written a first-rate, nonfiction account of his voyaging, *Cruises with Kathleen;* it proves that the boat lives up to her billing, and then some.

The original Vancouver 27, whose sail plan is not shown, had running backstays and an inner forestay, but no forestaysail was drawn. She also had a pair of aft lowers, but only a single forward lower. Donald Hamilton's Vancouver has the more normal, traditional rig involving paired lowers fore and aft, and he sets a loose-footed forestaysail and a near-masthead roller-furling genoa in good weather. For Don's single-handing offshore, this seems an eminently sensible rig, although someone whose sailing was less demanding could probably eliminate the running backs and the inner forestay entirely and have an adequately stayed mast 95 percent of the time.

Some other seagoing attributes are worth pointing out, such as the small ports and self-bailing cockpit with a high bridge deck (as in the flush-decked Frances), the straight keel for underbody work aground, anywhere there's a flat bottom and a four-foot tide, the well-protected propeller aperture and rudder heel. Down below, she has a hanging locker for wet gear where it will do the most good, and a chart table that's equally convenient. The settee will convert, if required, to an upper-and-lower, but the two sea berths amidships should be exceptionally comfortable, while the head compartment makes good sense up forward. With the small Yanmar diesel under the companion ladder, there is a special stowage space for a life raft under the cockpit sole.

What does a boat like this sacrifice? Room, to begin with, and light-air performance as well. Compare her with the Paceship 26, and the differences are obvious, even on paper. But in serious weather of extended duration, such as most coastal cruisers can and do avoid, the Vancouver or the Frances would almost certainly be safer, easier and more comfortable boats, especially for a shorthanded crew.

Racer-cruiser or cruiser-racer?

PACESHIP 26

Designer: C. Raymond Hunt Associates
Builder: AMF Paceship,
Box 1345, Waterbury,
Connecticut 06720
LOA . . . 26′4″
LWL . . . 22′6″
Beam . . . 9′6″
Draft (keel) . . . 4′6″; (centerboard) 2′7″–6′7″
Displacement . . . 6,000 lb.
Ballast (keel or centerboard) . . . 2,200 lb.
Sail area . . . 337 sq. ft.

When the American conglomerate AMF bought the Nova Scotian firm of Paceship, two of the prime assets were the 23- and 26-footers designed by John Deknatel of Ray Hunt's office. These cruiser-racers were exceptionally fortunate vessels, being both fast and roomy, and they continued to appear after the other Canadian Paceships died off. I very nearly bought a 26, and had the

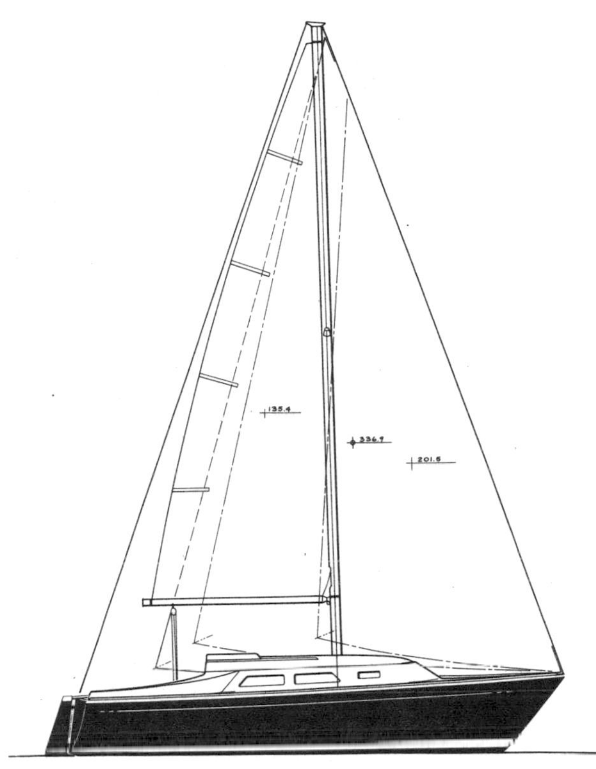
135.4
336.9
201.5

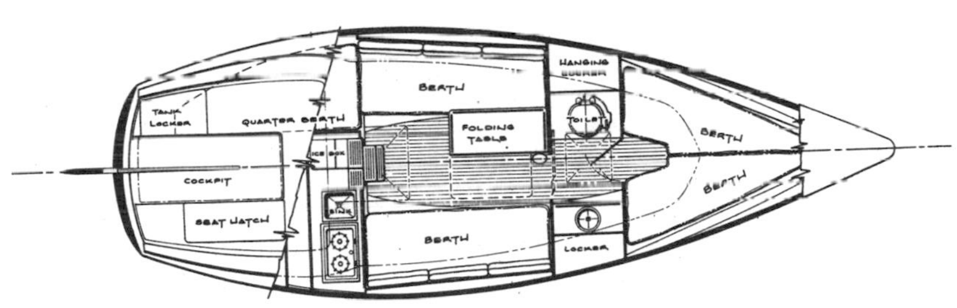
TANK LOCKER
QUARTER BERTH
BERTH
HANGING LOCKER
TOILET
FOLDING TABLE
BERTH
BERTH
ICE BOX
COCKPIT
SINK
SEAT HATCH
BERTH
LOCKER

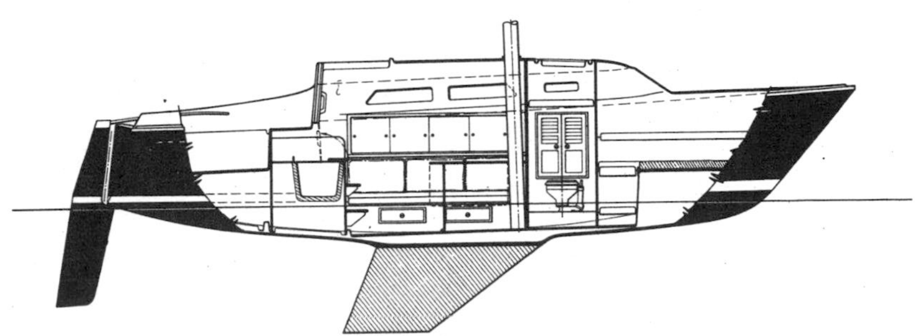

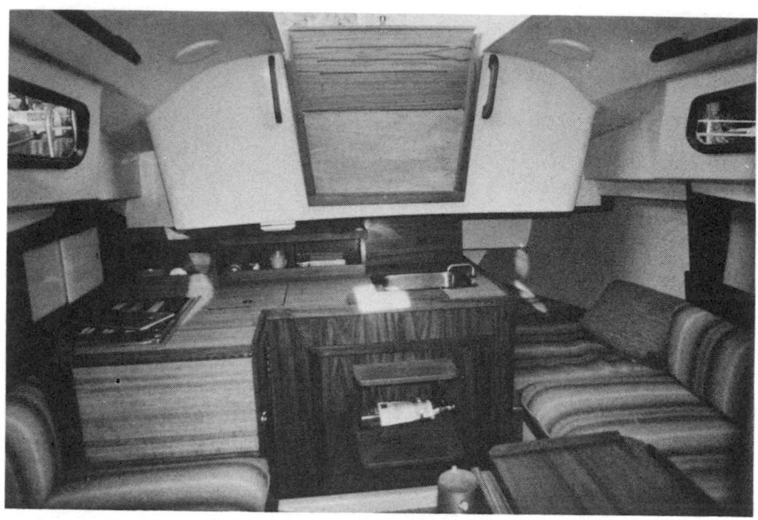

privilege of sailing a centerboard version for several days, and she still seems to me an exceptional boat in every way. (She was nosed out, as it happened, by another AMF boat, the 2100 described earlier, which better matched our sailing habits and our bank account at the time.)

In terms of exterior appearance, the Paceship 26 has always seemed to me very much a plain-vanilla boat, with her masthead sloop rig, straight trunk cabin, and high freeboard, unrelieved by any curve to the sheer. Her cockpit is quite large, with comfortable seat back—coamings and a good sail-handling setup. She has the slotted light alloy toerail popularized by C&C yachts, and a foredeck anchor well, and she is available with either a small inboard diesel or an outboard mounted on a less than attractive transom bracket. The diesel of course has the reputation for reliability as well as the capacity for generating electrical power in quantity, while an outboard is far cheaper. With the centerboard version especially, the inboard's propeller shaft is rather exposed to damage and fouling, while the bracket-mounted outboard can be battered if the boat is berthed stern-to.

Under sail, the Paceship 26 is a pleasure to handle. She is quick and nimble and her big sail plan gives her a lot of power in the light to medium breezes typical of most American sailing waters in summer. As the wind increases, the 26 develops a marked weather helm that warns the skipper to reef; if he does not, the boat begins to spin out into a broach when heavily overpowered. By reducing sail in a timely fashion she can be kept on her feet and moving fast in most weather conditions.

Down below, the 26 has an exceptionally practical arrangement for the kind of limited cruising most people enjoy. She has five berths, including a large quarterberth to port, a lobby-style head compartment that extends the width of the boat, and a good galley made better by a fold-down shelf at the forward end. The icebox is exceptionally large, although dry-food and utensil stowage is rather limited. About the only drawback to her interior is that the forward cabin has no light or ventilation when the head compartment door is closed.

Not as handsome or as trendy as many boats, the Paceship 26 is a remarkably practical cruiser-racer with a good turn of speed and superior accommodations for the cruising family.

ERICSON 30+

Designer: Bruce King
Builder: Ericson Yachts, Inc.,
1931 Deere Ave.,
Santa Ana, California 92705
LOA . . . 29′11″
LWL . . . 25′3½″
Beam . . . 10′6″
Draft (deep keel) . . . 5′10″; (shoal keel) 4′0″
Displacement . . . 9,000 lb.
Ballast . . . 4,000 lb.
Sail area . . . 470 sq. ft.

The 30+ is Bruce King's development of his earlier Ericson 30, with an underslung instead of transom-hung spade rudder and fractional rig having an extra 20 sq. ft. of sail. Like all the King designs for Ericson, she is an exceptionally good-looking yacht, with first-class performance and a very large interior.

The deck layout is up to date, with a T-shaped cockpit and halyard winches

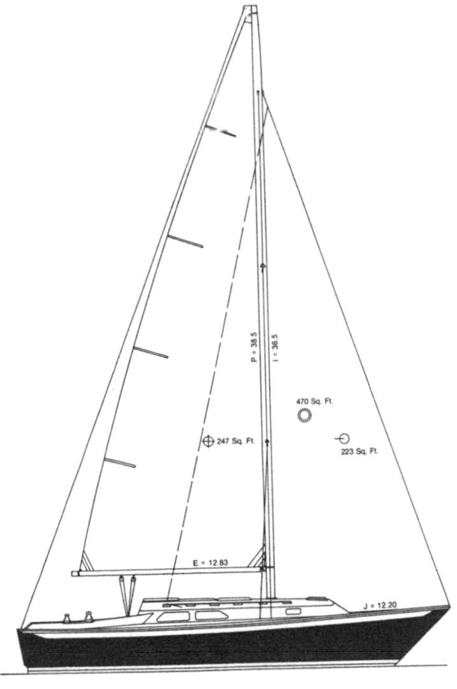

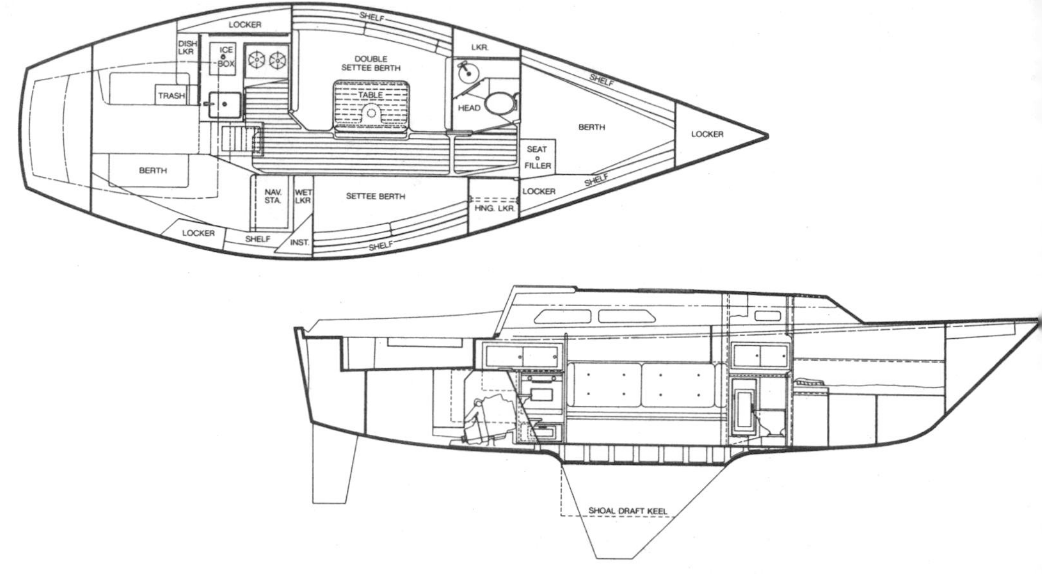

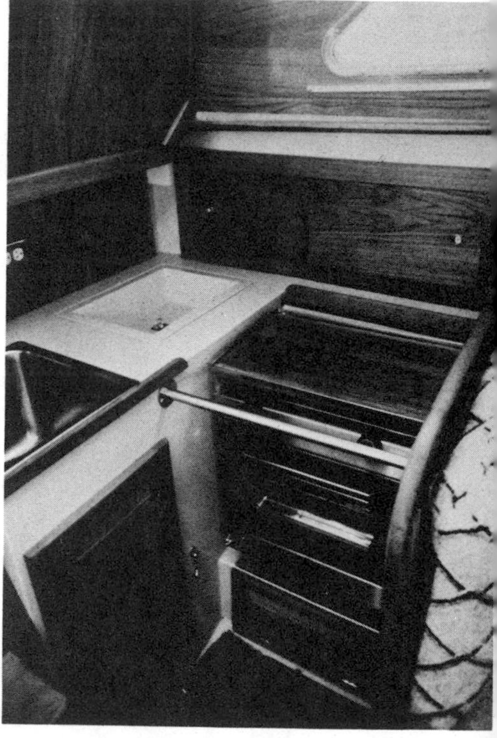

mounted on the after end of the deckhouse roof. With the chainplates located right into the cabin sides, there are good, safe walkways along the side decks. The mainsheet's ball-bearing traveler runs across the bridge deck, a feature about which opinions remain strongly divided. I was once quite opposed to this location for a traveler, feeling certain my children's fingers would be squashed by the slider every time the boat tacked or jibed. In practice, however, this does not seem to happen, and certainly the bridge deck is a very handy place for this essential piece of sailing hardware.

The performance of the Ericson, with her seven-eighths rig, seemed to me very good: She handles well, accelerates quickly, and tracks even in strong winds with little effort. Under power, her 16-hp. diesel should be quite adequate, and her 25-gallon fuel tank is claimed to give the 30+ a range of 175 miles at cruising speeds.

The Ericson's accommodation is set up for the kind of weekending and daytime voyaging most Americans prefer. Of her four sleeping spaces, two are double berths—the forward triangle (it is not a V at all) and the convertible dinette amidships. The only sea berths, both to starboard, are the settee facing the dinette and the quarterberth abaft the nav station. For the occasional offshore passage, two sea berths are probably adequate, and in warm climates the two doubles will be very comfortable at anchor, with opening hatches above each.

The navigation station is a clever installation more or less wrapped around the head end of the quarterberth, as shown in the plan overview. It should allow the skipper/navigator to construct a tight and self-contained nest with everything right at hand. A small but welcome foul-weather gear locker is built into the forward part of the nav station, at a logical point for sailors coming below to shed wet gear without soaking down the rest of the cabin (a larger hanging locker is forward).

Although attractive, the galley is somewhat less functional than it at first appears, having rather a shortage of working counter space. But the icebox is large, and there is an unusual and effective hatch for trash, leading to a container in one of the cockpit lockers. All in all, the Ericson 30+ would be a fine yacht for day racing and for the kind of cruising where one comes to rest at anchor or in a marina each night—and this, after all, is what 95 percent of cruising sailors do virtually all the time.

J/30

Designer: Rod Johnstone
Builders: J-Boats, Inc., 24 Will St., Newport, Rhode Island 02840.
J-Boats Europe, Hamble Point Marina, School Lane, Hamble, Southampton So3 5NB
LOA . . . 29′10″
LWL . . . 25′0″
Beam . . . 11′2″
Draft . . . 5′3″
Displacement . . . 6,500 lb.
Ballast (keel) . . . 2,100 lb.
Sail area (main and jib) . . . 443 sq. ft.

Although it runs counter to one's natural assumption, the J/30 is more like a cousin than a sister to the immensely successful J/24. The 24 is really an

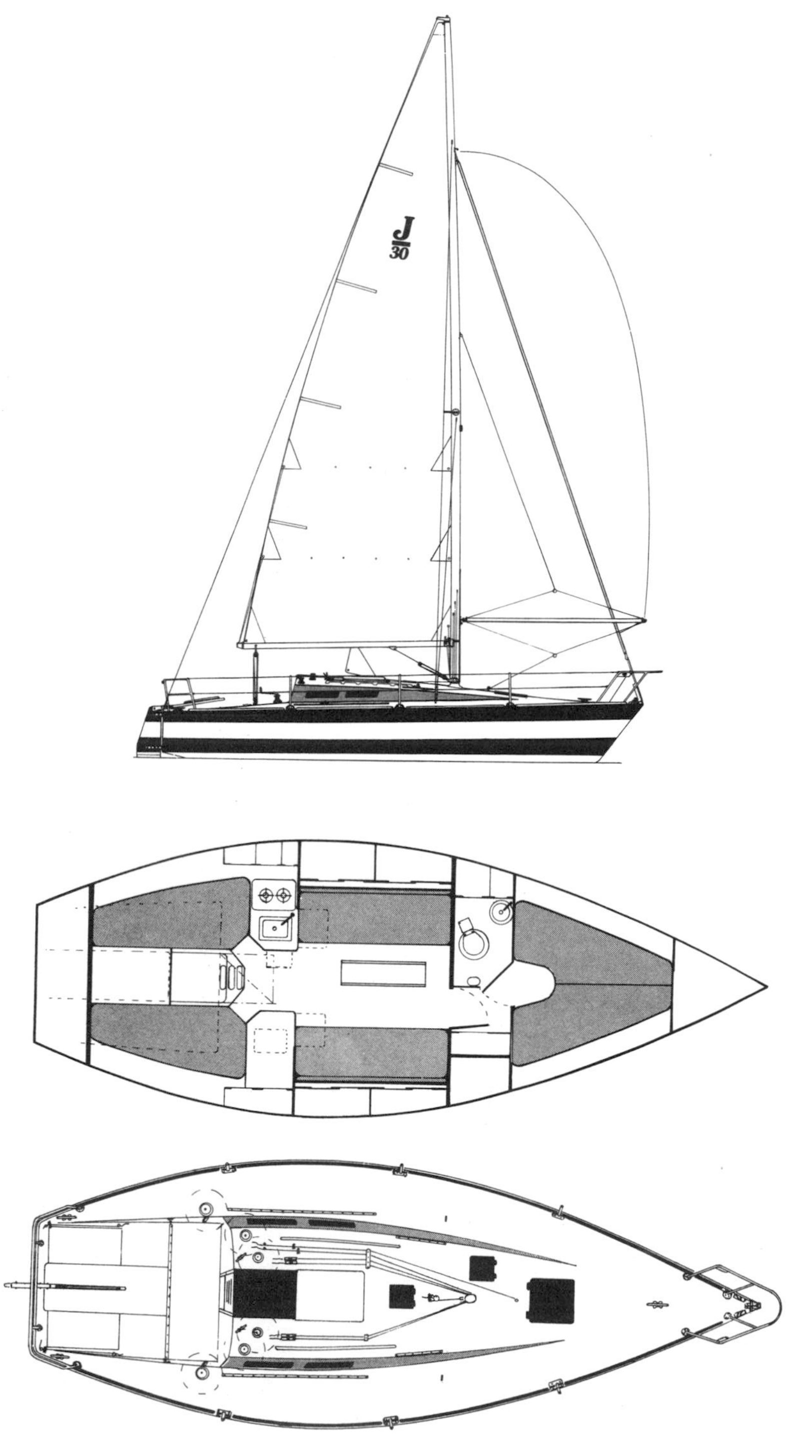
J
30

all-out racer with light and sometimes skittish performance and very little in the way of accommodation, while the 30 is a tough little seagoing boat that does best in heavy airs and provides a considerable amount of livability in a fairly simple interior. The 30 is definitely a racer first, but she has far more versatility than the 24—partly a function of increased size, but also deriving from a somewhat different design aim.

As a sailing boat, the 30 has all the fashionable gadgets that racers cannot live without today—permanent vang, adjustable backstay, halyard winches on the cabin roof, jib tracks well inboard—but she does eschew some of the wilder flights in favor of the strict one-design approach that the Johnstone brothers found paid off so handsomely with the J/24. And thanks to the 30's increase in size, the sail-handling gear is not so bunched, making it both more comprehensible to the less than expert eye and more usable by sailors for whom racing is not in the blood.

A look at the J/30's specifications reminds the viewer that she is an extremely beamy yacht for a 30-footer, and that beam is carried well aft to provide a great deal of genuinely usable room down below. Her layout combines the imaginative and the well proven, and offers four sea berths out of a total of six. Although the interior is simple and relatively unadorned, the decor is bright primary colors with a white overhead, giving a remarkably cheery feel to the cabin. Access to the 15-hp. diesel is simply superb, the galley is on the small side but realistically adequate for light meals both hot and cold, and there are clever touches that enhance the limited space available in a boat this size. For example, there is a folding shelf at the forward end of the galley counter and chart table to increase work surface when necessary; a contoured door-locker provides excellent bottle stowage; the chart table surface slides aft, revealing the icebox access.

The great success of the J/24 was based on Johnstone's recognition that a goodly segment of the American sailing public was ready for a racing boat that combined sophistication and simplicity and performance. The J/30 is a restatement of that basic theme, but in a considerably different key. While I would not seriously recommend the J/24 as a cruising boat, I'd have no hesitation in putting forward the J/30.

Foreign accent

DUFOUR 2800

Designer: Michel Dufour
Sales agents:
Dufour, Inc., Seven River Rd.,
Cos Cob, Connecticut 06807
LOA . . . 27′1″
LWL . . . 22′6″
Beam . . . 9′7″
Draft (deep keel) . . . 4′11″; (shoal keel) 3′11″
Displacement . . . 6,175 lb.
Ballast . . . 1,985 lb.
Sail area (main and jib) . . . 330 sq. ft.

The Dufour people have a mystifying way of naming their models: While the Dufour 29 is, reasonably enough, 29′4″ overall, the 2800 is only 27′1″, as the number employed refers to kilograms of displacement. In the same vein, the Dufours 31 and 35 are those numbers of feet in length, while the new 1800 is—you guessed it—about 25 feet overall, and weighs 1,800 kilos. In any case, the 2800 is an excellent example of the Continental style in high-quality cruising yachts. Like the early Arpège, Dufours have maintained a reputation

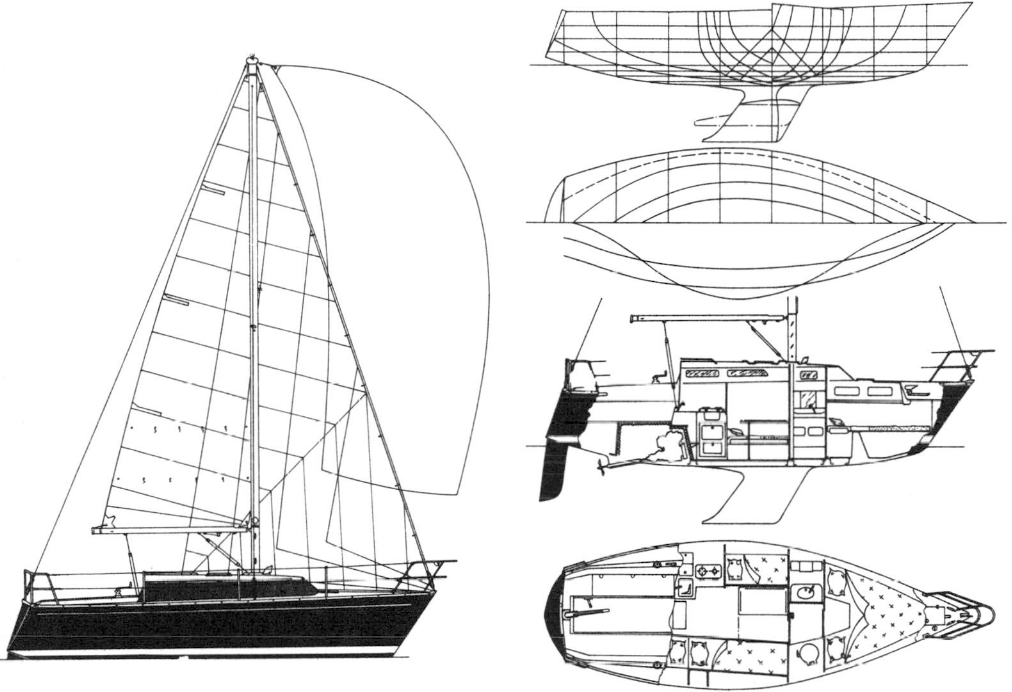

as excellent sea boats, well built and well arranged for serious voyaging. Hence they may seem a bit too purposeful to the more easygoing American eye, but for the sailor who takes his voyaging seriously, they have a great deal to recommend them. The 2800, for example, is a rugged little yacht that sleeps five, with three seagoing berths; she has a remarkably efficient galley that comes complete with silver, dishes, and cups; a sliding chart table recesses into the quarterberth tunnel; and she has a lobby-style head compartment running the width of the boat.

Her cockpit is large by European standards, where the climate is more conducive to snuggling, and she is an easy boat to handle, with a standard masthead sloop rig that is rather modest by American standards (compare her sail area, main and jib, to that of the J/30, an only slightly heavier boat).

The current crop of Dufours are rather high-sided to the American eye, but this impression is largely the effect of different paint styles here and overseas. U.S.-built boats usually incorporate a broad stripe of contrasting color just below the gunwales to lower the apparent freeboard. Dufour, by contrast, uses the same kind of color band to lower the height of the deckhouse, which is not high to begin with, leaving one with the impression that the boat's sides are higher than they are.

Construction of the Dufours is absolutely first-rate, but perhaps the most remarkable thing about them is the completeness of the inventory. As noted above, it includes cutlery, but it also comes with a CQR anchor, 15 meters of chain and 33 meters of nylon warp; pulpit, stanchions, and lifelines; halyard and sheet winches; complete galley; and a diesel engine with a control panel that even includes a battery load indicator.

Idiosyncratic short-hander

GOLDEN TOPAZ 7.7

Designer: Deborah W. Berman
Builder: Ken Fickett for
Sag Harbor Marine, Inc.
P.O. Box 395
Planetarium Station
New York, New York 10024
LOA . . . 25′4″
LWL . . . 19′7″
Beam . . . 8′0″
Draft . . . 3′3″
Displacement . . . 3,598 lb.
Ballast (keel) . . . 1,498 lb.
Sail area (sloop) . . . 304.5 sq. ft.; (cutter) 316 sq. ft.

Deborah Berman is an unusual designer not only because she is female but also because her boats are both imaginative and practical, being derived from her own considerable sailing experience. She first came to my attention in 1973, when she turned in a design for a 24-foot, hard-chine sloop with, of all things, a Chinese lug rig; despite the unfamiliarity of the sail arrangement, the boat won first prize in the amateur category of *Motor Boating & Sailing*'s design contest. Since then, Ms. Berman has gone on to become a teacher of design, and has created this little cruiser for limited production.

Designed for short- or single-handed coastal cruising, Golden Topaz is intended to provide separate cabin accommodations for up to four people, an efficient galley, and a surprising amount of storage space. Most of all, however, she is a serious cruising boat. The sloop rig is somewhat more unusual, having a boomless, roller-furling main and roller genoa arranged so that all lines can be handled by one person in the cockpit. The cutter rig is more orthodox, but it too allows for quick sail reduction and easy handling, especially in heavy weather. Auxiliary power can be a 6-hp. diesel located beneath the cockpit sole or a similar-size outboard in a cockpit well. Or one might feel that a small, handy boat like Golden Topaz required no engine at all—she could probably be moved through calms with a pair of jointed sweeps.

The accommodation concept is quite unusual, and it shows the result of lots of practical experience cruising in small boats. No stowage space for bulky sails is needed. They roller-furl or stow on booms. Thus, there is room for a

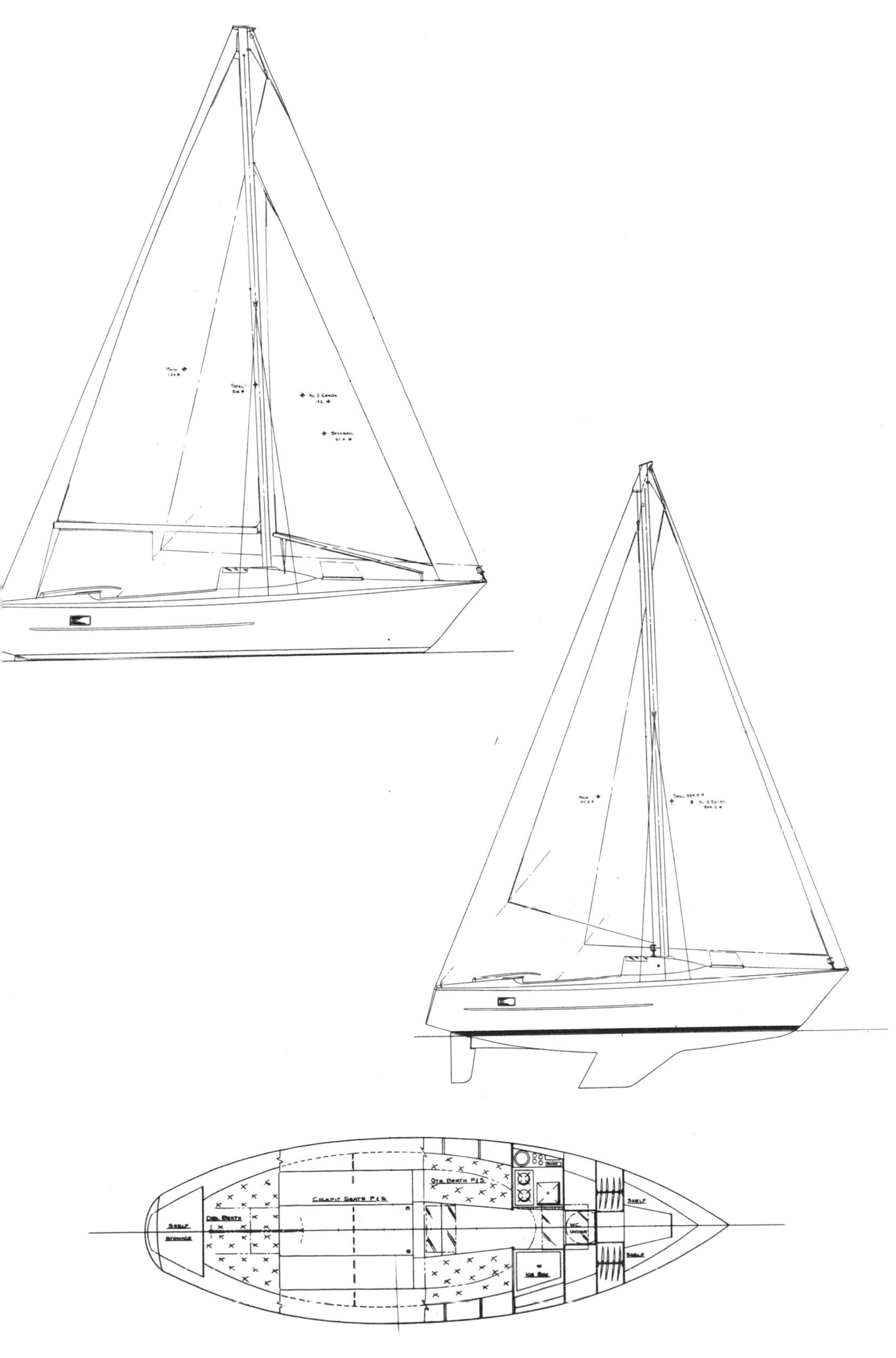

Main
124
Total
316
No 2 Genoa
192
Staysail
61.8
Main
Total 304.5
Shelf
Stowage
Dbl. Berth
Cockpit Seats P & S
Qtr. Berth P/S
W.C. Under
Ice Box
Shelf
Shelf

substantial galley and two hanging lockers. The foot-to-foot quarterberths and aft cabin shelf also make maximum use of the interior.

Although her unfashionably low rig makes her seem underpowered to the casual observer, Golden Topaz does in fact carry plenty of sail for her displacement. The sloop rig has a sail area:displacement ratio of 21, while the cutter has a ratio of over 22. This may seem remarkable, but it is due to her light displacement—she has a displacement:length ratio of 214, which is normally characteristic of light to moderate racers or light cruising boats.

With very little required in the way of mechanical equipment, Golden Topaz can be one answer to the need for an economy boat, where the cost goes for the vessel, not for gadgetry.

Classic statement

MAID OF ENDOR

Designer: John Atkin, Box 5, Norotou,
Connecticut 06820
LOA . . . 20′3″
LWL . . . 18′6″
Beam . . . 7′8″
Draft . . . 3′4″
Displacement . . . 5,200 lb.
Ballast (keel) . . . 1,100 lb., (interior) 400 lb.
Sail area . . . 335 sq. ft.

Practically no one can draw a classic small cruising yacht with the élan of John Atkin. His love for and knowledge of the traditional illuminates his designs and makes them stand out, and none to my mind is more striking than this tabloid cutter. A good seven feet shorter than the Dufour 2800, she carries slightly more sail in her gaff rig, and is within a thousand pounds of the larger yacht's displacement. As one might expect, construction is wood—in keeping with her style—and heavy. Although she is beamy and solid, her vast press of sail and her fine bows should give her a good turn of speed, especially off the wind. Were she mine, I'd be inclined to compromise tradition to the point of having that jib set up for roller furling.

With her small cockpit and easily reduced rig, Maid of Endor should be able to take relatively heavy weather with equanimity. Her cabin is a very small space, but a properly constructed wood cabin can be cozy almost beyond the modern sailor's understanding, and it would not be hard to imagine spending a rainy day at anchor stretched out on a berth with one of those books you can never seem to read elsewhere—*War and Peace,* maybe, or *Moby Dick.*

The plans call for a small gasoline inboard, which would presumably now be replaced by a similar-size diesel. One could hang foul-weather gear behind the companionway ladder and stow a surprising amount of gear under the

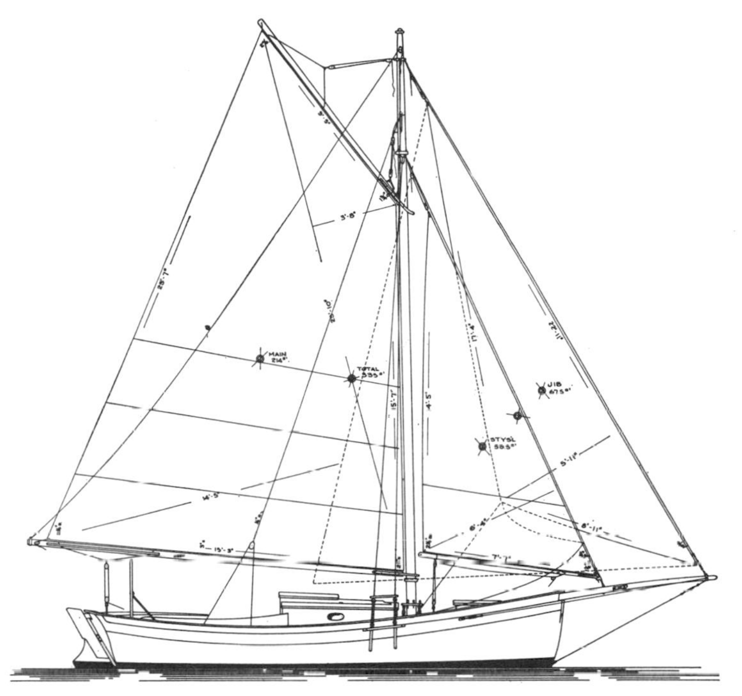
MAIN 214□'
TOTAL 355□'
JIB 67.5□'
STYSL 58.5□'

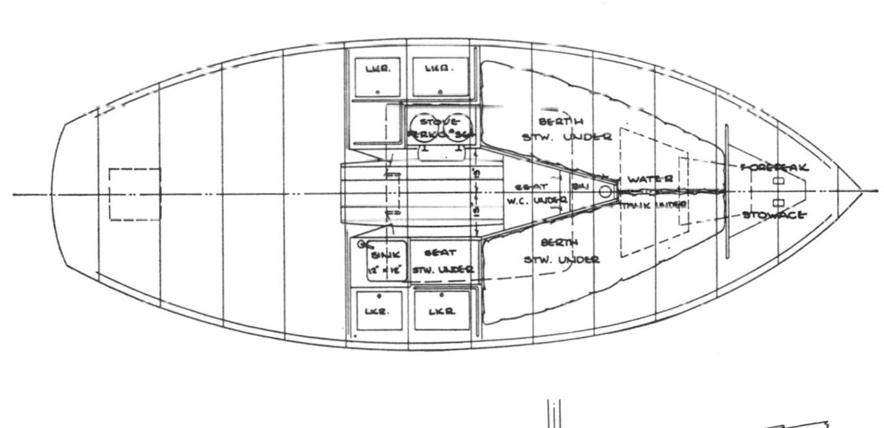
LKR.
LKR.
STOVE
BERTH
STW. UNDER
SEAT
W.C. UNDER
WATER
TANK UNDER
FOREPEAK
STOWAGE
SINK
SEAT
STW. UNDER
BERTH
STW. UNDER
LKR.
LKR.

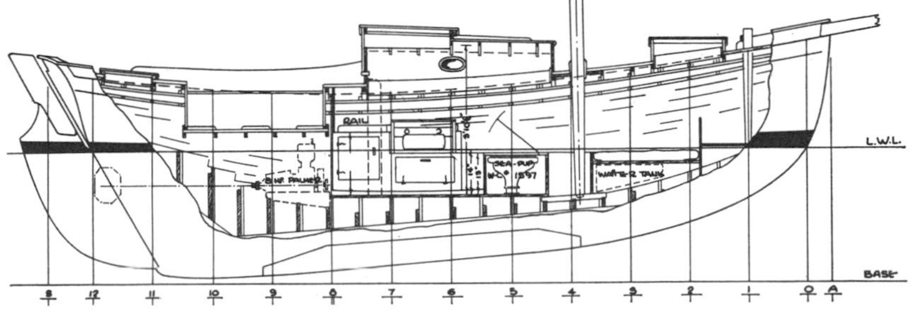
RAIL
WATER TANK
L.W.L.
BASE
8
12
11
10
9
8
7
6
5
4
3
2
1
0
A

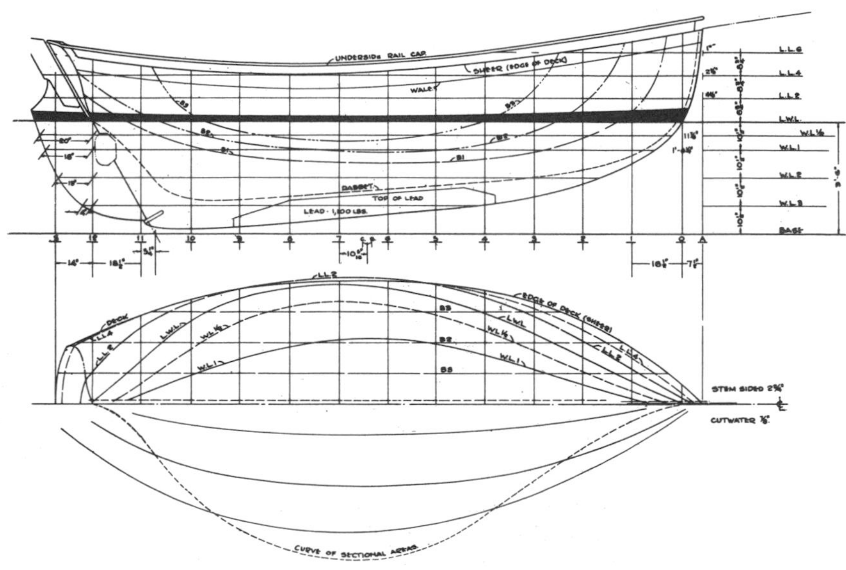

berths, in the several lockers or the lazarette. An absolute dazzler in any fleet, Maid of Endor could be something of a surprise in terms of her cruising potential as well.

Twin-keeler from England

WESTERLY CENTAUR
Designer: J. Laurent Giles
Builder: Westerly Marine Construction, Ltd., Aysgarth Rd., Waterlooville, Portsmouth, Hants. PO7 7UF
LOA . . . 26′0″
LWL . . . 21′4″
Beam . . . 8′5″
Draft . . . 3′0″
Displacement . . . 6,150 lb.
Ballast . . . 2,800 lb.
Sail area . . . 330 sq. ft. (approx.)

One of the most successful boats ever produced by England's Westerly Marine, the Centaur even achieved considerable popularity in the United States, a difficult feat in the face of transport costs and import duties. Like all the Westerly cruisers, she emphasized accommodation, with berths for five or six (depending on one's attitude toward the size of the converted dinette). The Centaur had a pair of quarterberths and a small but functional V-berth forward cabin. A sizable hanging locker was across from the enclosed head and the galley was linear, facing the dinette. For some curious reason, the icebox, under the head end of the starboard quarterberth, never really made it into the galley counter.

Like all Westerlies of the period, the Centaur had a very simple decor, being largely white inside, with some color accents from the upholstery, and a little wood trim at the aft end of the main cabin. This made for a surface that was bright and very easy to keep clean, if a little sterile.

The snug masthead rig featured roller reefing on the mainsail and Terylene (Dacron to Americans) running rigging before it was generally employed. The choice of engines was interesting: One could have a bracket-mounted 9.5-hp. outboard, a 7-hp. Volvo Penta MD 1 diesel, or a four-cylinder, 32-hp. Ford gasoline inboard.

Her cockpit, quite adequate by American standards, was very large for small British cruisers, and while her big cabin house took up a lot of space, there was adequate working room on side decks and foredecks. Her salient feature, of course, was the twin-keel underbody which allowed her to sit upright in the many British harbors that dry out completely at low tide. If American anchorages ever become sufficiently crowded, twin keels may yet become popular here as well, and a tough, seaworthy little yacht like the Centaur could be appreciated more fully on this side of the Atlantic.

The Centaur represents what might be called the middle period of Westerly yachts. The earliest models were very odd indeed to American eyes, and a good example is the Nomad, plan and profile of which appear on page 7. The 22-foot Nomad was itself a development of Westerly's first cruising yacht, and it had the same heavy emphasis on accommodation still visible in the Centaur. Like the later model, the Nomad had an enclosed head compartment, remarkably complete galley and separate forward cabin. She also offered "almost 6′ headroom" in the main cabin, another theme that appeared in all the Westerly yachts, however small, and not an easy trick to achieve when one considers the commitment to twin keels.

In a 26-footer like the Centaur, of course, there is a considerably increased cubic footage for the designer to play with, resulting not only in headroom for most adults throughout the accommodation, but also a relatively larger cockpit and a few extra inches everywhere. The Centaur has a displacement: length ratio of 284, which makes her a moderate cruiser in that category, and a sail area: displacement ratio of 15.7, indicating she is well canvased for a cruising yacht. What these ratios cannot take into account, of course, is the twin-keel underbody, which in my opinion will reduce her normal sailing speed inordinately.

The new wave of Westerly yachts, just appearing on the U.S. scene, show a turn away from the traditional Westerly characteristics. In addition to the racing yachts, denominated GK 24 and GK 29, a line of fast cruisers seems to be in the offing, and only the future will tell how the public will receive them.

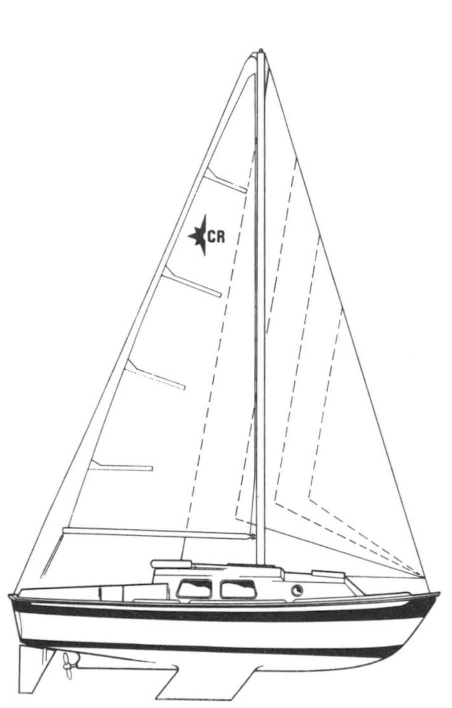

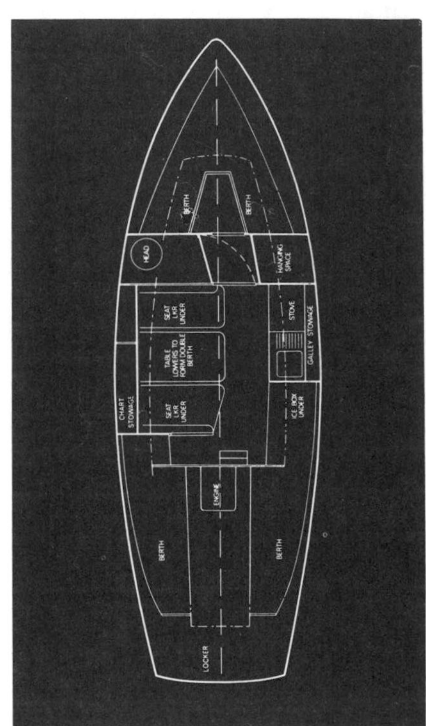

IV

Sails and Sail Selection

The trouble with most sail wardrobes is that they just happen: The boat may come with working sails, or the owner strips his checkbook to buy what he assumes will be her ultimate wardrobe, and later discovers that mistaken first purchases have more or less boxed him in in terms of future acquisitions. It's important to envision a complete sail wardrobe at the time one buys the first sail—even if the next purchase is two or three seasons off (and if it is, you get some kind of willpower medal).

If yours is a class boat, see what sort of sails the other owners of similar craft in your sailing area have bought. It will also be useful to discuss the whole thing frankly with your sailmaker. (It sounds quaintly Old World to speak of "my sailmaker," kind of like referring to "my tobacconist." But you *can* think this way, and you should, as discussed below.) Bear in mind, however, that other owners are likely to justify their own purchases, and sailmakers are in the business of selling sails. You can always buy sails you lack, but you can only dispose of an unwise purchase at a stinging loss.

One other thing to bear in mind if the boat you're buying is new, and that's the hardware associated with anything beyond working sails. Most manufacturers sell genoa and spinnaker gear as installed packages, and both are far easier to attach to the boat while she's under construction than afterwards.

For instance, the standard genoa gear package consists of matching lengths of sheet track, sliding cars and stops, snatch blocks and sheets. Prices are normally about what you'd pay for the gear itself, but of course the price includes installing the track, and if your boat has a molded headliner that extends under the side decks, this can be a complex operation. Do be sure, if

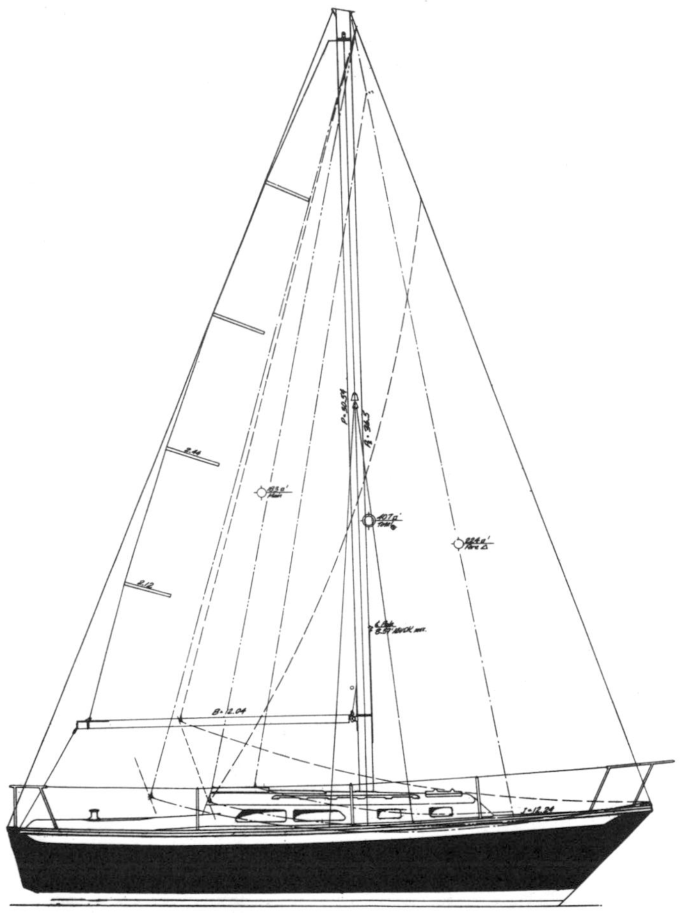

Relatively complete sail wardrobe, less spinnaker, is indicated by dotted lines on sailplain of this Ericson 29.

you sign up for this option, that the track is secured by machine screws with large washers to distribute the load or—better still—is backed up with an aluminum plate or length of quarter-inch plywood.

Spinnaker gear normally consists of pole, halyard, masthead block, sheets, blocks and pad eyes for the quarters, topping lift block and halyard, foreguy and block, and mast track, with car. Although there is more gear involved, the installation is probably no more complicated than that of two genoa tracks. Still, the mast track alone can mean two or three afternoons' work with tap and die—with the mast out.

Even if you don't envision a spinnaker in the near future, spinnaker gear (unlike electronics) is probably an optional extra that will enhance the resale value of the boat, and that will do her no harm. If the gear does not come as a package, having the builder install the track alone is probably a sensible investment.

Mainsail and . . .

One begins with the unavoidable mainsail, taking care that it has a reefing system compatible with the boat's hardware, and that its cloth weight makes sense for the kind of sailing breeze you're likely to have. It may well be that your boat comes with main and working jib in the base price. More than likely these will be bottom-line sails, adequate as to cut but less than overwhelming in terms of material, stitching, or small details (such as leech lines). If the sailmaker who provided these sails has a loft in your vicinity, then it will probably be all right to take the canvas as is. But if he is halfway across the country, or outside it altogether, it's a good idea to negotiate for a price reduction on condition that the sails be omitted. Don't expect a price reduction commensurate with what top-quality sails of that size and weight would have cost: That, after all, is why the builder is throwing these sails in—because he gets them at a double discount, once for quantity and once for quality.

Still, it's a mistake to start off with basic sails that are less than good. You ought at least to be assured—by the sailmaker, not the boat dealer—that the sails coming as standard in your boat's base price will have the same service from him as ones that are made to order.

When a headsail is included in the base price, it's almost always a working jib or lapper, and the latter has become nearly a synonym for the former. The first sailboat I owned had these two sails, and they were adequate for a full season before I began to dream of more versatility. But I was a beginner, and you are probably not. If you are, main and working jib are a good beginning combination, if you have the willpower to watch other boats with more elaborate canvas sail past you. Spend a season learning what your two sails can do under all conditions, and you'll be a better sailor for it.

When yours is a light-weather sailing area, the conventional working jib may be purely frustrating, and even a 110 percent lapper will be too small too much of the time. If that's the case—if the boats you see are nearly always under main and genoa—then you ought to consider beginning with a reefing #2 genoa and a mainsail. The reefing #2 is, in effect, two sails in one, giving you a medium-large headsail for average and lighter than average conditions, and a sail equal to a lapper but lower down (for less heeling moment) for heavy weather.

Finally, if you have a twin-sticker, your basic wardrobe will of course also include a mizzen.

Sail weight is pretty much a function of sail size. Today's polyester (Dacron or Terylene) sailcloth is so strong that we are able to get away with far lighter

A reefing #2 genoa in its full configuration on a Pearson 28. Unlike the main, the reefed jib must have its foot laced to keep from scooping up seas.

sails than our ancestors did, and for most of us a lighter than average sail will be more fun and more useful than a heavier one. As to the cloth itself, there are any number of compositions of the artificial material from which they are made. Basically, it is a matter of the relative amounts of fiber and resin filler in each bolt of cloth: Sails that are heavily resin-filled are smooth, shiny, and impressive to look at when new. They are also absolute hell to furl or reef, being both slippery and stiff. The filler leaches out after a while, leaving a shapeless bag.

More expensive cruising sails have the shape properly cut and sewn in, with little or no filler. These sails are soft to the touch and relatively easy to fist (the old-time sailor's highly descriptive term for clutching a sail with the knuckles, not the vulnerable fingertips). Any good sailmaker has access to this kind of material, but if your boat is sold with a suit of sails included in the base price, the chances are 20 to 1 the sails will be resin-filled off-the-rack bargains.

The mizzen is almost certainly the most neglected sail on the boat, with the working jib a close second. Mizzens are cut like mains, and many sailmakers use the same weight fabric, or even heavier, on the grounds that a mizzen will be left up after all other sails have been lowered in storm conditions. This seems to me a fallacy: A mizzen leads a hard life in the dirty air off the main, and it deserves to be created to perform a decent job in standard conditions. If you anticipate a lot of stormy-weather sailing, it will probably make more sense to get a storm mizzen as an extra sail—it will be very small and can be quite flat-cut (because it is always working closer to the wind than the mainsail due to the latter's backwash). In my opinion, and after two ketches, a mizzen should be the weight of cloth its own size would call for if it were a mainsail. It should also have at least one and preferably two reefs—for balance as much as anything else—and you should be able to reef it without leaning over the transom, which means leading the reefing and outhaul lines well forward along the boom.

First add-ons

Having spent as much time as you can bear with your basic sails, you're ready to branch out. What you next acquire will depend partly on what you bought first, partly on sailing conditions in your cruising waters, and partly on what you now perceive to be the boat's needs.

If you started with main and working jib or lapper, you'll now want either a #2 or #1 genoa jib. The terminology of genoas is still most confusing. Most people describe genoas by number, with #1 being the largest and #3, #4 or even #5 being the smallest. The only thing they have in common is the fact that, by definition, a genoa is low cut and overlaps the mast. After that, anything goes.

As noted earlier, the size of a given genoa is usually stated in terms of a percentage—180 percent, 170 percent, 150 percent, etc.—of the LP, or luff perpendicular (see page 52). If you plan to race your boat, the handicap system under which you compete will pretty well determine the largest LP you can carry. If you don't race, or don't race very much, your largest genoa's LP is up to you—there's nothing that says you can't carry a sail whose clew is sheeted right to the lee quarter. It is, however, probably a waste of sail and money, and will make for a lot of difficult sail handling.

In practical terms, people who sail in predominantly light-weather areas like southern California, the Chesapeake and Long Island Sound, or the Mediterranean, will usually find that a 180 percent genoa is about the maximum they can usefully employ. Many others find that 170 percent is just about as good. Although there is no firm agreement in detail, most authorities seem to feel that beyond about a 150 percent LP, overlap doesn't prove a whole lot on the wind, and only serves a purpose off the wind if the jib is fully boomed out.

The genoa numbers, then, are relative—one's #1 genoa is the largest in the collection, whether it be 150 percent or 180 percent. Some sailors have two #1

170 percent # 1 genoa on a 28-foot Great Dane sloop. This sail is cut to allow a tack pennant that raises the sail's foot enough for the helmsman to see under it.

genoas, a heavy and a light, cut to the same dimensions but of slightly different cloth weight. This seems to me the kind of thing that makes some sense for racers but little for cruising people.

A #2 genoa may be either a heavy #1—depends who's counting—or a slightly smaller, slightly heavier sail, usually with a luff that's as long as that of the #1, but a slightly shorter foot.

The difference is not great, but if the boat seems significantly underpowered even by a lapper, I'd go for the #1, while if the smaller working jib, fitting the foretriangle or even a smaller area, seems adequate more than about a third of the time, then a #2 will probably make more sense.

At the same time, you may now be ready for a spinnaker. It seems to me a mistake to wait too long before buying this sail, as it is to wait too long before jumping into a swimming pool: Many cruising people have managed to convince themselves that a spinnaker is just too much for them, and have settled for second-rate sailing as a consequence. If your normal crew is just you and another person, or just you, a regular spinnaker may indeed be more than you care to cope with. In that case, I'd recommend one of the proprietary "cruising spinnakers." They are no harder to set or strike than a genoa and can significantly liven up downwind performance.

For the ketch or yawl owner, probably the mizzen staysail ought to come even ahead of the spinnaker. It's an easier sail to cope with, and a more basic addition to the rig than the spinnaker. When ordering the spinnaker or the mizzen staysail, do keep in mind the graphics of what you're up to: You have the chance to create a really striking visual effect with these two sails, or an equally eye-catching visual disaster.

Roller genoa

One other kind of genoa perhaps merits a separate discussion. The roller-furling headsail, seen more and more aboard cruising and even racing yachts, has some technical requirements of its own. This sail rolls up around a wire or a flat spar (or a grooved rod, so it can be taken off easily). In order for the sail to roll evenly, successive layers of edging cannot lie one atop the other, so the sail's foot is cut upward, with a clew that's high off the deck. This has the disadvantage that it's not nearly as efficient going to windward as a deck-sweeping sail, and the corresponding advantage that it's far easier for the helmsman to see beneath and the sheet lead stays constant as the sail is rolled away. It does require a sheet lead way aft, which can cause some problems getting the sheet to the winch at a functional angle.

This kind of high-cut genoa was for years called a *reacher* on this side of the Atlantic and a *yankee* by the British and some Europeans, and both terms arose before roller furling was at all common.

A roller-furling genoa is easy to spot because of the edging of sunresistant material on leech and foot.

No matter what sailmakers claim, a roller-furling headsail will not set very well when partially furled. If cut flat by a skillful loft, it won't be damaged by setting when halfway unrolled, but it will be high off the deck, will have a very peculiar-looking draft, and will almost certainly require to have the sheet leads moved aft. A roller-*furling* sail isn't a roller-*reefing* sail unless the roller mechanism is specially strengthened for the heavier loadings.

Even so, the roller-furling #1 genoa is an increasingly popular cruising sail, and justly so. It seldom requires a man to go forward to handle it, except when the line on the furling drum overrides, comes adrift, or jams. It will not have as taut a luff as a normal genoa, which means that the boat will lose a few degrees of pointing ability, but it can be carried right up to the last minute and then furled in a flash, leaving the foredeck clear for line handlers or the anchoring detail. On balance, it's a hard sail to argue against.

There are numerous proprietary brands of the basic roller-furling arrangement, and most of them seem equally good. On a small boat, the temptation is to make the furling line of very small diameter Dacron. This is probably a mistake, as it will just be very difficult to handle when rolling up the sail under any load at all. Five-sixteenth-inch braid or even three-eighth-inch (1″ circ) is far easier to deal with. Another frequent error is trimming off the furling line too short: Remember that the sail will be rolled under varying degrees of tension, depending on circumstance, and the more tension on the sail—i.e., the tighter it's rolled—the more line will be required to furl it. When first measuring the furling line, one tends to hand-roll it around the roller drum evenly under light tension—the optimum method. In real life, the line is apt to bunch up somewhat, calling for a greater length of rope for the same amount of furl. Having rolled the sail completely up by hand the first time, lead the rope through all the required fairleads back to the cockpit. Then measure off enough extra line to make it possible to take three turns around the primary sheet winch, with a goodly amount of tail—this will come in very handy the first time you have to furl in a squall. Then add five more feet for good measure and cut.

When setting up your own roller-furling gear, the second most common mistake, after locating the furling drum too close to the headstay (see page 57), is to have an unfair lead off the drum to the first fairlead on deck. If the furling line is to have a fighting chance of spooling evenly, it must come through the fairlead directly onto the drum, without dragging on either lip. If the lead isn't fair, the furling line will bunch up somewhere on the drum, and you'll simply have to relocate the fairlead bull's eye.

Finally, make sure you always furl the sail under some kind of load: It can be luffing while it's being furled, but the sail should be carrying a little air, and the furling line be under a little tension, or you'll get what fishermen call a backlash—one layer of line jammed under another.

If you have a roller #1 genoa, then your progression from that point will be a little different than if you have conventional headsails. For one thing, you *can* use the roller jenny as a storm jib, although it's not good for the sail and not good sailing. So you should probably plan on getting a smaller jib that sets from the headstay, forward of the roller stay (unless you have the kind of roller gear that permits you to remove the roller jenny without striking the whole jibstay).

If you have a double-head rig on your cutter, chances are your jib is a yankee, and if you have a bowsprit (or even if you don't) that it's on a roller. In this case, you don't have to worry about providing a working or storm headsail, because you've already got one, in the guise of your working staysail. Whether it's on a boom or not, this sail should be cut with at least one set of reef points. It should also be as big as the staysail triangle allows.

You will next, with a double-head rig, probably want to invest in a dramatically large #1 genoa/drifter for light airs. If you have no extra headstay forward of the roller stay, this sail can even be set flying. On light-air days it can be a considerable improvement over the boat's standard pair of headsails, especially in the smaller boats we're dealing with.

Finally, the sail collector may want to round out his suit with a genoa staysail, which, as the name suggests, is simply a staysail cut to set under the genoa and overlap the mainmast by a good deal. It is a pain in the neck to work with, and is probably only worthwhile if your voyaging includes long close-reaching stretches without the need to tack.

Completing the standard suit of sails

Assume you have your main, working jib or lapper, #1 and #2 genoas, and your spinnaker. What other sails might you have use for? This is the modern sailor's equivalent to the question of how many angels can dance on the point of a pin, or how high is up. We are talking here of an investment of several hundred dollars or pounds that may possibly return you a quarter of a knot. And that only occasionally.

If your sailing area is notoriously light-winded, you may want a drifter in addition to your #1. Sailing in Long Island Sound, I found I used my Hirondelle catamaran's drifter as often as the #1 genoa, and either of them four or five times as often as the working jib. Its usefulness to you will depend both on the local weather conditions during the sailing season and your attitude toward light airs: A drifter, cut from three-quarter-ounce nylon, operates at the edge of no wind at all, and it's easily blown permanently out of shape if one holds on to it after the breeze has attained five knots or so.

Probably more practical is a cruising-type single-luff spinnaker ("Flasher," "Shooter," or other proprietary name) in addition to your regular chute, for when you're sailing short-handed or reaching (assuming your standard chute is fairly full cut). On the other hand, you may want to have a second spinnaker proper—a star-cut to complement your tri-radial, or vice versa.

The kind of staysail hoisted with a spinnaker varies tremendously according to the sailmaking theory of the moment. Tall and thin or short and long-footed, the spinnaker staysail is definitely a luxury.

What about storm canvas? Few coastal cruisers have much call for it, or much knowledge of when and how to set it. My own feeling, which goes strongly against tradition, is that of the two classic storm sails, one is definitely a waste of money for most people and the other is marginal, depending on the rest of your sail wardrobe. The old-fashioned storm trysail laces around the mast or runs on a separate reinforced track alongside the regular mainsail track. It can sheet to the end of the boom, or directly to a block on the quarter. And you will probably spend your entire coastwise career without ever removing it from the bag.

A storm jib, on the other hand, is a must, according to how it relates to the rest of your suit of sails. Rather than try to define such a jib by size, let's say that you require a sail that'll take your boat to windward in winds and through seas as fierce as the boat's fabric can stand. That may be your working jib—perhaps with a set of reef points—or it may be a separate sail entirely. My own feeling, subject to any number of caveats, is that a boat with a big foretriangle, so designed that she'll go to windward with a headsail alone, may be best off with a working jib one weight heavier than what would normally be called for, while a boat whose design requires both a reefed mainsail and a small foresail to claw up in heavy weather should probably have a storm jib.

If you do get a storm jib, make sure that it has a wire strap permanently fixed to its head and running the length of the jibstay: The pressure of wind in this sail is great, its luff is short (meaning that there'll be a lot of rope above the winch drum), and if you are going to make yards to windward, you'll need the straightest luff you can get. In addition, it's probably a good idea to splice separate sheets into the clew ring, because in the nature of things a storm jib will be subject to a lot of flogging, and it will be almost impossible to resnap a runaway shackle.

And then there are always what I call ego sails—ones whose shape or function are designed to express some personal opinion of your own or to make up for some deficiency in an otherwise adequate rig. For instance, I once owned a rather stumpy-masted 30-foot ketch. Her sticks were short because her keel was so shallow, and she needed every inch of canvas she could set. On a beam or broad reach, there was the mizzen staysail; on a run, the spinnaker; going to windward was best not thought of; and that left close-reaching. For that heading, we had a sail called a mule, one that might more accurately have been named a main backstaysail. It filled the area between main and mizzenmasts not occupied by the mainsail, with its head at the main masthead, its tack at the base of the mizzen and its clew sheeted through the same block that served the mizzen staysail halyard. It had ordinary piston hanks along its luff, which attached to the main backstay. On a close reach it would give the boat somewhere between a half and three-quarters of a knot, but the real reason I had it was that it was amusing, striking, and individual.

There are other such sails—jib topsails, mizzen spinnakers, you name it. I've even seen a mini-mizzen designed solely to allow a ketch to ride easily at anchor without weathercocking back and forth. The point is that she's your boat, and within the limits of the enforced laws of man and nature, you can do as you please.

How to buy sails

Another chapter of this book deals with costs and purchasing generally, but sails are something of a special case, so it may make sense to deal with their acquisition here. As noted above, your new boat may or may not have a set of working sails included in the base price. Your secondhand boat will certainly have sails as part of her equipment, but their worth is questionable. In either case, you would do well to establish a working relationship with a sailmaker, even if all you want at the moment is a professional cleaning and repair at the season's end.

Choosing a sailmaker is not like choosing a spouse, but there are a few resemblances. For one thing, it pays to get a partner who understands and sympathizes with the kind of sailing you plan to do. (This, of course, requires that you be honest with yourself and him; it's unfair to ask a man to be both a sailmaker and a mindreader.) Another resemblance to marriage is that the mistakes created by the two of you will linger on and fester, so it's worth some trouble to avoid as many of them as possible.

Most sailmakers who advertise in yachting magazines cite the racing records of their customers. It stands to reason, because a race won is something tangible you can put in an ad, and most sailmakers have the idea that cruising sailors don't buy sails anyway, since they have no interest in skillful sailing.

In looking for a sailmaker, I'd keep three criteria in mind. In no particular order I would . . .

1. avoid the sailmaker whose ads deal exclusively with racing success, especially victories by clients in hot leagues like the SORC or the Admiral's Cup;
2. look for a man who has made sails for a number of boats of your class, not as a bulk order from the manufacturer but for individual owners on their own recognizance. If there are no boats of your class around, look for the man who makes sails for boats of similar type;
3. buy locally. For one thing, it's a lot easier to take a torn, dirty, or unsatisfactory sail back in your car than to pack and ship it, and for another, the sailmaker is going to be a bit more careful if he knows you can and will be on his doorstep when something's wrong.

Buying locally doesn't mean buying from the smallest sailmaker in the area. Even the biggest loft of the world's largest sailmaking firm is a tiny business by normal standards. You have every right to be treated with individual attention, and you can reciprocate by not wasting the sailmaker's time in idle visiting, and by scheduling your order—and the ensuing necessary discussion—for the slack time, which is usually in the fall before New Year's.

When you first go to a sailmaker, try to establish in your own mind a sail wardrobe to aim at and a schedule with which you plan to time your purchases. If the sailmaker has a good deal of experience with your boat's class, listen carefully to his suggestions; he probably has a better idea than you do about what will be a useful sail and what won't. At the same time, bear in mind that sailmakers tend to be intensely conservative, especially the ones who've been heavily involved in racing. For many of them, it's literally impossible to visualize a mast without black bands top and bottom, and there are some things they simply cannot imagine because the racing rules expressly forbid them.

If your sailmaker is racing-oriented, be wary of suggestions for sails that are only of use to racers. Some of the largest, most international lofts are known in the boating trade for their "staysail-of-the-month" approach to their customers. Highly specialized sails or ones with a very narrow wind range will be equally annoying to the cruising skipper who wants everything on his boat to have at least two uses.

Secondhand sails

Not all sails are new, and there are two ways you may encounter used sails. First and most common, of course, is when you buy a secondhand boat. Nearly always such a boat will come with at least three sails and often with quite an impressive array—eight bags, ten or even more. This may or may not be a boon to you. If possible, you should sail your secondhand boat before making a bid, and try to set all the sails in her inventory, even if the prevailing breeze of the moment is wrong for some of them. What you're trying to do at this point is simply decide what's worth keeping, and how much your bid should be scaled down in consequence.

There is no clearly defined working life for synthetic sails, but it doesn't hurt to be suspicious of anything that's more than five years old. The boat's basic wardrobe—main and genoa, as a rule—will have taken the roughest beating and will get the same treatment from you. Very likely you'll have to consider replacing one or both within the first season. Spinnakers can take an astonishing amount of abuse, including being almost literally exploded in heavy winds, and still recover. So a much-patched chute may not be in as bad shape as it looks.

When checking the boat's sail wardrobe, allow the owner to set the leads and various tensioning devices, then observe the result. If the jibs have a maximum draft that's sagged back about two-thirds the way from the luff, they will make nice awnings, but not much else. Mainsails whose leeches remain

The kind of treatment this Tartan 27's main is receiving will surely shorten its working life. The stretch marks between panels aren't new.

hooked no matter what are similarly incurable. Forget about any sail with a machine-gun rattle along the leech. And be very cautious about sails that show the telltale pencil marks of recutting.

If possible, get off at a distance and watch the boat sail by under various sail combinations. A blown sail—one whose shape has been permanently altered by stretching—is unmistakable from a distance, but it may be surprisingly hard to discern the problem from directly below.

The other way to pick up used sails is from a sailmaker or sail broker. From time to time sailmakers have customers whose plans change or who cannot pay for the sails they've ordered. The sailmaker may give you a good price on one of these in order to get them out of the loft with some slight profit. Occasionally he'll even throw in a bag or cover as well. In buying someone else's sails, it's important to bear a couple of things in mind. First and most important, if the item in question was cut for a boat of your class, or even one that's generally similar in dimensions and displacement, it'll probably be quite adequate for cruising, if less than perfect for racing. Even a sail that has nothing to do with your own boat can be useful: I once bought secondhand the genoa from a

210-class daysailer to serve as the #3 genoa for my 30-foot ketch. It worked out amazingly well, providing the length of foot and shortness of luff I wanted in a heavy-weather sail for my tender cruising boat.

At the same time, don't expect too much from a sail that was cut for another boat, and very possibly with another owner's idiosyncrasies in mind. You may end up paying more for alterations to make it fit than you would for a new sail. While much sailmaking mumbo-jumbo is just that, and while sailboats have been jury rigged with just about any piece of cloth you can name, a sail that was designed for your boat, her rig, and your cruising area will normally work best.

Buying a sail from a secondhand dealer is perhaps the most usual way to acquire an inexpensive addition to your boat's wardrobe. There are only a few sail brokers and they advertise in the back pages of sailing magazines. Their wares tend to fall into three categories. First are the unused or nearly unused sails placed with them by sailmakers whose clients have disappeared or by owners whose boats (but not their sails) have come to grief. Second are sails that have had a considerable portion of their lives used up in service and are being replaced (usually by racers) with something newer or trendier. And third are the unsatisfactories, the ugly ducklings that have been recut and recut and are still not what the original owner wanted.

Obviously, sails in the first category are simply new sails, while ones in the second should have a decent amount of life in them, should have something approximating their original shape, and should be priced accordingly. The third group may or may not be of use to you, but they can normally be recognized by (as noted above) the pencil marks of redesign for recutting as well as the sewing itself. Used sails are sold on approval, as a rule, with the understanding that you will spread them on the floor or lawn and check them out, but not sail with them. It pays to have independent expert advice if you are uncertain of your own ability to recognize a dud—so take along a friend.

For the cruising skipper who has no racing blood, secondhand sails seem to be a most logical purchasing decision, especially if you're reasonably knowledgeable and your boat is of a common size and class. The racing skipper, alas, will probably not find someone else's sails worth having, except perhaps as backup or cruising canvas, allowing him to spare his best rig for competition.

Sail-handling gear

Not all that long ago, the only winch on a sailing yacht was the one that raised the anchor. Now winches have become both necessities and status symbols: If one is to get a pleasurable level of performance from today's cruiser, winches are indeed necessary, but nowhere near as many of them as some people think. Indeed, in the past couple of years there's been a move toward the reduction of at least one category of winches, those that serve halyards. Paradoxically (it seems at first) this reduction has come among the racers, who have always seemed the most gadget-happy.

There are two reasons: money and weight above the waterline. It's hard to say which is more important to the serious racer, but there's little doubt which is more convincing to the cruiser. And typically, it's been the racers who've managed to show the cruisers how to get the same work out of fewer, cheaper mechanical aids. But we're getting a little ahead of ourselves.

Anchor duty aside, there are two main functions for winches aboard a modern cruising boat. The first, as suggested above, is to increase the pull on halyards; the second is to provide the same additional effort on sheets. The two jobs are similar, but not identical. Generally speaking, a sail is raised and lowered fairly infrequently in the course of an average sail. With the notable exception of the spinnaker, when a sail is lowered, it comes down with little or no tension on it, often on the run. By contrast, a properly sailed boat will have its crew tending the sheets regularly, even when they're not racing. The sheets must come in easily—fast without loads, and then more slowly under heavy load—but they must also ease off the drums without skidding or jamming the line.

Boats of the size we're discussing generally have at most three halyard winches—one each for the jib, spinnaker, and mainsail. If there's a mizzenmast, no winch ought to be necessary for the mizzen itself, especially if a gooseneck downhaul or Cunningham is fitted, nor for the mizzen staysail, which is set flying. As most but not all sailors learn early on, the mainsail halyard runs down the starboard side of the mast, the jib and spinnaker

Halyards led aft through cam cleats to winches on the cabin top.

halyards down the port side—assuming all three terminate on the mast in the first place. More and more small cruisers have the first two halyards led back over the cabin top, aft where a wincher can get at them while kneeling on the bridge deck or standing braced in the companionway. In very small cruisers —say under 25 feet overall—or ones that are especially fine in the bows, simply sending a crewman forward can take half a knot or more off the boat's speed, and so there's a good reason to keep people back in the cockpit when possible. Also, by means of stoppers (of which more below) it's possible to run all the halyards to the same winch, stopping off instead of cleating each line when its hoisting task is done.

Assuming that the halyard winches don't interfere with the main hatch or a cabin-trunk-mounted mainsheet, the cabin-top location seems to me a very good one. The mainsail can be raised and lowered without leaving the cockpit, and this is a definite advantage. Don't ask too much of the arrangement, however, for there are a number of things you cannot expect of it: For one thing, it makes reefing a bit more complex—instead of having a man at the mast who tends both halyards and reefing gear, one now requires someone in the cockpit besides the helmsman to man the halyard, while another person either cranks the roller reefing or secures the jiffy-reefing hook.

Nor should you expect to be able to drop the jib in a tidy heap without going forward. Jibs nearly always drop about halfway down the stay, then catch some wind and have to be handed down the rest of the way. And sometimes wrestled and sat upon. A trained hand at the mast-mounted halyard winch can usually slack the halyard with one hand and pull down the jib luff with the other, while with the deckhouse mounted rig, one sailor has to be on the foredeck and another aft to avoid the halyard's getting tangled as it runs.

If you have a good power-of-three or -four tackle on a gooseneck downhaul, you probably don't require a main halyard winch at all, but if you don't have such a handy rig, the sheer friction involved in getting a 30- or 35-foot luff up all that track will mandate a winch, although it may be a very small one (see the table for sizes of winches according to sail size and winch function). Do not under any circumstances accept the old-fashioned reel halyard winch with its deceptive and untrustworthy brake handle. There is virtually nothing good that can be said about it, and it's seldom seen except in the catalogs of hardware firms specializing in the arcane.

A jib halyard winch, on the other hand, is very important on nearly any modern yacht. It's usually the same size as the main halyard winch, but should if anything be somewhat larger. One may fairly ask why have both a jib and spinnaker halyard winch, and if you're a cruising person exclusively, the answer is that there's no good reason. One does of course need two separate halyards, but there's no reason why both cannot lead to the same winch.

As noted above, the spinnaker is the only sail that's normally lowered under heavy tension (although a mainsail is under some tension when being roller or jiffy reefed). It's a good idea to have a halyard stopper fitted a short distance above the winch, just as a safeguard. If you have a similar stopper fitted for the jib halyard, you can leave the raised jib up, and properly tensioned, while raising a spinnaker in addition—as when sailing on a beam reach.

If you have a roller-furling headsail, you'll need an extrahefty winch to put tension on its luff, and perhaps a two-part tackle in the halyard as well. Roller genoas seem almost never to be adequately tensioned, and those sagging luffs account for much of the poor windward performance in otherwise good cruising boats.

With a proper tackle system, as discussed below, there is no need whatever for a mainsheet winch on a 30-footer, with the possible exception of a catboat.

A small cruising boat's primary sheet winches are perhaps her most important pieces of hardware, constantly in use when the boat is under way, and frequently employed as mooring cleats or even for winching the boat off a sandbar. They should be oversize if anything and should, in my opinion, also be self-tailing. This is particularly important if the boat is sailed shorthanded, as it means the person at the helm can also trim the sheets without excess effort. It also means that two people, instead of three, can handle the boat under main and genoa at almost maximum efficiency.

Among the various brands of self-tailing winch I have no personal preference, but it does seem to pay to have winches you can service yourself, to the point of stripping and regreasing them once a season. In complex machinery that's subject to hard service, it does seem that the best costs extra. I doubt, however, whether any but the larger boats will need two-speed self-tailers

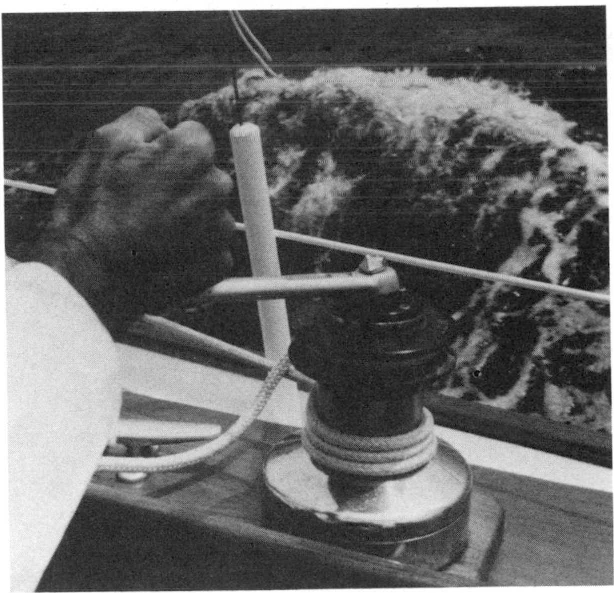

Self-tailing sheet winch. The cleat is a safety factor.

unless racing is your primary concern. The mechanical advantage of single-speed winches is enhanced by using a longer rather than a shorter handle (most manufacturers make at least two lengths), assuming there's room to swing it without hitting a lifeline stanchion or piece of the mizzen rigging. It can be most annoying not having enough room for a complete turn of a winch handle.

While on the subject of handles, make sure that your winches have the star-shaped universal handle sockets. Keep a pair of handles in the cockpit when under way, buy one of the inexpensive plastic kind for the halyard winches, and keep a spare below. Some people invest in locking handles for the mast-mounted halyard winches, but these seldom seem to lock properly somehow, and you can realistically expect to lose a handle now and then, usually during a moment of struggle up forward. You will lose fewer if you have a pocket at the base of the mast in which to stick the handle when not in use.

Secondary winches, slightly smaller than the primaries, are standard on nearly all racing boats, but for a cruiser they seem to me largely an affectation. If you're buying a new boat, they are certainly something you can skip the first year (but do make sure that the winch pads are accessible from below, in case you change your mind later). You may find it useful to have a small snubbing winch for the spinnaker pole topping lift, which can operate under considerable tension in a 30-footer, but again, it's worth going without for a season to see if you really need it. This winch will normally be mounted on the cabin top, and you'll want to be sure that installing it after purchase won't mean ripping out some of the headliner. Most better boats now have some means of access to the underside of the cabin top, whether it's screw-in plates or zippers in a fabric headliner.

Finally, you may, halfway through your first season, feel that life would be a lot easier if you had a small winch for the roller-furling genoa gear. Chances are, however, that there's something wrong with the gear, probably with the critical first lead off the furling drum, which must be exactly in line with the drum opening. If necessary, the furling line can be—should be—rigged so it can be led direct to one of the sheet winches in case you ever do have to furl a big jenny full of wind.

Blocks and track

The proper trim of headsails, and thus their most efficient performance, depends to a great extent on the location of the trimming points, the blocks that initially change the direction of a sheet as it comes off the clew of the sail. Probably the most common form of adjustable lead is a track running along the deck from just abaft the shrouds to the beginning of the cockpit coaming, or even further aft. Along this track runs one or more cars that are adjustable as to location by spring-loaded or screw pins fitting into holes in the track.

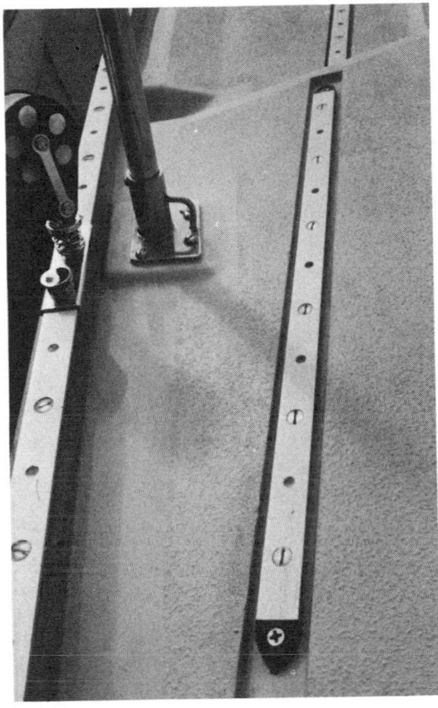

Inner and outer headsail sheet tracks. Recessing the inner one will prevent stubbed toes, but will also collect harbor dirt.

Another popular form of track, identified especially with the C&C line of sailboats, consists of a black anodized aluminum toerail pierced every couple of inches and running from bow to stern. No cars are used here, and the snap-shackle blocks are made fast directly to the track, as are fenders, boom vangs, and anything else one wants to attach.

All the elements of a headsail sheeting system are sooner or later going to be under great tension, and some parts will be under far more stress than others. The standard type of block used for the initial headsail sheet lead is called a snatch block. Because it opens at the side and has a snap shackle below, it's easy to change lines, to change locations along a perforated toerail, and to strike the block itself below at the end of a sail—a good idea from the point of view of maintenance, and a better one from the point of view of security. The fact that a snatch block opens at two points means that it's not as strong for a given size as a standard block, and it can also cause problems with awkward sheet leads that put unfair stresses on the block's attachment to the track or car.

Few of today's blocks will explode or collapse—though I've seen it happen. What's more likely when you use a too small block is a gradual deformation, first noticeable as a slight binding when you try to spin the sheave with the block under no load. After a while, the block becomes deformed to the point that it's nothing more than a fairlead. It pays to get blocks of the proper size, or even a size larger, according to the manufacturer's recommendations.

If you employ turning blocks as well as sheet blocks, bear in mind that the load on the former type of block can be half again as much as on the latter, or even greater. Turning blocks are often fixed cheek blocks and can sometimes serve a dual purpose as primary blocks for the spinnaker sheet and guy.

It may be that in spite of every adjustment you can make, your headsails just don't seem to find a proper sheet lead along the track your boat carries. The jib may sheet in so tightly that it persistently backwinds the main, or its lead may be out so far that the sail lacks drive. Check with your sailmaker if you have reason to suspect either condition is hopeless, given the possible leads on the boat, but don't waste his time until you've tried everything. It may be necessary to move the track or recut the sail. Of the two, recutting the sail is probably easier and cheaper. Moving the track means redrilling all the bolt holes, sealing the old ones and bedding the new fittings, and then trying to cosmeticize what you've done.

V

Fittings and Gear

All but the smallest cruising yachts have foredeck hatches, usually mounted at the leading end of the trunk cabin. These hatches come in for a lot of abuse, both in use and, later, in words. Many of them are inadequate both in design and construction. A proper forehatch should be large enough to get out of while wearing foul-weather gear (about 21 inches on a side is minimal), large enough to admit the biggest bagged headsail without snagging, strong enough for the heaviest crewmember to stand on without trepidation, capable of being propped open at various heights and staying there, and waterproof when dogged down tight.

This is a fairly heavy order, and on smaller yachts it may not be possible to achieve every aim. In practical terms, perhaps the most important thing is that the hatch should be waterproof. There are few more annoying things than wet bunks, and a dripping forehatch can soak down an amazing expanse of cabin. While forehatches are far less prone to leaks than companionway sliding hatches, there are three things that can produce drips. First is the insertion of a separate piece of Plexiglas in the hatch surface for additional light in a cabin that can otherwise be rather tomblike. The small port is a natural water trap, and unless it's perfectly bedded will begin to drip.

In more and more new boats, the forehatch is recessed into a cabin top that slopes gently down to the foredeck. While this looks streamlined as anything, it simply provides a path for any solid water that finds its way on deck and, unless the hatch is securely dogged, can guide a breaking wave right into your sleeping bag.

Finally, many hatches are flexible in themselves, with little stripping around the edges and only a single screw-down fitting to exert pressure and make the setup weathertight. A well-designed hatch should be scuppered around its edges, with rubber stripping to seal it tightly. Unless the hatch is quite solid,

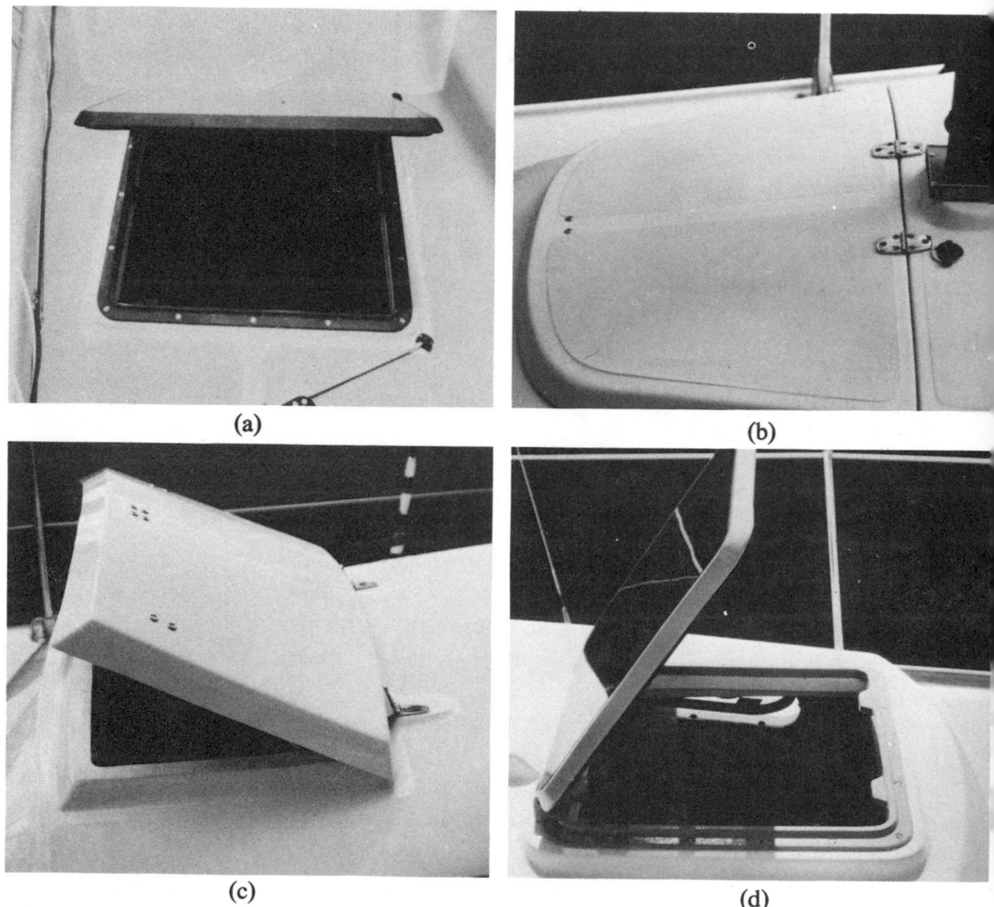

(a) (b) (c) (d)

Forehatches: (a) on the foredeck itself, this one will be a waterscoop in heavy weather; (b) not a whole lot better, with only one securing point on the forward edge; (c) built-up lip should make some difference, but the plastic seems a bit flimsy; (d) good quality metal-framed hatch on a raised base—easily the best of the lot.

two screw-down fittings on the forward edge will probably be required to dog it tightly. When closed, the hatch should have no protruding edges that will snag sheets as the boat is tacking, although there's probably no way to prevent a hatch that's partially open from eating every sheet that comes near it. Perhaps the best one can do is rig a piece of shock cord from the forward side of the mast above the highest extension of the open hatch cover, running down to an eye on deck forward of the hatch. It's not a perfect solution, but it will help.

The cabin top is a tempting place to stow gear, but there are any number of good reasons for finding other locations. Just about the only things that belong on the cabin top are ventilators, which may be in the form of the

(a)

(b)

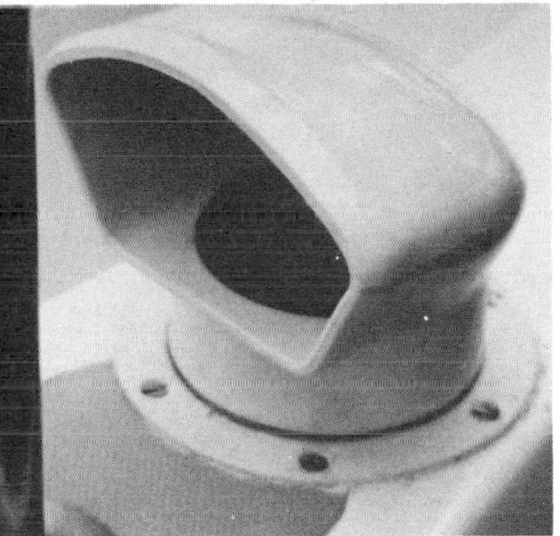

(c)

Vents: (a) traditional dorade style, with PVC ventilator on a wood box; (b) less attractive, but functional (note the too-small drain hole in one corner); (c) not a dorade at all, this ventilator is adequate for airing the engine compartment, but keep a watertight cap handy.

familiar dorades or as small hatches, letting in light as well as air. Obviously all of these openings have to be as watertight as possible, but they are seldom completely so. It's therefore a good idea to make certain that there's nothing immediately below a ventilator or hatch that's likely to be spoiled by wetting, because sooner or later it'll be doused.

Many boats—and not the most expensive, necessarily—have a fiberglass shell, the trunk or tank, into which the companionway hatch slides when it's fully open. This is an excellent feature and one to look for. Not only does it protect the hatch when the boat's in use, but it also reduces the incidence of leaks at the forward end of the hatch—a spot that's very prone to them. Finally, a hatch tank is a good place on which to mount an instrument console—it's at eye height for the helmsman and offers perhaps less distraction than anywhere else. Besides, such an installation frees up the after side of the cabin for crewmembers to lean against.

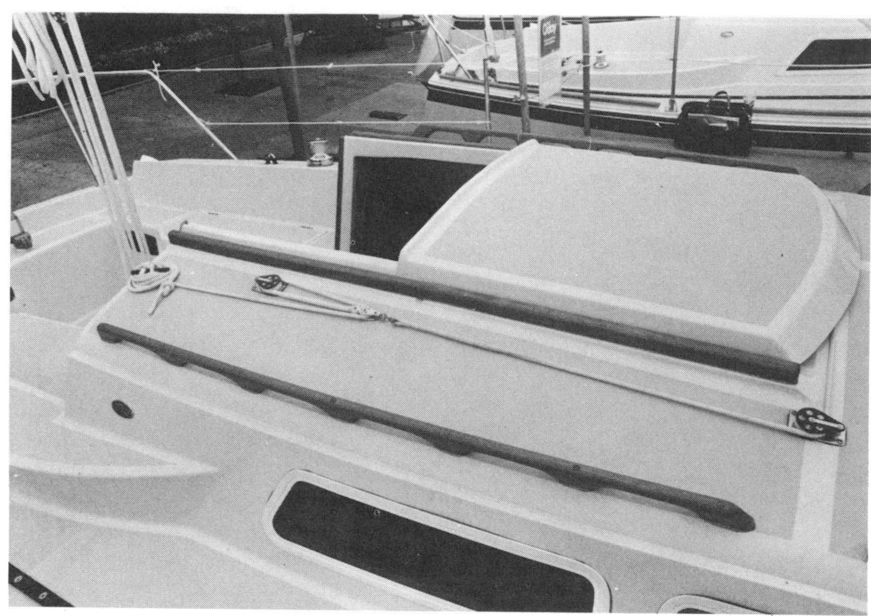

Main hatch without a trunk, like this one, will encourage leaks under its forward edge. (Tackle is for a centerboard pennant.)

Proper main hatch of tinted Plexiglas slides forward into a protective trunk which, if well bedded, should be leak-free.

Cockpit and steering

In small cruising boats, the cockpit is the sole center of action under way. There are at least two major reasons why this should be so. To begin with, when you're sailing shorthanded or single-handed, it will be both more efficient and safer to have all the principal controls within reach—even distant reach—of the helmsman. Second, unlike larger yachts, the small cruiser is very sensitive to weight changes, especially forward.

While most boats' cockpits are carefully thought out, they tend to be compromises: The designer has to allow for sailing the boat with a cockpit full of guests as well as with no one besides the skipper. Shop around for a cockpit layout that matches your sailing intentions, and you'll probably do well to find one that comes halfway, with the flexibility to allow you to customize it the rest of the way. Let's examine what's needed from the separate points of view of skipper and crew.

The person at the tiller or wheel should first of all have maximum visibility around as much of the compass as possible. With modern deck-sweeping jibs,

Well-engineered, high-tech cockpit of the C&C-designed Mega. The helmsman can also handle the mainsheet, while headsail sheets go to cabin-top winches.

a substantial portion of the view forward and to leeward will be blocked much of the time. The person at the helm should be able to sit down on the leeward side and see around the largest genoa, while someone else keeps watch to windward. The person at the helm should—must—be able to see over the cabin top while sitting comfortably. Being just able to peer over the hatch trunk while sitting bolt upright on two cushions isn't good enough.

The primary steering positions will be windward and leeward sides under way, and probably standing up on the centerline under power. While sailing, the helmsman should be able to see whatever sail trim gauges the boat may possess, as well as the speedometer and depth sounder. Under power, he or she should have easy visibility of the latter two, as well as of the engine instruments.

In addition to visibility of instruments and the water ahead and to either side, the helmsman should be placed so he can see what the crew is up to. Some boats have their steering arranged so the skipper is well forward in the cockpit and some of the crew are working behind his back. Besides being potentially dangerous, it makes for less effective sailing.

Steering efficiency depends to a certain extent on the boat's own good or bad habits, in part on the location of the rudder vis-à-vis the other elements of the cockpit, and in part on one's personal preferences. Many people new to sailing have wheel steering installed in even small cruisers, probably because it reminds them of their cars and works the same way. Some will get a wheel because it can provide a better mechanical advantage than a tiller. Some just feel it makes for a saltier ambience.

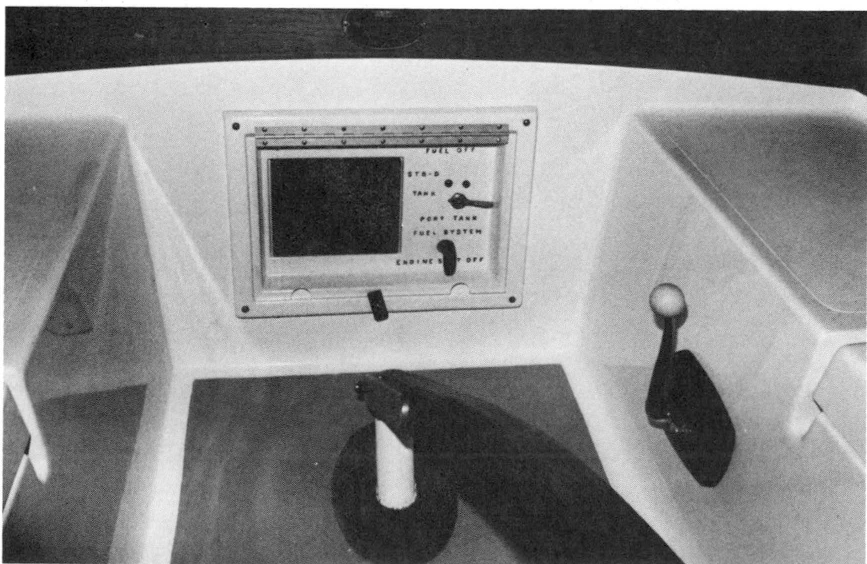

Engine panel behind the helmsman is likely to be forgotten. Clear plastic panel will protect the gauges.

It seems to me that in boats 30 feet and less in length there is probably no reason to have a steering wheel at all. This doesn't mean I'm against wheels in smaller cruisers, just that I think the buyer should be aware that the extra money he's spending on yet another piece of machinery that may go wrong in an embarrassing moment isn't necessary from the boat's viewpoint. It may, however, be an appreciable element in your enjoyment of the boat, in which case it cannot be argued against.

If you're approaching the decision from a neutral location, here are some things to consider: As far as steering efficiency and sensitivity go, a tiller is almost certainly superior to a wheel. If your boat is so hardmouthed that you need the gearing advantage of a wheel to handle her helm, then you've got a large problem with the boat's balance, and obscuring it with a wheel isn't really addressing the situation. Few small-boat cockpits are properly engineered for a wheel anyway. It is probably almost impossible to edge your way past it, and more often than not, a person of average height standing behind the wheel of a small cruiser will find the backstay abrading his scalp.

And having said all that, it's only fair to add that one of the ego-boosting delights of owning a sailing cruiser, however minuscule, is to stand behind her "destroyer"-style steering wheel feeling like the king of the world.

Since you, or someone, will spend long hours steering the boat, the helm area should be as comfortable as possible. For me, this means some kind of back support when sitting, good footing when I'm standing, someplace to rest my free arm when sitting on either side, and most of all, a means of bracing myself

Not an ideal cockpit: The wheel (an owner's option) is too small and the spokes are a nuisance; the cabin top is high to see over easily; and the single-point mainsheet lead is right where one might want to sit.

when the boat is laid over. When the boat comes about or jibes, it should be easy for the person at the helm to get across without becoming enmeshed with tiller or mainsheet (only practical experiment will tell you).

For long hauls, there should be a reasonably secure place to put things—the small pigeonhole lockers built under wide cockpit coamings are a definite asset to any boat, and prefabricated units can be installed in many coamings by the owner. Finally, the cockpit should be properly engineered so that the person at the steering is neither standing nor sitting in a pool of water no matter what heading the boat is on or what her angle of heel.

As noted above, the person steering should be able to reach and handle both the sheets and the engine controls while still being able to steer. This sounds obvious, but it's not necessarily so.

For some reason, more than a few inboard engine installations have the ignition well out of reach of the steering. This seems to me both irritating and potentially dangerous. The only minor advantages are that the ignition, when below, can be somewhat protected from the weather and from boat thieves. But when you are coming into a slip under power and the engine stalls as you reverse it, you want to be able to reach that key fast. It's also possible (if rare) for a running engine to refuse to go out of gear, in which case the only answer may be to turn off the ignition.

The crew are workers some of the time and passengers the rest, and the cockpit layout should reflect that fact. Under way, the crew's primary functions are to act as lookout and to tend the sheets. This means that their seating should be so arranged that they can easily see forward, and they should have access to the primary and secondary winches without moving from their observers' positions. In addition, the winches should be capable of being operated with the boat at an extreme angle of heel—easy on the lee side, but often something of a problem when trying to winch in a recalcitrant spinnaker guy while the boat's on a screaming reach.

From a purely functional point of view, I find it easiest to operate a winch if I can belly up to it, while standing on the cockpit sole with my feet braced. Tailing can be accomplished while sitting down—in fact it's sometimes easier to throw all one's weight onto a line when one is not standing. In small cruisers, however, there is seldom enough room in the cockpit to allow for a clear standing space alongside a primary winch, and one must make do while kneeling. The problem is sometimes aggravated in the case of secondary winches, usually located aft of the primaries: It can be quite difficult in a small cruiser to operate the secondary winches without becoming involved with the helmsman.

On many new small cruisers the sheet winches are moved to the cabin roof, flanking the companionway hatch. This of course means that the sheets must have a fairlead upward from the sheet or turning blocks on deck. It can also mean a great increase in sheeting efficiency, as the sheet-tending crewmember can stand in the companionway, out of the cockpit action, with the winches

Cluttered by lines, but an effective layout. Note access to sheet winches, deep coamings for back support.

more or less at chest level. When the sheet winches and the halyards and lifts all come back over the deckhouse to the cockpit, it can make for a splendid work center. Tails of halyards and sheets can simply drop into the cabin, which keeps confusing spaghetti out of the cockpit. Such an arrangement can be very efficient when one knows the ropes—literally—but it can be chaos for a stranger. I have found that color coding the lines and the cleats to which they lead is perhaps the simplest solution, and labeling each cleat with a self-adhesive vinyl tag helps new sailors become aware more quickly of what they're doing.

When the crew aren't working, they want to be as comfortable as possible. A boat whose cockpit has a bridge deck at least fifteen inches wide provides useful extra room with the potential for shelter abaft the cabin trunk. Most boats have seats running down either side of the cockpit. Ideally, these should be not less than fifteen inches wide, with good back support and with a narrow enough space between them athwartships so a crewmember can brace his feet, legs slightly bent, against the low-side seats. I've been aboard a number of boats where the cockpit was just too wide to do this, and the inevitable result is a tangle of bodies on the lee side when the boat is tacked quickly and someone loses his or her balance. The only amelioration for a too wide cockpit is to bolt a two-by-four to the cockpit sole and use it as a heel brace.

It's a truism to say that the cockpit seats should be adequately scuppered so they drain on either tack, but there are still a number of boats whose cockpits collect water, especially in the corners. Scuppers should be capable

Minimal dodger, this one keeps the companionway dry, although it won't protect the occupants of the cockpit much.

of being cleared with a piece of wire, because they will sooner or later collect enough gummy grit to clog.

Some builders suggest that their boats' cockpit seats will serve as fair-weather berths—and some will. But bear in mind that a comfortable seat width for most people is fifteen inches, while very few people have shoulders that narrow. Speaking as someone who has slept on a seat just over a foot and a quarter wide, I can vouch for the fact that one gets rather little rest under these circumstances. It is, however, possible to extend the width of a cockpit seat by means of a foldover flap; it's been done on the Herreshoff America catboat with good results.

One of the best inventions of the sailing age is the folding cockpit dodger. Nearly any sailing cruiser's cabin top will accept one, and they make a tremendous difference in cockpit comfort on cold or windy days. The basic dodger is simply a baby-carriage hood covering the companionway hatch opening. It keeps water out of the accommodation while admitting air, and there is usually enough shelflike room at its forward end to stow a folded chart or binoculars.

Better for most people is a dodger that runs nearly the width of the cabin top. Not only is there far more usable dry shelf space but it provides much more shelter to the occupants of the cockpit. About the only drawbacks are that it's difficult to see ahead, even through the little plastic window, and it can be hard to work one's way forward along the side deck without leaning on the dodger frame and twisting it. Though many people do not, one should make a point of folding the dodger down flat when it's not needed.

One other piece of canvas much used in tropical climates is the Bimini top, named after the similar device invented for small sport-fishing boats. Unless

An exterior rudder, whether transom-hung or not, needs heavy pintles and gudgeons like these.

one is a dedicated performance sailor, the Bimini top will not interfere with one's sailing enough to make a difference, and it can be a godsend for people with tender skins. A proper Bimini top has a tubular frame, as opposed to a cockpit shelter that's just a rectangular piece of cloth with poles through hems at either end, usable only at anchor. One can cut down the amount of necessary framing by integrating the forward end of the Bimini with the dodger frame. In fact, it's possible to go the whole hog and tent in the entire cockpit with side pieces and screens, although this kind of thing seems awfully involved for most people.

As much as one may try to make a cockpit resemble a living room, it still has the boat's steering system in the middle of it, and it will be good to do some thinking about the various types of steering that are possible in a small cruiser. There are essentially two ways of attaching a rudder to the boat. The simplest is to hang it on the transom, hinged somewhat like a door. Not only does this have the important advantage of being easy to get at and quick to repair but it also obviates a through-hull fitting—always something to avoid if possible. In addition, by mounting the rudder at the very aft end of the boat, one maximizes its leverage and makes it most effective.

There are two obvious drawbacks to the transom-hung rudder: First, it necessitates mounting any outboard engine off center, which makes it less efficient. An off-center outboard will steer a tight circle in one direction, and a wide one in the other, and when moving ahead in a straight line, the outboard has to be cocked off slightly. The other disadvantage is that it's much harder to set up wheel steering with a transom-hung rudder, although it can be done. And finally, there are many people who find transom-hung rudders aesthetically unpleasing, although I don't happen to agree.

The other type of rudder is mounted beneath the stern, entirely underwater or nearly so. It can be hung from the end of the keel or from a separate skeg, or it can depend solely from its own rudder post. In any case, the rudder post comes up through the bottom of the boat and through the cockpit sole, usually via some sort of tube that provides a watertight shaft. An accident to the rudder, however, may easily damage this tube and cause a leak into the hull (just as a shock to a transom-hung rudder may tear it right off its gudgeons).

The type of rudder also has an effect on the cockpit's layout. A transom-hung rudder normally has a tiller coming over the afterdeck, involving itself with the boat's mainsheet traveler, if she has one. While the tiller can be swung upward to clear the cockpit, it can only swing down to a certain point, the exact amount determined by the height of the cockpit and the pivot point of the tiller itself. The tiller attached to a through-the-hull rudder normally comes up out of the cockpit sole, hinged to a fitting that sometimes seems designed to snag clothing and even flesh. If the boat has wheel steering, the binnacle will usually be forward of the point at which the rudder shaft emerges from the cockpit sole. It's necessary to make sure that an emergency tiller can fit over the top of the rudder post and have sufficient play to allow the boat to be steered if the steering packs up.

The most common type of wheel steering on today's cruisers calls for a binnacle fixed more or less in the middle of the cockpit, with the throttle and gearshift on its column and the compass, plus perhaps a speedometer and depth sounder, on top. With the stainless-steel "destroyer"-style wheel, this makes an impressive and effective steering system with a great deal of mechanical advantage and a reasonable amount of feel, transmitted upward from the rudder, through the system's cables.

If you're considering this kind of wheel steering, there are several things to look for. First, can you—or the tallest member of your regular crew—stand at the wheel without grazing his or her head on the backstay? Can all the regular helmspeople see the compass and any other binnacle-mounted instruments without bending down to peer into the dials? Is the compass itself so located that it can serve for taking quick bearings fore, aft, and athwartships? And finally, do the position of the binnacle and the diameter of the wheel impede fore and aft movement in the cockpit? In a small boat with the standard bench seats, it's almost inevitable. A few boats, among them the C&C 29 and the Independence 31, have T-shaped cockpit wells, with the crossarm of the T located at the wheel. Not only does this design make it easier for crew to move past the wheel but it also makes it possible to tend the jib sheet winches while still standing, a definite plus in terms of efficiency.

Whatever the location of the binnacle, a stout grabrail on its forward side

Easily accessible rudder shaft under aft seat, keyed for tiller.

will protect the compass and give the watch on deck something to cling to in bad weather. Make sure any metal so close to the compass is nonferrous.

About the only other conformation of wheel steering is the forward-facing wheel hooked up to a transom-hung rudder, as on many catboats. The gear box abaft the wheel makes a convenient saddle-type seat, and the whole thing saves much cockpit space. Some people, however find the seating position hard on their backs.

Engine gear

Chapter X in this book treats power plants as functional elements, but here toward the beginning it may be helpful to examine separately the accessories you'll want to consider buying to get the most from your power plant and make it last as long as possible. The basic problem with power plants and sailors is that the two are an inimicable combination, oil and water. It sometimes seems to me that a sailor is never so deeply satisfied as when his power plant fails, fulfilling his darkest suspicions. Assuming, however, that you'd rather have your auxiliary perform as advertised, let's consider how to get the most result for the least effort.

Begin with instruments, because fewer and fewer small inboard engines have them. Most new marine engines, gas as well as diesel, have a couple of alarm lights for low oil pressure and overheating and perhaps a warning buzzer (for when the engine dies with the ignition switch still on). If you have any interest in how the engine works at all, this kind of embryonic dashboard is unsatisfactory. It may cost more to get a useful one, but it can be done, and for your own peace of mind it should be.

The proper instrument panel for any inboard engine has four instruments represented by dials, not lights or buzzers; a couple of ancillaries not on the instrument panel are also recommended.

For monitoring the engine's health under way, a water temperature gauge and an oil pressure gauge are indispensable. Start with the recommended readings in the engine's owner's manual, but don't be panicked if the gauges fail to register in the "safe" zone: They may be indicating real trouble, they may simply be registering the fact that the engine is new, and they may not be properly calibrated. A good mechanic can tell you quickly which is the case.

The ammeter tells you only whether the battery is charging or discharging, and how much. What it tells you about the state of the battery is secondhand information, but worth having.

The tachometer is really more of a navigational instrument than an engine gauge, but it can be informative about the kind of work the engine is doing relative to its normal capacity. As an indicator of speed through the water, the tachometer is as accurate (when the boat's under engine alone) as most speedometers, and to do without it is to handicap yourself needlessly. It is, by the way, possible to rig a tachometer with an outboard engine, although a decent speedometer will, in this instance, probably be more helpful.

Fuel gauges on any boat are suspect, and on sailing boats they're doubly so. Unlike automobiles, boats are constantly jiggling up and down relative to a fixed reference point. The fuel in the tank is moving, too, and the readings have to be damped heavily in order to be readable at all. In addition, the odd shapes of many marine tanks make readings down toward the bottom of the tank nearly useless. When you first get your boat, try to arrange for her tank to be dry. Then fill it to a quarter of rated capacity, note the gauge reading, fill to a half, and so on. If the fill pipe is a straight shot to the tank, a stick marked in fractions will be as good as the gauge and maybe better.

Batteries and accessories

The final engine-related gauge I'd recommend, and one that's being fitted to more and more small inboards, is the battery condition meter. This is essentially an accurate voltmeter with an expanded scale, reading from about 9 to 15 volts. It's normally part of the engine's switch panel, although it's possible to purchase these units separately. In some respects a battery condition meter is more informative than an ammeter, since it will tell you both the voltage available from the battery (or batteries) and, by extrapolation, the approximate rate of charge. On my own boat, I hit the battery meter as soon as I go below upon boarding and just as I kill the main battery switch before going ashore. Also after every use of the electrically powered marine sanitation device, or any other unusual current draw.

The battery condition meter is of course something that's available to outboards as well as inboards, and it's perhaps even more valuable for the former, as there is otherwise virtually no way to know the state of the battery.

Most boats with inboard engines, and some with outboards, arrive with a 12-volt battery as part of the standard equipment. While a single battery is adequate for an outboard-powered engine, nearly all inboard-driven boats will require two batteries. The standard small-yacht battery has a capacity of 60 ampere-hours. This means that, at full charge, it can nominally deliver 60 amps for an hour, and then it's flat if it isn't being charged. It can also deliver 20 amps for three hours, or 3 amps for 20; the product of amperes and hours indicates the rated capacity of the battery.

But this is strictly nominal. Given the vagaries of wiring systems and the marine environment, it is generally a mistake to expect more than half the rated amp/hour capacity from a battery. And how do you figure the amperage you need? List all the electrical gadgets aboard driven by the ship's battery and note their hourly current draw, then figure out the maximum number you might be using at once over an extended period and add up their hourly rates, multiply by two, and there you are. Most electronic devices aboard will have their amperage noted somewhere on the casing or in the owner's manual. The following list will, however, give you some idea of what's involved:

Navigation lights (red/green/stern)	2 amps
masthead anchor light	0.3 amp
wind indicator	0.3 amp
depth sounder	0.3 amp
speedo/log	0.3 amp
compass light	0.1 amp
electric bilge pump	10 amps
refrigerator	8 amps
VHF-FM transceiver	3 amps (transmit)
	0.2 amp (receive)
self-steerer	4–13 amps

According to marine engine expert Conrad Miller, a 60 amp/hour battery is adequate for starting circuits of a marine gasoline engine, if one has another battery to serve the accessory circuits listed above. Diesel engines, which have a very heavy current draw during the starting process, require a heavier battery with greater amperage—check the engine manual for recommendations. For safety's sake, it's an obviously good idea to have both elements in a pair of batteries capable of starting the engine by themselves. On exceptionally cold days, it may take both batteries together to get the engine turning over, especially if it's a diesel.

AC and DC panel conveniently located under bridge deck. Three-position battery switch is next to circuit breakers.

The best battery setup calls for a pair of 12-volt batteries connected to a multiple safety switch with four positions: *1, 2, Both* and *Off.* As you can guess, this allows you to draw from either battery or both at once, and you can also disconnect both batteries so that any leakage in the electrical system—and many boats have such leakage, caused by moisture—will not drain the batteries flat during the course of a week. Normally the engine will have a generator or alternator attached, and an ideal arrangement calls for separate generators or alternators for each battery. On a small boat, this is probably overkill. But when you're at anchor, do make sure that whatever electrical devices you're using are drawing from the accessory battery, not the engine-starting unit. Never switch off the battery when the alternator is running or you'll blow *everything.*

If you're buying or replacing batteries, make sure that they have an extended guarantee, and that it covers marine service. Many otherwise excellent batteries with three-year guarantees specifically exempt use in a boat in the small print of their warranty literature. If your boat is diesel-powered, be sure that the engine-starting battery at least is rated for the extra demands of diesel service.

Installation of batteries is important, both for safety and efficiency. When they are charging, batteries emit explosive hydrogen gas, so it's a good idea to keep them clear of any spark source. At the same time, the longer the run of wire between the battery and the engine, the more power will be lost. Most well-engineered small cruisers have the batteries in a compartment adjacent to the engine, but bulkheaded off from it, with the shortest and most direct run of wire possible between battery and starter motor. The wires themselves should be heavy gauge, with easily cleaned terminal fittings.

A good many manufacturers still don't provide adequate security for their battery installations, and indeed batteries are heavy enough so that they'll normally stay put from weight alone. Still, a tipped battery is no joke, and yours should be installed in a plastic or fiberglass battery box that's *strapped* in place to prevent tipping. The box should have a top, not to keep the battery from falling out (we're talking about weekenders, not Cape Horners), but to prevent short circuits caused when a tool or other piece of metal falls across both battery terminals.

Even if your boat's engine has a generator or alternator, a battery charger is a useful piece of insurance. If by some bad luck your battery should be drained, the engine-driven alternator won't be much help in starting. Jumper cables, like the ones you carry in your car, will probably not work too well, simply because the distance between two adjacent boats is so great. You'll probably have to take the battery to an electrical power source to recharge it, and the handiest one will be a marina electrical socket. Because batteries are so unwieldy, a carrying handle is a good investment that takes up little space. The charger can be a standard portable automotive unit, with a maximum charge rate of about 15 amps.

About the only other battery accessory you may be inclined to get is distilled water. Unless your boat's freshwater supply is horribly tainted, however, it will probably be quite adequate for topping up, and lugging a quart of distilled water about can be quite a nuisance.

Tools and spare parts

Unlike the long-haul cruiser, the weekend voyager doesn't have to contemplate rebuilding his engine a thousand miles from anywhere. A certain assortment of tools is important, to be sure, but the small-boat owner has the temptation of carrying too much rather than too little.

Over the years, I've found it convenient to divide my tools into those pertaining to the engine and those having to do with the rig, the sails, and the ground tackle. Although this practice requires two containers instead of one, it seems to shorten searching time. There are, of course, some tools that serve for working on the engine or the rig, and these can either be duplicated or (more normally) set in the more convenient box or bag. When I had a very small cruiser—a 17-foot gaff-rigged catboat with a 3-hp. outboard—I was able to concentrate all the boat's tools in one handy rigger's bag. This small container was vinyl, with a drawstring top and approximately eight pockets of varying widths around the outside perimeter. While it didn't protect the tools as well as a rigid box might have done, it made access to the most frequently used items easy and it was simple to stow.

Since then, I've accumulated more gear, and that first bag has multiplied to become a bag for bosun's gear, a box for tools, and a second box for spare parts. I don't recommend this growth, I just record its likelihood.

In any case, my toolbox is now steel (I had a plastic one, but it wasn't man enough for the job) and rather prone to rust when the paint is scraped off. It contains the following items:

- *Wrenches:* I have a three-eighths-inch socket ratchet-drive set graduated in sixteenths of an inch from three-eighths to seven-eighths of an inch, with extension and angle-drive attachments. I also have a set of combination open-end/box-end wrenches graduated in eighths of an inch from three-eighths to three-quarters and a large adjustable crescent wrench with a maximum opening of about one and a half inches. I have a set of Allen wrenches for set screws, seldom used but invaluable when needed, and a special deep-socket thirteen-sixteenths of an inch drive wrench for spark plugs. The only addition worth contemplating is an oversize adjustable open-end wrench for plumbing fittings, especially the ones associated with through hulls.
- *Pliers:* I carry a pair of long-nose pliers, standard slip-joint and long-handle slip-joint pliers, a wire cutter and stripper and two pairs of Vise Grips, sometimes called mole grips. These last are perhaps the single indispensable boat tool, serving as wrench, pliers, cutter, and hammer (not to mention propeller-shaft lock). One pair of Vise Grips is small, the other large, and I use them about equally.
- *Power tools:* It's probably better not to carry unnecessary power tools on a small cruiser, as they live a short and unhappy life in the dampness. But I find that a three-eighths-inch electric drill, a power sander, and a saber saw are very useful. Get the double-insulated variety, even though they cost more; the chances of electrocution are much reduced. For the drill there is a set of bits up to one-half-inch diameter and a hole saw attachment for making larger openings. The saber saw has an assortment of blades for both fiberglass and wood. A well-cured glass hull will eat saw blades like popcorn, so a considerable number are required for any serious work. When sanding, a rotary sander is useless on wood that's going to be varnished. Get the belt variety, with an assortment of wet-and-dry sandpaper.
- *Other hand tools:* For on-board emergencies, I have a hand drill that's a pain to use, but better than nothing. I also carry a ratchet screwdriver with assorted standard and Phillips-head blades: There is no quicker way to strip a screw than to use a driver blade that's too small. Other useful items include a hacksaw with a couple of extra blades, a Surform tool and a pair of files, a magnet on an extension arm, for fishing ferrous items from the bilge, a battery-powered trouble light, a steel tape measure, a level, and last but hardly least, the final argument, a hammer.

Assorted fasteners are always useful. My toolbox includes wood screws, machine screws, cotter pins, and rings—all in a variety of sizes, and all stainless steel. Several sizes of stainless-steel hose clamp are also extremely helpful. Do be sure that the hose clamps' innards are stainless, too, or the little screw mechanism may well rust and freeze or fall out. I carry a couple of kinds of waterproof tape in the bosun's bag, but silver duct tape has now superseded every other kind for virtually every use afloat.

Lubricants are always necessary on a boat. I carry penetrating oil to break things loose, lubricating oil, a big spray can of WD-40, and two kinds of grease—the relatively thin stuff that's used for outboard gear cases, and the nearly solid water-pump grease for applications where the lubricant has to stay put.

Although it doesn't live in the tool kit, I also carry a Swiss army knife and find it as useful as all the other items put together (always excepting the small Vise Grips).

"Spare parts" is an inadequate term for the collection of miscellaneous bits that every cruising boat acquires as time goes on. For the sake of categorization, it might help to divide the subject in two. First and easiest consists of the spares that go with the engine:

- Spark plugs (a complete set, and not the ones removed from the engine at the end of last season)
- Diesel injectors
- Complete fuel filter or fuel-filter elements
- Lube oil filter and enough oil for a complete change
- Transmission oil or grease (for outboards)
- Extra gaskets or gasket compound
- Cooling system hose
- V-belts for alternator/generator and water pump
- Fuses and bulbs
- Impeller for water pump
- Shear pins for the outboard
- Extra prop, if yours can easily be removed without hauling the boat

If you have an unusual or discontinued engine, consider carrying the following more elaborate spares: ignition points, condenser, distributor cap and coil, voltage regulator, generator/alternator.

Less easily catalogued are the spares and leftovers that accumulate at the bottom of the box: through-hull fittings bought but never installed, an extra turnbuckle complete with toggle, clevis pins too large and too small for anything on the boat, crimp-on electrical terminals, copper wire, clamps for gluing, tubes of epoxy cement and epoxy putty, sandpaper—you see what I mean, and my only additional suggestion is that, once a season, you sift through your collection and discard anything too hilarious.

Electronics

The first piece of electronic equipment most cruising skippers purchase is a depth sounder. Probably not because they stand in urgent need of one, but because it is quite cheap and its function seems terribly useful. In fact, while it is certainly handy to know how deep the water is, a depth sounder will seldom prevent your running aground. In fact, you might argue that it increases the chances of grounding by giving the helmsman an erroneous feeling of security: By the time you realize that the figures on the dial indicate the depth of water under the middle of the boat, it's often too late to tack away.

On the other hand, if your sailing is done in areas where the bottom shelves gradually and with reasonable predictability, the standard depth sounder can give timely warning that you're running out of water and had better turn fairly soon. Only when you are approaching a steep-to shore is the depth sounder really deceptive. I have been aboard a boat that was aground forward with the depth sounder still reading twenty feet.

For serious coastal navigators, however, the depth sounder is a very useful tool, enabling a skillful pilot to form a mental picture of the bottom contours, which he can then match with the charted depths. When crossing some salient underwater feature, such as a riverbed or abrupt shoal, it's quite possible to derive a solid line of position from the soundings, and it does serve to check the depth of an anchorage when dropping the hook. Certain types of depth sounder will also reveal (to a skilled interpreter) a good deal about the composition of the bottom directly beneath the boat.

So a depth sounder is probably a good long-term investment, even if you can't get the most out of it right away. There are, however, several types and each has assets and liabilities.

Until fairly recently, far and away the most common unit was the type now known as a fishfinder. Its circular dial went from 0 at the top to 60 or 100 feet (as a general rule; often a switch enabled one to convert the feet scale to fathoms). When the sounder was on, there was a persistent flash of light at 0 and another opposite the depth below the boat. The characteristics of this second flash gave important clues to the hardness of the bottom and the abruptness of its slope. Occasionally there would be transient flashes between the 0 and the bottom reading; sometimes these were meaningless indications that the unit's power was turned on too high and, by reducing the *gain,* the intermediate flashes could be eliminated. Other times, the flashes remained, and indicated fish or debris between the top and bottom. In sophisticated fishfinders, these intermediate readings can be most informative to the person who knows what he's looking for; to a navigator, they remain a pain in the neck.

Assets of the flashing-light set are its low cost, the fact that (once the positions of numbers around the dial have been memorized) it's easy to read approximately even when the dial is relatively far from the viewer, and the possibility of reading the bottom as well as the depth. For many people, the movement of the light flash up or down the dial gives an easy-to-comprehend notion of the bottom contour, but this seems to depend on the viewer.

Drawbacks are that the flashing light is hard to read in anything approaching direct sunlight, one can never get more than an approximate depth because of the width of the indicating flash, one must learn to interpret which are meaningful flashes and which aren't.

Seldom seen today, but common a few years back, the needle indicator displays depth across a generally rectangular dial. The depth indication is always precise (not necessarily accurate), can be read in sunlight or (with a panel light) darkness, and requires no interpretation for intermediate readings, which are damped out of the system.

But a needle can be difficult to see at any distance, its movement back and forth across the dial leaves, for most people, little memory trace of the bottom configuration, and its apparent accuracy is only a reflection of the needle's fine point, not the instrument's precision.

The currently fashionable version is the digital depth sounder. It reads out in arabic numerals that are visible in anything but bright sunlight, and its indications are unequivocal—or so they seem. Like the needle indicator, the digital unit gives no indication of bottom composition, although it does have a gain knob that increases or decreases the strength of the signal. Many digital units have the annoying characteristic of *hunting*—reading out a series of random numbers—when first turned on, and some are so sensitive that only fine tuning can prevent them from hunting erratically and without warning, even after running for some time. While the digital unit is easiest of all to comprehend, it doesn't seem to have the ability to project in most viewers' minds a sense of what the bottom contour is like. This of course is not a failure of the instrument but a characteristic of the human mind, and perhaps those who have never known anything but a digital instrument can find its series of numbers provide a continuous message and not just a collection of bits. Finally, the sensitive digital sounder will record intermediate objects between top and bottom, but the sudden intrusion of such a depth in digital form can be very unnerving to the novice pilot.

One may gather from the foregoing comments that the classic flashing-light sounder is my favorite, and on consideration I'd agree, but it's a personal decision that I wouldn't lean on too heavily. If someone were to offer me a free depth sounder of reputable make, I wouldn't worry too much what its indicator system was.

Depth sounders, being popular in small outboard-powered fishing craft, can be powered either by internal batteries, an external 12-volt system, or both. The amount of current draw is not great—a tenth to a third of an ampere is normal—and most self-powered units employ a single 9-volt battery that can be run for many hours before going flat. Other sounders work only off the boat's own 12-volt system, and unless your boat's primary storage battery is very small indeed, this is probably a better choice if one has to decide between self-powered and boat-powered. For my money, however, the best system has a throwover switch enabling it to draw current from internal or external batteries as required.

There are two parts to the question of where to install a depth sounder. The best location for the transducer—the device that transmits the subsonic signal to the bottom and receives it back again—is often nowhere near the best location for the indicator head or dial. Since the principle of depth sounding rests on the relatively constant speed of a radio signal through water and thence back to the indicator head, the length of wire between head and transducer is critical. Although the amount supplied may be far too much, don't clip it and shorten the coil; you may distort the readings.

Generally speaking, the transducer head should be installed so that it's perpendicular to the bottom when the boat is moving. In a sailing boat, this is an ideal state, as the boat normally heels while under way; thus a transducer that's correctly aligned on starboard tack will be considerably off on port, and vice versa. The normal compromise is to install the unit on the centerline for operation with the boat level, and trust to the width of the cone-shaped radio signal to produce a moderately accurate reading when the boat is heeled. Some skippers who are ultrafinicky about their navigation have transducers on either side of the keel, with a throwover switch that allows either sender to read on the dial. This is probably unnecessary for anyone who doesn't navigate professionally.

The best location for the transducer is a third to halfway back along the waterline length, and as far below the waterline as possible, without placing the transducer in peril. The idea is to place the sender-receiver in unturbulent water, low enough so it'll be below the surface no matter how the boat heels. There should be a certain amount of keel below the transducer to protect it if the boat is grounded accidentally or while it's in the slings: A transducer is, after all, a through-hull fitting, and it can be pushed out by accident.

Since the curve of the hull will probably prevent the transducer from aligning correctly vis-à-vis the bottom, it's often necessary to build up a base that produces the proper alignment. One good system is to make a wood cylinder of the correct diameter, then saw it on a diagonal that will provide a proper fit both inside and outside the hull. Another way is to bed the transducer in a pad of one of the popular epoxy putties. This means that a matching base will have to be built up inside the hull, so that the locknut on the shaft of the transducer will screw down level and seal the through-hull.

Although I've never had a problem with a through-hull depth-sounder transducer, I always feel a little nervous about the head protruding through the bottom and, even more, about its threaded stalk sticking up from the inside of the hull: Pictures of someone kicking it or some piece of equipment knocking it loose keep entering my mind.

One way most owners of fiberglass hulls can avoid drilling a hole in the boat is to mount the transducer in a well inside the hull. The British-made Seafarer echo sounder, in fact, offers a kit that makes it easy to do just that. It consists of a plastic cylinder that fits tightly around the wide base of the transducer, a generous supply of epoxy putty, some fluid to fill the tube, and a screw cap to seal it, with the transducer inside. To install the unit, one cuts the cylinder to fit the inside hull contour of the boat as closely as possible. Then sand any interior paint off, fit the cylinder so that it's perpendicular to the sea bottom with the boat at rest. Build a fluidtight packing of putty around the tube's base, fill it with the oil supplied, insert the transducer, seal the top, and there you are.

The idea is that by immersing the transducer in a conducting fluid—for one I owned, it was simply cod-liver oil,—the transmitted signal will go freely from transducer head to sea bottom, only slightly weakened by the hull. On the boat in which I installed such a fitting, the sounder's range—nominally 60 feet—was hardly affected at all, and the depth indications were quite accurate. The only drawback was that the installation preempted a small bilge compartment completely, as nothing loose and heavy could be stowed there. In-hull transducer installations are usually quite adequate in noncored fiberglass hulls, but a wood or foam layer will kill the signal.

As noted above, the length of cable between transducer and dial is normally quite adequate. Indeed, if anything it's too long for most smaller boats. The extra is most easily coiled tightly and neatly alongside the transducer, while the operating length is stapled (with properly insulated staples) to the bulkhead and thence to the sounder dial. The location of this readout will often be conditioned upon the location of the yacht's switchboard or batteries (assuming you're running the sounder off 12-volt power), as the power cable is usually a good deal shorter than the transducer cable. Given the limited number of circuits on the average small yacht's switchboard, it's quite acceptable to double or even triple the sounder with other navigation-oriented devices. On my boat, the same circuit breaker copes with depth sounder, ADF and VHF-FM, without difficulty.

If you plan on using your sounder only as an alarm, the indicator dial can be installed anywhere it will be visible to the helmsman on either tack, in full daylight. A digital sounder can be mounted on the steering-wheel binnacle, and a frequent combination calls for the compass in the middle, flanked by speedometer and depth sounder. I have always found such installations distracting, as the person at the wheel must look down to see what's going on, and in moments of stress this can present orientation problems. If the eyesight of skipper and crew will permit, a location on the after-cabin bulkhead or, better yet, on a console mounted atop the companionway hatch tank, is perhaps easiest to read while keeping one's eyes on the road.

Boats where this is impossible, or that use flashing-light indicators difficult to read in sunlight, sometimes carry the indicator mounted on the midships bulkhead at the forward end of the main cabin. It is usually close enough to read—especially when one doesn't have to be too precise, as with the flashing-light indicator—and dark enough in the cabin to make the light stand out.

But if you have any ambition for using the depth sounder as a navigation instrument, it should be located where the navigator can see it. The forward end of the saloon isn't a bad place, especially if the boat has a forward-facing navigation table or even one that faces outboard. One way to compromise is to mount the indicator head on a hinge, so it can swing out into the companionway, visible to the helmsman, and then back inside, where it can be seen by the navigator and locked away from view when the boat's put to bed. The most elegant (and costly) solution is to get a set with dual indicators, but this seems like overkill for most of us.

When using your depth sounder, you'll have to make a continual mental adjustment for the difference between the true depth of the water and the depth from sounder to bottom. For instance, if your boat draws four feet and the transducer is mounted two feet below the waterline, the depth indicated on the sounder will be two feet less than what's really there. This kind of difference is of little or no consequence in deep water, and it can actually be a small safety factor in the shallows. Adjusting for it becomes second nature after a while, although when one is very tired it can be a distinct effort to remember whether to add or subtract for true depth. Some expensive units have an internal adjustment to eliminate the ambiguity of a permanently inaccurate reading, and this is certainly a desirable feature if it doesn't cost too much extra.

Finally, a number of depth sounders, especially digital models, offer a built-in depth alarm. This audible warning may be preset at the factory for a given shallowness, or it may be capable of being set by the operator. While it's a tempting idea, the alarm can be an unmitigated nuisance in real life. A decent-sized shoal of fish or even a temperature shear between cold and warm currents below the surface can trigger a sensitive alarm, which is guaranteed to wake up your liver bile even when your intellect is positive there's twenty fathoms under the keel.

Speedometers and logs

The electronic depth sounder is a fairly ancient piece of equipment, dating back (in small boats) some twenty years or more. Reliable speedometers for sailboats are a considerably more recent development. For many years, about the only two pieces of equipment available were miniature versions of the classic taffrail log and elementary pitot meters. The first read distance by means of a weighted impeller on the end of a line towed astern. So many revolutions equal a nautical mile, and with the aid of a watch one could quickly arrive at a speed; or relatively quickly. The real, enduring function of the taffrail log, as the name states, is to register miles traveled, not speed.

The pitot meter, derived from similar devices on aircraft, registers speed by the pressure of water in a tube or against a pivoted shaft. The faster you go, the greater the pressure. The problem is that you have to be going rather fast to register anything at all, and at the speeds normally attained by sailing craft this type of indicator is quite unreliable.

Why have a speedometer and log at all? The primary reason for most people is navigational. It's a lot easier to maintain a good dead-reckoning track if you have not only an accurate notion of your speed but also a good idea of distance traveled—one cannot watch the speedometer constantly, and a log will average without human optimism.

Aside from immediate navigation, a good speedometer will help you keep track of how your boat's speed is doing during the course of the boating season: As time passes, slime and then weed grow on the bottom, and both will slow the boat. By keeping careful track of speeds through the water at various combinations of heading, wind speed, and sail, you'll be aware in short order if the boat's average is dropping.

For the short-haul yacht whose skipper is interested in racing, the speedometer and log are most useful of all. Not only does he use them in the conventional navigational manner but he also employs the speedo when tuning the rig and training his crew. Even with a less than accurate speedometer, the relative alterations in speed caused by a good versus a bad sail combination (or trim or helmsperson) is obvious right away. You need not be beguiled by the noise of a boat crashing inefficiently through the water—one look at the speedo convinces everyone to ease the sheets on a reach and let the boat back up on her feet, where her progress, while less dramatic, will be faster.

Although there seems to be a plethora of speedometers and logs on the market at the moment, most of the acceptable ones are much the same. Let's dispose of the variants first.

The traditional taffrail log, which can now be hooked into a speedometer, has a lot going against it. In its favor is the fact that it requires no through-hull fitting and, apart from the possibility of being taken by a big fish, it is most reliable. Opposed are its cumbersome size and location—right on the transom, in most cases—the fact that it can only be employed on the open sea, where other boats' propellers won't gobble it up, and the related fact that one's own boat can pull it into the propeller, if the skipper forgets to retract it when going astern. A good taffrail log is not cheap, and while it's salty as hell, it really belongs out in deep water, well away from land. Inexpensive variants of the taffrail log, which have in common with their legitimate parent a friction device dragged through the water well behind the boat and a transom-mounted indicator, have most of the log's drawbacks and little of its accuracy. But blue-water sailors will usually have one tucked away somewhere as a spare.

That leaves the two viable small-yacht units: the paddlewheel and the hull-mounted impeller. The latter is popularly known as a Sumlog, which is (like Fathometer) a trade name for one type of unit. Basically, the impeller indicator is a neatened-up version of the taffrail log, in which the log's weighted torpedo-shaped prop is fixed to the boat's hull instead of being towed at the end of a line. The connection to the indicator dial is mechanical, which means that there can be installation problems (see below) and noise, as the indicating cable spins inside its protective tubing. In addition, these units seem subject to fatigue in the cable, which causes it to wear out and snap after a few seasons. In addition, the impeller attracts plastic bags and seaweed with a collector's greed, and it's not at all unusual for this style of unit to stop abruptly. The solution may simply be reversing the boat sharply (a bit difficult under spinnaker), or it may involve putting over a diver with a knife.

As the reader may have guessed, I've been shipmates with a couple of units of this type, and while they are cheap, efficient when they work, and easy to understand, they have more drawbacks than necessary. I vastly prefer the paddlewheel indicators, and judging by the large variety, so do most people.

These devices are truly electronic and relatively easy to comprehend, even for me. Essentially, they consist of two parts connected by an electrical cable. The transducer is a miniature paddlewheel that is recessed in a tube set into the hull so that only the tips of the wheel blades protrude. (The tube, obviously, is sealed at its inner end.) On one blade is a small magnet, and on the inside of the tube a piece of ferrous metal and a sender. Each time the wheel makes a full turn, the magnet passes the ferrous metal register and the sender dispatches the news to the second part of the speedometer or log—the indicator head. You are in fact generating a small current and measuring it. Here the number of revolutions in a given period is translated into speed through the water or distance traveled through the water. (That "through-the-water" is important; think about it for a minute.)

Electronically speaking, it's a relatively simple device. About the only thing that throws it off is the need for the boat to attain an initial speed that will break the paddlewheel magnet free and start it spinning. Once this happens, the unit will usually register accurately up and down the scale. The wheel is sufficiently protected so that it can't pick up waterborne debris, nor is it likely to be damaged in the normal course of operations. There are times when its location can be critical, however, and it's important that the unit be completely recessed into the hull so that no collar is raised to disturb the waterflow past the paddlewheel.

Readout of these units can be either by means of a needle or, more recently, in liquid crystal display (LCD) digits. What suits you is what's best, and there's no arguing with taste. If you choose a digital unit, be certain it can be read in direct sunlight; and if yours has the conventional needle display, it will probably be easier to read if the scale is slightly expanded for lower speeds around S:L .9 or less. Obviously, any unit should be capable of being illuminated, and the better ones have variable illumination (bright light is for maximum sunlight, by the way).

All but the most basic units are capable of being adjusted, as the boat's hull design will probably influence the speedo/log's accuracy. Once the unit is installed, it's worth spending a day (and that's what it will take) running speed trials to calibrate both log and speedometer. Adjustment details for your unit should be included with the instrument, but the basic procedure involves running the boat back and forth over a measured mile under power, preferably in a situation where current isn't a factor. Then, having established a clocked speed for the known distance, calibrate the speedometer and the log to register this amount. It's a good idea to check both units occasionally, when running a known distance at a steady speed, to make sure they're still reading reliably.

Most paddlewheel speedometer/logs are retractable for cleaning. The tube containing the wheel fits snugly inside a permanent through-hull fitting, held in place by a screw-down collar. Unscrew the collar and the tube can be withdrawn into the boat, accompanied by a surprisingly forceful gush of water. A dummy tube is inserted in the through-hull, and screwed down to stop the flow. If one is reasonably coordinated, the amount of water admitted during the replacement of one unit with the other shouldn't exceed a quart or so, although it may seem like a good deal more. If a boat is tied up in water where weed growth is a serious problem, it's a good idea to replace the impeller with the dummy tube whenever the boat will sit unused for more than a few days. Some units have a gatevalve/stop cock so the job can be done dry.

When buying a retractable through-hull unit, be sure that the tubes are held in place by a half dozen threads on the retaining collar. Although all the parts involved are carefully made of strong plastic (sometimes bronze), it's happened that a carelessly hauled boat has pressed the real or dummy impeller against a hauling cradle, popping the plug and filling the boat. In addition, when a boat is on a cradle, supported at only a few points, its hull can temporarily distort enough to make a through-hull tube break free if it's not securely emplaced.

As with any through-hull, the speedo and/or log should be located where you can get at them without too much trouble. If it's a retractable unit, it should be easily accessible from all sides, yet enough out of the traffic pattern to avoid casual jars from crewmembers or sliding gear. The dummy impeller tube, freshly greased, should be stowed adjacent to the primary transducer unit. The ideal location itself will probably be on centerline in the forward part of the hull, where laminar flow of the passing water is easiest to attain, and down low enough so the sender won't rise near the water's turbulent surface on one tack. (Some demon racers have paired speedometer/logs, one for each tack.) It's very difficult to locate a speedo sender where it won't break free of the surface when the boat is on her beam ends, but you ought to be able to locate it where it will register accurately at normal angles of heel—say to twenty degrees or so.

Obviously, the transducer should be well clear of other through hulls, especially ones like depth sounders or engine-water intakes that obtrude from the hull. This is one area where the miniature propeller type of unit has a slight edge, as it stands sufficiently free from the hull to escape most turbulence, nor does it require to be located where it can easily be withdrawn into the hull, as this isn't possible with such a unit. If you have a direct-discharge head, don't site the impeller in line with the soil pipe for obvious reasons.

Location of the instrument head is a matter of convenience, with most units. Impeller-driven mechanical speedometers will offer some tactical problems as the sender cable cannot be bent sharply around corners but must be radiused easily to avoid jamming the spinning cable. The best lead is straight forward or (with a reversing accessory) aft in a nearly straight line from through-hull to indicator dial; curves in the cable should be gradual. Units with electrical cable connections are not so sensitive in their positioning, and the length of the wire is generally the only determinant. It's advisable, obviously, to have the readout dial in a spot where you can get at the back for any necessary calibration, and where incoming wire connections will be dry.

My own feeling is that, if one's pocketbook permits, the best combination is a speedometer and log on separate dials, but reading off the same through-hull sender. Ideally, the log is the navigator's business, as he or she is directly concerned with distance made good through the water, rather than with the boat's speed of the moment. The person at the helm, on the other hand, needn't be distracted by elapsed distance but should be aware of speed increases and decreases deriving from sail trim and helmsmanship. If your boat has a chart table, the log dial should be near it, and the best logs have double readouts —a cumulative reading from the unit's installation and a resettable face, sometimes called a trip indicator.

As with the depth sounder, the helmsman's view of the speedometer will be far more efficient if he or she doesn't have to look away from the horizon to see how fast the boat is going, losing touch with the steering in the process. Bulkhead mounting is good, but a unit inset into a container atop the main hatch tank is probably best. If you have the traditional taffrail log, however, your options are virtually nonexistent, as the instrument is designed to be screwed into a deck fitting back by the transom, a superbly inefficient place for either navigator or helmsman unless he has a fully swiveling head.

Direction finders

Of the relatively common yacht instruments, the radio direction finder has been until recently the glamour item. That place is now being taken by Loran, but until cheap, mass-market Loran-C (a few years off yet), the RDF will continue to be bought, installed, and misused with happiness by the majority of cruising sailors. If you were to ask any skipper why he'd bought an RDF or ADF (automatic direction finder), he'd undoubtedly tell you it was for position finding. Yet relatively few yachtsmen employ their RDFs for regular positioning, and fewer still trust the results.

If you plan to use your RDF seriously, I would go for a unit that had beacon, AM commercial, and possibly VHF-FM (especially if you don't have a VHF-FM transceiver). Commercial FM, CB, and the marine band are harmless, but not worth paying extra for.

There are other features you'll want to check for. A null meter is, after all, the essence of the set. Some people find aural nulls easier to achieve than visual ones on a dial. It's best to have the capability of receiving both. Another useful knob is the beat frequency oscillator (BFO). This will enable you to pick up the silent carrier wave of a frequency and pin it down even when it's not transmitting. It will also unscramble SSB transmissions for you.

A sensing circuit, to resolve 180-degree ambiguity, is also handy. Because of the nature of the directional antenna, you may be seem to be receiving a signal either from the transmitter you're tuned to—or from 180 degrees in the opposite direction. In most cases it's fairly obvious which is the case, but sometimes an accurate position really depends on resolving 180-degree ambiguity, and this feature is very useful then. Headphones are also good to have—a boat can be a noisy place, and if you're trying to pick up a weak signal, the ability to screen out ambient tapping, creaking, and whining is handy. Also, if you're DF-ing at night, the radio will drive everyone else aboard nuts with its reiterated Morse patterns, and by plugging in the earphones you normally cut out the set's integral speaker. Standard phone is a single one-ear insert that can become quite uncomfortable after a while. If you have the talent, or a friend has, rig up a set of real headphones. They may appear overdramatic, but they'll be worth the trouble.

Every direction finder has either a built-in (or attached) compass or a pelorus located under the pivoting bar antenna. To use the latter, the RDF must be fixed in place, aligned in a fore-and-aft plane. Most European sets have the attached magnetic compass, and most American sets have the pelorus. You have to take your choice.

Power for the RDF is provided by integral batteries, usually C or D cells; by a 110-volt house-current outlet; and/or by hookup to the yacht's 12-volt system. If you employ the RDF sparingly, integral batteries can last a surprising length of time—a couple of months of weekend use would be quite ordinary performance. And if you forget to turn the unit off, only its batteries go flat, which can make a difference. On the other hand, when you're trying to bring in a marginal beacon, less than peak battery performance can be hopelessly inadequate, so always keep a spare set of long-life batteries. Being able to tap into the boat's 12-volt system means that you can usually expect superior performance from the RDF, as long as the boat's battery is in even passable shape. My own inclination is to look for a set that has both capabilities, as many do. One-hundred-ten-volt power, on the other hand, offers little advantage to the cruising sailor, and about the only argument on its side is that you can plug into house current and use the set for practice or entertainment during the off season. Considering the low price of small AM or FM radios, this is not an adequate argument.

The automatic direction finder (ADF) is a close relative of the familiar RDF, but with some differences. To begin with, it is considerably more expensive—about twice the cost for an ADF whose other features are similar to a given RDF. In return for the extra money, one gets enhanced ease of taking bearings. To use an ADF, one tunes the desired frequency and waits (if it's a multiple-use beacon frequency) until the correct beacon comes on the air. Press the direction-finding switch and the bar antenna automatically homes on the null, which you read off the instrument's pelorus just as you would with a standard RDF. There is a 180-degree ambiguity indicator and a null meter, which really serves only as a tuning aid or sensing circuit.

What's interesting when using an ADF is watching the automatically activated antenna "hunt" the signal. Even when the null is located, the antenna will continue to move a degree or two, according to the various demands of boat motion and deviation. Many experts feel that an ADF is intrinsically no more accurate than an RDF, but it's unquestionably easier to use. What you have to give in return is an increased drain on the unit's electrical supply, be it integral or ship's battery. When the ADF is operating in the direction-finding mode, a small electric motor is driving the antenna, and the effort involved uses up D or C cells rapidly. While many RDFs have only a single power source, all ADFs are capable of drawing from 12-volt power as well as D or C cells. If you decide on an ADF, you should make sure to hook it into your boat's electrical system so that you have the choice of power when you need it. You may also want to consider a combination unit, which can operate as either a standard RDF or an ADF.

If a substantial amount of your navigation is done in fog or out of sight of land, an RDF is definitely a primary navigational tool. When one adds in its monitoring and weather-receiving functions, the advantages become very strong indeed. As I've suggested, however, the standard RDF with extraneous bands is not used too often in its direction-finding mode, and if all you want is music, you're probably better off with a cassette player. At all events, practice with it and learn its shortcomings—which can be considerable (refraction, compass error, interference, etc.)

Radiotelephones

Along with other electronic devices, radiotelephones have been enjoying a great burst in popularity in recent years. At least part of the reason is that as everything else increases in price, radiotelephones and calculators show a modest decline, while in many cases increasing their efficiency.

The most valid reason for buying a radiotelephone is that it is a first-rate tool for summoning help in an emergency. The U.S. Coast Guard and British Coastguard have a network of SSB and VHF-FM stations covering the entire coastline of their nations, as well as the shores of the Great Lakes and many rivers. 2182 kHz and VHF-FM Channel 16 (156.8 MHz) are monitored twenty-four hours a day, and in the United States CB Channel 9 is reluctantly watched when it will not interfere with other operations. All VHF-FM transceivers are required by law to have Channel 16, as all SSBs must have 2182 kHz, and these frequencies are used constantly to initiate calls. It's a rare occurrence to be unable to raise anyone on 16 or 2182—more often it's a question of wedging your transmission in. But remember that these are distress frequencies and must only be used for initial contact—don't clutter the air with useless chatter, you may need to call for help yourself one day.

The second good reason for having a transceiver is business, under which we can include the need of some people to remain in touch with offices or associates or family; the requirements of making marina or dinner reservations, or arranging for spare parts or repairs; or simply the need to make and modify cruise plans when voyaging in company with other craft. Many boat owners accept being cut off once they set sail—indeed many, like me, find this a major asset of the cruising yacht—but an increasing number of others use the radiotelephone afloat the same way they use the landline telephone at home, without fully realizing the differences between the two.

Finally, although it is a minor reason, most marine VHF-FM radios carry the listen-only crystals for one or two of the weather channels on coast radio. As the VHF-FM antenna is normally mounted at masthead height, as opposed to the RDF's far shorter whip, the transceiver's pickup range is far greater.

Volume production of VHFs has indeed brought prices down. Not as far as CBs, to be sure, but a great deal lower than SSBs. What are we talking about in money? Prices change very rapidly, but somewhere between two hundred and five hundred dollars would seem to blanket it. This is a considerable range, and there are several features that will determine what you pay. When deciding on a set, it's important not to be stampeded into accepting features you neither need nor want: The authorities have issued recommended channelizations for radiotelephones, but these suggestions—and that's all they are, beyond the minimum two-channel legal requirements—are based on the conviction that people who buy radiotelephones will want to talk all the time. It is inconceivable to officials—or radiotelephone manufacturers—that a person who says he wants a unit only for emergency communications really means it.

For that reason, although you are required by regulation to have only three channels (16, intership safety 6, and a ship-to-ship in the United States, or 67 in the United Kingdom), it's impossible to buy a set that is built to accommodate these three and no others. True, you don't have to buy crystals for the other channels, but simply having the channel capability adds to the cost of the set. The smallest standard VHF-FM transceivers on the market today, therefore, are twelve-channel units. The next up in complexity are sets with fifty to fifty-six channels, and then there are the "international" sets with eighty-two receive and fifty-five transmit channels, which is simply ridiculous.

You can buy portable, battery-powered VHFs with up to six channels, but the 1 to 3 watts they put out, and the short antenna, will be hard put to compete with the standard 25 watts (the maximum allowed power) and masthead whips. By shopping carefully, it's possible to get a VHF with antenna, sixty feet of wire, crystals for channels 6 or 67 and 16, the Coast Guard working frequency of 22, two ship-to-shore and one ship-to-ship channels, plus the two principal weather frequencies for about the same price as a portable unit.

Things to look for in buying a conventional VHF-FM in the United States are, first, the necessary number of crystals for the channels you want now, plus vacant channels for later expansion if you feel that's a possibility; weather-receive channels for the two primary NOAA channels (labeled WX-1 and WX-2); and an antenna pretuned to the crystals in the set, which means that all you have to do to install the unit is screw down the mount, lead the antenna wire up inside the mast, and fasten the antenna at the masthead. No FCC-licensed technician is required to tune crystals and antenna, and while your transmission may not have total efficiency with the "el cheapo" antenna normally supplied in such packages, it should be quite adequate for nearly all use.

The other three possible communications systems for small cruisers are citizens band, single-sideband MF, and ham radio. The latter is of course a worldwide network of radio amateurs with the widest possible capabilities, but it really has little application to the coastal cruiser, as you can't use it to call another boat (unless he too is a ham), a marina, or the Coast Guard. SSB on the old medium-frequency band is also impractical for most small yachts. To begin with, the FCC requires that one carry a VHF-FM short-range transceiver before it will issue a license for a medium-range set; in addition, SSB sets are temperamental and expensive, and most of the yachts your size, not to speak of marinas, won't have this equipment.

About the only rival to VHF-FM aboard small cruisers these days is the omnipresent CB radio yet to arrive in Britain. It's far cheaper than VHF-FM, has a far greater body of people who own sets and listen to them, and it has the kind of short-range potential for calling home direct, without the trouble and cost of a marine telephone hookup. After a lot of interagency muttering, the FCC and the U.S. Coast Guard finally agreed that the latter would monitor CB Channel 9 at many of its bases. Both the Coast Guard and the FCC strongly dislike CB, in part at least because it is almost entirely out of government control. But hundreds of thousands of citizens were using it, and private emergency organizations were setting up shop to cope with the government absence, so the federal agencies bowed to reality and agreed to allow the Coast Guard to stand by the semiofficial CB emergency channel when such monitoring would not interfere with other CG listening watches.

In technical terms, the Coast Guard has a strong basis for its preference for VHF-FM as the "official" small-craft emergency communications system. VHF-FM has greater and more predictable range, it is less affected by static interference, less often blanked out by intervening geography, less crowded with madmen and imbeciles. By and large, the sailing cruiser is unquestionably better off with VHF-FM in most situations. About the only three things that might make CB the choice are (1) an absolute need for some radio link, and the need to pare every penny—a good forty-channel CB with antenna costs less than half the price of a twelve-channel VHF-FM with antenna; (2) a short cruising range, within a few miles of a base station; (3) presence of REACT or other CB emergency group in the area, as well as a large number of other boats—usually outboard-powered fishermen—so equipped.

Miscellaneous electronics

There are a number of other electronic devices that can make your boat—at least in theory—safer, more comfortable, and more accurately navigated.

After some experience with most of them, I'd be inclined to say that few if any are really essential, and their usefulness will depend in large part upon your orientation toward them. If you get along well with gadgets, if you are conscientious about dials and warning lights, they will probably serve you well. But it's only proper to warn that a large number of skippers invest in fancy electronics and then lose interest in them, leaving another vacant mounting bracket when the device succumbs to moisture and inattention.

Perhaps the most popular cockpit indicators these days, after compass and speedometer, are the various wind instruments. There are essentially two, although one appears in at least two separate modes. The simplest is a masthead anemometer, or wind-speed indicator. My suspicion is that the cruising skipper can detect gross changes in apparent wind strength quickly and accurately enough to make the necessary sail changes provided by his limited sail wardrobe. There are inexpensive, hand-held devices available at modest price that will second-guess the beginning weather prophet until he or she can correlate sea state and the sound in the rigging with wind speed.

In a somewhat different category are the wind-direction instruments. They come in two varieties. One indicates wind direction (relative to the boat, of course) right around the compass, or from 0 degrees to 180 degrees on either side of the boat. A reasonable set of shroud and backstay telltales will do just about the same thing, as will a masthead wind vane. Somewhat more useful, especially at night, is the close-hauled wind indicator, which shows on an expanded scale the relative wind direction from about 10 degrees to 50 degrees on either bow. Once you've developed reliable data on your boat's best close-hauled headings (which will depend on wind strength and sea state as well as headsail), a close-hauled indicator can save the nighttime helmsman a lot of worry and make up a great many miles. In the daytime, however, the familiar jib luff woolies will serve about the same function and should do it better, as they relate wind direction not to boat heading, but to sail performance, which is after all what's you're concerned with.

Another electronic device that's become more popular in the last few seasons is the electrically driven autopilot for tiller-steered cruising sailboats. Typically, this unit has a low current draw and can supply up to a hundred pounds or so of steering force—but not continually. It will operate aboard boats up to thirty-five feet or so overall, but it's obviously at its best on small yachts with well-balanced sail plans.

Basically, the unit consists of a compass hooked into the autopilot mechanism, itself connected to an electrically driven piston. As the boat swerves off the preset compass course, the autopilot engages the electric motor, which operates the piston hooked to the tiller and brings the boat back on course, after which the unit drops back into its idle mode. Many experienced owners of small cruising sailboats have used such units for hundreds or indeed thousands of coasting miles. The only requirement for such a device is that one recharge the operating battery from time to time, but it probably draws little more power than the running lights, unless the boat is seriously off balance.

The other facet of tiller-steering autopilots is that, since they operate off a compass, they are indifferent to changes in wind direction or even to the complete absence of wind. Unlike wind vane selfsteerers, electrical autopilots will operate perfectly well with the sails down and the wind at flat calm. The only precaution to take is that the boat under power be as well balanced as she is under sail, to avoid the unit's discharging any more than necessary. On the other hand, while a compass-activated autopilot will hold a boat on course under sail, except in the case of gross wind changes that overpower the unit, it will not respond to small directional changes in the wind. Thus, where a wind vane will get the most from the apparent wind and keep the boat sailing at a preset angle to it, the autopilot will keep her slogging away toward her objective. It's a nice question which is better for the small cruiser.

At least one long-range cruising sailor, Donald Hamilton, has voted quite emphatically for the autopilot. Proprietor of a small ocean cruiser, the Bob Harris-designed Vancouver 27 (see Chapter III), Hamilton finds the autopilot very handy for coastal navigation and feels that the time saved by merely dialing the course, as opposed to setting up vane steering lines and then, as often as not, resetting them, makes the autopilot used more often. It is a powerful argument.

With some modern autopilots, one can have the best of both worlds. The unit can operate off a compass or off a wind sensor, according to choice. If the extra cost of this option is possible, and if you habitually sail alone or short-handed, it may well make all the difference. If you do go for such a unit, however, it will be quite important to invest in two batteries, as the chance of running down your engine starting battery is that much greater.

Among navigational devices of tomorrow that are already present today, Loran looms large on the immediate horizon. This is essentially a receiving unit that records the incredibly small time differences between the arrivals of two signals simultaneously transmitted from different points. This time difference between two stations (a "master" and a "slave") can be translated into a line of position, and these lines are transcribed on charts for many yachting areas. The Loran receiver reads out a position line as a series of digits, and the navigator simply matches it with the nearest one on his special chart. He then dials another pair of transmitting stations and gets another LOP the same way, and voilà—there he is. Many new sets read directly in latitude and longitude. A good Loran set is said to provide precise, repeatable positions to well under a quarter of a mile, which is not bad. Loran coverage along the coasts and several hundred miles out to sea is generally excellent, the only problem at this point being the shortage of Loran charts. It is safe to say, however, that in a few years all major boating areas where Loran might be used will be covered by these special charts.

Till now, the relatively high price of Loran-C (there was also a Loran-A service, but it has closed down) has kept most small-boat skippers from acquiring sets. Its ability to produce good positions with a minimum of mental or electrical drain has stimulated the market, especially among small commercial vessels, to the point where the cost of Loran sets has begun to tumble, like VHF-FM before it. Given today's and tomorrow's inflation, of course, a price tumble isn't as dramatic as it used to be, but we're talking about prices in real dollars that have virtually halved in the last few years. As large companies like Texas Instruments and the Japanese electronics firms enter the field, look for sets to become both better and cheaper, and look for Loran to become as popular as RDF, and probably rather more heavily used.

No sooner has one electronic marvel arrived than another seems to be looming on the horizon. The newest contender is satellite navigation (SatNav, or sometimes NavSat, for short). As you might guess, this system derives earthly fixes from the positions of transmitting satellites circling the earth. The receiver picks up an absolute position, as opposed to an LOP, whenever a satellite is high enough over the horizon to transmit one, and it is the ultimate in navigational simplicity from the operator's viewpoint.

In relation to Loran, it has both advantages and drawbacks. To begin with, its coverage is worldwide, and while there are now only enough satellites to provide fixes every hour or hour and a half, there promise to be more in the near future. And its use could not be simpler, as it reads out in latitude and longitude, currently accurate to about two or three miles. Unlike Loran, its readings require no correction factors.

Disadvantages are that its price is now about twice that of Loran (although it is coming down faster than Loran), in the neighborhood of $2,500, or £1,000; its positions are less precise than those of Loran, when the latter have been corrected for chart errors; and as noted above, it provides new positions only periodically, not continuously, which makes it best suited for navigation well offshore by cruisers rather than racers.

Ground tackle

There are few areas of boating lore where opinions are so firmly and loudly held as in the field of ground tackle. Everyone knows exactly what you ought to have, and is willing to prescribe at the slightest opportunity. At the same time, most experienced cruising folk, when closely questioned, will admit having had their favorite anchor drag under otherwise perfect conditions. What this suggests, at least to me, is that (a) there are a lot of lucky sailors around, (b) anchor type is not so crucial as many think, and (c) you should probably never trust any anchor more than you have to. At least one world-famous cruising sailor routinely carried six anchors, and many well-seasoned voyagers feel unhappy with fewer than four. But in a small cruising boat with limited range this is normally unnecessary. Before trying to decide which anchor or anchors you require, it will help to set some requirements within which you can make a rational decision.

First question, to my mind, is what do you expect the anchor to do? This seems foolishly obvious, but it's more complex than it looks: Do you need ground tackle that will hold the boat at occasional local anchorages under reasonably predictable conditions and in very similar bottoms, or will you be ranging far enough to need a rig that will hold your vessel regardless of weather, in a wide assortment of conditions? Were I, for instance, cruising a two-berth catboat in the shallow waters of New York's Great South Bay, where the bottom is nearly always hard sand, I'd be inclined (for reasons that will become apparent) to opt for a single Danforth slightly larger than the prescribed size: On a small boat, even the so-called storm anchor is no great weight to lift or stow, so why have a minuscule working anchor as well?

But if I were cruising only a dozen miles north, in the deep waters of Long Island Sound, where bottom varies from sand to mud to rocks and back again, I'd probably want at least two anchors, of different types. Same boat, different requirements.

The normal minimal recommendation for even the smallest cruising yacht is two anchors. The working anchor, like the working sails, is for everyday use, while the storm anchor is for conditions when you're hanging the boat's safety and maybe your life on the hook. Serious long-haul cruising people, whose boats are seldom under forty feet in length, often opt for the heaviest anchor they can manage as their storm hook, and they are right. This is overkill for a small cruiser. In modern, lightweight designs, a fifteen-pound anchor should be quite large enough as working anchor for a 30-footer, and a twenty-pound anchor is quite big enough for storm service. Going up to the heaviest anchor an adult can manage without a windlass, which is probably going to be about thirty-five pounds, hardly proves anything.

Of all the anchors available in the United States today, the Danforth, its variants and imitators, are collectively the most popular. Part of the reason is convenience and the marketing skills of the manufacturer, but mostly the

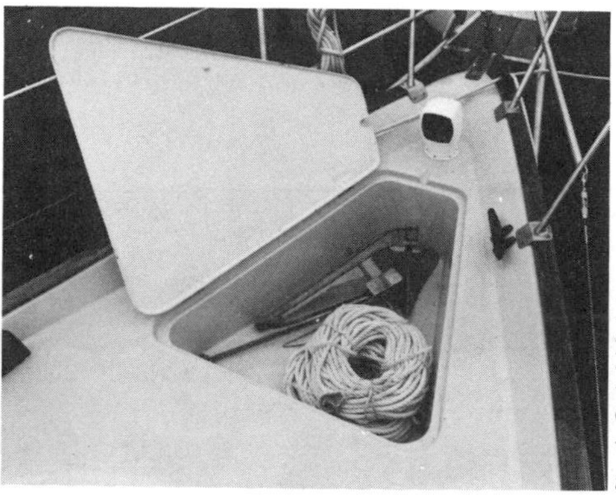

Ideal anchor stowage well has space for suitable Danforth and CQR Plough, as well as made-up rode of adequate length. Note that with this type well, anchor rode cleat must be offset as shown.

proliferation of Danforths derives from the fact that it's a superb anchor for a wide variety of common anchoring situations. It features a pair of extra-broad, flat flukes whose area gives the hook tremendous holding power when they are properly dug in. These flukes are quite sharp, a necessity when digging in a relatively light mass of metal.

The Danforth is ideal in sand and superior in mud, the two types of bottom that every cruising skipper searches out. It is, however, an anchor that's prone to bring up heavy, dripping samples of mud bottom, as the flukes seem well calculated to act as shovels or scoops as the anchor breaks out.

The crown, a squarish hinge that connects the flukes with the shank, is engineered to allow a precise angle of attack for the flukes relative to the shank. According to the manufacturer, this angle is one of the secrets of the Danforth's great success, and one of the reasons why less carefully made imitations frequently show an amazing decrease in holding power. On most Danforths, it's possible to make fast a trip line at the crown so that a snagged anchor, if it has been buoyed in advance, can be withdrawn backwards.

The Danforth has a built-in stock, the crosspiece to which the flukes are welded, so that it almost always lands flat on the bottom, ready to dig in. The only drawback to this arrangement is that if the anchor doesn't bury the stock as well as the flukes, the boat can swing back over the anchor at the change of tide and foul the stock with the rode, effectively tripping the hook.

The shank is long and fairly thin, and it's not unknown for a deeply dug-in Danforth, when subjected to a sideways pull in attempting to break out the hook, to develop a severe bend in the shank. It doesn't seem to do any great harm to bend the shank back straight again, as long as heat isn't applied and as long as the angle between flukes and shank remains the same.

The Danforth comes in standard and "hi-tensile" versions, which are the same except that the latter style can withstand a somewhat greater stress. There's also a quick-release trippable version known as the Sure-ring. In this, the shank has a slot running its length, with a sliding ring in the slot. The rode is made fast to the ring, and if pull on the anchor is reversed from the normal direction, the ring slides to the crown end of the anchor, which then pulls out backwards. It's an effective way to avoid a trip line, but obviously not a rig you'd want to turn your back on. Personally, I prefer the trip line.

There are many imitators, both more and less overt, of the original Danforth. Some are cheaper, but not a whole lot. Having had good experiences with various Danforths for something like thirty years, I cannot see any reason to have anything but the genuine version aboard my own boat. This is not to say that the Danforth is the only anchor I like, but it's the only Danforth-shaped anchor I carry.

For a flat and relatively unobtrusive object, the Danforth can be a real problem when chocked on a foredeck. What seems like a logical way to stow the anchor turns out to be a perfect trap for sheets and headsails, and frequently the chocks themselves can be torn free from the deck. If there is no other place to stow your Danforth, it will help to set a small eye in the deck just beyond each end of the stock. Run a strap from one eye, over the stock, the crown, and the other end of the stock to the second eye. This should keep passing lines from catching under the extended stock.

A recently developed chock for Danforths consists simply of a pair of stainless-steel brackets suspended from the forward end of the bow pulpit. The anchor's stock fits in the brackets and it hangs with the end of the shank perhaps secured to the tack fitting. This is all very well much of the time, and will probably pose few problems until one has a spinnaker or other light-air headsail to cope with. There is, in terms of sailing efficiency, the additional fact that it would be hard to find a worse place to locate an anchor's weight than high off the deck ahead of the bow.

If your boat has a deep cockpit locker—and most fiberglass boats do—one good place to stow the hook can be in a vertical chocking arrangement bolted to a bulkhead inside the locker. Unless the locker is filled to overflowing, the anchor shouldn't pose too much of a snagging hazard, and the rode can be coiled and hung right alongside it. The only problem, of course, is that this spot is hardly ideal for one's primary, everyday anchor, being so far from the bow.

Of course the ideal stowage spot for a cruiser's working anchor is in a recessed anchor well built into the foredeck. Here it will be out of the way, unable to snag anything, including tender toes, and ready to go. A proper

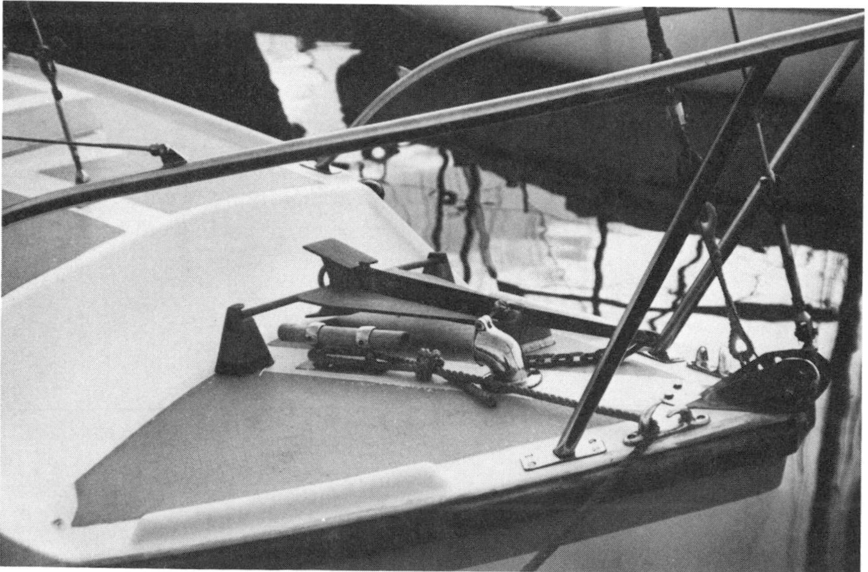

On a small foredeck, even a Danforth is obtrusive. Sheets cannot catch under ends of stock, but could get under shank. Note that chain pipe faces aft to minimize leaks from spray.

anchor well should allow for the anchor to be chocked or lashed down, should provide adequate space for the working rode—say one hundred or one hundred and fifty feet—to be loosely coiled around the Danforth, ready to run, should have an overboard drain big enough to allow grit and mud to pass, and should have a stoutly backed ring or eye to which the anchor rode's bitter end may be made fast. Not a really tall order, but it's surprising how few anchor wells meet all the requirements.

A storm Danforth can be an even greater stowage problem in today's flat-bilged boats. Probably the second-best location is under a berth, if it will not fit beneath the floorboards. Again, a way of securing the storm anchor is necessary, as a loose twenty- or twenty-two-pound anchor bashing about under the floorboards can cause a surprising amount of damage in short order. A couple of eyes bolted through a bulkhead, with shock cord tie-downs, will serve quite well in keeping the hook from picking up enough momentum to break free. The storm-anchor rode is very prone to being shoved and pushed into corners. It should be at least half again as long as the working rode, and longer if you can manage it. It should be carefully coiled and stopped off, because when you want it to run free, you don't want two hundred feet of half-inch spaghetti to deal with.

The favorite anchor of many deep-water cruising sailors is the plow—or plough, if you prefer the British spelling. The original plow is a British invention, marketed under the trade name CQR. (Say the three letters quickly. Get it?) Other plows are now made by a number of manufacturers, including

There is no efficient way to stow a CQR Plough on deck, but this set of chocks and tie-downs is as good as any.

Danforth, of all people, and some of the European imitations of the original CQR have achieved very bad reputations indeed. It seems to be a matter, as with the Danforth, of a small engineering error seriously degrading a valuable idea.

The plow has two primary appeals, one genuine, one cosmetic. It is a very versatile anchor, and is an adequate instrument for most types of bottom although it is probably not best in any given one: The Danforth, for instance, is its superior in sand, as the grapnel is in coral or the old-fashioned kedge is in rock; but the plow works in all these settings, which is no mean accomplishment.

In its naked condition, the plow is a very unfriendly device to try to stow. Hinged just above its plow-shaped double fluke, it will not lie flat, nor will it stand upright. It is just sharp enough at its point to pose a menace to feet and sails, and no chock will really hold it well. About the only way to stow a plow ready for use is socked up tight in a bow roller and, since to many skippers this looks salty as hell, that's where most plows end up. Despite the weight —which is slightly more than for a Danforth of equivalent holding power— this is almost certainly the best place for the plow to be. With its plowshare pointed down and aft, it will seldom snag sails, though it can reach out and grab docklines and mooring lines.

The third unspecialized anchor is the old-fashioned yachtsman's anchor— the shape you think of when someone says anchor. The standard kedge might best be described as semifolding; that is, its stock slips through the shank and can lie alongside it, making it possible to stow the anchor in chocks on deck. It's a matter of a minute or so to slide the stock back in place, and lock it so that it's at right angles to the two flukes. Some types of yachtsman's anchors, notably the ones sold by Paul Luke of East Boothbay, Maine, break down into three pieces—stock, flukes, and shank—for convenient below-decks stowage. Here the process of reassembly will take somewhat longer.

Although it is as old as the hills, and then some, the yachtsman's anchor was engineered into a sophisticated device by the Herreshoffs and others. The trouble is that it's a bit hard for the layman to tell an expertly designed kedge from a bad one. Generally speaking, the visible key is the fluke shape. Sharp, narrow flukes of a diamond shape are designed for penetrating hard sand or clutching at rock or coral. Wider, flatter flukes are for softer bottoms. Avoid flukes shaped like the spade symbol on a deck of cards: These tend to be too blunt to penetrate most bottoms in the weights used aboard yachts, and they also tend to catch coils of rode as a yacht drifts back over its anchor with the change of tide. Remember, when one fluke of a yachtsman's anchor is buried, the other one is lying there waiting to snag something just above the bottom.

Although many tradition-oriented yachtsmen swear by the kedge, it is seldom seen anymore except in areas where a rocky bottom is the rule. There it has an edge over just about everything else, including the specialized grapnel, which is a far weaker construction.

A boat equipped with a bowsprit has a convenient spot from which to hang a made-up kedge, and a skipper who is willing to consider wandering over the sea with such a contrivance swinging from up forward doesn't care about weights in the eyes of the boat anyway. Many shorthanded skippers run the rode back to a cleat alongside the cockpit coaming, so that they can release the hook without leaving the tiller. If you do this, be sure not only that the line is led free both back and then again forward, but that it is secured somewhere at a reasonable scope.

There are, at this writing, several other types of anchor available. Indeed, after a long stagnation, anchor design seems to be an active field again. Of the new designs, the Bruce anchor, developed in the oil fields of the North Sea, and the Wishbone, which has a fairish vogue in southern waters, seem most popular.

The Bruce anchor has been in use for a relatively short time and has attracted a number of partisans. It is a one-piece unit with no moving parts, shaped vaguely like a plow whose single fluke had been hammered out into a concave shape. Its strong suit is said to be the ability to grab and hold in a variety of bottoms on short scope, and it was developed to hold drilling rigs in place in relatively shoal, rough offshore waters. My initial experience with the Bruce anchor, in both soft mud and hard sand, was very positive, but a subsequent test in a gravelly bottom was less fortunate. I personally feel that it has considerable promise, but that I want to learn its ways better before making any flat pronouncement.

In one respect, however, the Bruce stands out: It is even more difficult than the plow to stow on the average small yacht. Because it doesn't adapt its shape at all, virtually the only place to put it is in a roller chock over hanging the bow, and there it would probably be no more (nor less) prone to foul than the plow.

The Wishbone is a development of a British anchor invented a hundred and fifty years ago. Its shape is reminiscent of a Danforth whose flukes are joined along the centerline and surrounded by a V-shaped frame. Many skippers in south Florida and the Bahamas swear by it, and it does not seem to have the Danforth's propensity for picking up bits of coral or rock. At the same time, one gets a good deal less fluke per pound of anchor than with the Danforth. It would be somewhat easier to stow and less prone to snag passing lines. My own impressions are not fully formed enough to have a fixed opinion on its holding capacity.

Although not normally figured into ground tackle systems, the cleats, bitts, and chocks; are accessories to consider carefully. Nearly all mooring cleats are too small (see the table in Chapter II), and it is worth the trouble to replace the anchor cleats if they are disgracefully tiny. Certainly they should be through-bolted, with backing plates and washers to spread what can be a considerable load. Anchoring aside, consider that if your boat ever has to be towed off a sandbar by the Coast Guard, it's the bow cleat they'll probably use, and the initial tug will be a beaut.

Make sure that your cleats are properly faired off, so that no sharp edges, either from bad design or poor casting, will rip the line. The same applies to bitts, and doubly to chocks, which are often among the worst-designed pieces of hardware on any boat. Many boats now have a single or double chock cast as part of the tack fitting and forestay chainplate. There is nothing intrinsically wrong with this setup—indeed, it can be the strongest possible arrangement. But because nearly all boats dance at anchor to a certain extent, the anchor rode will saw back and forth all night (or all week), and when the boat is pitching at anchor, the rode will attempt to leap out of the chock.

The best such integral chock is a double—one slot each side of the tack fitting—with the sides of the chock not only rounded off but slightly flared, to minimize chafe (see photo on page 172). A roller, either metal or rubber, is a plus, as long as there's enough side left above the roller to keep the line in place. Ideally, you should be able to insert a locking pin from one side of the chock to the other, above the rode. This will certainly keep it in place.

What comprises an anchoring system? The stressed elements include (but are not limited to) the anchor itself, one or more shackles, chain, line, and the cleat or bitt on the anchored boat. Obviously, all the components should be of more or less equal strength, although it is sometimes useful to have an extra-heavy segment of chain for its weight alone.

Begin with the anchor. Most manufacturers provide tables of claimed holding power in various types of sea bottom. Your boat will seldom exert anything like the forces claimed as maximums: As an instance, I once anchored a 37-foot ketch of 25,000 pounds displacement in a 20-knot breeze, with a dynamometer made fast to the anchor rode just beyond the bow checks. The yacht in question

Reasonably good locker for a Danforth. Note single roller chock at bow; rode made fast to cleat would necessarily chafe on pulpit leg.

exerted about as much resistance as a vessel reasonably could, having six feet of freeboard forward, a long, straight keel and a complicated rig with upper, lower, and intermediate stays. The maximum pull on the anchor line never exceeded a hundred pounds, and while it would have been considerably more in a fully developed sea, it was nowhere near the rated holding power of our 12-H Danforth in soft mud. Holding power is thus rated with a built-in safety factor, and the other parts of the system should be consistent with the anchor.

Perhaps the first place most people err is in the size of the shackle connecting anchor and chain. Quite often chain of appropriate size has links too narrow to accept the proper shackle. There are two ways of getting round this. First is to increase the size of chain, and second is to purchase a length of chain with oversize shackles at the ends, such as is frequently sold by chandleries specifically for yacht ground tackle. The question of how much chain is a hard one to answer. In coral-infested waters, I would want an all-chain rode if the boat's stowage and my back would handle it. In other areas, I think three to five fathoms is probably adequate.

A second shackle links the chain to the nylon rode. Nylon is, in my opinion, clearly superior to any other natural or artificial rope for anchor or docking lines, because of its great strength and elasticity. A proper eye splice, with five sets of tucks around an eye of the same metal as anchor and shackle, will complete the connection. The pin of the shackle should be wired into place—again, using wire made of the same metal as the other components of the system, usually hot-dipped galvanized steel.

The rode's length depends of course on where one plans to anchor. It's thus

Very poor arrangement of bow hardware. With a nearly vertical rode, chafe on fiberglass gunwale would be inevitable.

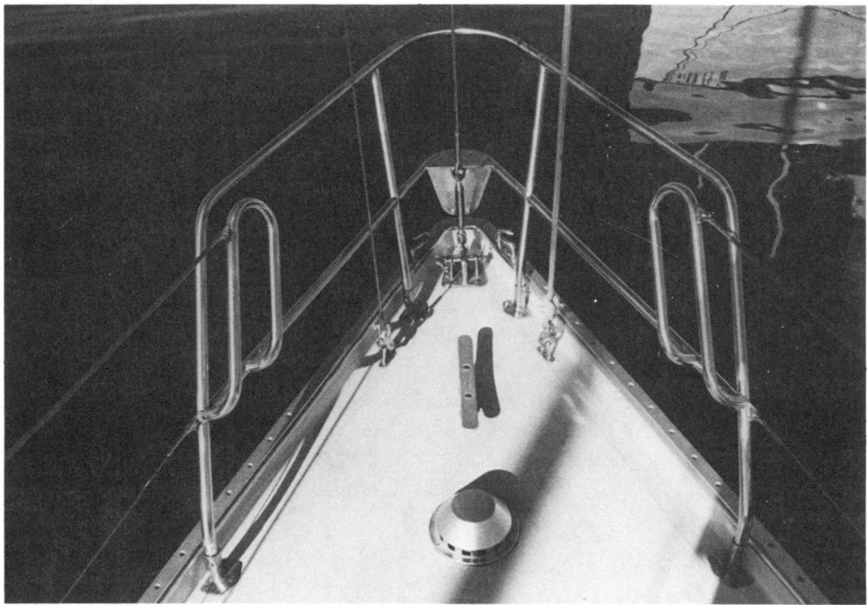

On a Danish sloop, a single deck cleat and two skene chocks make an adequate lead. Note also bow pulpit overlap to accommodate jib foot.

Proper bow rig, with double chocks, double roller leads, pinned to prevent rodes from jumping free.

impossible for me to prescribe absolutely, except to suggest that a working anchor rode for a small cruising yacht should seldom be less than a hundred feet in length, while the storm anchor rode should probably be at least half again as long. Bear in mind that with the usual 5-to-1 scope, a rode of a hundred feet will allow you to anchor with reasonable security in only fifteen feet of water. (Scope, expressed as the ratio of rode to water depth, is measured from the boat's chocks, not the water's surface.)

It's a great convenience to have your anchor lines measured off in convenient increments, and while it's easy to use an indelible pen, removable plastic tags allow you to cut the chafed end off an anchor rode and simply move the tags to new locations.

The bitter end of the rode should be made fast to a strong, well-backed fitting in the anchor locker. If the rode is all chain, it will be convenient to have the last few feet rope, so that in an emergency you can cut the line where it comes through the deck pipe, rather than fumbling about below.

In addition to the anchor chock, a pair of secondary chocks should be installed on the toerail forward. It's impossible to specify exactly where they should be, but they're primarily for docklines and only used for anchoring if you set two hooks at once. The *skene* chocks with overlapping horns are probably best, of a size able to take one-inch line (some yacht club or fuel dock will have it). Again, the edges should be both faired and flared, and the chocks themselves should be through-bolted as they can by subjected to considerable accidental loading.

VI

Safety

Perhaps the best way to define safety for the active sailor is negative: Safety is the avoidance of stupid, needless mistakes. One may in the end take far greater risks, but only in the full knowledge that one is doing so. The mistakes to be avoided may not be of one's own creation: A good deal of boat safety is undoing the carelessness of others, or rethinking a boat to suit one's own particular requirements.

Another aspect of safety afloat is the systemic one. When I first outlined this chapter, I listed a number of essential items of equipment and left it at that. It was a conventional approach. Sitting down to write, it occurred to me that, at least in part, we are trying to organize a boat to avoid a number of definable problems—sinking, fire, man overboard, to name a few. Doing this requires equipment, to be sure. It also requires organizing that equipment according to the boat's design, the conditions she is expected to encounter, the abilities of the crew. The sheer size of the boat has little to do with it: John Guzzwell sailed the tiny *Trekka* safely, almost uneventfully, around the world, thanks largely to superb organization of his resources. Planning ahead is of the essence.

As crashing is the bête noire of flyers, sinking is the normal bane of sailors. In recent years, designers and safety experts have paid more and more attention to the possibilities of "unsinkable" pleasure craft, especially in small sizes. Nowadays even a ballasted sailboat of considerable size can be made practically unsinkable. The problem is often more acute, however, with smaller cruisers, where every interior inch is important to the accommodation.

Of the two basic ways to achieve unsinkability in a small boat, one is natural, the other artificial. The first involves positive buoyancy conferred by the material from which the boat is built, and of course the most obvious instance is an unballasted vessel made of wood. If the rest of the load is not too great, a small wood boat will float even if awash by itself. So will boats whose construction embodies a substantial amount of foam flotation (usually sealed between layers of fiberglass cloth). This normally makes for an extremely thick hull if the boat carries any ballast at all.

Another method, seen in the unballasted Stiletto overnighting catamaran, involves the use of an ultralight honeycomb material, called Nomex, between layers of fiberglass cloth. The individual cells of the Nomex may be fractured if the hull is pierced, but because they don't interconnect, the amount of flooding of the hull material (not the inside of the hull) is restricted to a space a little larger than the fracture itself.

Most cruising multihulls are or can be made nearly unsinkable by means of the air trapped inside the lightweight hulls. Of course a multihullist's chief fear is not sinking but capsize, because although the overturned boat can float for days or weeks, it will not right itself.

Since most small cruisers are ballasted monohulls, however, the easiest and most practical way to make them unsinkable is to add blocks or containers of flotation in strategic areas. The big problem with a swamped boat floating at gunwale level is its instability. Awash, it seems ready to roll slowly over into total capsize when struck by the smallest wave. Putting flotation in the most logical unused space—beneath the floorboards—just accentuates this tendency. To keep a swamped boat upright, the flotation material has to be as high as possible. Along the sides, under the deck, in the forepeak and lazarette—all these are good places. Even so, if the boat ever does fill with water, she will probably be less than truly stable as long as the mast is up.

The flotation material itself may be either sheets or blocks of closed-cell foam—Styrofoam or one of its relatives—or air tanks. Foam has the advantage that while it can be punctured or even shredded, the bits remaining still supply flotation. It can be carved more or less roughly or poured as a liquid to fill a given space precisely, then sealed with a protective covering of fiberglass. Air tanks work as well as foam, as long as they remain intact, and that of course is the problem. A bow air tank, especially, is vulnerable to puncture after which it may or may not be strong enough to contain the inrush of water.

At this writing, positive flotation really doesn't seem to be a practical method for protecting ballasted monohulls above about twenty-five feet. The trend of federal regulation has been toward requiring positive flotation in small craft, but for the foreseeable future, the boat that will float when holed or flooded is more than likely to be a multihull or a nearly unballasted daggerboarder.

Avoidance of leaks

This being the case, the next question is how to reduce the likelihood of sinking in the "sinkable" boat. The answers fall into two categories: avoidance of serious holes in the first place, and efficient bailing systems in the second. In larger vessels, compartmentalization is the first and most obvious way of reducing the amount of water that can get into the hull in an accident. Although this seems out of the question for the size of boat we're talking about, it does apply to a limited extent. There are three obvious places in a small cruiser where a lot of water can come aboard, and where proper design can contain it.

The first is way forward, in the eyes of the boat. Most cruisers have a forepeak of sorts—the useless triangular space at the very bow. In some boats, that space extends far enough aft so that a collision at waterline level will flood the forepeak, but not the rest of the boat. Look for a sturdy bulkhead that's unpierced (or at least capable of being plugged) to well above the waterline, and that's watertight.

Boats that have a separate outboard motor well aft where the lazarette would normally be can have flooding problems there. I once owned a 25-footer whose after bulkhead, while strong, was less than watertight, and we nearly sank running free on a blustery day, when the lazarette engine well filled with water, which then worked through cracks into the cabin. Be sure that your boat's outboard well, if any, is perfectly sealed from the accommodation.

The cockpit itself can be a major source of flooding, if the boat is ever pooped by a following sea, or if the cockpit drains are plugged during a continued heavy rain. The best solution is a bridge deck, which at the worst will convert the cockpit to a gigantic bathtub, with the overflow running aft over the transom. If the companionway has a low step, however, it may pay offshore sailors to be sure the lower slides are extraheavy, tightly fitted, lockable, and set in reinforced tracks.

Pooping is, for most of us, a rare event. Far more dangerous are the holes in the boat that we take for granted, especially the through-hull fittings below the waterline. It's a good question how many such fittings are necessary in the first place, and it's quite possible to have a boat with no through-hulls below the waterline at all. Even if this seems impractical (and it probably will) you should aim for as few such fittings as you can get away with, each one easily accessible and capable of being sealed or plugged.

Let's examine the more common such through-hulls and see what can be done to make them less dangerous.

Boats with inboards will require a raw-water intake below the waterline. This supplies seawater (salt or fresh) that either cools the engine directly or cools the self-contained freshwater system, then exits through the exhaust. A proper raw-water intake should be a heavy fitting (I prefer bronze), carefully bedded to the hull inside and out, and fitted with a large backing block to spread the load. Inside the hull should be a seacock or—less desirable—a good-quality gate valve. The hose leading to the engine should be secured to the valve pipe by double stainless-steel hose clamps. It can be transparent, but should be reinforced and should lead as straight as possible, to avoid any chance of kinking. A freshwater filter in the line ahead of the engine is not a bad idea at all, given what's floating around these days. Because it's possible for the valve to fail, there should be a shaped wooden plug nearby, just in case.

The raw-water intake will normally be located close to the engine, low enough in the hull so the cooling system can draw water even when the boat is heeled. The intake valve should be easily accessible inside the engine hatch. Some authorities suggest that the seacock should be closed when the engine isn't being used. This seems to me likely to lead to running the engine without any raw water and, without a water-temperature alarm, seizing the whole unit. I would say, get the best-quality valve and trust it.

Perhaps the old-fashioned marine toilet is the cause of more serious leaks in yachts than any other single piece of gear. The system involves a small intake and a large exit valve, each of which should be securely seacocked. Leakage can come from either direction, and frequently does, and the fault is seldom in the seacock. Usually the problem is a blockage in the valving system of the head itself, and the leak is so slow no one notices it. A point to check is that the intake should be sited ahead of the exit—better still, on the opposite side of the keel—so that you don't suck in your own discharge. Although the old-fashioned marine head is now illegal in U.S. waters, the same problems occur with Type I flow-through MSDs.

The only genuine answer is to turn the seacocks to "off" (which should be labeled) when the head isn't in use. Seacocks are far more positive closures than any rubber or plastic valves, and it is not wholly humorous that the main valve in a marine toilet is known technically as a joker. The ideal answer, like so many ideals, often falls flat because the human element fails. As someone who is less than methodical about keeping head seacocks closed, I can hardly be accusatory, but that doesn't invalidate the prescription.

The typical speedometer-log through-hull, with its miniature paddlewheel recessed into a removable plug, has a potential for danger that fortunately seldom materializes. There should be no leakage at all around a speedo-log installation. I use ordinary water-pump grease—heavy and resistant to dissolving—to caulk between the impeller plug and its through-hull tube. If the unit is not fitted with a stop cock, one must expect about a quart of water to enter the boat when one replaces the dummy plug with the real impeller. If it cannot be retracted and is left in place when the boat isn't being used, the impeller will soon pick up weed and barnacles; it's better to plan the location of the impeller so that a sudden jet of water won't damage anything than to leave it in all the time.

The depth-sounder installation should also be leak-free. Again, unless the exterior transducer is knocked or jarred severely, it should be quite dry after being properly bedded. Once the bedding compound bond with the hull has been broken, however, you'll probably have to haul the boat and redo the installation to stop a dribble. As with similar through-hulls, a tapered, soft wood plug that fits the through-hull hole is a good idea just in case the whole unit is wiped off by a rock. Remember not to coat the surface with antifouling paint.

The propeller shaft of an inboard engine leaks a little all the time, and you might as well get used to it. It could hardly be otherwise, since the rapidly spinning shaft pierces the hull, and a certain amount of water inevitably finds its way inside. The leak will be through the stuffing box, a bearing located where the shaft goes through the hull. The main nut at the forward end of the stuffing box can usually be tightened or loosened, and it requires a certain amount of experience to determine the proper tension. For most shafts, the nut should be hand-tight: A small drip will occur when the shaft spins, but little or no water will enter when the shaft is stationary. If the nut is too tight, the stuffing box will quickly become hot to the touch with the engine running in gear.

The problem with stuffing boxes is that they're nearly always in an inaccessible part of the bilge, so that you have to hang by your heels to see what's going on. Fortunately, you can usually diagnose what's happening by touch alone. Do be sure, however, that you can get at the stuffing box fairly quickly in an emergency, and do be sure that your toolbox contains a wrench large enough to fit the main stuffing-box nut. Stuffing boxes often contain a winding of special cord around the shaft, compressed by the nut as it's tightened. This packing should be replaced every season, and the stuffing box itself checked for leaks perhaps every month. Most—but not all—stuffing boxes require to be greased periodically. The builder or dealer will know how often.

When a yacht's rudder post goes through the hull, it too is prone to a certain amount of leakage, though far less than the stuffing box. A proper rudder installation has the post inside a tube sealed at both ends, but a serious accident can cause sudden and serious leakage around the rudder. Short of hauling the boat, there isn't a lot you can do about this.

While many builders are conscientious about through-hulls below the waterline, they may be quite oblivious to the dangers of the same kinds of fittings at or slightly above the boot topping. Aside from the fact that cruising boats are occasionally loaded below their marks, there is also the problem of sailing well heeled for long hours at a time, with an above-waterline through-hull exposed to continual or repeated immersion. The ideal answer—seldom seen on small production yachts—is to have the same seacocks on all through-hull fittings, whether below, at or above the waterline.

It's unrealistic to expect a stock builder to alter his product or wrench his production line out of shape for one safety-conscious customer, so if you do want above-the-waterline through-hulls to be closable, you will probably have to arrange for that yourself. Given the nature of plastic fittings, it isn't hard, but it will be fairly expensive. You may be better advised, unless you do a lot of heavy-weather sailing, to double-clamp the hoses and trust to luck. Just as a toilet bowl's rim should be above the boat's waterline when she is at rest, a galley or head sink should be high enough to prevent water from pouring in even when the boat is heeled. The galley overside outlet should be just above the waterline, so slop of the waves helps keep it clean of grease buildup.

The kind of through-hulls we're discussing here include sink drains, of course, but perhaps even more important are the cockpit scupper drains. In most stock boats these are of minimum number and size, yet they're absolutely vital. Unless your boat's cockpit sole is very high above the water, your leeward drain may actually flood the cockpit to a depth of two or three inches with the boat heeled. The first sailboat I owned had this unlovely characteristic, and as a result we sailed with a large supply of wine-bottle corks. The cockpit drains were normally unplugged only when the boat was at anchor.

What we should have done, of course, was buy longer lengths of reinforced hose and cross the drain pipes, so the leeward drain in the cockpit connected to the windward hole in the boot-topping, and vice versa. This should be standard practice, and is a point to check.

There are several problems inherent in small-boat cockpit drains. First, the pipes usually run through the lazarette, where it's easy for loose gear to pinch them closed or even tear them free from their connections at top or bottom. If they are at the forward end of the cockpit, they get involved with inboard engine installations, and it may be impractical to cross them.

The normal drain installation consists of a plastic through-hull fitting in the cockpit sole, connected by tubing to another in the hull. Unless the run of tubing is nearly straight or the curves are very easy, the piping is likely to pinch itself closed. Or if not closed, the aperture will be so reduced that a little dirt and a few matches will jam it. This is the big argument against crossed pipes—that they are so prone to blockage. A proper installation may require an L-bend pipe on the through-hull, to allow the initial lead of tubing to run straight. In any case, a semi-flexible wire—a stiff coathanger will do—of the proper length is a good investment, and reinforced transparent tubing will allow you to see the location and nature of any jam.

Most yachts have scuppers at two or three points along the deck, and water simply runs down the hull, leaving untidy tracks along the way. Some boats have internal scuppering to carry the water inside the hull from deck level and release it via a through-hull at the waterline. Personally, I would stick with the old-fashioned smeary scupper rather than punch another hole through the hull. If your boat does have this kind of scupper, though, be sure you can get at the line from inside, in case the fittings or tubing let go.

A final potential source of intermediate-height leaks is the exhaust pipe of an inboard engine. A well-designed boat should run with the exhaust clear of the water, but there will be times when a pursuing wave overtakes her; likewise, nearly all boats have the exhaust several inches above the waterline with the boat at rest. But if she is overloaded, or taking on water from another source, the exhaust could be immersed to deliver the coup de grace. The good exhaust installation will have a standpipe arrangement just inside the transom, to prevent any siphoning of water from outside into the engine. And you should have a large plug to seal the opening in the winter and if you go offshore frequently.

Topside leaks

Topside leaks are almost always more annoying than dangerous, but if you do get caught out in desperate weather—and it can happen quite close to shore —the boat's watertight integrity may be all you have left.

The companionway is perhaps the most critical spot, since it's normally the largest potential hole and the one that's most often open. As noted earlier, a bridge deck will reduce the companionway's exposed area, and solid slides or doors, securely mounted and lockable, will take care of the rest. If you're pooped, some water will undoubtedly get below, but in that kind of weather it's going to be very marshy in the cabin of a small yacht in any case. What you want to avoid is a breaking sea cascading down the ladder. I was pooped just once (so far) in a 25-footer. We weren't expecting it, as the seas were high but nowhere near breaking, until we went over a shallow patch and the bottom grabbed at the passing wave and broke it. The sound was remarkably like an express train, and the cockpit was filled even as we took off on one of the wildest rides I've ever had in a keelboat. Although there were no slides in the companionway, the boat's bridge deck kept all but about five gallons of water out of the accommodation. It was enough to soak everything, but had no effect on the boat's buoyancy, the important thing.

In a knockdown, the cockpit locker tops can easily flip open and allow a large sluice down into the lockers. In many small yachts, that means drowning the engine as well, and if you don't get the boat upright quickly, you can be in real trouble. The answer is of course strong, lockable closures. For many years the only catch available was a misbegotten gadget called the draw latch, perfectly designed to take a dime-sized patch of flesh off the back of your calves. Now, the draw latch is still used by some builders, but better ones either recess it into a concave fiberglass dimple in the cockpit side or use some other form of closure. Perhaps the simplest and among the most secure is a length of wire or chain running down from the inside of the cockpit locker lid, through an eye, and forward to the main cabin, where it can be secured (often after having been transmuted to a rope tail). This closure is easy to release, requires no cockpit locks or hardware, and has considerable positive security. It's not quite as watertight a fastening as the old-fashioned draw latch, but at least it will prevent the secured hatch from opening wide and admitting many gallons of water at once. Once your boat is fitted out and stowed for voyaging, it's a good idea to survey her quickly for loose gear that may come adrift in a knockdown. Most people think of batteries in this connection—and quite properly, too—but other dangerous pieces of equipment include storm anchors loosely stowed in cockpit lockers, icebox (or other interior) hatches that are not hinged, and cooking utensils, including the stove itself.

The early fiberglass pocket cruisers had very simple forward hatches that nearly always leaked at the slightest excuse. Proper design has made these hatches less prone to drips, and a desire for ventilation has increased their number so that even a 27-footer may have hatches forward and aft of the mast (not counting the companionway itself). Accounts of pitchpolings and of decks being swept by seas frequently mention the dislodging of loosely attached hatches, and the skipper whose sailing takes him into heavy seas ought at least to give the matter a thought. Extremely lightweight hatches—single plastic moldings with hinges and a cheap catch—are asking for trouble, either from boarding seas or burglars. A proper hatch should have solid hinges (ideally two sets, so it may open forward or aft), a hefty latch, and a fiberglass lip that's built up from the deck to prevent leakage.

It was about a half century ago that the dorade vent first made its appearance as an antidote for water coming down standard ventilators. The design has been worked over but never really improved, and it remains the best design for primary boat ventilators that must (or should) be open all the time. The dorade consists of a vent scoop mounted at one end of a small deck box. Air drawn into the scoop enters one end of the box, along with whatever rain or spray it may bear. The water falls to the bottom of the box and drains out small scuppers, while the air reaches the cabin by means of a vent pipe at the other end of the dorade box. Simple, effective, and, if not foolproof, far better than anything else yet devised. While there is little chance of taking dangerous amounts of water through a standard vent, one can expect to soak down a considerable portion of the boat during a driving rain or a savage beat to windward. Even the dorade will be overcome if a green sea strikes it, so it's a good idea to install the vent so that its cabin intake is over something the head, the galley sink—that won't suffer from occasional wetting down.

Ports in small yachts are at once a blessing and a curse. Because they tend to flex in a subtly different rhythm from the rest of the vessel, they will leak after a while no matter how good the bedding and bolting. The only solution is periodic rebedding. But a leak, while annoying, is no serious danger. What is to be avoided are the large-size ports that may simply pop out if a sizable sea strikes them. Not only will the boat's cabin be inundated, but the whole deckhouse structure, which depends to a certain extent on the port itself, can be compromised. If your boat has ports with an individual area of over two square feet, it's a very good idea to devise some form of storm protection, especially if you're an offshore sailor. The simplest thing is perhaps suitably shaped sheets of three-eighths- or half-inch marine plywood, capable of being secured by four or five bolts (the bolts themselves, heavily loaded with bedding compound, can remain in place until needed).

Pumps

In its search for better governmentese, the Coast Guard has invented the term "dewatering" to replace the several activities we all used to describe as

Well-scuppered cockpit seats. Pump handle opening is accessible to helm, but will collect rain and spray.

"bailing." And while it remains true that the most effective dewatering device is a frightened crewmember with a bucket, there are easier ways of getting the sea back where it belongs, both on ordinary days and in emergencies. In general and practical terms, the two primary choices are manual and electric bilge pumps. The manual are divided into fixed and portable subcategories.

My own feeling is that any boat with a substantial bilge area ought to have at least two pumps, probably one fixed and one portable. Other boats, such as multihulls, with very shallow bilges may in emergency be bailed more effectively with a bucket than a pump. In dealing with everyday seepage, a pump's real usefulness is its intake hose's ability to reach down into deep sumps and into otherwise inaccessible corners.

The best manual pumps, to my mind, are the so-called diaphragm type, which will pass surprisingly large wads of semisolid material along with a large volume of water. They can also be opened and cleaned in short order if they ingest something so big that it cannot get through the mechanism. Diaphragm pumps are offered in a number of shapes and installations, but the best all-purpose unit is the type that mounts in the vertical side of a cockpit locker. The removable handle can be operated up and down while sailing if necessary, and one may pump the boat's interior from the cockpit *with all hatches and seat lockers closed.* If you have only one pump aboard, this should be the one.

The intake hose should run to the boat's bilge sump, usually a molded-in well in the keel so located that loose water in the hull will eventually run downhill to it. (Parenthetically, this will be facilitated by limber holes in all thwartships floors, so water cannot collect in pools here and there.) Some boats have no orthodox sump, or are so designed—catamarans, for instance—that water collects in more than one spot. Rather than invest in an expensive double pump system, one may get two intake hoses hooked to a single Y valve, so the pump may draw from either hose at one time. In my old Cheoy Lee Bermuda

30, the main bilge pump had a throwover valve enabling the pumper to empty the sealed icebox sump as well as the bilge—an extraordinarily well-thought-out arrangement.

It's surprising how difficult pumping a boat's bilge manually for even a few minutes can be to the average sedentary sailor. A fixed pump mounted on a cockpit seat so the lever is pushed back and forth instead of up and down is a lot easier to work, but the necessary rubber collar will take far more of a beating from collected rain and sunlight in this horizontal location than in the harder-to-pump vertical alignment. The pump handle should be as long as the surrounding limits will allow, as leverage is a great help in this situation.

A portable bilge pump can be just as good as a fixed one, or even better, since it can be moved to the site of the pumping or even to a disabled boat alongside. Most portable pumps seem to be the archaic "navy style," with a handle that one pulls and pushes to work a piston inside a cylinder. Except for seniority, there is little to recommend this design: It is far harder to operate than the lever-action diaphragm; it is prone to clogging and cannot be opened easily for field repair. Far better to invest in a small diaphragm pump with an extralong handle, mounted on a piece of marine plywood. One stands or kneels on the plywood while working the handle. It is very effective.

An electric bilge pump is a great convenience, especially in a leaky boat, but it is to my mind definitely a luxury on the size of boat we're taking about. Only if there are medical reasons for avoiding extended pumping is an electric unit really necessary. It should, in my opinion, be wired on its own fused circuit direct to the batteries, so that if an accident kills the switchboard the pump will still operate. Unless your cruiser has a non-self-bailing cockpit (seldom seen or tolerable on even the smallest yacht) an automatic switch is probably not a good idea. There seem to me to be far more cases of pumps burned out and, indeed, whole electrical systems destroyed by automatic pumps than there are of boats saved in the owner's absence.

Strictly as an emergency measure, one should not underestimate the value of the engine saltwater intake hose as a pumping device: Removed from its through-hull valve (which is of course closed) and plunged into a full bilge, it can add a significant pumping capability as long as the engine is running. In this case, however, an in-line filter before the engine is vital, as a serious leak will usually carry into the bilge an assortment of pump-clogging debris.

Fire

Fire is a major fear aboard any yacht. Not only can a fire develop quickly in a small boat, but there's often no place for the crew to go. As with other dangers, however, fire risk can be reduced by reasonable planning, good maintenance, and sound equipment.

The first question to consider is where in your boat a fire is likely to happen. Unless you smoke in bed, and fall asleep doing so, the possibilities are limited. The marine stove is the most likely source, if not the most dangerous, followed by the engine and fuel system, the oil-fed lamps if any, and the electrical system.

With their tendency to flare up when being lit, their ability to be blown out while still feeding vaporized fuel, and the fact that (because of their low heat level) they are on so long, alcohol stoves probably account for more shipboard fires than any other marine device. Because most of these fires are relatively minor, few are reported, but every skipper has a horror story or six to relate on the subject.

The dangers from both alcohol and kerosene derive from their nature as liquid nonexplosive fuels. They may flare up, but they won't blow up (though they can soak into wood or fabric and then present a hazard), and, while different techniques may be required to fight alcohol and kerosene fires, preventing them is much the same problem. Propane, butane, or compressed natural gas (CNG) present instead the danger of explosion. Quite often a large bang from one of these units will be followed by no fire at all, the fuel having expended itself in a single dramatic gesture. Here, prevention is 95 percent of the problem.

Fire prevention in connection with a galley stove may be divided into two areas: the stove's surroundings and its installation. Any galley stove should be

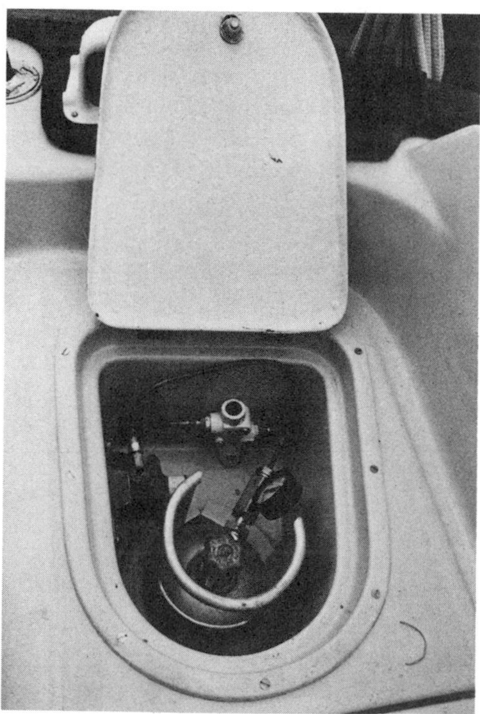

Gas bottle stowage in cockpit: Bottle is braced against shifting, and compartment is vented over the side.

so located that its flames won't ignite nearby curtains or woodwork when a pan is removed from a burner without turning it off. Remember that if the burner is in direct sunlight, it will be almost impossible to see the flame: you must get into the habit of turning burners off as a matter of course. There should be no curtains directly over the galley stove— often a difficult prescription to fill—nor should there be easily combustible shelves or lockers where they can be heated by a neglected burner. Normally this means something like a foot above the burner and six inches all around, but if you're in doubt, test with your hand.

Dish, pot, and food lockers shouldn't be located behind the galley stove, so that you have to reach over the burners to get at the items they contain. Nor should a fire extinguisher or blanket be bracketed so that you might have to reach through flames to get at it. Liquid-fuel stoves should be contained in an enclosure that won't burn or blister when burning fuel escapes, as it inevitably will, and runs down the sides of the stove.

The installation itself is very important. A boat stove operates in an exceptionally difficult environment, and most such stoves want nothing more than to give up the fight. And unlike stoves on powerboats, those on sailing cruisers ought to be capable of heating things even when the boat is bashing to windward on her ear.

The first installation requirement, then, is an effective gimballing system. A good many small cruisers today arrive from the builder with two-burner pressure alcohol stoves recessed into the galley countertop. This seems to me an adequate installation for powerboats, but is acceptable for sailing craft only if you have another, gimballed stove available for cooking under way—because you won't be able to do so safely on this rig. A safe gimbal system will allow the stove to remain horizontal at the boat's maximum heel angle when under sail—say 25 or 30 degrees for a small monohull. Further, the stove must not become top heavy when there are pots on both burners. And finally, there should be fiddles in the form of rails and movable clamps, so you can clamp a pot in place on the burner. In a very small cruiser, you may be best advised to opt for a self-contained single-burner swinging stove that's mounted on the bulkhead. I had one of these for a couple of years, and if the cook is good at planning ahead and the crew is tolerant, it can suffice. Such units, which can utilize semisolid fuel (like Sterno), alcohol, kerosene or disposable bottled-gas containers linked directly to the burner, are quite safe, because they're accessible all around, there are no fuel lines to speak of, and the pot is actually cradled in the burner. The only thing to be wary of is keeping the burner far enough below the overhead and away from bulkheads to avoid charring paintwork or igniting curtains.

Most smaller boat stoves have self-contained fuel tanks. They are difficult to fill and likely to run out halfway through cooking a meal, which can make for an exceptionally unpleasant session filling the hot stove. Every time you use the stove, look around the bases of the burners and along the fuel-line joints for pinhole leaks, evidenced by tiny flames. An alcohol or kerosene pressure stove should probably be tightened up and regasketed every couple of seasons, or anytime you see a flame leak.

Boats over about twenty-seven feet are now arriving with larger stoves—two or three burners and an oven—having a separate fuel tank. While the usefulness of an alcohol-heated oven seems to me debatable, it's at least an extra pot and pan locker, and keeping it filled with utensils will help it counterbalance weights on top. Most stoves with external liquid-fuel tanks have a pressure pump on the tank, a fuel-line valve, a copper fuel line from tank to stove, interrupted at the stove end by a flexible hose that maintains the connection when the stove swings in its gimbals.

It's very important that the fuel line be safeguarded for its entire length. Inspect the bulkhead apertures through which the rigid line passes, making sure that the metal tubing is padded to avoid chafe. Make sure also that it's secured to the bulkhead with padded brackets and that bends in the tubing are radiused easily and not crimped. The rubber-hose connection should be armored (cased with metal braid) and secured with clamps to the tubing, whose end should be beaded or ridged. One should be able to shut off the pressurized fuel supply at the stove—by turning off the burners—and at the tank, and one must make sure that the tank, which is frequently in a less than accessible spot, is reachable in a hurry.

Propane, butane, or natural-gas installations are regarded as being more critical than alcohol or kerosene, if only because gas can blow up with remarkable force. I once saw a sizable cruiser opened along the gunwale like a sardine tin from the force of a propane explosion in the lazarette. On the other hand, millions of people around the world cook with gas for decades without serious incident, and if one is careful, there should be no problems.

The self-contained camper's stoves that attach to bulkheads offer few problems, because the can connects directly to the burner. Just be certain that the connection is positive and leak-free (a small amount of liquid soap around the joint will bubble a warning in most cases). Stoves with external tanks, by contrast, require greater care. Essentially, one should follow the same precautions with fuel lines as with a liquid-fuel stove, but there is the additional need to stow the gas bottle securely. Assuming your boat was designed to handle bottled gas, there should be a special locker that drains overboard in which the gas bottle and its spare replacement will fit securely. The locker should be padded or the bottle lashed or braced in such a way that it's immobilized: Not only will motion put a stress on the fuel line but it will also tend to chafe the paint off the gas bottle, which can begin to rust out.

Like any fuel line, the gas bottle's should have shutoffs at both ends. In addition to the manual shutoff on the bottle, I installed in my last boat a solenoid switch operated remotely (by electricity) from the galley. With this unit, made by Marinetics of California, there is a red light always lit when the gas supply is reaching the stove, and it makes an excellent reminder. Also, one can shut down the gas line without climbing out on the deck—a fact that makes this safety practice more likely to be followed.

Much has been made of the fact that while butane and propane are heavier than air, and will sink into the bilge if they escape, natural gas is lighter, and will rise—presumably out of the boat. This is an advantage, but it seems to me somewhat overemphasized. If the natural gas escapes in a place where it cannot dissipate by rising, it will collect just the same. A good overhead vent above the stove might be a good investment here.

Cabin heaters, used in northern climates for warmth and elsewhere for a shippy atmosphere below, can also be quite dangerous. Personally, I have found that the galley stove serves quite well as a cabin heater: Simply invert an old-fashioned ceramic flowerpot on a burner—the loose-pored pottery will absorb moisture and emit a nice, dry heat to the cabin.

If you are installing a cabin heater yourself, be absolutely certain that there is adequate insulation around it. Follow the maker's instructions religiously, and remember that air space is one of the best possible insulators. My principal objection to cabin heaters (which I think look nautical as hell) is that their stovepipes always seem to be located so that they're certain to be grabbed by a passerby losing his balance. To a certain extent the same remarks apply to the picturesque kerosene cabin lamps that are installed but seldom used in so many yachts. Probably such a lamp should only be lit when the boat is at rest and the quite considerable heat and soot from the chimney will be caught by the smoke bell directly above.

It seems fairly likely that within a decade there will be no more inboard gasoline engines in American boats. The U.S. Coast Guard has made installations of these units progressively more difficult by tightening regulations, while small diesels have become more and more commonplace, cheap, and lightweight. As most remaining gasoline installations are likely to be elderly, it's doubly important that they be regarded with suspicion and maintained with care. Unless your boat's engine installation is more than about ten years old, chances are it has been done in accordance with safe practice. To be sure, here are a few clues to look for.

First, does the fuel line lead from the top of the fuel tank, and are there no petcocks or other valves for drawing off fuel on the tank? The direct thinkers who installed the Atomic-4 in my old Cheoy Lee ketch took the fuel line from the bottom of the tank so gravity would keep the supply running. Which was fine until the day the carburetor float stuck and I arrived aboard to find five gallons of gas in the bilge. The same builders had thoughtfully installed a plain, old-fashioned faucet at the bottom of the tank, alongside the fuel line, presumably in case I should ever want a cup of gas with my cereal. I eventually sealed it off when it began to leak after a few years.

But that was before Coast Guard regulation. Only a couple of years ago a lot of boats were still being delivered with inadequate or nonexistent ventilation for fuel and/or engine compartments. You need at least one intake and one exit vent for each engine or fuel compartment not essentially open to the atmosphere. The intake vent tube should go at least halfway down to the bottom of the compartment, and the exit tube's mouth should be as low down in the compartment as is practically possible. This usually means no lower than the top of the bilge sump, if this element is in the engine room. The ventilators themselves should be capable of being cocked into or away from the wind, to provide a good draw and outlet and it is not a bad idea to install a powered blower in the exit line, locating it well above the bottom of the bilge.

My own choice for ventilators are the flexible PVC type, in whatever conformation suits the boat. They do not snag lines, will not stub toes, can be kept clean with ordinary scouring powder, and can be removed and capped in bad weather. The vent tubing leading down from them should never be less than three inches in diameter, and should consist of flexible tubing (PVC is most common) stiffened either by molded-in ridges or by wire. The point here is to keep the tubing from kinking (and thus partially closing) where it bends.

Fire extinguishing

But in spite of the best practices and intentions, fires occasionally start on pleasure craft. Correct fire extinguishers, properly located, are necessary—and equally important is knowing in advance how they work and taking care of them. U.S. federal regulations prescribe fire extinguishers for all but a tiny minority of engine-powered vessels; other countries have similar regulations, or at least recommendations. Technically, this means that an engineless cruiser doesn't have to carry one. Since, however, one's galley stove is probably just as dangerous a fire hazard as the engine, and perhaps more so, it would be foolish to skip carrying an extinguisher if you have a cooking device aboard. And to carry matters one step further, what happens if a boat near you catches fire? Of the two times in thirty-odd years of boating when I've used a fire extinguisher in earnest, one was for a galley fire in my own boat and the other was for a fuel tank explosion-cum-fire in a powerboat next to mine.

In determining what the small cruiser ought to carry in the way of fire extinguishers, it's useful first to see what's available that meets the government's fire extinguisher regulations. Virtually every marine dealer (and thus every yacht) now carries only one type of hand extinguisher, the "dry chemical" unit. The extinguishing agent in virtually all of these is a powder propelled by a CO_2 cartridge, and the contents are named "dry chemical" because it's a rather more impressive term than sodium bicarbonate—baking soda—which is the basic ingredient. There's nothing wrong with powdered baking soda as an extinguisher. But it is an unholy mess to clean up afterwards, as the jet-propelled, talcum-like stuff gets into every crevice (that's what you paid for), from which it can be vacuumed for literally weeks afterwards. It is also relatively cheap, because of mass production of the typical 5 B:C type units, which are the minimum size acceptable by the U.S. Coast Guard. Since 10 B:C units are only half again as costly as the 5 B:C type, but have twice as much extinguishing punch, it seems to me that the small cruiser's primary extinguisher ought to be the large size, with smaller ones as backups—but we're getting a little ahead of ourselves.

The *B:C* in the official designation means that the extinguisher is rated efficient against flammable liquids (engine and cooking fuels, for instance) and fires in live electrical components. Some few, more expensive dry chemical units have a different chemical composition and are accordingly rated effective against Type-A fires as well as B and C. Type A, as you might expect, are fires in normally combustible solids such as wood, paper, rubber, etc.

The best galley fire extinguisher, in my opinion, is the CO_2 unit, included on all Coast Guard lists but very hard to find in the average marine supply store. Carbon dioxide, which has no aftertaste when sprayed on a suddenly flaming pan of bacon, for example, is very expensive as a first purchase. Most people would rather stick with the known and inexpensive dry chemical unit, and sacrifice a meal if necessary. The same goes for freon extinguishers, which I have never seen but which are (at this writing) still approved, and foam, which comes in large and bulky containers seldom seen aboard yachts.

About the only frequent use of CO_2 has been in fixed and automatic engine-room fire extinguishing systems aboard powerboats, and these costly installations are now being replaced, in many cases, by a new extinguishing agent called Halon. While not cheap (a unit that will handle a 75-cu.-ft. area goes for the price of a good dinner ashore for four), the new units seem to me excellent automatic protection for cruising sailboats with gasoline engines in relatively inaccessible spaces.

Finally, one ought not to forget the very efficient fire extinguishing agent with which the boat is normally surrounded: water. It will dilute alcohol in stove fires until it cannot support combustion, and will of course extinguish all Class-A fires as well. The problems, however, are two: One wants to avoid taking too much water aboard, as it will create a situation as bad as the fire it's extinguishing; and second, water is no good against live electrical fires (it will conduct the electricity) or against flammable liquids, which will usually ride on top of the water, still flaming away.

Firefighting strategy

In a marine fire, one often has only a couple of minutes to do whatever is going to be done before matters are out of hand. Firefighting strategy is fairly basic in a small cruiser, but a little preplanning is possible. First, determine as best you can the danger areas where fire is likely to occur—engine and fuel compartments, galley, cabin heater, and oil lamp. Now try to picture what would happen if a fire were suddenly discovered in each place; consider your courses of action if you were on deck and the fire below, and if you were below and the fire were between you and open air.

My own feeling is that one ought first to have an extinguisher in the cockpit, right near the helm. It should be instantly available, yet shielded from the weather—not an easy thing to accomplish. Probably the best location is a bracket just inside a cockpit seat locker, but not on the underside of the hatch, as the extinguisher will fall free every time you slam the lid. Ideally, you should be able to see the extinguisher's pressure gauge when you open the hatch, so you'll be alerted if the compressed air charge is leaking.

Down below, you will of course want an extinguisher near the galley stove. But not too near. Bear in mind too that if the galley is aft, the engine compartment is immediately adjacent: The extinguisher should not be so placed that an explosion in the engine area might wipe out the bracketed extinguisher—also so that it can be reached from the cockpit in case the cook is the other side of the fire.

Beyond that, it seems to me that there should be one more extinguisher forward, especially if your pocket cruising yacht is compartmented. Should the worst occur, the occupants of the forward cabin may want an extinguisher to buy time while they extricate themselves through the tight forehatch.

Fire extinguishers should be overhauled every season or annually—ask your local marina, and if they can't help, call your fire department. Apart from this expert treatment, you should get into the habit of looking at the extinguisher gauge every time you pass. It's a matter of a second or less, but you may be surprised, as I have been, to find the pressure suddenly way down on one unit, for no perceptible reason. And if you have an extra beyond the legal requirement, you won't be so reluctant to take the depleted extinguisher ashore and have it refilled.

Beyond that, any extinguisher should be turned in for recharging any time it's been used, even momentarily. This is especially important for the dry chemical type, which are virtually one-shots. Once the initial burst of powder is released, some of it is bound to get into the nozzle and shutoff, and while you may be able to get several bursts from the instrument, it's more than likely that there will be a slight jamming, and thus a slow leak, in the nozzle someplace.

Man overboard

For most skippers, particularly those who have done any single-handing at all, the thought of man overboard is perhaps the most chilling of all. The first thing to remember is that there is almost never an adequate excuse for someone's falling overboard: It is nearly always carelessness, sometimes equipment failure, but it should not have happened. The prevention of man overboard is a perfect instance of combining proper equipment and proper procedure. Let us consider first the gear and then how to make best use of it and general good seamanship.

The basic personnel-retention system is your boat's pulpits and lifelines. Notice the plurals. Boat buyers are much more sophisticated about lifeline systems than they were only a few years ago, when screwed-down pulpits were common. That's not to say that all such gear is good yet. Some of it is junk by the most generous definition, but more and more gear is at least adequate.

The basic lifeline system for a cruiser is well specified in the Offshore Racing Council's list of safety gear for ocean racers. Their prescription is interesting. For cruiser-racers rating more than 21 feet (which is to say, boats 25 to 27 feet overall and longer), the rules require a

> fixed bow pulpit (forward of headstay) and stern pulpit (unless lifelines are so rigged as to adequately substitute for a stern pulpit). Pulpits and stanchions must be through-bolted or welded. . . . Taut double lifelines, with upper . . . line . . . at a height not less than two feet above the working deck, to be permanently supported at intervals of not more than seven feet. A taut lanyard of synthetic rope may be used to secure lifelines, provided that when in position its length does not exceed four inches. Lower lifelines need not extend to the bow pulpit. Lifelines

Asking for trouble: Handling the jib on the bowsprit can be very tricky. A roller-furling unit would be a good idea.

need not be affixed to the bow pulpit if they terminate at, or pass through, adequately braced stanchions two feet above the working deck, set inside of and overlapping the bow pulpit, provided that the gap between the upper lifeline and the bow pulpit shall not exceed six inches.

Yachts rating less than 21 feet are required to carry only a single taut lifeline not less than 18 inches above the working deck, plus bow and stern pulpits (or an arrangement of lifelines as above, substituting for a stern pulpit). If the lifelines are more than 22 inches above the deck, a second, intermediate lifeline must be fitted. For races held in protected waters only, no stern pulpit is necessary, and lifelines need be carried only to the midpoint of the cockpit.

The ORC is mute about the actual construction of the lifelines and stanchions, but in his authoritative manual, *Skene's Elements of Yacht Design,* Francis Kinney quotes the following for a boat 25 feet on the waterline and 10 feet longer overall. Since the size and heft of the lifeline system relates more to the humans who may be thrown against it than to the size of the yacht, Mr. Kinney's figures seem to me to be worth passing on. For the lines themselves, he specifies plastic-covered quarter-inch wire of 7×7 construction, with a five-sixteenths-inch turnbuckle. The stanchions (height not specified) are to be 1 inch outside diameter, Monel or stainless tubing, with a .083 inch wall thickness. The stanchions and pulpits are to be weldments of the same tubing and all vertical members are to be through-bolted to oak backing blocks.

Certainly these specifications are hardly perfect in terms of retaining people in the boat. A lifeline 18 inches off the deck will hit the average person at just about knee height, while a two-foot line will strike most people at mid-thigh. In either case, a line may do more to topple a standing crewmember than retain

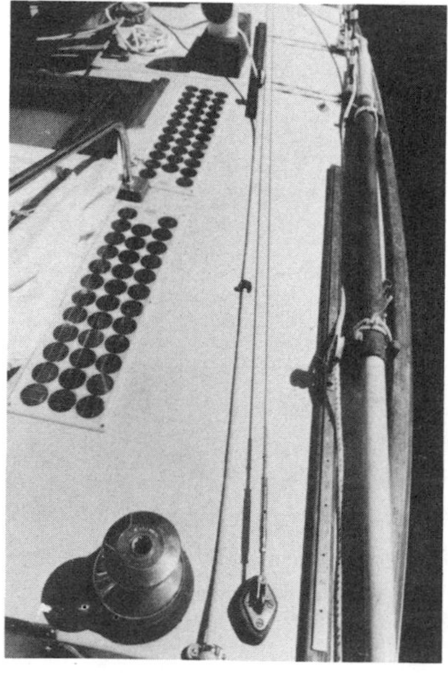

Jackline along the deck allows a crewmember to hook on at cockpit, work all the way forward without unhooking. Note also solar panels, sweep lashed on deck aboard this engineless Frances 26.

him. But one must remember that a sailboat's foredeck, especially today, is not a playpen but an area over which sails must move relatively unimpeded. It is better for crewmembers to adjust their working stance than to add lifeline stanchions that are unrealistically high.

Workers on deck in rough weather will probably find themselves braced more often against a good toerail than a lifeline anyway. Although seldom seen on small boats, a toerail that's three inches or so above the edge of the deck will make a good bulwark to place one's feet against. Likewise, when working forward in heavy weather you'll want to hook on your personal lifeline. Snapping it to the boat's lifelines is tempting but not a good idea, if only because of the leverage created if you do go over the side. Better support is obtained from a wire jackline, running the length of the working deck on either side, and shackled (in rough weather) to pad eyes through-bolted forward, and also level with the cockpit coaming. With this device, which I first saw aboard a 30-footer that was embarking on a single-handed circumnavigation, a sailor may snap on as he leaves the cockpit and not have to fuss with hooks again as long as he's on deck. By making the jackline quarter-inch 7×7 wire (stainless but *not* plastic coated), one may eliminate much of the stretch that makes any rope safety line such a tenuous-seeming device. Obviously, the jackline should not impinge on a fiberglass deckhouse or other structure, or it'll saw its way through in short order.

If this is not possible, so-called ears, or loops, on the bases of the lifeline stanchions will at least make good strong points for harness safety-line attachment, although they won't help with the problem of moving forward and aft. These ears are also excellent for making fast preventers, barber-haulers, and vangs.

More and more stern pulpits are now being built with integral hinged boarding ladders. To my mind, this European innovation is even more important and useful than the last great bit of continental engineering, the foredeck anchor well. Such a ladder makes man-overboard recovery much simpler, especially from today's high-sided cruisers, and it is also a marvelous, out-of-the-way location for the swimming and dinghy ladder. Some ladders are even engineered so that they can serve as gangplanks when the boat is moored stern-to a pier, but this seems rather a lot to ask.

Finally, if your boat has a very strong transom-hung rudder, like the ones seen on many pseudo-Colin Archer designs, it's not a bad idea to put a couple of steps on the rudder itself, one just above the waterline, and another a foot or so higher, to serve as handholds and footholds in emergencies. This rig doesn't substitute for a regular ladder, but it may be a worthwhile supplement.

In heavy weather or after dark, it's important that all hands on deck be protected from falling overboard by appropriate safety harnesses, with adequate emergency equipment, so that they can be found if by some chance they do go over. There are numerous makes of harness on the market, and among the best of them seem to be the units marketed in the U.S. by the Atlantis foul-weather-gear company. In selecting one or another, here are some points to consider: First, one ought to be able to move about the deck in severe conditions without ever having to be completely unhooked from a strongpoint; this implies a double safety line with two snap hooks, or a single extralong line with one hook in the middle and another at the end. The hooks themselves can be either the so-called carbine hooks used by mountaineers or heavy-duty snaps, but they should have positive locks so that they cannot come undone accidently. The lightweight, spring-loaded bronze hooks that are sometimes seen just don't seem heavy enough for an adult's harness, although they're adequate for small children, who can't undo the heavier hooks.

Second, if one's weight ever does come on the safety line, it will probably take up with a savage jolt. The normal attachment point for the safety line is about at the midpoint of the ribcage, with the main element of the harness encircling the chest just under the arms. It's held up by a pair of integral webbing suspenders that invariably twist and make donning a wet harness in the middle of the night one of the more ingenious physical tortures since the rack. A way to avoid the twisting and struggling, and of minimizing the jolt if the harness is ever used in earnest, is to secure the harness onto the outside of a float-coat (see life preserver section below), either by stitching the harness permanently in place or affixing it temporarily with Velcro patches. Either way, one shrugs on the jacket and the harness at the same time, and the padded jacket will absorb at least part of the shock of one's weight coming abruptly onto the straps. If a jacket seems too heavy or hot, you may use one of the life vests that has a cloth cover over Ensolite closed-cell foam. (This fact, incidentally, makes Velcro attachments especially appealing, as one may attach the same harness to jacket or vest as preferred.)

Obviously the link or buckle joining the two ends of the harness belt must be at least as strong as the snaphooks, and as easily released if necessary. One would think that it would be at least as obvious to have all the metal parts rustproofed as well, although this detail seems to have escaped the attention of many harness makers. Personally, I have had better luck with galvanized snap hooks and buckles than with apparently stainless ones, which invariably begin to rust (the snap hook springs are never stainless) after the damp harness has been hung, (as sooner or later it will be,) in a stuffy foul-weather-gear locker. Finally, the harness belt should have a couple of D rings for attaching a sailor's knife, pliers, or other tools.

Part of the personal safety rig should also be a small man-overboard light and a whistle. In the former category, opinions seem divided as to whether the light should be fixed or a flashing strobe. My feeling is that a swimmer in steep seas will be obscured, along with his light, a good deal of the time anyway, and a fixed light maximizes the amount of time he'll be visible from a low, heaving deck. The whistle should never, I feel, be the standard police variety with a little cork ball, as this tiny sphere will soon become even tinier shreds, eliminating the whistle entirely. Far better is one of the minuscule flat plastic whistles made to military specifications with no moving parts. They are sold by many chandlers and appear virtually indestructible, as well as being capable of emitting a whistle of physically painful intensity; at all events it should not be metal if you are likely to be afloat in freezing weather.

It's possible also to carry a small dye marker and an envelope of shark repellent. While I have no intrinsic prejudice against the former, dye markers do tend to let go at odd moments, and it seems to me likely that one worn on the person, and subject to being flattened, will probably result in a yellow foredeck rather than a mark for the search party. As for shark repellent, I have yet to read of a substance that has been proven to repel sharks, and indeed I recall seeing some research that indicated certain long-favored repellents (including one used for a while by the U.S. Navy) attracted certain sharks while being ignored by others.

Man-overboard rig

What's suitable for festooning a presumably active deckhand and what ought to be attached to a man-overboard rig set up in the rigging are different things. The latter appliance stays immobile till wanted, and so it can contain more items of gear—provided that they don't interfere with launching the device quickly. To see what I mean, let's consider all the elements a complete man-overboard rig might be comprised of.

The basic part is the life preserver, most commonly a horseshoe buoy. This is a semirigid shape of closed-cell foam, enclosed in a removable vinyl cover of yellow or international orange. The open ends of the horseshoe can normally be closed by a short length of plastic-covered wire with a snap hook at one end. The horseshoe lives in a plastic-covered steel bracket or a plastic pocket secured to the stern pulpit or to the mizzen shrouds of a ketch or yawl. The idea is that the helmsman can flip the buoy instantly over the side in aid of a person overboard, but the bracket, which has to compromise between quick release and a secure grip on a valuable piece of gear, is frequently less than successful. In addition, the short line between the open ends of the buoy is all too often snapped in such a way that it has to be unhooked before the horseshoe can clear the bracket.

Since the short line is only a secondary part anyway, I leave it unhooked when the horseshoe is in its bracket, but some busybody inevitably tidies up by snapping it—through the bracket, as often as not. To this imperfect device there attaches a bewildering array of gear:

1. A floating strobe light, hung upside down from its own bracket alongside the buoy and activated by being turned right side up.
2. A whistle.

3. A drogue, or small sea anchor, to keep the lightweight horseshoe from skipping over the sea in high winds. (Obviously, someone must deploy the drogue before the rig goes over, or it must be so arranged that throwing the rig will automatically release the drogue.)
4. A man-overboard pole, attached (if one goes by IOR rules) to the ring by twenty-five feet of floating line. The pole is ballasted to float upright, at least in moderate winds, and to meet IOR standards must be long enough to carry a flag eight feet above the water. The flag is normally the diagonally divided red and yellow International Code letter *O,* meaning "man overboard."
5. Dye marker, required by IOR.
6. Shark repellent.

Getting this tidy lot over the side in calm water can be an operation, and a little imagination will suggest what's involved in springing it when the waves are high, the wind is howling, it's pitch-black and raining buckets and you're petrified by a real emergency.

Ocean racers, who look at these matters more seriously than most people, often construct long tubes under the decks of their boats, with an open end in the transom. The horseshoe buoy sits in its rack on the rail, and the pole, attached to it, lies in wait in the tube. Heaving the horseshoe tugs free the pole. Most cruising yachts, however, aren't equipped like this, and if they carry a pole at all, it's usually lashed so securely in a bracket of its own along the backstay that five minutes' work is required to release it, and you may or may not remember, as it goes over, to slip the little protective envelope off the tightly rolled flag at the top.

With the possible exception of number 6 above, each of these items has a real utility, so one cannot simply dismiss the rig as ridiculous, although it is obviously impractical. One can, however, take steps to set it for the least amount of hassle. Your own ingenuity is the best guide, but here are some suggestions: First, combine the man-overboard pole and the strobe light. This makes one less string, one less lumpy piece of gear to tangle in the ejecting process. Man-overboard poles with a built-in strobe at the top are somewhat more expensive than the two items sold separately, but they seem to me to be well worth it.

Make sure that your horseshoe is set in its rack ready for release, with nothing hooked to the frame. Some horseshoes have small pockets sewed to the vinyl cover. These are ideal for the whistle and the dye marker. The drogue should be carefully inserted in a vinyl envelope (most come with something like this) which is itself attached to the pulpit or ring bracket, so that heaving the ring pulls the drogue out in a streamed position, clear of the boat. The pole is probably best located upright along the backstay, with its base in a socket —an ordinary flagpole socket will do. The little protective cover that keeps the nylon *O* flag from deteriorating in sunlight can form the upper end of the holding system. By stitching the cover tightly to the backstay with sailmaker's thread, it will make a sort of socket of its own. Be sure the flag is stuffed into the cover, not wrapped around the staff.

To launch the rig, lift up on the pole to clear the socket, then pull down and throw it over. Now lift the horseshoe, which will be straining at its leash, and release that, streaming the drogue as it goes. Practice will help make the motion foolproof and will illustrate to all hands why correct stowage is vital.

When sailing shorthanded well offshore, many sailors fasten a length of line to the helm and trail it astern. If a man alone on deck falls overboard, he grabs the line (a knot on the end will help), is towed along, and makes the boat alter course and come up into the wind, thus alerting the watch below or allowing the man in the water time to climb back aboard.

Flares and EPIRBs

In emergencies, of course, one wants a more attention-getting device than the ordinary running light. Under the general heading of emergency, we can include times when you want some other vessel to approach and also when you want him to sheer off. The traditional nighttime distress signal for small cruising boats has been the hand-held red flare, a close cousin to the highway flare carried in many cars. About the only major difference is that while a highway fusee has a spike for jamming it between cracks in the paving, the nautical flare has a wooden handle.

Flares come in two colors, white and red. A white flare means nothing more than, "I'm here, watch out for me." Its primary purpose is to indicate your position to a large and closing vessel; it is also an acknowledgement of having seen somebody else's SOS. A red flare, on the other hand, is a call for help: It means, "I am in distress," and is an invitation for another craft to come near you, so don't employ the one if you really mean to pass on the other's message.

Better than hand-held flares, although somewhat less reliable, are the aerial variety, also white and red, and with the same significance. A hand-held flare can only fail to ignite; an aerial flare may not fire, and even if it attains full height, it may then not burst. But if it does work as it's supposed to, an aerial flare is noticeable for a far greater distance than a hand-held one. The best aerial flares are the parachute variety. These are larger and much more expensive than the ordinary meteor-type flares. The former rise to the top of their trajectory, then descend relatively slowly under a small parachute, burning all the while. White parachute flares can be used in emergencies to illuminate a goodly stretch of sea, although they will destroy the night vision of anyone in the area. Meteor flares rise to the same height, but arc swiftly down to the sea again. They are considerably less likely to attract the attention of someone not actually searching for you.

Standard aerial flares are fired from a wide-barreled, breech-loading Very pistol, which comes in either 12-gauge or 25-mm. muzzle diameter. There is not a great deal to choose between the two sizes, but do make sure that your flares match your pistol. When using the pistol, remember that it has a mule-like kick and brace yourself before pulling the trigger.

In recent years, pyrotechnics manufacturers have come out with hand launchers, often referred to as "pen guns" because they aren't a great deal larger than an oversize fountain pen. These units shoot small flares in various colors, but in my opinion they aren't nearly as visible as the larger, old-fashioned variety. Pen guns, like the Very pistols, often come under state and local firearms or handgun regulations. Check with your local Coast Guard Auxiliary or police about this. There is no question that large numbers of mariners do carry Very pistols, even in the waters of the U.K. and states like New York, which have strict gun laws, and practically none of these pistols are licensed. Let your conscience be your guide.

In the daytime, even the brightest red or white flare is a pale imitation of its nighttime self. Under most conditions, a hand-held orange smoke signal is a far better attention-getting device, and virtually free from the slag problem that bedevils flares. Orange smoke works well in all but high winds, but there is nothing better. A proper distress-signal kit contains both day and night signals. There are numerous other distress signals, many of which are packed into commercially produced distress-signal packets. A stainless-steel signaling mirror is not a bad device, especially when one is being searched for by professionals who know how to look. And a large red or international orange flag will help search-and-rescue personnel distinguish your boat from the others.

There are other distress signals more or less recognized by trained people alert to their meaning. One is a large red or orange rectangular flag with a square and a circle, both black, on its surface. Another consists of the International Code flags *N* over *C.* A third is, of course, the national or yacht ensign flown upside down. Personally, I doubt that any of them, except perhaps the last, would attract much interest from the average passing yacht.

There are, after all, two parts to a successful distress signal: giving notice of the situation and guiding the rescuers to your position. The first part is frequently the more difficult, especially when one is depending on visual distress signals in this increasingly electronically oriented age. A couple of years ago I was privileged to attend a Coast Guard–sponsored display of day and night visual distress signals, held on the waters of Chesapeake Bay. My feeling afterwards, like many others, was that visual distress signals are better than nothing, but that they have a long way to go before they're adequate.

By and large, a good visual distress signal will attract the attention of a trained person who's already looking for you, and will guide him to your location. So how do you alert him in the first place? One of the most promising developments in recent years has been the emergency position-indicating radio beacon, or EPIRB. The standard offshore EPIRB is closely related to the aircraft ELT (emergency locator transmitter); It transmits a wordless alarm signal on two frequencies monitored by military and civilian aircraft. This signal will be reported to the Coast Guard, who can then dispatch units equipped with special RDF equipment to track you down.

Technically, EPIRBs require an FCC license, which now costs nothing and is no great problem to acquire. They are also supposed to be restricted to vessels that regularly venture well offshore, which doesn't really apply to the kinds of yachts we're discussing. Still, a coastal racer or cruiser could hardly be harmed by carrying an EPIRB of the standard type. Just coming into use as I write is a far more useful device, the Class C EPIRB for inland craft. As designed, this unit will transmit on VHF-FM channels 15 and 16 alternately, and will have a relatively short range. It will be receivable by any vessel with a VHF, of course, but only specially equipped units will be able to home on it, since special direction-finding gear will be required. The price will probably be well under a week's wages, and it should provide excellent distress signaling capability for those whose sailing is within ten miles or so of shore.

An EPIRB's self-contained battery is designed to operate for an extended period, so if you ever have occasion to set one off, let it transmit continuously. Don't do as so many panicked mariners do—turn the set on for five minutes, then off for a couple of hours: This makes direction finding virtually impossible. In coastal waters, someone will hear you fairly soon, so once you've activated the device, leave it alone.

When the Coast Guard comes after a distressed vessel, they use both direction-finding gear and radar, and small pleasure craft make rotten radar targets by and large. Although there is still considerable disagreement about what is an adequate size for small-craft radar reflectors, just about all authorities agree that most yachtsmen, abetted by the reflectors' manufacturers, mount their reflectors in the most inefficient position possible. The ordinary yacht-style radar reflector consists of two slotted squares of aluminum (sometimes foil-covered cardboard) so joined that they are at right angles to each other along a common axis. A third square is inserted at right angles to the plane of the first two, and the resulting shape yields eight three-dimensional triangular corners which presumably catch the incoming radar signal and, rather like a jai-alai player, shoot it back whence it came. The problem is that the units are mounted with the first two squares in a diamond shape relative to the horizon, and the third horizontal to the horizon, which many authorities feel is minimally efficient in reflecting and amplifying the radar signal. It is far better, they say, to hang the reflector in the aptly named "catch-rain" position, when it is more likely to do its job efficiently.

First-aid kit

Virtually all crusing yachts, large and small, carry something that's labeled a first-aid kit, but few of these containers are adequate for even minor emergencies. I'm not for a moment suggesting that the average weekend cruiser needs the sort of elaborate Dr. Mitty surgical chest that strikes terror into one's crew, but it is a good precaution to consider the ordinary and peculiar first-aid requirements common to sailors and prepare for them.

By ordinary, I mean the standard injuries that boating flesh is heir to—near-drowning, scrapes, cuts, rope burns, insect and jellyfish stings, splinters, sunburn and of course seasickness. There are numerous reasonably priced first-aid kits that are equipped to deal with these common situations, but they are often without seasickness remedies. If you have a family physician who's also a yachtsman, ask him what he carries aboard—he may be able to advise you in terms of your own family's situation, without even getting into prescription drugs.

By peculiar first-aid problems, I refer not only to sailors' regular problems, but also those peculiar to your own crew. These can require anything from foot powder to digitalis, and such special remedies are, I think, best sequestered from the primary first-aid kit, in a special watertight container plainly marked both outside and on the container for each remedy—who, what for, how much and how often, and expiration date if applicable. Finally, a good first-aid kit must be keyed to a good first-aid pamphlet or book. There are now several good ones, listed in the bibliography. It doesn't matter which you select, but make sure that your medical supplies match the recommendations of the doctor-author in each case, or there's little point in having the instructions.

In your log, or wherever you keep such information, you should have a checklist of the first-aid kit's contents. Any time an item is used, it should be checked off and replaced. Twice in the past season, I have seen extremely well equipped and elaborate high-seas kits come up short when someone wanted a Band-Aid—although each had started the year with a couple dozen at least.

Life rafts

Although not one in a hundred small cruising yachts carries one, the life raft is gradually assuming its proper place as a primary self-rescue tool when all else fails. There are several types and designs of rafts, but all share a common characteristic that is worth thinking about. As a Coast Guard official in the safety equipment department once remarked, a raft is not a miraculous device, but simply another vessel, smaller than the one you're abandoning. It may or may not do its job, but it demands the same qualities (if not the same details) of seamanship that its predecessor did.

For most skippers of small yachts, a life raft is something one carries only if required to do so by offshore racing equipment rules. And it is fair to say that for most of us, the primary life raft decision is whether to invest in one in the first place. Probably not, for most of us in inshore waters: A thoughtful weighing of the odds suggests that it would probably be better to spend the money—as much as a fifth or a quarter of the parent vessel's cost—on better equipment for her. For those who do race, or who regularly venture offshore, the question of life rafts deserves serious thought. The first point to make, I think, is that one's dinghy—however good it may be as a dinghy—is simply not qualified to serve as a proper life raft, for two important reasons.

First, a dinghy is designed as a conveyance and load carrier, not a life-supporting vehicle; the demands of the two uses are quite different, the most obvious being that a proper life raft, with a canopy overhead and an inflatable bottom beneath, is designed to protect survivors from exposure, quite as dangerous to them as drowning. Second, in case of a yacht's sinking, she is likely first to have undergone a protracted agony that will have left her crew in near shock. A life raft is engineered to be launched and inflated with the minimum thought and effort, and she carries her own emergency supplies, which makes it unnecessary for the skipper or crew to remember to take them off the parent vessel.

So if you need an emergency boat as an adjunct to your yacht, only a proper life raft will serve. The question, of course, is: What's a proper life raft? Although its definition is inadequate, the ORC has made a stab at one, and it will provide a starting point:

1. capable of carrying the entire crew;
2. designed and used solely for saving life;
3. have at least two separate buoyancy compartments, each of which must be automatically inflatable; each raft must be capable of carrying its rated capacity with one compartment deflated;
4. must have a canopy to cover the occupants;
5. must have been inspected, tested, and approved within two years by the manufacturer or other competent authority; and
6. must have certain safety equipment "appropriately secured" to each raft, as follows—sea anchor, bellows or pump, signaling light, three hand flares, bailer, repair kit, paddles, knife.

For long-distance races only, the ORC further requires emergency food and water. Coast Guard authorities would say that the emergency water would be more important than some other things, and should be carried on all rafts.

An international convention on the Safety of Life at Sea (SOLAS) has formulated far more stringent criteria, especially as regards construction. Any raft advertised as meeting or exceeding the SOLAS standards is a first-class device, and should be considered top-of-the-line safety gear.

In recent years there has been a considerable controversy over raft design, between an inventor-entrepreneur named James Givens and the life-saving establishment, including the U.S. Coast Guard. A self-taught expert, Givens became convinced that because they had a tendency to capsize standard life rafts were basically unsafe in rough seas. Righting them—assuming it could be done—sapped the strength of the occupants to a point where they might succumb to exposure or fatigue. Givens has produced a raft that bears his name, and which is equipped with a massive water chamber below the body of the raft (which is itself much like standard rafts). The idea is that when the raft is inflated by pulling the ripcord, the water chamber sinks below the raft and fills in a matter of a minute or so at the most. The stabilizing effect of this chamber, says Givens, will prevent the raft from capsizing.

The Givens raft has now been approved by the U.S. Coast Guard. It seems to many detached observers a significant contribution to life-saving technology, although the same people may reject the idea that standard rafts, without the massive water chamber stabilizers, are inherently dangerous. For one thing, they have saved too many people to be viewed negatively. Since costs of standard and Givens rafts are in the same ball park, it appears to this observer that if one sails in an area where short, steep seas are prevalent, the buoy raft is well worth considering over others. In other onshore areas, almost any SOLAS raft or even the yacht-type version of the same (usually with abbreviated accessory kits and no inflatable double bottom) will be a significant addition to one's safety gear.

Whichever raft one selects, it's important to mount it properly so that it can be launched easily in emergency. For my money, the only type of raft container worth having is the rigid fiberglass canister—the old-fashioned valise pack not only admits water (which may freeze in cold climates and damage the contents) but also allows the raft to be damaged by careless crewmembers tramping all over it, something perhaps more likely to happen in a small yacht than in a large one. The canister should be of the type that will open by hydrostatic pressure if the parent vessel sinks, and then allow the self-inflating raft to bob to the surface. The raft's location, then, should be in a place where it can float free without snagging, yet not be washed overboard by a breaking sea. It should also be someplace where a battered crew can get at it without having to crawl over a wave-swept deck. In most modern yachts, the best place will be well aft, where the boat's design can best support the extra weight, perhaps at the aft end of the cockpit, where the canister can serve as an extra seat.

VII

Getting a Boat

The normal way to acquire a boat (if "normal" is a word to use for such an act) is to buy her, either new or secondhand. One can also build her oneself, either from scratch or from a partly complete version. My purpose here is to examine the advantages and disadvantages of each course of action. To put my cards immediately on the table, I have bought and sold a number of completed boats, both new and used, with and without brokers, and I have—just once—become involved in attempting to complete one from a hull-and-deck molding. Each experience has its lessons, some more instructive, and painful, than others.

Most prospective boat owners face only the question of buying new as opposed to buying secondhand. For many years, the primary factor in this decision was financial: One balanced the considerable savings implicit in a used boat against the degree of decay and disarray one was virtually sure to find. In recent years, however, the picture has changed markedly, and while there are still excellent reasons to buy either new or used, they are not necessarily the ones that existed only a few years ago.

Buying new

Perhaps the main reason to buy a new boat—or a new anything—is the intangible and satisfying sense of newness it imparts. There is no point analyzing this wholly subjective feeling. You know what I mean. There are, however, some quite genuine reasons for preferring a new cruising boat to one that's been ravished—er, *owned*—before. First, you will have no previous owner's mistakes to undo. The additional winch, wrongly sited; the tiddly wooden rack still unused in the main cabin; the unfortunate color scheme—all of these can be real annoyances, genuine devaluators of even a fine boat (and the possibilities should be borne in mind by you, every time you pick up a screwdriver to attach some new gadget to *your* pride and joy: How will that look to the next owner?).

On a more positive note, with a new boat you can make many of the essential equipment choices yourself, not having to accept or at least seriously consider previous owner's purchases. If there are major equipment options, such as a steering wheel or a pressure water system, it may well be far cheaper to install such devices when the boat is being built than to work between decks afterwards. In addition, a new boat escapes the visible and invisible aspects of wear and tear. This can be something as obvious as a badly chafed sail, as easy to overlook as a chain locker bulkhead beginning to delaminate, or as impossible to see as a corrosion problem in the mast step.

In terms of decoration, a new boat is far easier to personalize than one that someone else has imposed his own personality upon. It is often surprising how permanent small details of decor can be. Every plaque leaves a nail hole or four, and even glued-on curtain rod bases cannot easily be removed without traces. Practically speaking, an owner is certain to install equipment at heights and distances convenient for his eye or reach, and they may not work well for you at all. Like what? How about the increasingly popular bulkhead-mounted steering compass—any owner will instinctively saw his locator hole in the main bulkhead at a spot just below his own line of sight. And he will invariably choose a compass of a make you don't particularly care for.

One occasional gambler's benefit in a new boat is the "introductory price." Of course this is at least partly a gimmick to get a new class of boat rolling, but it can be a genuine savings as well. It is not at all unusual for a new class to make its first few boat-show appearances at a base price that's significantly lower than the competition's. Should you bite? There are several things to weigh carefully.

First, why is the price so low? There are only four likely reasons: the boat itself is built less carefully, of lower quality materials (and fewer of them); or it's built in an area or by a method that allows significant savings in construction costs other than materials; or the pricing is a deliberate, temporary inducement to get a healthy class started fast; or the builder has simply underpriced his product.

Of these possibilities, the first is, alas, the most common. There are some fairly common clues that suggest when a boat is the product of skimping. First, look at the standard hardware. Is it husky and of good brand-name quality? Marine hardware is a truly international commodity these days, and British Lewmar winches, French Goiot hatches and American Harken blocks are seen everywhere. Beware of vessels with anonymous hardware, or stuff that's suspiciously small compared with gear on other boats of the same size.

Then compare the boat's displacement with others of the same dimensions (not just length, but beam, hull depth, and keel weight as well). To a considerable extent, materials equal cost, so that less material means a cheaper boat. One has to be careful, of course, as modern design and construction have produced ultralight vessels of great strength and high quality. The thing to watch out for here is very light weight and suspiciously low cost—a properly built lightweight is a sophisticated and complex product and cannot be all that cheap.

Finally, one of your best safeguards is reputation. Not only the reputation of the builder, as this can go up and down in a remarkably short time, but also the reputation of the designer, whose name is likely to be more enduring, for good or ill. I am personally wary of vessels that carry no designer's name at all, and only a little less suspicious of boats whose design is credited to the builder's own "design team." While many builders can and do maintain a long-lasting relationship with a single naval architect, only the very largest can afford to operate their own design departments, and even they will usually pull in an outside accredited architect for at least part of the job.

It is possible that a boat's low price may be due to some savings inherent in semi mass production or locally low labor or materials costs. This situation obtained throughout the Orient up to about ten years ago, and one could buy a beautifully (if somewhat idiosyncratically) built boat from Hong Kong at a great break. Such is not the case anymore: You save on the hand-detailed woodwork, but you don't get the sophisticated construction, and the extra costs of shipping and duty equalize the final price. Some builders now offer package-deal boats, sold on the old Henry Ford theory—you can have any color you like in your Model T, as long as it's black. These builders set up a careful production line that allows an undeviating construction schedule for a sailaway boat. The result is indeed inexpensive, and the process is quite respectable, but in order to maintain the low cost, the builder is truly unable to make any optional alterations in his schedule.

Bringing in a new model of boat at a very low price is an old and tried tactic, and one that appeals to the gambler in many buyers: If the boat catches on, its price will undoubtedly rise rapidly in only a few months, and your early-bird investment will look pretty good. I bought a 30-footer once for about $13,000 (yes, it was a while back) and within six months the price had gone up $1,500. Of course, if the boat fails to catch on, the builder's early in-the-red sales will just make his eventual demise more spectacular, and you may wind up owning a pretty good boat that's a design orphan and hard to dispose of. Perhaps worse is the situation in which a boat *almost* catches on, after an initial low-price offering. The builder, fighting inflation, isn't making anything, yet he doesn't dare raise the price. What does he do? You guessed it—he cheapens the product, dropping a layer of mat here, eliminating backup plates on the hardware there, until by the time he does go under, his boat has the reputation of being a real turkey.

I've had good luck with initially low-priced boats, but I think the key here is not allowing yourself to be entranced by the price. If the boat is a front-runner in all respects, price aside, and would be one of your short list of three or four even if her price were level with the top of the field, *then* throw the price factor into your decision-making process.

The final reason for a low price on a new model—a simple costing mistake by the builder or importer—isn't as silly as it sounds. It happens in every industry, including the theater: When the stage production of *Around the World in 80 Days* opened, it was a couple of weeks before some bookkeeper figured that, with every seat in the house sold, the show was still losing several thousand dollars a week. Likewise, a number of very good builders have discovered, after selling their first half dozen boats, that the price simply isn't high enough for them to make any profit. A man may be a brilliant builder and a rotten accountant, and the boat business seems very prone to this kind of thing. It is especially rampant in the field of importing, where costs are tricky to figure, and many a beginner has simply translated the European builder's price into U.S. dollars, with the freight and customs charges thrown in.

The results to the buyer of accidental low pricing of a model are much the same as if the builder does it on purpose: If he recovers in time and gets his price up while maintaining customer acceptance, the builder or importer will survive, and you, the early buyer, will be in the catbird seat. If he goes under, which is of course somewhat more likely, you'll have a less valuable boat—although if she is an import, she may already have an unassailable international track record.

New boat drawbacks

There are also some common disadvantages to buying new. Most new boats, even the so-called sailaway packages, are far from complete by any rational standard. While it may be safe to take them away from a pier with the gear that they carry upon delivery, it's far from satisfying. No matter how carefully one budgets, there is invariably a considerable amount of material that has to be bought before the boat is truly well found. And many boats arrive with only half the bare essentials or less as part of the base price. There is a logic to this pricing, and it may help to understand it. Builders who figure that their boat is aimed at the beginner in the market, or even the person making the big step up from daysailer to cruiser, are more and more inclined to reverse previous practice and come up with "package" boats—ones that include as close to a complete inventory as the manufacturer can arrange.

The reasoning is straightforward: A buyer who hasn't had cruisers before will be unlikely to have accumulated that trove of carryover gear, from anchors to blankets to compasses, that people somehow acquire as they go from boat to slightly larger boat. Likewise, newcomers to cruising will not be freighted with the iron-clad prejudices as to equipment and location that old-timers—or more often, medium-timers—so often display. Face it, Danforth and Ritchie and Sestrel are all excellent compasses, but there are people who will insist on one or another and who will not be budged; these folks have probably lived with a brand and come to love it.

Some builders of boats aimed at newcomers to the market go on the opposite tack. They are the ones who aim to fluster a buyer with a deliberately low base price, trusting that this is the figure that will stick in his head, and that he won't become steadily more appalled as he begins to add up the list of "optional" extras—mainsail, stove, berth cushions—that the builder so thoughtfully makes available.

More often, a builder aiming at the experienced cruiser will offer as standard items those upon which consensus has been achieved—a diesel inboard, for instance, or four-inch foam mattresses on the berths—while leaving as much running room as possible for options that will help the new owner personalize his yacht—the aforementioned compass, or sails, or wheel steering. If you are the kind of person who feels that a builder has a taste in gear that matches your own, you're fortunate. If not, then you will need to work the equipment accessories into your base-boat budget.

A cruising sailboat, even a small one, is a complicated device and is more than likely to have a certain number of flaws when she's delivered. These can range from bad engineering—an inboard engine exhaust that admits following seas, for instance—to poor workmanship, and they may or may not be covered by warranty, but the odds are regrettably good that you will wind up coping with most of these difficulties, even if it's only chivvying the dealer into living up to the warranty—that is, if you've bought new.

By the same token, your new boat may have arrived with installations or gear that are as advertised but somehow not *quite* what you had in mind. These are really your problem, and you will have to deal with them as best you can. My own feeling, in this respect, is that you can go to boat shows armed with reams of information, can arrive with the experience of years of cruising on your back, and yet a new boat can fake you out just the same, until you've had a chance to sail her and cruise her. Buyers of larger yachts are sometimes able to spend a week or two aboard their boats before purchase, if the models in question are part of a charter fleet somewhere. People buying boats of the size we're talking about don't have that option, because very few 30-footers are economically viable as bareboat charters. You can, of course, query owners—and you should—can arrange to crew aboard a sistership—which is an excellent idea, too—but it takes a couple of weeks of solid experience to realize that the companionway grabrail is about two inches too far from where your hand naturally falls as you go up or down the ladder in a seaway.

Often a newly offered model of cruising yacht has to be bought on faith. One has faith in the designer, the builder, maybe even the sales agent, but all of them can be wrong. The question of a totally new model goes back, of course, to the previous remarks about introductory prices, but many new models arrive without any inducements, or even the negative inducement of a long wait before possible delivery. (Parenthetically, I have a considerable suspicion of boats offered for sale before there is, as it were, one for sail: With fiberglass boats, the main initial expense is tooling and the mold, and I would not invest in a production fiberglass boat until the mold exists and has coughed up at least five boats.)

When you buy new, you buy, more often than not, at list price. There is no lowering of the cost as there's supposed to be in a secondhand model. This problem affects the do-it-yourselfer and bargain hunter more than the average boat buyer, who would go after a used craft in mint condition and pay a new-boat price for it. But the fact is there—you seldom get a break on a new-boat price, and if you do, it's worth being a bit suspicious.

These days, the prices of secondhand cruising yachts tend to be considerably more than the same boats cost when new. Nearly all of this apparent rise in cost is inflation, although some few boats, such as the Tartan 27, may undergo a genuine appreciation beyond the illusionary rise. Still, it is no good looking at the price of a well-used Triton and expecting that a like-new version is going to cost the same kind of money. At the very least, you're looking at another 15 to 20 percent and a good deal of genuine, if unseen, wear and tear.

Building it yourself

A certain number of skippers, having surveyed the market, decide to build their own boats, either from scratch or from a kit. The reasons are various: Some simply don't have the cash for even a down payment on a boat of the size they require. But they can muster enough to start building, or at least they think they can. Others cannot find precisely the kind of boat for them, despite the profusion of designs and redesigns on the market. Others, and these are the rarest, feel an urge to create something of their very own, and somehow decide that their own boat will be better built and more personal than any off-the-shelf model.

Although it is not something I'd do, one cannot summon up an absolute argument against building one's own boat. The most telling counter to most people who announce they're going to do so is to inform them in detail of what they're letting themselves in for. I propose here to examine more or less what is involved in building a boat from various starting points, but first, at the risk of seeming absolute, I would like to suggest some vital attributes for the home boatbuilder.

First and foremost, he or she must be a first-class amateur craftsman. Any botcher can build a bookcase or even a dinghy, but when you attempt something as sizable and consuming as a cruising yacht, you must be really competent. Just as a word in your ear—the average home builder has enough problems squaring off corners, but how about a construct where some of the corners are square but many are not, and some of the primary lines are curves? Think about it.

Second, the would-be builder must love building. Otherwise, what is the point of it all? Better get a second job you do like, and pay the proceeds to a proper builder. Perhaps even more important, the amateur shipwright's family and/or associates must share both his love for boatbuilding and his dream. Otherwise they are unlikely to be around till the end.

Third, the builder must know enough about boats to know when it's essential to stick with the plans and when it's possible to branch out a little. Nearly everyone who builds wants to inject something of himself in the construction, but there are places to do it, and places to avoid a personal variation like the plague. One of the principal reasons for the bad reputation of many of the late Arthur Piver's cruising trimarans was the fact that a number of the home builders could not believe the designer had truly intended three-eighths-inch plywood sheets. Far better, they thought, to have half inch. But Piver had calculated a weight for his yachts. Making the hulls significantly heavier turned seabirds into sitting ducks.

A man who was building a monohull called me recently to inquire about the possibility of adding four feet in the middle. This kind of thing has been done with relatively undemanding commercial vessels, so I suggested he ask the original designer. Too much trouble, my caller replied. Well, I said, there are a lot of books on design in the public library. . . . But no, he answered, he couldn't understand any of them. He finally hung up, I'm sure carrying away the feeling that I was part of an establishment plot to thwart his joy. He will, I have no doubt, produce a horrendous turkey and will be lucky (if he takes it to sea) to escape with his neck.

If you are determined to build your own boat from scratch, you'll need a number of things (besides the attributes outlined above). First, you'll require a good set of tools. Nothing really extraordinary: If you have a tool inventory that would serve to build a small weathertight structure ashore, it will probably be adequate to produce a small cruising yacht. (See the Bibliography for books on boatbuilding, most of which contain lists of the necessary tools.)

Second, you will need a place to build her. This can be your backyard or a vacant lot, but you'll need to check the local ordinances and the neighbors first. Many people found Noah a difficult neighbor, and you may appear no different to a lot of folks. You will also, depending on the boat's size, need access to the water. It's surprising how many people forget this part, but one reads continually of the builder who has had to partially dismantle his boat to get it under a bridge or between two buildings on the way to launching. Unless the climate in your part of the world is unusually benign, you'll also need a weatherproof enclosure under which to build, at least until the hull is sealed in. A scrap-lumber, open-ended shed is probably best, but it too costs money.

Last, you'll need a design. There are several routes to go in finding one. Since yachts have been built for some time, it's likely that somewhere there's a design that's ideal for you, or as near as makes no difference. The difficulty is in isolating it from so many. My own feeling is that it's best to look for the designer first, and then the design. Yacht architecture is still a very personal thing, and most designers soon develop a definite style. Partly, of course, it is a matter of draftsmanship, but there is far more to a designer's character than the way he or she draws.

Your search—and this may well apply to a person looking for a stock boat as well as one intending to build—may most easily begin by reading the boating magazines that feature a regular design section. Chances are considerably against your finding just the right boat in the cross-section of a monthly design report, but you may well begin to notice that your eye is consistently drawn to the way one designer (or several) expresses a cruising concept. The architect who interests you may have published a drawing that has a look you admire, even though the boat itself won't do. Write and ask if he has a book of study plans (many do), and try to be as specific as possible about what you're looking for. It may just be that the person you write has created the kind of boat you want and has done it for a stock builder you haven't run across.

Suppose you run across a stock designer's plan that appeals to you. How can you tell from the magazine article or the study plan if the boat is technically adequate? Well, the answer is that you can't. If the boat you like has appeared in a national magazine, chances are it's respectable: Boat magazines are besieged by architects, and they have become very cautious about which designs they print. The boat may not be a performance world-beater, but she probably comes from an architect with a sound reputation, and she is probably at least superficially adequate—or labeled controversial, if that's her claim to newsworthiness.

But how to determine if a designer is worth consulting just on the basis of an advertisement or a word of mouth? To be honest, it's virtually impossible. Here are a few clues, information a designer will usually volunteer anyway. First, what are his technical qualifications? Although there are still very talented people around who are self-taught yacht designers, I would insist on an engineering or naval architecture degree. The two main home-study courses, NMMA/Westlawn and Yacht Design Institute, are quite adequate as qualifiers. In Britain, membership in the Royal Institute of Naval Architects may—but not necessarily—mean a qualification to design yachts; possession of Southampton's diploma in yacht and boat design, however, does. Next, what has he or she designed that's been built? It need not be a boat you particularly admire, but the owner should be accessible for checking. Or it can be one of a series for a builder, large or small. Obviously, if your designer has created something that's nearly what you want, and it's been built several times, the chances are he can alter it to suit you, or that he knows for sure such alteration is impossible. Either information is valuable.

In the matter of credentials, by the way, anyone can call himself a yacht or boat designer. The term has no official meaning and implies no degree. An architect, on the other hand, is something else, but it is still worth asking the details of the architectural degree.

Finally, ask what the architect's fee schedule will be, and what services he provides. Unless you are buying a stock plan or one that's only slightly altered, chances are you won't get a flat cash answer, as the architect's fee for an individual design will usually run about 10 percent of the boat's cost, and part of the architect's job is supervising the construction to some degree. If you are building her yourself, he should be aware of that fact and be prepared to handle your queries and possibly your psychoanalysis as well.

A stock or semistock plan is much cheaper than an original design, for obvious reasons. It should be something between five and ten dollars per foot of boat, for the rights to build one hull, and reasonable consultation, for a stock plan; and somewhat more for a stock drawing that requires alteration. Do not, whatever else you plan, buy a design with the idea of altering it yourself. As noted earlier, the results of this kind of thing, even with the most forgiving plan, can be utterly disastrous. Unlike racers, cruising boats are less critical in terms of where weights are placed or in details of materials and rig, and it is often possible to effect sizable changes in the basic format without ruining a boat's performance; but the designer is the one to do it, because presumably he knows where the critical points are, and in all likelihood he has run a certain number of possible changes through his mind already and evaluated their effect on the boat.

Most stock plans for cruising yachts are offered for construction in any one of several types of material, and often with one or another rig. The latter changeability isn't wholly a good idea: While a long-keeled heavy boat can perform in much the same way whether she is rigged as a ketch, cutter, or schooner, what all this means is that she is probably no great shakes in any mode. A proper mating of hull, keel, and rig is a genuine marriage, and you can't toss a different partner into the bed without there being a somewhat jarring note. If, on the other hand, the hull design is so lackadaisical that a partnership with any rig is equally acceptable, then the level of acceptability is probably pretty low.

Materials are somewhat different. Given proper strength through engineering, the practical difference among materials is a question of weight. That is, a given strength in wood, fiberglass, or aluminum will produce quite different weights of hull. The heavy material may mean that a lighter keel is necessary, resulting in a boat that's more tender than a lightweight hull of the same shape, with the extra weight in the form of lead ballast. But the point is that an engineer can compensate for these differences in weight and in construction detail, and alter a plan to adapt to any one of several materials without significantly altering its characteristics, at least where a cruiser is concerned.

Kit boats

Completing a kit or from a bare hull would seem at first like a wholly different order of difficulty. After all, isn't the hardest part already done? Perhaps the single best-known and most ignored fact about boatbuilding is that the cost (if not the complexity) of the hull is only a minor fraction of the tab for the completed vessel. The engine, spars, deck gear, and sails all still cost the same. The relative percentages are in a state of flux, as hulls become cheaper and quality interiors more costly, thanks to the shortage of woodworking craftsmen. Kit builders, seeking personalized interiors, feel that they can also save a great deal of money. Maybe.

On the face of it, there are few builders in the kit business, but when one puts the clamps on a builder, especially during periods of economic drought, it is surprising how many production boats can suddenly become available in partly finished form. A part-finished sale in the hand, after all . . . Most serious kit producers offer their boats in several stages of finish, beginning with the truly bare hull—a shell that may take four years or more to finish—at about a sixth the cost of the finished vessel. Next in line as a general rule is a kit that includes the hull, the deck, cabin, and cockpit molding installed, ballast properly glassed in or bolted on, and main bulkheads in place.

Although this second package represents an advance in several major areas, bypassing considerable expertise and heavy tools, there are a lot of critical areas remaining, even before one gets to the actual woodwork. Many builders offer as the next stage a so-called sailaway model, which runs about half the cost of the finished yacht. Sailaway here is an even more misleading word than usual, although the boat in this condition may indeed sail and you may, if you have a lot of Neanderthal blood, even camp out in her while working. Sailaway means the rigging is in—spar, chainplates, and the other essential bits, and perhaps the engine as well, depending. Finally, some firms offer a nearly finished version, with electrical system and plumbing installed, main and ancillary bulkheads in place, and the main elements of hull furniture—bunks and counters—in place. The cost is about 80 percent of the showroom version, and what really is there left to do?

Nothing truly vital, perhaps, but all the tricky, fiddly bits that differentiate a workboat from a yacht, and probably a difference of 50 percent in the resale price. The joinery remaining is the kind of thing that takes hours even for a professional—careful measuring, cutting, offering up (that supremely expressive carpenter's phrase), and recutting. The boat can, of course, be sailed between bouts of work, which may be an important safety valve or an additional delay factor.

Aside from the design and construction of the company-supplied parts of the kit boat, perhaps the most important thing from the point of view of the amateur builder is a source of information and encouragement at the plant. This may be a single person, the mother superior of the kit customers, or it may be good literature or it may be both. At all events, the road to a complete boat is a long, rocky, and lonely one, and expert guidance is very important for most people.

Buying a used boat

Most people, of course, buy a completed boat, and it will probably be the second-largest single purchase (after their home) that they make. There are a number of considerations here; let's start with the buyer of a secondhand cruiser—a "preowned yacht," in the loathsome jargon of some ads. The first question is whether to go after her by yourself or use a broker. There is, of course, no reason why you cannot do both, and if you are looking for an unusual boat it will probably make sense to work both sides of the street.

A broker sells time. Yours. In return for 10 percent of the purchase price (which he receives from the seller, who normally tacks it on to what he wants to receive), the broker saves you the time and effort of chasing down individual listings, or working painfully through hundreds of classifieds in the Sunday paper or boating magazines, of hours spent driving from one boatyard to another. Instead, one goes to a broker's central office, states the requirements, and examines the listings, choosing perhaps half a dozen that may suit. Not all of them will be available still, of course, because the boats will have been sold and the broker not advised, but it can still mean a significant saving in time and frustration. If the broker is a large one, you may be able to cover several states in a single visit, since most people who list with a single broker will list with all the ones they can think of, unless constrained by policy in the marina where their boat is kept. Many boats are listed with a central broker who farms out the listing to others: He gets part of the 10 percent even if another broker sells her.

Once you've picked out a list of possibles, the broker makes the arrangements to look them over, either in or out of the water, depending on the season. He will accompany you to the boat, will at least try to answer your questions from his own fund of knowledge (and misinformation) about the standard designs. If you come to the point of making an offer, the broker will relay it to the owner and will act as middleman in the negotiation that follows. Here his role is delicate: The more the boat is sold for, the bigger is his percentage, but unless the boat is sold at all—and by him rather than someone else—he gets nothing at all. This position produces a certain degree of honesty in the bargaining phase: The broker cannot be expected to advise you as to whether the boat is truly right for you—how can he read your fantasies anyway?—but he can probably be relied on to have a good feel for when one or the other party in a negotiation is seriously out of line. In this area, at least, his advice is well worth listening to.

Once an offer has been made, "subject to survey," in the old phrase, the broker's role is to grease the skids. It is obviously not a good idea to use him as the source of one's surveyor, since the broker at this point is committed to the sale, but do by all means take full advantage of his expertise in terms of sales taxes, registration changeovers, and the like. Once the sale is accomplished, the broker's role is done, he has "brought buyer and seller together," and he is out of the picture. There is no warranty at a brokerage, unless the broker has told you some ascertainable falsehood that caused you to buy the boat in question, and very few brokers would be caught in that trap.

In using the services of a yacht broker, then, you are paying for your own convenience, and not a great deal more. In buying larger boats than we are talking about here, the broker may have all sorts of elaborate secondary functions, and this kind of sale, where the commission runs into the thousands instead of the hundreds, is what brokers live for and on. From a broker's point of view, the sale of a 30-footer is good business but not a dream come true, and selling a 25-footer has got to be done quickly if it is to make money. The truth of the matter is that selling used boats is a time-consuming business for the broker, and about the same amount of search time can be involved for a small boat as for a large one.

If you plan to use a broker, then, you will only have his serious attention if he feels that you're serious, too. The way to convey this impression is to come with a carefully distilled list of requirements, preferably in terms of stock boats you're interested in. And if, in putting together such a list, you find it a mass of contradictions, it probably means that you aren't really near buying a boat —and shouldn't be let out loose with your checkbook.

You will also find, as you arrive at the broker's, that half the juiciest boats in his ad are no longer available, if they ever were, but there will also be suitable boats that weren't in the ad because they missed the deadline or just didn't seem as attractive as some others.

Try to eliminate as many obviously unsuitable boats as possible on the basis of their written descriptions. And be wary of the "specials" that may be thrust at you—vessels outside your size or price range that you're urged to "just look at." Chances are the broker is trying to get a recalcitrant seller down by running a string of nonoffers past him, or else he thinks your description of what you want isn't what you really mean (and this happens all the time). Finally, don't diddle around: If there isn't anything on his list you like, say so. Make sure he has your outline of the boat you're looking for and move on. You'll probably hear from him before the week is out, after he's had a chance to beat the bushes by phone.

Ten or even 5 percent of twenty thousand is a lot of money, and you may well reason that it would make a lot more sense to do your own looking and spend the savings on equipment. It's unlikely to work out that way: Sellers feel the same way you do—after all, the money is coming visibly off their asking price—and they'd like to get that extra cash, too. It is reasonable to expect to split the commission's difference between buyer and seller—not a negligible gain for either.

Whatever you do, don't engage the services of a broker to locate a boat and then go behind his back to avoid paying the commission. Even if the argument from decency doesn't move you, you may well find yourself so mired in legal problems that you'll wish you'd played it straight.

Without a broker

Buying without a broker means you have to do your own research. My feeling is that the so-called regional boating publication—*Soundings* in the U.S. is a perfect example—and the boating sections of big-city newspapers are the best sources of information for buyers interested in boats under 30 feet. In Britain, the national boating magazines' classified sections cover virtually the entire coast. Here especially you need a good idea of what you're looking for, a knack for reading between the lines, and decisiveness: A good boat will disappear like smoke if the price is right.

If you're set on a popular fiberglass boat of recent vintage and particular make, you will perhaps be best off by letting the first two or three go by, just to get a feel for what's going. Work up a price comparison sheet, including brokered boats (take 5 percent off the asking price), to determine what the current hoped-for price range is. Be wary of "loaded" boats, especially ex-racers, with lots of gear you have no use for. By and large, the boat that's been casually owned for a season or two will be the best bet pricewise. The owner probably never got involved enough to screw her up too badly, and he wants out for one reason or another. Be wary of the semipro fixer, who's bought a battered hull and has cosmeticized it with a quick once-over for his profit. This is the nautical equivalent of a used-car salesman and deserves the same respect.

Sometimes your best bet will be the careful owner who's had a yacht for years and has lovingly kept her in mint condition. Chances are he knows what she's worth, and will want it, but your chances are good of getting a trouble-free boat. One of the worst people to buy from is the gadget-happy ignoramus who's loaded a boat with gear he doesn't understand and expects to get the cost back—at the original retail—from you. Until he's been exposed to the marketplace for a while, it won't dawn on him that gear, especially electronics, doesn't really add much to the essential value of a boat.

But suppose you've finally found the boat you like. The price is a bit high, and you make an offer anyway. After a bit of haggling (or maybe none) you and the owner come to agreement. At this point, what do you do?

First thing is to seal the bargain with a deposit on the agreed-upon purchase price, subject to survey. The amount of deposit is flexible—1 or 2 percent is quite enough usually. Even if you have no intention of having the boat formally surveyed, always include the phrase "subject to survey" in your preliminary offer and contract. Not only does it give you a legitimate out if the boat proves to have a serious problem, but it also puts the owner on notice that he'd better fix those half dozen little problems he's let slide because the boat was for sale anyway and he's lost interest in her.

Next step is to get from the owner a complete inventory of all the gear that goes with the boat. It is best to walk over the craft and make notes, to avoid misunderstanding later. Even the best-organized owner is likely to forget some item until the last minute, when a discussion about whether it goes or stays can needlessly complicate the sale. The offer to buy should state explicitly that it is conditional upon all the boat's gear being in working order. If there are to be exceptions—the speedo that hasn't functioned all season—you should know about them now.

Sail trial

Obviously a sail trial is the only way to determine what's in good shape and what isn't. Most owners don't want to be in the boat-ride business and are reluctant to take any but really hot prospects out. As a matter of common decency, you shouldn't ask for a sail trial unless you're genuinely serious, but if you are, then you're certainly entitled unless it means commissioning and launching a boat that's been hauled. In that case, you may have to take her at her owner's word, at least partly.

Sail trials are almost invariably conducted in unsuitable weather—a flat calm or a howling gale is normal—and so you will have to do a fair amount of extrapolating from slim evidence. Go armed with a checklist and make sure that you perform the following functions at least:

Under power, steer a straight-line course at various speeds, to determine if the helm pulls hard in one direction or the other. Except in the case of outboards, this kind of thing is not curable. Does the engine idle without stalling? Can it go from full ahead to idle to full reverse and back without stalling? (When you're handling at close quarters, this can be very important.) How about turns? Will she turn easily under power? Can she hold a straight-line course? (This is asking a lot. As we shall see, propeller torque will almost always drag her off to one side or the other.)

Entering and leaving a slip: Most sailing boats handle badly under power, particularly astern, where there is never any propwash over the rudder, since their engines are small and the rudders aren't efficiently located for this function. It is probably unrealistic to expect any boat with one propeller to back straight under inboard power—her stern will almost certainly hook left or right. If the curve is predictable and not cripplingly sharp, you're in the ball park. Try a crash stop from full ahead. You're not interested in the engine's ability to resist a stall as much as in its power to halt the boat's forward progress. Boats with folding props are especially reluctant to do much of anything under engine, and it is a good idea to check that the prop will unfold at least a majority of the time. If the propeller shows a significant problem in opening when the boat's engine is placed in gear, see if the owner will replace it. He may have the original two-blade the boat came with.

Motorsailing, see if the boat will hold a course to windward unaided, under power with the mainsail and then with main and jib. This is not a buy/don't buy attribute, but it's a plus if your boat can make her own way motorsailing, as many can.

With the engine on, check all the dashboard instruments—if there are any. An instrument that's dead will probably have to be replaced in toto. Also check the dashboard light. Make sure the radio, RDF, depth sounder, and other electrical gear function properly. What about the bilge pump? The electrically driven toilet, if any?

You should try at least to set every sail in the inventory, even though it's unlikely that you'll have appropriate weather for some of them. Obviously, the main, working jib and genoa(s) are the most important sails, and equally obviously, they will almost certainly have the most wear. Don't expect perfection, but remember that badly fitting sails will probably not set any better for you, and a headsail that's blown completely out of shape is probably only suitable for use as an awning. It's a good idea to make a note of the proper track setting for each headsail sheet lead, as this will save you time and trouble later on. It may well be that there is no proper lead for some sails—this is especially likely in the case of storm jibs—and you will have to consider the cost of creating one.

Be sure the mainsail and reefing genoas, if any, get checked after reefing. See if the boat will heave-to with jib aback and tiller to leeward. Keep a wary eye for blocks and winches that seem too small or fenders and docklines that are old or inadequate: Many owners try to save a few bucks by trotting out old garbage at sale time.

Take the boat through a couple of tacks and jibes. She won't handle too well, unless you're already familiar with the type, but what you're looking for are obvious problems—winch handles that don't clear the stanchions or shrouds when someone's grinding, for instance, or a headsail that persistently hangs up on some forward projection. Note how many degrees she tacks through—more than 90 is very poor these days. Even if you don't set all the sails, make sure the halyards run easily in their sheaves, and that they're not hopelessly worn in critical spots.

The trick here is to walk a careful line between accepting something you'll have to repair almost immediately, and expecting a new boat for the price of a secondhand one, which is unreasonable.

If the sail trial reveals no egregious faults, you will only have the survey to perform or commission. If there are serious problems arising from the sail trial, try to settle them on the spot rather than deferring them till later.

Surveys

As to surveys, they are a chancy proposition all around. You, the prospective buyer, pay for the cost of hauling the boat (if she is in the water) and blocking her if necessary. (Try to get the yard to haul her late Friday and leave her in the slings over the weekend. This gives the surveyor time to do his number, and if you can consummate the sale, you may even have time to scrub the bottom and slap on a coat of antifouling—with the yard's acquiescence—before relaunching.)

You also pay for the survey, which normally includes the surveyor's travel expenses as well as his hourly fee. What do you get in return?

You get one man's opinion as to the condition of the boat, now and in the future. A good surveyor will not offer a direct opinion about how good a deal you're getting or even how well the boat will perform. His job is to evaluate the boat's condition in terms of what she would normally be expected to encounter—including predictable bad weather. If, therefore, you have some unusual requirement for the boat—that she be in condition to sail from the East Coast to Spain, for example—tell the surveyor in advance, so he can adjust his sights upward. Likewise, if you are buying a semifinished boat, be sure to inform the surveyor just what level of unfinishedness you think you're buying so he can tell you what you really have.

An ideally complete survey would require the complete dismantling of the boat, since it would involve checking every piece of material and every fastening. If this is impossible in a wooden boat, where screws can be drawn without too much pain, how much less achievable is it for a fiberglass yacht, where a good gelcoat can conceal disaster? With the advent of molded headliners, even the boat's true interior is often sealed off forever, and the surveyor has only tiny clues to tell him what he needs to know.

A decent survey of even a small cruising boat will take the better part of a day, and for the most part, the surveyor will want to work alone. He will probably be willing to give you a verbal report when he's done, time permitting, but the real evidence of his work is the written survey that will follow. It is this that will determine (in some cases) if you buy the boat at all, and how much or little your initial offer is adjusted downward. The survey is your property—you paid for it—and you need not show it to the owner at all. But if you want some correction or repair to be made, you will obviously want to have the document in front of both of you, and you may even require some amplification from the surveyor himself.

Clearly there are two extremes in a survey's results. The first is a boat that's absolutely clean, free of fault entirely. This is highly unlikely, if only because nearly every builder skimps somewhere, and most surveyors know by experience where each manufacturer hides his fast ones. It may not even be a matter of fault, but only of judgment: A surveyor may, for instance, be wholly opposed to butane or propane stoves in any form; he is entitled to his opinion, but he should state whether a suggested defect is a matter of legality, or generally accepted practice, or of obvious mal- or non-feasance.

At the other extreme is a boat whose survey reveals a situation so dangerous and costly to repair that it makes purchase of the vessel foolish. There are very few things in a boat that cannot be fixed one way or another, and the question is whether you have the stomach (and the bankroll) for the repair. Most surveyors will be able to give you at least a running estimate of how much a suggested repair will cost, and you should expect to have such an estimate except where it's a case of some item's being in need of complete replacement, in which case you can look up the price yourself.

Most stock boats' surveys lie somewhere in the middle: There are defects and one or two may be expensive, but there are no crippling problems. The normal procedure at this point is to take the survey up with the seller and negotiate. He may offer to rectify the problem at his expense, or he may knock something off the price, or he may tell you to get stuffed—take the boat or leave her. Except in the last case, where you will be governed by the kind of bargain you think you're getting, as well as your own skill and desire for the boat, the better choice is to get the estimated cost of the repair knocked off the selling price. This way, you have control of the repair, at least to some extent, and there's a better chance of its being done properly. Probably the seller will counteroffer: He'll fix it himself, or he'll give you part payment of the estimate. You have to decide if the adjustment is adequate.

From all the foregoing, it will be plain that the surveyor's skill is of the essence if a survey is to have any meaning at all. How can you tell if a surveyor is good? Well, unless you've used him before, you probably can't. But you can take some steps to tilt the odds in your favor. To begin with, you must make sure that the surveyor is unconnected with the seller, with your broker or with the boatyard. Most good surveyors are quick to disqualify themselves if there is even the breath of a conflict of interest, simply because there's plenty of work without this kind of problem. One good, if time-consuming, method is to check among your friends who have bought boats in the past couple of years: Did their experience with the boat after purchase invalidate anything in the report? Were there any problems the surveyor didn't spot? There almost always will be, but it's a matter of degree: My brother-in-law bought a boat and had her surveyed in due course. The examination failed to detect a gross breach in the gelcoat at the joint with the exterior metal keel, one that resulted in the boat's absorbing gallons of water over the next months, and requiring a serious repair later. This is unforgivable, but a pipe concealed behind a headliner may burst, without any predictable warning.

A good surveyor almost always has a good local reputation. If he is unknown, don't take the chance. Look for someone with actual construction and repair experience. Many boatyard managers do survey work after they're retired, and they are frequently excellent judges, as they've been ideally situated to get a track record on most builders. Builders, like the rest of us, tend to make the same mistakes over and over again, and a man who's repaired a lot of them knows where to look for the traces of a given manufacturer's habitual problems.

A man who's been around for a long time is also at an advantage. Of course he must be sound of wind and limb, and be acquainted with recent developments in the particular type of material he's examining, but he should also have the perspective to know the standard errors and problems characteristic of different eras in boatbuilding. In this respect, buyers of fiberglass boats are lucky, as commercial fiberglass construction dates only back to the end of World War II, and there are many surveyors around who have seen the progress of glass construction from its very beginnings. In Britain, when in doubt go to Lloyds, who only employ the best and who can't afford to be biased.

Another advantage of longevity in the trade is that a given manufacturer, if the brand has been around awhile, has probably gone through a number of financial and design stages, even within the run of a single model. There is one boat of which I'm aware, a 35-foot sloop, that's been in production for nearly a dozen years (an exceptionally long time in this business). The first dozen hull numbers of this model were excellent boats, superbly overbuilt, at least in part because the builder didn't have the expertise to cut corners, or the need to. But after these boats, he ran into financial problems and reacted, as most manufacturers do in this situation, by beginning to shave the specifications. His 35-footer sold the next fifty hulls on the reputation of the first twelve, but the boats were nowhere as good as the initial dozen, and the firm's reputation, unstained at first, declined until they were widely known as producers of a well-designed but distinctly shoddy vessel.

At this point they were bought and refinanced, and the 35-footers from hull 62 onward returned to the original specifications, although it took several years to restore the firm's reputation. This kind of information, largely unknown to the public, or available only as distorted rumor, is the conversational small change of the boat business, and a good surveyor will approach our case history 35 with real suspicion. Once he's seen the hull number, however, he'll know whether to expect the worst or not. That kind of knowledge only comes with time, and it's worth the price.

There is in my mind a genuine question as to whether the buyer of a small, used cruiser really requires a formal survey. Unfortunately, there are no clear-cut guidelines to help you decide. At one end of the spectrum, a 17-foot catboat with overnighting accommodations ought to be surveyable by any moderately intelligent buyer working with the aid of one of the several books on the subject (see Bibliography). On the opposite end, a nearly new 30-footer, costing more than the purchaser earns in a year, is just too big an investment to buy without an expert's opinion. The gray area is mostly located around twenty-five feet, where today's small cruisers begin to become both costly and complex. One rule of thumb that may help is to compare the estimated cost of a survey with the cost of a year's insurance on the boat in question. My personal feeling is that if the two are equal, or if the insurance is more costly, then get the survey.

In any case, you won't want to commission a survey until you are pretty certain the boat is acceptable: From your point of view, you don't want to pay to hear your worst fears confirmed, but to be prevented from making a costly mistake or be told that you've made an acceptable decision from one point of view. For this reason, you should become knowledgeable enough to perform a quick once-over survey of your own, one that's admittedly incomplete but informative as to the boat's probable quality. Ideally, this lick-and-a-promise should be capable of being done in about fifteen minutes, and should logically consist of disqualifying negatives: Three (or however many) strikes and the boat is off your list.

The "preliminary survey"

What should such an instant survey consist of? Obviously it will not include items that ought to be checked beforehand, such as the boat's basic design suitability, or things that can be worked out later, such as its total cost with required options. Basically, what you're looking for are indicators that the builder knows his craft and has taken it seriously. You cannot expect to make decisions about the boat's total fabric from a quick once-over, but you can look over some fairly important pieces of evidence. Like the following, for example:

1. Sight along the sides of the hull, looking for "hard spots"—places where the side has obviously been forced outward by some inner structure, usually a bulkhead. This suggests bulkheads that have been wedged in place, and it definitely means that there will be continued stress, and perhaps eventual failure, at the bulges. Very few fiberglass hulls have the kind of clean, fair run that was characteristic of a well-built wood boat, but there should be very few, only minor, hard spots.
2. The chainplates hold the rig in the boat. Check to make sure that they're properly made fast to the vessel. Older boats almost invariably fastened the chainplate to the hull sides, through-bolting them and them glassing over the exterior in some cases so the plates—straps, really—were only visible inside. This is perhaps the strongest structural way of accomplishing the end of holding the mast up, but it may not be feasible in today's designs, where it's often important to sheet genoa jibs flatter than formerly, which in turn means inboard chainplates bolted to main bulkheads. This is quite acceptable, but the bulkheads or built-up reinforcements should themselves be heavily secured to the hull with fiberglass; the plates should be heavy stainless steel, and they should be secured by lockwashers and standard nuts, or standard washers and locknuts.

3. The primary thwartships bulkheads are the main stiffeners in a fiberglass hull, as noted earlier. Make sure they're properly glassed to the hull itself: A six-inch overlap of the glass fabric is none too much. Check also to be sure that there are enough bulkheads. There should be some support, not necessarily a full bulkhead, every six or seven feet: Chain locker, forward end of V berth, head and hanging locker, galley and chart table, fore and aft ends of the cockpit, lazarette—all these are logical sites for thwartships stiffeners.
4. Through-hull or -deck fittings are crucial and usually easy to check. Look for real seacocks, not gate valves, on through-hulls below the waterline, and some kind of valve with a shut-off for every through-hull anywhere near the water, including the exhaust of an inboard engine. Through-deck fittings should have marine plywood, fiberglass or stainless-steel backup pads, in ascending order of preference, with lock washers and nuts of adequate size.
5. Check for the telltale tracks of topside leaks—around ports, hatches, chainplates, the hull-to-deck joint—and underwater leaks around through-hulls.
6. Finally, check the exposed edge grain of any visible wood. It should be sealed, or you're inviting delamination and/or interior rot. This includes bulkheads, hatches, and doors, and the deck itself, if it's wood-cored. It is especially important to seal the edges of plywood, which is perhaps the most common interior wood still used.

Obviously, this brief list doesn't begin to be a serious survey, but a builder who's lacking in all or a majority of these basic indicators is probably someone you'll regret doing business with later. And there are so many critical points in a boat that you'll never see, why take chances on the ones you can? If a boat passes this thumbnail survey, then it's probably worth passing on to a professional for his appraisal.

Buying from a dealer

Buying a brand-new boat is yet another experience. A good amount of the time the boat you inspect isn't the one you'll buy, a situation that creates its own problems; and of course you're inspecting the vessel in the artificial setting of a showroom, with professional assistance to keep it glossy. As with so many other transactions in the marine field, it's important for you to work with a reliable dealer (unless of course you're buying direct from the builder). This is just another layer of reputation for you to check, and there are no easy rules of thumb to follow: A first-rate influential dealer can get the best service from even a mediocre builder, while a lackluster dealership winds up with the short end of the stick from even a normally honorable builder. The ideal, obviously, is to ensure that both builder and dealer have first-class reputations.

If the dealership is in a marina, spend a couple of weekend afternoons talking with other new-boat owners who've bought models in the same line you're considering. Ask specifically about the condition of the boats as delivered, and what the dealer did to cope with warranty problems. A careful dealer will ensure that most problem boats are squared away before they're delivered at all, but the next best compromise is a dealer who's willing to rectify the builder's mistakes—and in anything as complicated as a cruiser, there are bound to be some. Find out, if you can, if the dealer has his own people who are able to handle routine problems—a good mechanic, good rigger, top-quality fiberglass patcher and painter. And try for a dealer near you. Not only is it convenient, but it's going to be a lot harder to ignore you if your complaints are local calls.

Check about financing, if that's something you're considering, and about trade-ins as well. Although it will be much more difficult, you will also want to make a few checks on both the dealer's and builder's financial condition. If you have a stockbroker, and the builder is a publicly held company, you can probably get a copy of the annual report. If not, it is much harder. As for the dealer's reputation, it doesn't hurt to start with the local Better Business Bureau to see if there are any complaints registered. Ask for a bank reference, since he's going to be playing with a lot of your money. If there are any rumors of financial irregularity, no matter how slight, pay attention to them: Unlike large companies, boat dealers can often vanish without a trace and with very little advance warning.

Your inspection of the general ambience should tell you a good deal. A yard that's apparently on the verge of dissolution may just be a character establishment, but more likely it's a place where the owner hasn't the cash to put things right. By the opposite token, a brand-new, spick-and-span place with every conceivable facility may be on the verge of collapse from overexpansion. What you want, I think, is something in the middle—an established dealer with good but not grandiose facilities, which have obviously been taken care of. If he has several lines of top-quality sail and power yachts, that's a plus, too—even if those aren't the lines you're interested in. The most popular boats are desirable dealerships, and the builders can pick and choose.

One of the most important aspects of buying a new boat from a dealer is the matter of fitting out and commissioning. Among the more unavoidable extras in any new-boat options list is the item headed *makeready* or commissioning. What does it entail? Essentially, a boat dealer usually receives his vessels from the factory by over-the-road transport, and this is most often the case with smaller cruisers like the ones we're talking about in this book. The boats are to a degree broken down and packed for shipping, and in most cases many of the options, being the dealer's sales prerogative, are installed by him.

A rough delivery trip can mean a boat that's not only dirty but physically scarred, with leaks (especially around ports and fittings) that it didn't have when it left the plant, a certain number of interior fittings shaken loose or off and, in this imperfect world, some options you didn't order and/or a shortage of the ones you did. It is essentially the dealer's job to fix all this, then to rig the boat's spar and step it, check all the electrical systems, including the ones his people have installed, and commission the engine, which often entails a good deal more than just turning the key.

When the dealer is also an importer, his job is even more complex, since it involves dealing with a foreign nation, with transit by ship as well as truck, and with Customs. In some cases, the overseas dealings are genuinely bizarre. The boat business is awash with stories of boats that arrive with critical parts missing or with some others badly installed. A good dealer's commissioning can save you more work than you can easily imagine, and a bad job can make a mediocre boat worse. Some of the work, in addition, may well come under warranty, either the builder's or that issued by the maker of the part or system in question. It is very important, when ordering a boat, to read the builder's warranty carefully, and to ask, if it is not clear, what other warranties apply and how they are serviced. It is hard, in the euphoria that surrounds buying a boat, to remain businesslike, but it will pay in the long run to have everything spelled out, in writing if at all possible.

One way to improve your chances of good service is to order your boat so that she arrives in a generally slack period, say mid or late summer. True, you won't have the entire season to play with her, but you will probably have the undivided attention of the builder's craftsmen, should anything be amiss.

VIII

Small-cruiser Galleys

The ideal galley should be capable of turning out multicourse gourmet meals, but should take up only one-tenth the cubic space of an apartment kitchenette; it should have vast stowage capabilities for hot and cold, wet or dry foods, but none of this stowage should impinge on the other areas of the boat; it should have a kitchen's normal counter workspace, but this surface should take up virtually no room; it should be in the middle of things, so the cook can participate in the ship's life, yet it must be clear of crew and gear moving forward and aft. And it should be able to do all these things at an angle of 30 degrees off the horizontal.

There are no ideal galleys.

Most of today's boatbuilders pride themselves on designing their vessels' interiors for people they still think of as "the little woman," or "the first mate," so it should come as no surprise that the results are uneven, to say the least. On the one hand, boat designers are intelligent men (and a few very intelligent women), most of whom have done some cooking afloat, so they know what's required. On the other, the marketing department has told them that it's the wife who makes the sale, and the boat's galley should look as much like her twenty-first-century kitchen as possible. The trouble is that a galley is not a kitchen, in the shoreside sense of the word. True, in larger yachts it's possible to fit in a very fair imitation of a house kitchen, but when we get below thirty feet overall, the stark realities of seafaring tend to come through.

To get a sensible picture of what a galley is, you must first consider what kind of cooking you and your crew plan to do in your boat. The answers to a few questions will suggest what you ought to be looking for, and whether you have any chance of finding it in a small cruising yacht. To begin with, do you seriously plan to have the kind of full-scale meals afloat that you take for granted ashore, and if so, does your style of cooking require that you actually prepare the food afloat? If your answers to both questions are yes, then begin tomorrow by calculating how many perishable ingredients you use in a day's meal preparation, how much counter surface you routinely take for granted, how many burners your main hot meal requires to be in action at once.

By contrast, most experienced sea cooks restrain the creative urge afloat, letting it burgeon in a few splendid dishes while keeping the rest of the meal down to a minimum level of difficulty. Many quite good cooks prepare virtually everything ashore and just heat it up afloat, while others find that they can ring the creative changes with elaborate nibble food—open-faced sandwiches, salads, reconstituted goodies—that would not normally be acceptable ashore. They have three things going for them. First, most people get so hungry out in the fresh air that they will eat plywood; second, boating retains some of the aura of camping out, and if you cannot have ants and sand in your food, at least it can be burnt or underdone a bit, so you know where you are; third, the cook always wields the ultimate weapon: quitting.

Let's begin by examining a few of the standard galley layouts seen in the boats of today and the recent past, vessels you're likely to run into on the new or used market. To begin with, never take a galley for granted based on the boat's accommodation plan or photographs alone. The distortions of a good draftsman or a wide-angle lens can make a pictured galley very different from the thing you have to live with. Ideally, you should prepare a good complicated meal in a galley before judging it. Since this is impossible, perhaps the next best thing for the cook to do is arrive at the showroom with a complex recipe in hand, something he or she especially favors for eating afloat. With the galley in view, figure out first where all the ingredients and tools would go, then how the meal would be prepared, both under way and at anchor. Think in terms of arm's reach, of work surface, of having to reach across a flaming stovetop to the dishlocker.

Can you stand up—straight up—while cooking? If you cannot, it almost certainly means that you'll wind up not cooking under way. An open hatch is fine at rest, but it has a number of problems while the boat's moving. Cooking while seated is a maddening backbreaker for most people. Is there someplace to put your feet? This sounds like a dumb question, but a lot of galleys are back aft, where the boat's stern begins to tuck up; what appears to be floorboard on the plans is often an upwardly curving surface suitable only for flies or Spiderman. Can you pass food both to the saloon table—presumably forward of you—and to the cockpit? You'll probably be eating as many meals in the one place as the other. How is the traffic plan—are you using part of the navigator's precious area as an icebox top, or will the cook's rump get bumped by every passer-through? In rough weather, can you brace yourself, or brace with a strap, enough to get a cup of hot soup to the cockpit crew? All these are important points, and while you may get around each and every one, doing so will mean that your boat's galley is that much less useful, and other areas will have to take up the slack.

The aft galley

Perhaps the most popular galley in today's small boats runs the width of the cabin aft by the companionway. There are good reasons for this. For one thing, much of the area is unusable for anything else; it is in a part of the boat where the pitching is least felt, so the cook will last longer and the meals will stay put better; and it allows the cook in a small yacht to reach most of the working areas of the boat without moving too far from his or her work space.

The typical thwartships galley in a small cruiser has a stainless-steel sink to one side of the companionway, with its plumbing in a door-front locker below. On the other side is the icebox, nearly always top-loading, with a drain direct to the bilge. There is a locker on one side, and space for the stove on the other, and, as a rule, room for at least one utensil drawer. The most common

Aft galley in a Columbia 7.6 runs the width of the cabin. Removable ice chest to port replaces fixed icebox. Only accessible working space is upper companionway step.

problems with this sort of galley derive from the fact that the most obvious working surface is usually just where anyone ascending to or descending from the cockpit will put his feet. Sometimes, if the companionway is wide, a crewmember passing through has the option of putting his feet in the food, the sink, or even the open icebox.

On many boats, there is at least one quarterberth extending back under the cockpit. This may or may not interfere with the galley layout, in that a number of aft galleys extend over the foot of a quarterberth so that the sleeper is at least partially under a galley counter. You need to approach this sort of layout with caution, as all too often it means that the occupant of the quarterberth either cannot roll over, because the counter has insufficient clearance over the bunk mattress, or finds his feet interfering with the plumbing of the galley sink, which sometimes is located over the quarterberth tunnel.

A practical solution to this problem, at least in boats over about twenty-six feet, is to opt for an L-shaped galley to port or starboard, leaving the other side free for a proper quarterberth (or sometimes a quarterberth with chart table over—see Chapter VII). The L-shaped galley normally has the icebox aft, and usually the sink as well, while the stove faces the cook athwartships. This arrangement allows the standard two-burner stove to be gimballed, and also provides for a certain amount of drawer and locker space in the same module that holds the stove. The L-shape is not normally deep enough to allow for a restraining strap to run between the two corners of the unit, and while it makes for an extraordinarily compact galley unit, it is hardly ideal if you plan to do a lot of cooking aboard.

There is no question that the U-shaped galley, with the opening athwartships, is the most seaworthy installation for serious cooks aboard serious cruising yachts. The after arm of the U has the icebox, the crossbar contains the gimballed stove, often with oven below, and the forward arm holds the sinks, often double, with locker and drawer stowage below, outboard of the stove and aft of the icebox. A heavy webbing strap across the mouth of the U will make it possible for the cook to function in just about any weather when pots will stay on the stove (and the cook's stomach will stay down). This is a fine rig, but it does use up a lot of space in the most motion-free—and hence valuable—area of the yacht. If you are serious about cooking under way, and even more serious about eating full-scale meals under way, this is a layout to consider.

The linear galley

Back a few years, when the convertible dinette seemed almost *de rigueur* aboard cruising sailboats, it nearly always faced a linear galley. In this fore-and-aft arrangement, the icebox was usually toward the bow, followed by the

L-shaped galley in Mariner 28 combines with quarterberth.

sink, with the stove aft, near the ventilation provided by the companionway hatch. There was usually a locker below the sink, a drawer or two below the stove, and lockers outboard. Since the linear galley usually matched the dinette in length, and since the dinette was also a bed, the galley counter in even a small boat might be six feet long.

As a whole generation of seagoing cooks discovered, the linear galley is fairly easy to operate when the boat is on an even keel, and no real problem when the boat is heeled with the galley on the down side. The problems arise when you, the cook, are scrabbling your way up a continual slope to work at a galley that has suddenly risen to chest height. And in a small boat with a dinette, the passageway between galley and dinette is too narrow, nor is there any way to lash the cook in place. The linear galley is fine when the boat's at rest, but it can be a monster on the wrong tack.

Some few older boats of mid-size, such as the Tartan 27, and a number of very small newer boats have the galley as a counter just abaft the main bulkhead, sometimes split into port and starboard segments by the passage. Galleys of this type are almost always makeshift, places that say "galley" to the inexperienced buyer, but are nonfunctional under most conditions. There

Utterly minimal galley in a C&C Mega consists of two counter units facing each other amidships, with hydraulically operated daggerboard between them.

is usually a minuscule sink, a place for a stove opposite, and sometimes a too small, badly insulated icebox. Maybe even a small cubby for food stowage, but not what anyone in his right mind would consider a seagoing kitchen. Such galleys almost always require the operator to function sitting on a bunk, halfway swiveled around, and there is little ventilation because of one's distance from the companionway. A boat with this type of galley may be a fine little craft, and may provide much enjoyable cruising. But not for the cook.

Finally, there is the fragmented galley, which has bits and pieces of itself

Minimal aft galley unit—but where does the stove go?

Icebox is under companionway ladder, sink is to port—but foot clearance under counter is minimal.

scattered all over the boat. More often than not, this kind of thing is hopelessly optimistic, but it can work, and one should not condemn it out of hand. Perhaps the best example of an apparently disastrous galley that was in fact quite functional was aboard the 22-foot Hirondelle catamaran I once owned (see Chapter III). This British-built cruiser had a short counter, with sink and dish drain, built into the starboard hull. Behind the cook's back, when he was standing at the sink (as one could in the hulls of this little cat), was a counter across the bridge deck. By turning around, one could easily reach the waist-high cooker (British for two-burner stove with grill below), over which was a sizable locker for dishes and food. The only really mad part of the arrangement was the icebox, which was out in the cockpit and virtually uninsulated. At least the water from the melted ice drained between the hulls and not into the bilge.

Sliding galley unit retracts under cockpit seat. Stove fits in cutout, watertank is in unit, ice chest is under companion ladder.

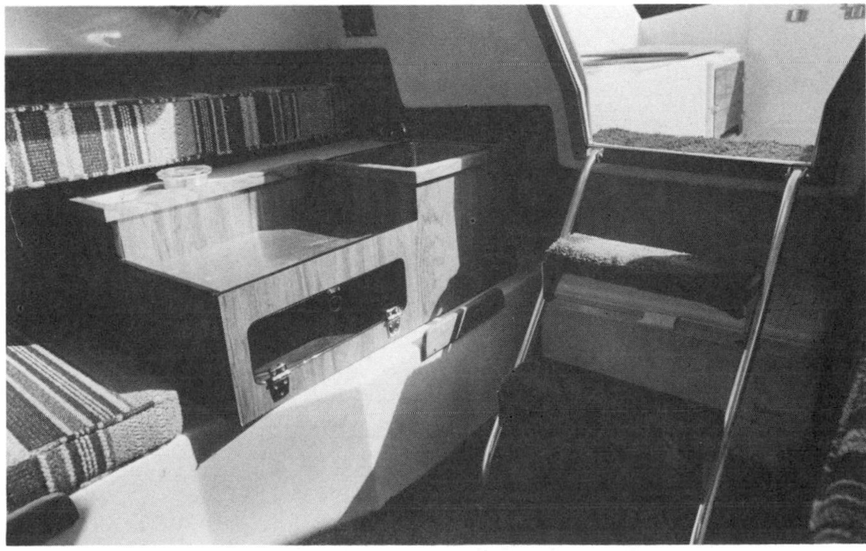

Folding shelf at forward end of galley doubles counter space.

By adding a portable ice chest, which sat on the quarterberth next to the sink, this carved-up cooking area became very practical indeed. We didn't even have to give up the quarterberth, as our younger son found the cavelike atmosphere, with the ice chest blocking off other people's access, to be just what he liked.

The trick, then, is never to take a galley at face value. Even at the risk of being thought a bit odd, it pays to simulate cooking a meal before making up your mind. And if the galley is clearly very limited, but the rest of the boat meets all your requirements, bear in mind that you are not buying a diner but a sailing vessel, and that virtually every port of call has lots of good restaurants, any one of them capable of turning out better food than you can get from even the best small-boat galley.

Creating extra stowage

The most important changes in the average galley have to do with increasing the amount of usable space in the basic installation through the addition of shelves, lockers, drawers, and other improvements that maximize the available unit. Let's look at a few obvious examples, some of which are regularly provided by builders as part of the standard or optional price of the boat.

The most significant lack in most small-yacht galleys is counter space, horizontal surfaces near the stove and sink for food preparation or just stacking utensils. Most galleys have at least one forward-facing thwartships side on which you can mount a hinged shelf: Raise it for use, drop it flat against the galley bulkhead when you're through. If there's a quarterberth abaft the galley, you may be able to mount the hinged shelf so it swings up into the access to the berth. One fine Canadian-built yacht, the CS-27, has a shelf that props into place forward of the galley, and another that swings up inboard of the gimballed stove. Virtually anyplace will do, just so long as you don't place a shelf where people will fall against it or lean on it as they're moving forward or aft. Shelves should always be fiddled—that is, they should have a guardrail at least one and a half or two inches high all around the edge, except for gaps at the corners (for sweeping crumbs and mopping spills). A shelf's supporting member should be strong enough to absorb the occasional lurching crewmember, and it should provide a positive lock to prevent the folding shelf from falling away without warning.

Every galley should have at least two drawers. The first drawer will inevitably wind up holding winch handles, fuel- and water-tank keys, snatch blocks, and bits of tarred twine too small for any use. The second drawer is for galley utensils. Even if the drawers open fore and aft, they should be provided with some form of positive lock. The simplest is just a notch that keeps the closed drawer from sliding open as the boat pitches or heels. To open, lift the drawer up and pull out. This is normally quite adequate, although sailing a boat off a substantial wave top can result in having silverware all over the deck. When buying a boat with this sort of drawer stop, look for a slightly loose-fitting drawer, as the wood joints that seemed so sloppy in the showroom are likely to swell in use afloat. Also make sure the drawer has some form of lock to keep it from coming completely out.

What if your galley has no drawers, or one that's too small? A proper sliding

CS 27 galley work space can be enlarged by raising hinged panel inboard of stove, placing wooden stove cover in slots forward of unit.

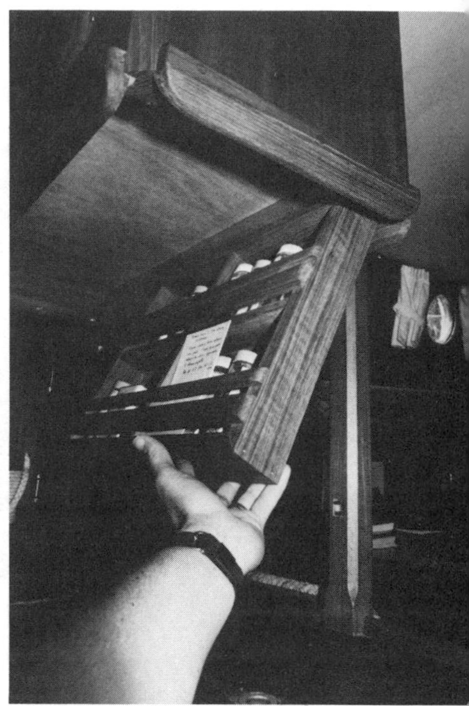

Fold-down spice rack secures under overcounter dish locker.

drawer isn't the simplest thing to build, but there are marine woodwork companies that specialize in building prefabricated drawers and cabinets, complete with sliders, for installation into fiberglass bulkheads with adequate space behind. These units are usually teak-fronted and plywood behind, and they are not cheap. But they come in a vast assortment of sizes and shapes, and you're almost sure to find one that will fit the available space.

What space? Well, there's usually a bunk alongside the galley, and the stowage under it is accessible only by lifting the mattress and a ply panel beneath. This is an obvious place, as is the galley counter, which often has a stowage area that's really inaccessible through the locker door that's the only standard way in. Or you may have a deep locker that's too high to be practical. Cover part of the front opening with teak-faced plywood and recess your drawer into that. If you're going to get a galley into a pocket yacht, it takes thought.

Don't neglect things like knife and utensil racks or dish and plate racks in the galley. There are frequently fiddled stowage areas on the galley counter outboard of the stove or back under the bridge deck. These stillborn locker spaces can be converted to real lockers quite easily. About the only thing to bear in mind is that any locker should have a stout catch on the door and adequate ventilation to keep it from being a mold breeder.

As the reader may have picked up already, there are four elements to a workable galley: stove, icebox, sink, and stowage space. It's possible to do without one or the other—the British have only recently come grudgingly to admit that iceboxes are not immoral—but by and large the elements are the same no matter where or how you cruise, although their size and efficiency may vary tremendously. People who cruise in hot weather most of the time can manage without a stove, and many Florida or southern California boats get very little use from their cooking arrangements. In most parts of any country, however, a workable stove is a necessity, especially in spring and fall when it can also be used to heat the boat.

Stoves

The most common boat stove, and one of the most exasperating appliances ever created, is the two-burner pressure alcohol unit, either gimballed or permanently locked in place. Generally speaking, this has an integral fuel tank, mounted between the burners, with a small hand pump that creates air pressure in the tank and thus pushes fuel along to the burners.

Similar in use to alcohol but far more efficient is common kerosene. Like alcohol, kerosene under pressure requires a preheated burner to vaporize the fuel. But you don't preheat with the kerosene itself. Instead you use stove alcohol. If the kerosene vaporizes properly and catches, you have a much hotter flame than you would with alcohol, with what seems to me less of an unpleasant smell. (This last judgment is hopelessly personal: I find both alcohol and kerosene unpleasant but not unbearable; many others cannot stand one while they can abide the other.)

If, as frequently happens, the kerosene fails to vaporize, you get the same flare-up as with alcohol, plus a generous dollop of smelly, oily, sooty black smoke. Kerosene is advertised by many old cruising hands as being available everywhere, but this is no longer true. In more civilized surroundings and expensive marinas, it may be hard to find, although in more remote places it's still widely used and relatively (for a petroleum product) cheap.

For my money, there is only one sensible fuel for boat cooking, and that's bottled gas. Of course I grew up with it in an assortment of beach houses, had my eyebrows incinerated as a teenager, and got used to its quirks. I don't for a moment underestimate its forcefulness. But everything is dangerous, sooner or later, and compared to the convenience and the efficiency it affords, the danger of bottled gas seems to me well worth taking a chance on. European cruising folk have been using it for decades, with no significant diminution in their numbers.

The problems with bottled gas—either propane or butane, and to a lesser extent liquefied natural gas—are that it is invisible, heavier than air (except for

LNG), and explosive, *and* that the normally level-headed U.S. Coast Guard has what can only be described as a panic-stricken fear of it unsupported by evidence.

There are also various solid-fuel cooking appliances. Many small boats of a few years back carried a gimballed Sterno-fueled one-burner stove called a Sea-Swing. This device fitted into a metal socket bolted to a bulkhead and could be removed and stowed when not needed. Its *raison d'être* was that the single burner would hold a small pan in the very worst weather and make it possible to get some kind of hot liquid into the watch on deck almost no matter what. On the other hand, mariners discovered the awful truth that Sterno is an extremely slow-heating fuel, and one could spend the better part of an afternoon trying to heat water for coffee. This device, good in its time, has now largely been replaced by a different single-burner heater (see below) with a different, more effective fuel.

Another old favorite is a pivoting grill that fits into a flagpole socket aft and extends out over the water. When the cooking is done, a flip of the wrist dumps the extra charcoal into the drink, neatly staining the transom. Although it's a somewhat cumbersome device, this type of grill avoids having red-hot coals in the boat—not a bad idea. Its only drawback, in my experience, is that if the handle isn't secured carefully, the whole thing can tip before you've finished cooking, dunking the dinner.

Charcoal on a boat can be desperately messy. There are two ways of handling it cleanly. First, you can prepackage the coals in double paper bags and staple them closed. The trick is to measure out enough coals for a meal into each bag, and carry half a dozen such bags in the lockers. If you have leaky lockers, put the paper bags inside a plastic bag which you can remove before cooking. Another way is to use one of the sets of coals that come presealed in cardboard, rather the shape of egg cartons. The cardboard has been treated with firelighter, so you only have to light it, and the operation is well in hand. I always carried a large closing canvas or triple-thick paper sack for the grill itself, as it will coat everything it touches with permanent black after use.

But let's return to the boat's standard stove. What size and conformation do you need for your normal cooking aboard? Except in the very smallest boats, a single burner is too little. To get by on one burner, you have to plan ahead, and do it carefully. It can be done, by such tricks as preparing boil-in-a-bag meals in advance and heating them in a pot whose liquid serves some other purpose (such as washing-up or coffee water). But it is a trial, and if you have any space at all, you'll probably want two surface burners.

As noted earlier, this is the standard stove for small cruising yachts. Many cookbooks have been written around the two-burner stove and its scheduling requirements, and I've found the number of burners (if not the stove itself) suitable for years. There are so many things a two-burner stove *can* do, in fact, that unless you have definite plans for living aboard and serving elaborate meals, two burners are probably quite adequate. It's important, when one's

Good-looking installation of stove-plus-oven—but how would one reach the sink foot pump with boat heeled on port tack?

cooking is restricted in this way, to plan the entire meal and dovetail the recipes so as not to get caught short of flames at a crucial moment.

One thing you cannot really expect to have with a two-burner stove, and that's any kind of baking. Although there are so-called stovetop ovens, usually made of folding sheet metal, these things are only adequate for such elementary jobs as heating up frozen TV dinners. Especially with low-temperature alcohol burners, the stovetop portable simply won't hold heat well enough to let real baking temperatures build up—although they will do an excellent job of baking you right out of your own cabin as they raise the temperature below.

The average two-burner gimballed stove has some balancing problems for cooking with the boat well heeled. Because it is itself quite light, and because it's so low that a tall pot stands well above its surface, the normal two-burner unit often cannot hold cookware in a heavy sea. For this reason, as well as to have another burner handy, quite a few skippers invest in one of the miniature single-burner units, such as the well-known Sea-Swing or the relatively new butane-powered Mini-Galley. These bulkhead-mounted units will function in the worst kind of weather, when all you really want is coffee or soup anyway, and they can also help out a larger stove under calmer circumstances, although their burner diameters are severely circumscribed.

The same part-time assist can come from a hibachi or grill, unsuited to preparing complete meals, yet a boon in providing an extra heat source as needed. The trick, of course, is to be realistic as well as foresighted about the kind of cooking you plan to do afloat.

More and more quite small cruising yachts have two- or even three-burner stove tops with regular ovens beneath. These can be fueled by any of the three standards—alcohol, kerosene, or gas—in ascending order of efficiency and convenience. A gas oven on a boat does not have a normal pilot light; if it has

Flush-mounted two-burner stove has removable wood cutting board.

anything at all, it's a pilot that must be hand-ignited before each meal, but that can remain on, to relight the oven's main burner if it's turned off for any reason. Alcohol and kerosene ovens have the same preheating requirement as do surface burners, except that they are much harder to get going and are prone to elaborate flare-ups.

One might suppose from all that has gone before that I regard gimbals as quite essential for a proper seagoing stove on a sailboat. Although I've been aboard successful cruising yachts whose stoves were not gimballed—sailed

Minimal galley on Seidelmann 25 has ice chest under companionway step, stove on rails.

1,100 miles in one—the absence of a cooking surface level with the real horizon always seemed to me an unnecessary handicap on the cook, who was already grappling with the task of cooking under difficulties. Only on quite large yachts or on multihulls can one get away without serious gimbals. In the latter, the amount of heel should be very slight, except in some trimarans with very small floats, and the pots and pans should be capable of being restrained by rails and movable clamps. In a multihull, the cook's chief problem is not angle of heel but a constant short, quick motion that can jump a pot off a stovetop, if it's not secured. Again, if a multihull does sail at more than about 10 degrees off the horizontal, you may be advised to invest in a portable gimballed burner in addition to the yacht's regular stove. If you do, be sure to get the lightest unit possible—almost certainly the camper's Mini-Galley—because of multihulls' great sensitivity to weights. (Not that one burner will make so much difference by itself, but it helps to start and stay in this weight-saving frame of mind.)

Even if a stove is gimballed, that doesn't mean it's been done effectively. This is especially problematical when one is dealing with a two-burner stove recessed into a countertop. If you stop to think about it, the difficulties become clear. Suppose you take a standard two-burner stove, about four inches high as it sits flat on a counter. If you locate the pivots of a gimbal in the upper edge of the stove, it'll balance perfectly no matter how the boat heels (pitching is a different matter)—as long as there isn't a large heavy pot or two on the surface. When they're added, it's like having two heavy adults stand up in a dinghy: instant instability.

Old-fashioned stove gimbals raise the pivot points well above the stovetop, so that even when the stove's center of gravity is raised thanks to the addition of a couple of pots the pivot is still higher. Obviously, this becomes less important when a stove has an oven, as the weight of the bottom unit will virtually always overmatch the weight of what's on the burners.

Another gimballing problem, especially prevalent with stoves having ovens, is swinging room. While the gimbal itself will allow the stove to do a complete somersault, there are almost certain to be stops somewhere along the way. Quite often a stove bottom will swing inboard as far as you like, but only 15 or 20 degrees outboard. It pays to check when you're buying the boat, as there is probably little you can do about it afterwards. My own feeling is that a gimballed stove that's meant for serious use should swing at least 30 degrees both ways—not that you'll be sailing at that angle of heel, but it's easy, when hammering along at a steady 20 degrees, suddenly to dip the rail to a sudden puff.

Even a well-gimballed stove should have sea rails all around, as well as a couple of pairs of portable clamps. These are fixed to the sea rail, either by spring pressure or set screw, and can be moved to virtually lock a pot or high-sided pan in place. You should get used to using them at all times, so it becomes a habit.

Iceboxes

Iceboxes on a small boat are a lot simpler and much more trouble-free than are stoves. One has virtually no choice, when buying a new boat, as to the type of icebox; it's just there when the craft is built, and you live with what you get. That being the case, I would only list some considerations about iceboxes to bear in mind when you're comparing galleys.

Begin by believing, hard as it may at first seem, that a good fixed icebox frequently isn't necessary at all on a small cruiser. You may be considerably better off with a portable unit, for several reasons. First, there are some really excellent portable ice chests on the market today, the Igloo and Coleman models being exceptional. Their construction matches or equals virtually anything you'll find installed in a boat. Second, a portable ice chest helps food arrive at the boat without defrosting: You have only to pack the chest direct from the refrigerator at home, and there's no long unrefrigerated hiatus between home and boat. If you take the further step of chilling off the chest before transferring food from the refrigerator, you will be that much more ahead at the beginning of your cruise. Most of the new small cruisers that offer removable iceboxes use standard sizes of the better brands. And most are, to be sure, on the small side. It's my feeling, based on considerable experience, that a forty-eight-quart-capacity chest is about the minimum you'll require for a week's cruise with four people, under average conditions; few if any small cruisers have portable chests that size, but of course there's nothing to stop you from buying a second chest and stowing it in a quarterberth, alongside the galley. Because, face it, you're seldom going on a week's cruise in a very small vessel, and the weekend jaunts can be handled by a chest of, say, twenty-four-quart capacity.

There are several things to look for in a built-in ship's icebox, and not all of them are apparent. First and most obvious are the twin matters of size and shape. For the average small cruising yacht, it seems to me that about six cubic feet is a fair size, assuming that it's a viable shape and has good insulation. Bear in mind that much of the box's contents will be ice, and that block ice occupies about a cubic foot per fifty-pound chunk. Since a hundred pounds of ice is not at all unusual for a starting supply at the beginning of a week's cruise, one ought to figure that nearly two cubic feet of icebox space will be preempted before any food goes in at all. (It is good practice, by the way, to chill off a boat's icebox before a cruise by putting in a hundred pounds of ice the night before you're planning to load, and then topping up to a hundred pounds again before putting in the food.)

Ice can be a very hostile element to food: If not packed immovably it can crash about in the box, smashing containers as it goes; as it melts, it turns the icebox's contents soggy. Ice makes a rotten shelf on which to stack food, yet it's often all that's available in the average small yacht's icebox.

Many iceboxes in linear galleys are up against the hull side, and have its shape, so that there's a steadily decreasing amount of usable space as one nears the bottom of the box. To get the most from the box, and keep items from sliding beneath the ice cakes and getting lost, you will have to chop the cakes roughly to fit the bottom contour, which of course causes them to melt more quickly. The better boxes allow the ice to sit on a nearly flat bottom and have a shelf or two about halfway up, to accommodate food such as produce that will suffer by being laid against the ice itself. More about shelves a bit later, but in the meantime, it's well to bear in mind that the bottom of one's icebox will often contain up to six inches or more of cold water, very useful in keeping cans and bottles chilled, but not of much consequence for anything else.

One aspect of shape that's often overlooked is the opening at the top of the box. Although one doesn't want it to be any bigger than necessary, it is a major pain in the neck—and often the knuckles—to have to wrestle a block of ice through a too small opening. A foot on a side is none too large, in my opinion, and allows for the variation in shape among cakes of ice.

Location is another problem, and one you can't do much about, short of getting another boat or rebuilding the interior. When shopping for a cruiser, one should consider one's cooking patterns and decide if the icebox is properly located to serve them. In a small yacht, the icebox top is nearly always the primary work surface in the galley, and it should be considered in those terms as well as in terms of access. In some yachts where the galley is aft, the icebox opening is wholly or partly under the overhang of the bridge deck. Having lived with this kind of arrangement for a couple of seasons, I have no hesitation in denouncing it. Not only is it very hard to load the box without simply dropping the ice straight down, but it is also nearly impossible to get a decent view of what's inside. Since any yacht's icebox is likely to become a semifrozen grab bag after the first couple of days at sea, it's important to be able to look down into the corners, and it will help a lot if the galley electric light shines down into the box.

The question of access is a complex one, and the best icebox I've yet seen in a cruising yacht had not one door but two. Though not often seen, a deck-loading box can be a great convenience as well as a terrible temptation to the crew on watch, who need only reach into the deck hatch to consume all one's beer in an afternoon. Seriously, though, a deck-loading box with a vertical door in the galley below is about the best compromise I've yet seen aboard a cruiser.

But if your boat's box is located normally—with a flush hatch in the counter surface—you'll have to make the best of it, and barring a few really bizarre locations, such as one seen in some British-built yachts where the top-loading box is under a settee cushion, the questions of location and access are not nearly as important as those of insulation and drainage.

The efficiency of insulation is partly a matter of the icebox's location relative to heat-producing elements of the boat—the engine, for one common example—partly a matter of the thickness and type of insulation, and partly a matter of the completeness with which the box is wrapped by its insulating material. It is very difficult to determine just how a boat's icebox is insulated by reading the sales literature. All builders claim that their boats' boxes are "well insulated" or "fully insulated," but few if any say how much or with what. Most of it is polyurethane foam or Styrofoam or a relative thereof, and while Richard Henderson, in *The Cruiser's Compendium,* recommends four inches of insulation for iceboxes in hot climates, you will usually be very lucky to see three, and two inches of insulation is probably more like average. If you find that your boat's box doesn't seem to be holding a chill, check the side or sides nearest the inboard engine, if you have one, and consider adding a layer of foam there. Be sure also that the box's lid is as thickly insulated as the sides —frequently in less well built yachts the lid is hardly insulated at all, and while cold air certainly sinks, some of it will escape by conduction through a poorly insulated top.

Most builders today either provide no drain at all or else drain the icebox directly to the bilge. Although the first design can be infuriating to live with, the second is almost equally bad, as sooner or later one is bound to have a disaster in the icebox that one does not want to pass on to the bilge. In the Bermuda-30, however, as in very few other boats I've seen, the icebox drained into a sump tank with a large screw top (for cleaning). The tank was emptied by the bilge pump, using a throwover valve. If you have the space in the bilge, and a mechanical bent, it is not too hard to set up such an arrangement for your icebox, and it will certainly keep unpleasant smells from the boat's interior.

Failing this, it is possible to hook the drain into a foot or hand pump that will empty into the galley sink and thence overboard. Or you may have a drain in the icebox that leads directly over the side. This kind of thing is seldom seen, however, because most iceboxes have their bottoms well below the waterline.

Water systems

Although more and more quite small cruisers have increasingly elaborate freshwater systems, I don't care to have one on my own boat. (On a borrowed or chartered yacht, well, that's another matter entirely.) It seems to me that the minor convenience of pressure water or heated water is well and truly counterbalanced by the cost and worry of taking care of the system in a hostile environment. Be that as it may, a working knowledge of basic boat plumbing is necessary to any cruising person, and it is not complicated, at least in principle.

The basic nonpressure system consists initially of a tank, which normally has a deck-level fill pipe. The fill is perhaps better located if it's off the deck itself, to prevent its taking in dirty or salt water through an untightened cap, but nearly all such tanks do have their fills on deck, and very little foreign matter seems to get in. Do be sure, however, that the cap of your water tank is plainly marked "water" and your fuel tank cap marked "fuel," "gas," or "diesel" as the case may be.

The intake hose leads more or less directly down to a secure fitting in the top of the water tank. Matching it is the much smaller pipe attached to the water-tank vent. The small opening at the upper end of the vent should be hooded, again to prevent unwanted substances from getting into the system. The vent should be located off a horizontal surface and preferably where you can keep an eye on it while filling the water tank, as a sudden gush from the vent tells you you're nearing the top of the tank. A water-tank vent probably should not be on the side of the hull, especially if yours is a boat that dips her gunwale frequently. Aside from the chance of pulling in a bit of salt water, there is a real if remote possibility that when sailing on one tack for a long time you may start a siphon and fill the tank entirely with salt (or at least exterior) water. I find the inside of a self-bailing cockpit or even the side of the deckhouse are good places for a vent installation. There will probably be a single water outlet from the tank. If it's located on the tank top, it will pay to have some sort of petcock at the tank's lowest point, to make complete draining possible. (A pump will never pump dry.)

Most small cruisers will have two basins with freshwater taps, one in the galley and one in the head. As a rule, these basins will each have a single pump-operated faucet (unless the boat has pressure or hot water). There are numerous pumps on the market, most of which are adequate to the service. In my opinion, the rocker-arm pump, in which the vertical pump lever is pulled and pushed alternately, is far superior to the plunger pump, in which one pulls and pushes an inconveniently designed handle in and out. Better than either of these, to my mind, is the foot pump. A small pedal a couple of inches off the deck is operated with a gentle tapping motion, producing a steady stream of water (once you get the rhythm) and leaving both hands free. In a small, lively boat this last is no small advantage.

So much for the basic system. If there is not one, you should install at the lowest point in the piping a cock to drain all the lines. If you don't drain them, and you live in a place where water freezes in the winter, it will and your pipes will probably burst. If you have two tanks, the withdrawal lines should run to a central fitting with three valves. You should be able to run both basins off either tank, or off both simultaneously, and you should have a third valve to drain off both tanks into the bilge.

Pressure water is not terribly complicated. An electric pump, usually keyed by a spring-loaded faucet, takes water from the storage tank and feeds it into the system where it stays under pressure until the tap is opened, which releases the system water and draws more from the tank. In some cases, an intermediate tank is used to make a regular flow of water easier in a multifaucet system. When the main tank runs low, the electric pump has to labor to fill the system

—and a laboring electric pump, one that runs for several seconds after the faucet is closed, is a sign that the water tank is nearly empty.

The simplest kind of automatic water system uses a single switch to turn on the water supply, and the type of system must be matched to the number of outlets being used.

Hot pressurized water simply adds another level of complexity. The water is heated by the yacht's engine, and it normally takes an hour or so of running time to bring the water to an appreciably high temperature. Usually a simple heat exchanger connects the engine's fresh cooling water to piping run through the boat's hot-water tank. The tank itself is so well insulated, in a good system, that it will keep water quite pleasantly warm overnight. A fancy unit will also have a connection to the boat's 110-volt shore power panel, so that when you're plugged in at the marina, the water heater is in automatic operation. The heater's piping is of course connected to a pressure system of its own. Compared to a house's hot-water system, to be sure, a boat's is small and slow. But many cruising people find it quite acceptable and a genuine addition to their comfort afloat. I freely admit to being a Neanderthal in this respect, as I find pressure hot water on my own boat just another expensive gadget to go wrong sooner or later.

If your boat does have pressure water, you should insist on having a hand or foot pumping system as well. It is not unknown for pressure water to give up the ghost partway through a cruise, and if you have a manual backup, your voyage need not be ruined. The manual backup need be in only the primary sink location, but it is a must—I can still recall being well out at sea in a large cruiser whose electric water system died, leaving us with no hand-powered backup. Until we hit upon an emergency method for tapping the tank, we felt very foolish squatting on top of a couple of hundred gallons of water we couldn't get at.

It is quite fashionable on long-distance cruisers to install a seawater pump that draws directly from over the side. The idea is that seawater can be used for much cooking, for washing the dishes before a freshwater rinse, and even for washing the crew (likewise, one hopes, with a freshwater rinse afterwards). The savings in water from the ship's tanks can be considerable with such an addition, but it is probably unnecessary on most small cruising yachts with only coastwise yearnings. For them, the water in which they sail is often unreliable as to cleanliness, and the next freshwater point isn't that far off.

IX

Living Space

Sleeping

The number of berths in a boat intended for coastal cruising is usually a matter of secondary importance. If you honestly plan to make frequent overnight passages offshore, then of course you need places for the off-watch to sleep in comfort while the boat is under way. But the key here is being honest about the kind of cruising you really do, and most of us do very little sleeping under way.

In the average small cruiser there are three main areas that can be used for

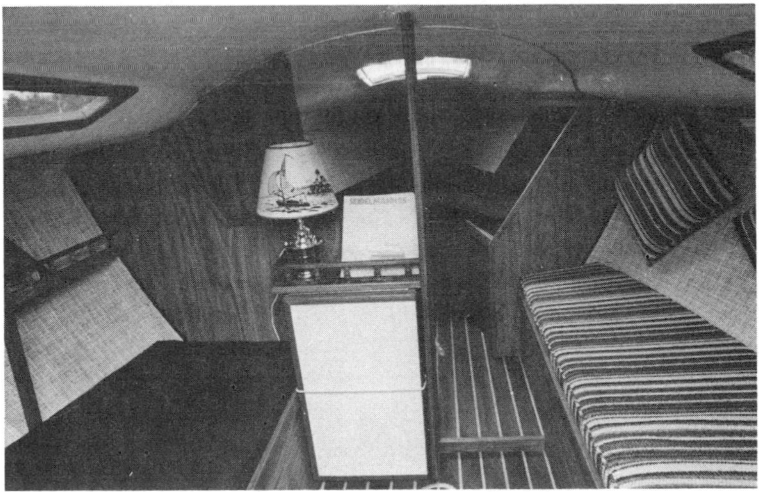

Looking forward in Seidelmann 25, open V-berth is forward; self-contained head is behind half bulkhead to port.

sleeping, at least occasionally: topside, which usually means in the cockpit; below in the forward cabin (if any); and below in the main cabin. Each location has its advantages and drawbacks, and in order to have an accurate idea of what you're in for, it may help to look closely at the whole problem of what a colleague of mine once referred to as "berth control." The question most people start out with is "How many berths do I need?" In that form, it's hard to answer. You have to know a lot more than just the number of the regular crew.

Begin by dividing all sleeping surfaces into two main categories—permanent and occasional. The number of permanent berths required is the key question, as the others can be improvised almost infinitely. For the purposes of this chapter, I'm calling a permanent berth any surface designed primarily for sleeping, and one that does not have to be altered in order to make it an adequate place to sleep. To divide yet again, permanent berths are either sea berths or they aren't (the same can be said of occasional berths).

Permanent berths

And a sea berth is one in which a crewmember can sleep while the boat is under way, without interfering with the vessel's operation. On a deep-water boat, sea berths are the most important kind, and a boat that cannot sleep half her crew under way probably has no business making offshore passages, except under very unusual circumstances. Most coastal cruising sailors, however, come to rest at night, whether at a marina or at anchor, and a real sea berth is only necessary when someone becomes ill or exhausted during a daytime

Quarterberths in sitting-headroom Frances 26.

passage. Even if you have absolutely no intention of sleeping under way, it's a good idea to have at least one sea berth in any cruising yacht, even if you have to do a little rerigging to arrange it.

There are four types of permanent berth, and all of them may be seen in the same 30-footer, although it is unusual. Beginning aft, there is the quarterberth, so named because it extends back, usually under the cockpit seat, into one or the other of the boat's quarters. Although most boats have only one quarterberth, there's no reason why you cannot have them either side of the companionway. Quarterberths are usually large singles, although I have seen doubles—and real ones—in relatively small yachts such as the C&C 29. Children excepted, normal people sleep with their heads at the cabin end of a quarterberth, and they can usually rely on a decent supply of fresh air—sometimes mixed with rain and/or spray—from the companionway.

The quarterberth on many offshore passages is reserved for the navigator (who is usually the skipper) or the cook, as this berth provides something of a nest, more or less out of the way of traffic, yet convenient to nav station, galley, and deck. A quarterberth is a good place for anyone whose stomach is not of the firmest, as the boat's motion is probably least at this point, and there is immediate access to the great outdoors.

The standard settee berth runs fore and aft along the sides of the main cabin. There is usually stowage above it, in drawers or lockers, and often below as well. When a settee berth is occupied, it's usually impossible to get at the drawers immediately above it, a fact that should be considered when deciding what goes into them. One of the design factors that handicaps the average settee is that a place wide enough to make a good seat is too narrow to sleep on, while a bunk of adequate width is a little too deep for the average thigh. Put it another way: A good settee is a bad berth, and a good berth makes a poor settee. Assuming you have a settee that's wide enough to sleep on, however, you can make it narrow enough for sitting, as we shall see below. The other drawback of a settee for under-way sleeping is that it's smack in the middle of the living area, and makes a poor place for anyone to get any rest on a passage.

Far better in many ways is the pilot berth, which is usually outboard of and above a settee, up against the yacht's side. In olden days, when no one worried about ventilation, many main cabins (then known as saloons) had a row of pilot berths along each side, each berth a little niche, with a draw curtain for privacy. One wonders why the occupants didn't smother. Today's pilot berth isn't nearly as isolated, although it is significantly out of the main stream of traffic. Like the quarterberth, however, it tends to collect materiel that has no home anyplace else, which can be exasperating to the person whose berth it is. The main drawback of a pilot berth is the difficulty of getting out of it in a hurry—or even not in a hurry—if the settee below and inboard is occupied by a sleeper. But a pilot berth is the ideal sea berth, far enough aft to have the best of the boat's motion, out of the way, and easy to secure in a seaway.

There are relatively few things a designer can do with the bow of a boat: It is unavoidably triangular, and even if you cut off the extreme point and call it a rope locker, the shape of the remaining space doesn't lend itself to much else than a V-berth. In boats above about twenty-three feet, most V-berths today are capable of being sealed off, to form a small but separate cabin, with the head and hanging locker between them and the main cabin. At anchor or in the marina, the V-berth is just fine, but under way it is often hopeless, especially in a small boat. There are three reasons. First, the forward space is where headsails tend to collect when not set. Even quite a small bagged headsail takes up an inordinate amount of space, and the accompanying dampness and smell (many headsails contain a resin that has the aroma of an ancient men's room) can be unpleasant. Second, a boat with fine bows will be surprisingly sensitive to the weight of a couple of adults well forward. Third and most important, the motion in the forward cabin of a small boat close-reaching or beating precludes anything that could be called rest, at least by an adult. It is not at all unusual for the hapless sleeper to lift clear off the mattress with every thrust of the bow, and whether he or the boat hits first makes little difference. Added to that is the rush of water right past one's ear, often coupled with an insidious chill and damp in a less than perfectly insulated hull. Having said this, it is only fair to add that many small children can sleep in a forward cabin no matter how violent the sea, although it is necessary to provide protection against falling to the deck. V-berths, then, are indeed permanent, but they are only usable at sea under certain conditions and by certain people.

Settee berths port and starboard in main cabin of Ericson 29.

Occasional berths

An occasional berth can be defined as an area that's used for sleeping part of the time and for something else at other times. A few years ago, when the mania for vast numbers of berths in tiny cruisers reached its height, it seemed possible to make just about any flat surface into a berth, and usually a double, and I have always wondered how many families were shattered by these tiny torture chambers. In the last couple of years there seems to have been a slight reaction against the extreme floating motel, perhaps best reflected in the ebbing number of convertible dinettes now being offered in small boats.

The convertible dinette is certainly the occasional berth in its purest (and sometimes direst) form. Typically, it is formed by a pair of bench seats, one facing forward, the other aft, with vertical padded backs. Between them is a table that can be dropped to rest on pieces of molding at the outer edges of the seats. The seat-back padding is removable and fits on the lowered table, and there you are. In the average small boat, the dinette is only barely large enough for two people to have shoulder room side by side on either one of the seats. When one lowers the table to make the so-called double berth, the inward slope of the hull causes the effective shoulder room of the berth to be noticeably less than that of the dinette.

Another version has a U-shaped settee around three sides of the table, which may have a drop leaf to enable someone sitting on the facing settee to use it as well. There is nothing wrong with this arrangement in a larger yacht, but in boats of thirty feet or so, the table tends to be too small for four dinner-size plates at once, which seems the least one might expect. A somewhat more workable variant is the L-shaped settee, which provides for a slightly larger eating surface.

There are numberless ways to make the table surface drop, and fortunately the cleverest ones have all died off. The most consistently workable seems to consist of sockets on the deck and underside of the table, into which a stout pillar fits. The pillar is simply removed at bedtime, and the only real drawback is its tendency, if not chocked in, to roll noisily around on the cabin sole every time the boat rolls.

In terms of sleeping, there can be several problems inherent in a dinette, although none of them is necessary. To begin with, the table almost certainly has fiddled edges—raised lips, to keep plates from sliding off—and a decent fiddle ought really to be about one and a half inches high. This in turn means that the cushions on which one sleeps ought to be at least four inches thick, if one is to avoid having a surprisingly sharp edge laid across one's back and calves.

The cushions themselves are often ill-cut, the builder having had to choose between a comfortable seat back and a comfortable mattress, and having decided that curved corners looked better. To make something approaching a consistent sleeping surface, of course, there should be as few ridges and

Fold-up seat back transforms settee into wide berth.

valleys in the cushions as possible, and they should fit tightly together with relatively little motion beneath a restless sleeper. If your dinette's cushions are miserable to sleep on, you can consider replacing the whole rig with a double air mattress, of imposing some intermediate leveler, such as a partly inflated air mattress or a backpacker's three-eighths-inch ground pad, between you and the cushions.

There is no question that a dinette/double berth dominates the small boat's main cabin when in use as a bunk: Until the sleeper(s) occupying it have got up, nothing can take place very easily, and frequently nothing can happen at all, as the sleepers' clothes necessarily festoon the galley and/or chart area.

The dinette can be a godsend to the cruising family with small children on a rainy day, as it gives a splendid place to play games, draw pictures, or play with midget autos. At rest it's not at all a bad place to eat, and it can even be used under way sometimes. But it is limited, and it is a compromise, which is to say that it performs neither function as well as the real table and genuine berth for which it substitutes.

Time was, and not so very long ago, when every cruising yacht had at least one pilot berth in the saloon, and below and inboard of it a pull-out settee, sometimes referred to as an "extension transom." In the pushed-in, or settee, mode, this piece of furniture made a seat of comfortable width, and when pulled out and locked, usually with a pair of barrel bolts, it formed a berth of reasonable width. It often had drawer stowage beneath it, and it was possible to rig lee cloths to keep the sleeper from falling on the deck.

All in all, it seemed a splendid compromise, but few are seen on small cruisers today. How come? Well, to begin with, it simply didn't work as well as all that. The jamming extension berth is a bitter memory to many cruising sailors of the last generation: As the wood swelled, the berth stuck, never all the way in or out, but somewhere in between. Go to sleep on it, and the boat was sure to lurch, closing or opening it abruptly. And the carpentry itself became more and more costly, in the era of molded modular interiors. There were other, cheaper ways of sleeping two people on the same side of the boat. Besides, as boats became fatter amidships, the need for sliding berths was less —there was just more room.

Another drawback to the extension settee is that it severely restricted fore-and-aft movement in the main cabin. If the dinette/double berth was a problem in this respect, the extension berth was often worse, making it just about impossible to get from the forward cabin to the companion without walking lengthwise over some sleeper. And finally, of course, the sleeper in an extension berth inboard and below a pilot berth could count on being trampled or at least pawed every time the occupant of the sea berth entered or left his enclosure.

In the end, then, the extension berth works if the required carpentry is first

Seat back lifts to make upper berth. Wire cable supports berth, but note full-length lee cloth.

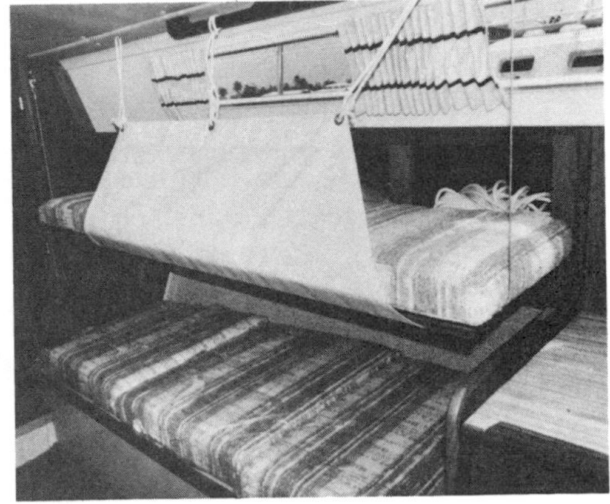

class, if there's a fore-and-aft passage even when it is fully extended, and if it is truly an occasional, i.e., emergency, sleeping place.

Folding berths

One common way of converting a settee into a berth is with a lifting or removable seat back. In this conformation, the narrow settee has a stowage space for bedding behind its back during the day. At night, the back is either hinged to swing up or is simply removable, often doubling the width of the berth. This arrangement can work very well indeed, as long as there is clearance beneath the swung-up back. One clever version of this setup uses as a seat back a simple padded board that fits into U-shaped slots in the bulkhead at the head and foot of the berth. At night, the board is removed and fitted into two alternate slots even with the inboard edge of the berth, thus making a padded bunkboard.

On some yachts, the swing-up seat back is even used to form part of an upper berth, an arrangement that can work, but that has some scaling problems in boats as small as the ones we're discussing here. There is seldom enough vertical space from cabin sole to side deck to allow for (a) adequate height of the lower berth off the deck, when it's a seat, *and* (b) a high enough seat back to make a berth of decent width, *and* (c) enough clearance between upper and lower, *and* (d) enough clearance between upper and the underside of the side deck or cabin overhead. It is, as you can see, a complex problem, and it's usually easier for the designer to swing the seat back up and out of the way, and leave well enough alone.

A type of occasional berth often seen in older craft, and still found in the first generation of fiberglass cruisers, Triton and its cousins, was the root (or stretcher), berth. At its simplest, this is nothing more than a stretcher formed by a piece of heavy fabric sleeved along its long sides to accept a couple of sturdy poles. The ends of these rods fit into holders on the fore and aft bulkheads, and the whole affair can be removed, rolled up, and easily stowed during the day.

A root berth (named, I understand, after a person named Root) is surprisingly comfortable, at least in warm weather. Instead of a single piece of cloth, it can be built up from webbing for better ventilation and greater springiness, and it can be made firmer by bridging the gap between the stretcher poles with other rigid members. If the cabin becomes cooled at night, a root berth can be quite chilly underneath, but a good sleeping bag or even an air mattress can provide the necessary insulation.

The normal location for old-time root berths was as uppers over the main cabin settees. A set of alternate sockets for the ends of the inboard pole, or a block-and-tackle to the overhead, allowed the occupant to adjust the angle of the berth to allow himself to sleep on the level, at least as long as the boat remained at more or less the same angle of heel—and old-time cruising yachts would only tack (if tacking itself were unavoidable) at the change of watch.

Size and shape

One great question concerns the proper size of berths, as well as the best design for combining support and comfort. To a considerable extent, it's inescapably a matter of personal choice, and partly a question of age: The young have the ability, it often seems, to sleep anywhere; when I was a teenager I could grab a few *Z*s on a coil of damp manila anchor line, a prospect that's notably unappealing today. Still, there are proven proportions for proper bunks, and design features that have passed the tests of long use under varying conditions.

Landlubbers who have never slept under way are always amazed at the narrowness of true sea berths. Yet at sea—especially in a small boat—one wants to be wedged in place, as even a few inches of constant to-and-fro movement can take the rest out of any watch below. British designer and surveyor Ian Nicolson gives a set of what he calls minimum dimensions for a seagoing berth to fit "a large (but not exceptional) man." The width at shoulders and hips is 1'9", width at the foot is 1'1" and at the head, 1'4". The berth's total length is 6'4", and if one were to divide the length into five equal parts, the area of greatest width would be 40 percent, that's 1'4", from the head end and 2'7" from the foot. More recently Roger Marshall in *Designed to Win* gives more or less the same measurements.

As Nicolson points out, these dimensions would be for that rare berth whose sides and ends rise vertically from the mattress. Where the yacht's side slopes outward, as it is almost certain to do along one long edge, the width dimension can be slightly less. As for the length, Nicolson suggests that it should always be at least two inches more than the occupant's height. This frankly seems to me truly minimal, but then I often sleep on my stomach with my feet adding an extra couple of inches by virtue of being flattened. Unless you have very precise knowledge of who's going to occupy which berth (and unless they are people who've reached their full growth), it's usually a mistake to accept berths of less than six feet as being full length, as they will simply be too small for too many.

While a narrow, deep berth is what's wanted for seagoing, that same spot can be very uncomfortable in a boat that's at anchor or tied up in a marina. Then, of course, the bigger the better, as sprawl space will be an aid to sleep and so will the ventilation derived simply from freely circulating air around the sleeper's body. It can be a dilemma, and the compromising answer only comes from being honest with yourself about how you're going to use the boat. As a general rule, a double berth ought always to be large, as by its nature it won't make a satisfactory sea berth. (On a long tack, to be sure, one person can sleep comfortably on the well-supported down side, but it's no longer a double.) Quarterberths, being supported on both sides, as a rule can be rather wide. Settees, especially the pull-out kind, should be wide, too, as you will probably want to wedge some cushions between yourself and the seat back or bunkboard for padding.

V-berths are something of an anomaly in terms of measurement, because the straight length along the boat's centerline isn't the true length of the berth, each side of which should be measured from head to toe. Although it is not a factor of size, it seems to be true of most people that they can only sleep well under way in a berth that runs along the yacht's fore-and-aft axis. The reason is simple enough: When a boat heels—and nearly any sailing boat heels a bit —a berth that's not lined up with the yacht's centerline will dip its head or foot, and as the boat rolls, the berth will seem to corkscrew. A thwartships berth, seldom seen on a small cruiser, will be virtually untenable in a moving boat, although it may be delightful at rest.

Mattresses are a real problem in yachts, both in terms of thickness and covering material. As for filling, some form of foam is now virtually universal. Closed-cell foam is better, but of course more costly. If you sleep aboard a lot or in damp climates, the extra cost will probably be worth it. Most people these days feel that four inches of foam between them and a wood or fiberglass bunk bottom is about right. Unless the foam is very firm, or you like a hard mattress, three inches is too little, and less is only adequate if the berth bottom is canvas or webbing. If in doubt, lie on your side and try to drive your hip bone into the material. If your hip bottoms out, you probably won't want to sleep on that surface.

Curiously enough, too much thickness in a mattress, especially a soft one, can result in a bunk that's very warm, since a good deal of you is totally insulated, retaining too much body heat for most cruising climates. If you're stuck with very thin mattresses, or a widely variable climate, the ubiquitous air mattress can come to your rescue.

Clearance above a berth mattress is important. In a small cruiser, one's berth is to a considerable extent one's bedroom, and it is more than just a place to sleep. Certainly any berth should have enough vertical clearance to permit one to sit up and read or pull on one's trousers, and you should be able to get in and out without inconveniencing the occupants of neighboring berths—or indeed the other occupant of a double. Look for handholds and grabs to make entrance and exit easier.

Berth supports

There are few less restful sensations than lying in one's berth calculating the chances of being dumped on the deck at the next roll. Proper support will give one the ability to relax and, eventually, to sleep, although few adults I know get sustained rest the first night or two aboard a boat. Supports for a berth may be permanent, temporary or jury-rigged, rigid or flexible.

In older yachts, pilot berths were, as noted earlier, virtually semiprivate roomlets, with curtains and high fixed bunkboards to retain the occupants. There are relatively few berths like this today, because the poor ventilation and accessibility are more than most people are willing to put up with in return for the certainty of remaining in their berth no matter what the boat's gyrations. The only new boats I've seen with the cubbyhole sort of support are a couple of racer-cruisers from Yamaha and an occasional deep-water cruiser from European builders.

If you do go for a boat with a permanent bunkboard, it must be high enough to hold you in when the boat is heeled, without your having the sensation of oozing over it. This is a hard matter to sort out at a pier or boat show, but in a trial sail in a decent breeze, you can lay the boat over to 20 or 25 degrees, get into the bunkboarded berth and see if you still feel secure. Because if you don't, the board is worse than useless. (And if you do, chances are the berth will be a real problem getting into and out of.)

Nearly all temporary bunkboards are fabric, sometimes webbing, although one occasionally sees a rigid hinged board. The most common type of support consists basically of a synthetic cloth trapezoid, with the longest edge screwed down into the berth's wood or fiberglass base, or sewn to the underside of the mattress. The screws themselves should be fixed through grommeted holes, to prevent tearing the fabric when it is strained. Two other grommeted holes are fixed in the upper corners, and short lines lead from these holes to fittings through-bolted to the overhead or fore and after bulkheads. The bunkboards will provide more support if the tie lines go upward to points directly above the ends of the board's longest edge: This way, their pull both stretches the bunkboard's upper edge and keeps it taut, and raises it as high as possible. The tie lines are easiest to rig and loose if they terminate in snaphooks, but it can be a mistake to splice both ends to the grommets and snaps, as the lines will almost certainly stretch a good deal under the weight of a body.

One argument against upward-leading lines is that their upper ends are probably going to be out of reach of the sleeper, who may need to get on deck in a hurry. But of course this problem can be solved by putting the snap hooks at the lower ends of the lines. Another objection is that in through-bolting a stressed fitting to the overhead—often one with a balsa core—one is simply inviting leaks right over the berths. There is a certain amount of reason in this feeling, and perhaps a better solution is to make the tie lines fast to the interior grabrails.

Ready-made bunkboards are often too short for real support. My feeling is that they should be at least four feet long at the lower edge, so there's air space at the head and foot (often interchangeable on midships berths), but adequate bolstering from shoulder to knee. In some cases, it's possible to split a double berth lengthwise with a bunkboard tied to the overhead, as well as one on the berth's outside edge, thus making two sea berths. It requires, of course, that the double's mattress be split lengthwise for at least the middle four feet, something that is often the case in dinette berths and that is virtually always true of V-berths forward (although here the boat's motion may still be too much for comfort).

It may also be necessary to rig partial-length bunkboards for quarterberths, especially if the bunks are very wide at the head end, and sometimes pilot berths will have rigid bunkboards for part of their length, and removable ones the rest of the way. The thing to avoid in any bunk support is a drooping, inadequate bunkboard, since it cannot be trusted and will sooner or later let you down, literally. I can recall, with insomniac clarity, one recent ocean passage when the bunkboards (affixed to pad eyes in the fore and aft bulkheads) became stretched out of shape, just like old headsails, to the point that crew-members rolled right over the distended upper edges. During a gale, one hand found herself pitched clear over the board, over the top of the intervening drop-leaf table, and onto the occupant of the down-side settee on the far side of the cabin. It's difficult to go on watch with any enthusiasm left after something like that.

Jury-rigged supports may be anything that comes to hand. If your boat has extension settees and a permanent drop-leaf table, you may be able to pull the windward-side settee all the way out and use the table, padded with a cushion, as a bunkboard. But make sure before you do this that the table is properly secured, preferably to a bulkhead at one end and a deck-to-overhead grab pole at the other; if, like so many boat tables, it's only bolted or screwed to the deck, the continued pressure of bodies will rip it free and perhaps destroy it altogether.

Stowage in a berth's immediate vicinity is far more important than many boatbuilders seem to realize. When you go to sleep tonight, glance over the top of your bedside table and the top of your bureau as well: Watch, keys, wallet, change, glasses—all get tossed down casually at home, yet these items, plus knife, gloves, flashlight, and cap, have to find some place near the sleeper afloat, too.

My feeling is that each sea berth should have a fairly deep fiddled shelf at its head end, so located that it will not bash a sleeper's head when he sits up suddenly, and big enough to accommodate the things I've listed, and perhaps socks and underwear as well, and even a book. A small locker or drawer can sometimes be set into the bulkhead at the head of a berth, if there's room in the adjoining cabin or area, for the same gear. In addition, there should be a gear hammock or an adjoining drawer where a sleeper's clothing can be stored. Ideally, each crewmember would have two drawers, one for clean and one for used clothing, but that's usually asking too much, and it will probably be adequate, during a cruise, to have dirty clothes relegated to a laundry bag hung —not thrown—someplace where there's decent ventilation.

Light and ventilation

Light and air are vital adjuncts to a sleeping space, although many yacht designers clearly adhere to the nineteenth-century thinking that considered fresh air a health hazard. Obviously, one will want to be able to darken a berth when its occupant is trying to sleep and something else is going on in the same cabin. This design requirement really has to be met at the boat's construction stage, and most builders with any experience are quite good at screening a cabin's lights from the sleeping areas. More and more berths have "personal" reading lights that scarcely impinge even on those in a berth directly above or below, but it should also be possible to cook a meal or plot a course without rousting the entire off-watch.

It's not hard to check: Simply climb into each berth in turn and look around to see what light fixtures are visible from where you lie, and how necessary they will be at night. A properly engineered main cabin will always have a galley light fixture that's screened both from the helm and from sleepers, and there should be a similar light in the navigation area. About the only nonspecific light useful in a cabin at night, with the boat under way, is a red-tinted safety light, spotted out of harm's way at the foot of the companionway, to help stumblers.

The head

It is not my purpose to suggest for a moment that readers of this book join the tens of thousands of cruising people who are disobeying the marine head regulations, whether out of ignorance, out of confusion, or out of a conviction that said regulations are a political ploy and don't clean up anything. That's for you to decide. What I hope to do, however, is to explain in reasonably clear terms what the U. S. marine sanitation device (MSD) regulations say, what they mean, and what's available to comply with them.

The regulations, to begin with, are drawn up by the EPA and administered by the Coast Guard. They divide the cruising waters of the United States, inland, riverine, and coastal, into three categories defined by sewage disposal. The first consists of "no-discharge" waters. In areas so defined, it is illegal to release any sewage over the side, whether treated or not. Such waters are usually closed-system lakes, such as New York's Lake George, but the MSD regulations allow a state to petition the EPA to declare any area no-discharge, if the state can prove a sound environmental reason for this judgment, as well as the presence of adequate pumpout stations to service marine holding tanks.

In point of fact, many boating people believe that the EPA is committed to no-discharge as a policy, and has been only too eager to certify states' requests for this status on the slightest excuse. State politicians, on the other hand, quick to draw attention away from more politically powerful polluters, have found "rich yachtsmen" a convenient, unorganized target. As a result, much of the Great Lakes and a number of California coastal harbors have been declared no-discharge zones. Since this designation is a continuing process, the boatman is well advised to check with his local Coast Guard district headquarters to determine the current boundaries of discharge and no-discharge zones in the waters around him.

The second category of waters, covering most of the main river systems and coastal waters, can be described as "limited-discharge." In these areas, one has the option of attaching to one's marine head a treatment device that reduces the coliform count of sewage to an approved level and then ejects it over the side. (One may, of course, also use a no-discharge device in a limited-discharge area, but not a treatment device in a no-discharge zone.)

Finally, there are offshore waters, those beyond the three-mile coastal limit, where no MSD regulation applies. It is worth bearing in mind that the demarcation line for the MSD regulations is not the same as the inshore line that divides the international from the inland rules of the road jurisdictions.

So much for areas. There is, in all of this, one gaping loophole that is especially applicable to owners of small cruisers, that are by their nature used mostly for overnighting or weekending. The MSD regulations apply *only* to vessels having installed head systems, and the Coast Guard has specifically excluded from this category all heads designed to be taken ashore (presumably) and emptied into a toilet or sewage system. Or your boat may have no head whatever—there is no law forcing you to carry one. It is, however, illegal to dump raw sewage into any no-discharge or limited-discharge waters. And the Canadian government has a record of hostility toward American boats with portable heads, feeling that these units are invitations to lawbreaking.

If you opt for an installed marine head, there are nominally three, but really only two, types from which to choose. Approved heads designated as Type I or Type II by the Coast Guard are in principle the same things: pass-through heads that treat the sewage to reduce the coliform count. Type I's do it somewhat less efficiently than Type II's, but neither one retains the sewage.

For practical purposes, Type III MSDs are retention systems. (Incinerators can also be Type IIIs, but they are absurd for small yachts.) Typically, the Type III head consists of a standard toilet which passes the sewage into a holding tank, which is then pumped into a shoreside tank, usually at a marina. As often as not, the marina collects the pumpout fee from the owner, and dumps the raw sewage back into the body of water in which you are sailing. There are also recirculating heads, like the ones on aircraft, that employ the same rinse water over and over, and that are also hooked into holding tanks. These latter units must be Coast Guard–certified, but a holding tank that stores sewage at ambient temperature, without treating it, has a *prima facie* certification, and need not be labeled as approved.

The boat you like will probably be offered new with one or another type of

MSD, take it or leave it, and the builder will be required to sell you an approved installation or none at all, but he is not allowed (at least in theory) to offer other than legal installed heads in the United States and Canada. Most boats in the vigorous tidal waters of Europe have heads that discharge directly into the sea—but how long this state of affairs will last is questionable.

What follows are my own, highly personal feelings about the currently available options in toilets. Begin with the extralegal portable head, usually known by some dreadfully cute name like Porta-Potti or Tota-Toilet. Such units are relatively inexpensive and consist in general of two elements. The top, which is also the seat, contains a tank holding a couple of gallons of flush water. When the toilet is used, the flush water cleans the bowl and then flows, along with the sewage, into the bottom part of the head, which is essentially an airtight container with a sealing valve. When the tank is full, it's carried ashore ("just like a briefcase," says one ad. Not like my briefcase, I respond), to be dumped into a standard head. In past years, these portable heads had a number of engineering problems: The valves leaked slightly, so that you would leave a dreadful trail as you marched resolutely down the pier, carrying your plastic "briefcase" and pretending you weren't aware of every eye on you. The deodorant sold to disguise the smell of human waste had its own distinctive, pungent aroma. In addition, it was colored blue, and would turn everything it touched a permanent cobalt. And finally, it was highly poisonous, deadly to a home septic system.

Recently, proper engineering and development have disposed of a number of these problems. The units are largely leak-free, especially if you avoid waiting until the last, overflowing moment to empty them. New biodegradable deodorants make it safe to empty tanks into a home toilet. Standard hold-down latches keep the toilets in place during heavy weather, yet do not disqualify them as noninstalled devices.

My own feeling is that if you can face the depressing task of emptying these heads at approximately two-day intervals, they are a very practical solution for the coastal or lake sailor. Not the least of their attractions is the fact that you punch no holes in the hull, have no machinery to clean, and can—if worst comes to worst—simply remove the whole thing for repair or replacement.

The drawbacks are, first, that even the largest has a limited amount of flush water and a limited amount of waste-stowage space. In my experience, a family of four will require to empty such a head's tank about once every two days, assuming normal frequency and no access to another head. For the small weekender, this is usually enough capacity, but if the unit has been employed even once, it is wise to empty it anyway, and this can be tedious. Second, your head compartment entrance and companionway must have the proper dimensions to allow the tank to be taken easily in and out. In one small boat I owned, the clearance was absolutely minimal, leading to much cursing and skinned knuckles. Third, you must have access to a nearby head in which you can dump the portable unit. Many marinas and yacht clubs aren't too keen on having their toilet facilities treated in this fashion, and you may have to become resigned to carting the tank unit home in your car—something you'll have to do anyway—in order to clean out the holding tank half from time to time. And fourth, you will sooner or later miscalculate and find yourself with an overflowing head and far from an emptying point.

None of these problems is fatal, and on balance it still seems to me the most desirable solution for small cruising yachts. It has—function aside—two additional advantages over many other devices—first, it requires no through-hull fitting at all, whether above or below the waterline; second, it is easy to clean the entire area by removing and hosing down the toilet itself.

If most of your boating is done in coastal waters, and you are frequently offshore, a Type III (holding tank) rig with a Y-valve throwover seems to me the best compromise for the medium-size cruiser that plans the occasional longer passage. It is important, however, to make sure that your vestigial holding tank is properly constructed and engineered, both from the point of view of resale value, and to allow for a later change in the Coast Guard's or EPA's position regarding throwover valves. No matter what the temptation, it seems to me that a holding tank of less than ten gallons' capacity is shortsighted, and a good venting system may at some point be a must. It is also important to ensure that the Y-valve throwover is secure from accidental meddling, and that you at least are clear as to which setting is which. If you do have a Y-valve, you will also want a standard seacock on the through-hull intake and exhaust as an additional safety measure.

What about the Type I or II units? At this writing, and for the foreseeable future, my personal impression is that the Type II is too bulky and the Type I too demanding of electrical power to make either really practical in the small auxiliary cruiser. The most successful Type I units typically have a peak power demand of 40 or 50 amps during their digestive cycle, and this kind of thing really requires a separate battery if your electrical system is to remain truly reliable. If you feel that a Type I unit is acceptable in terms of power draw, then shop carefully before deciding on a given unit.

Head compartments

In a small cruising yacht, the choices for head compartments are quite restricted by boat size and the rest of the design. One thing you can be sure of, and that's the fact that it won't be like your bathroom at home. On a boat of thirty feet or less, you're guaranteed a cramped, cheerless, chilly or stifling chamber that can, if not rigorously cleaned, pack more atmospheric punch than a tin-roofed outhouse in an equatorial July. To make matters worse, most Americans still carry around with them the spikier Victorian shibboleths about bodily functions, and many ladies in particular can by anticipation turn a necessary interlude into a major trauma.

Slide-out sink unit on CS 27 conserves space over head.

If, however, you're willing to scrap some of your preconceptions, you can fit a functional head that's relatively easy to clean and not too space-consuming into virtually any cruiser. The first thing that has to go is the standard notion of privacy, especially aural privacy. Unless your crew is deaf, everyone's digestive habits are fairly public in a 30-footer. If it's any consolation, the same is true on a boat ten feet longer. You can, and should, expect visual privacy, but in a small boat it may be foolish to require a rigid bulkhead between you and the rest of the ship's company.

What are the desirable attributes of a small cruiser's head compartment? First and foremost, the toilet must be functional and reliable. The latter term requires no definition, but the former may need amplification. The head must have adequate capacity for the crew and the cruising area. It must be physically suited to the anatomy of the users—and this is no joke: I have shipped with a head that could only be approached kneeling, like a peculiarly repellent idol, and with another that was too narrow for any but the slimmest hips (in his *Designed to Win,* Roger Marshall specifies as an absolute minimum a hip width of 26 inches).

Try sitting on it; let the males in the crew try facing it operationally—it may be that awkward height that that holds users half kneeling and half standing; try bending forward while sitting: Is there room, or do you bang your head against the door?

The head must be well ventilated, especially if the compartment is sealed off much of the time. No matter how religiously you clean the area, an unven-

In open-plan boats like Frances 26, head is often boxed in forward.

tilated head is a smelly head. Finally, it must be easy to clean, even around the back. Removable, portable heads have a big advantage in this department.

What are the choices in location and layout? Let's begin by addressing the question of where.

In the smallest cruisers, the head is usually spotted between the forward V-berths, and this is the standard, time-honored location in two-berth overnighters—but privacy is poor if the berths are occupied. In some boats, the head is exactly between berths, with a folding cover concealing the top and front. In others, it's offset under one berth. There is not a great deal to choose between the two installations, and the only thing to look for in either case is access around the head for cleaning and opening or closing the seacocks if the head is of the old-fashioned type. The smaller portable heads are ideal for these spaces, as are the old-fashioned fitted buckets over which the late L. Francis Herreshoff made such a fuss.

(In case you came in too late to encounter a fitted bucket, it is simply a wooden pail, strongly enough constructed for one to sit on, and fitted with a shaped detachable seat. The favored style in buckets was a cedar job with a rope handle long enough to allow it to be rinsed over the side. Obviously such a contrivance is virtually *prima facie* evidence of intent to pollute.)

In boats of twenty feet and up, the standard head location is usually a recess at the head (or aft) end of one of the V-berths, separated from the sleeper by a partial bulkhead forward and a full bulkhead aft. Often the head faces a hanging space, which allows for symmetry in the layout. There's usually a bit more access for cleaning in this arrangement, but the head is still very much part of the forward cabin, and really impinges on the entire accommodation as well. All this means is that scrupulous cleanliness is absolutely required. The flow of air below isn't restricted to any great degree, and a separate vent for the head area probably isn't necessary at all, especially if there is a forward hatch more or less over the toilet.

As boats reach about twenty-five feet (sometimes less) in length, one begins to encounter the separate head compartment, usually with stooping headroom. In this setup, the toilet can be closed off from view either between uses, during use, or both. Today's standard arrangement is a thwartships compartment, often with a sliding half door to close off the forward cabin V-berth and a regular door between the head and the main cabin. Typically, the forward hatch remains in the forecabin, so some additional ventilation and light are required in the head. The advantages are increased room and, in some boats, a sink facing the head (often the counter into which the sink is recessed is over the footwell for a main cabin quarterberth). There may well be a hanging space, behind either the toilet or the sink, and a small locker for first-aid kit, toothbrushes, toilet paper, and the like. If you have any choice in the matter, a hanging space or sail bin behind the head itself is less than ideal, even if it has doors. If it does not, the contents of the space or bin are sure to be spattered, and even if it does, odors will tend to permeate the area.

In boats a little bit larger than twenty-five feet, one sees the separate head compartment occupying one side of the boat amidships, with its bulkhead usually placed to reinforce the fore and aft lower chainplates (in those yachts so sturdily rigged as to have two sets of lowers). Personally, I find these emplacements can be poorly engineered, with the usual mistake being an attempt to miniaturize the head compartment of a much larger yacht—tiny locker, minuscule sink, handkerchief-size counter, cramped toilet and, as the coup de grace, a single poorly built towel bar that looks like a grabrail but only reveals itself as plastic as it comes away in your clutching hand.

If a boat has a small head compartment, it's probably better to omit the sink, or if possible to have a slide-out or fold-up unit that empties directly into the head (assuming one has overboard discharge: otherwise the holding tank will fill in no time). This is a standard design feature on many European cruisers, and it's beginning to appear on this side of the water as well.

In some boats the head compartment is located aft, by the companionway. As a rule the head itself is half recessed back under the cockpit, with a hanging space outboard under the side deck and a counter with washbasin at the forward end of the compartment. The door may swing open on hinges or slide fore and aft. Just in terms of its own efficiency, such a compartment makes a good deal of sense in a small cruiser: There is probably maximum headroom at the aft end of the deckhouse, and minimum motion in a sea; one's power-operated MSD is close to the yacht's main battery, for a short cable run; there is less need to disturb sleepers by tramping the length of the cabin to get from the cockpit to the head; and the hull shape at this point is probably full enough to offer a number of options in terms of placing a holding tank.

On the other hand, if you feel as I do that going to the head is merely an episode in one's seafaring day, and not a high point, then it may seem to you that using this prime space isn't a terribly logical choice for a toilet. It's entirely a personal decision, based on the needs and tastes of one's crew.

Eating places

The convertible dinette was one of those lightning-bolt ideas like the wheel, revolutionizing a whole body of thought. As first conceived, it added great flexibility to the main cabins of small cruisers, both power and sail, but eventually, like so many fine ideas, the dinette came to be applied somewhat too universally. Now it has ebbed to something like its proper importance, and it is possible to have boats with or without dinettes, and with good accommodations either way. In a very small cruiser, a proper dinette—that is, one that seats four people, either as two couples facing each other fore and aft or one each at head and foot and two along the outboard long side—will necessarily impinge on the boat's centerline. Think again of the spaces involved in locating the human body: According to Francis Kinney *(Skene's Elements of Yacht Design),* a standing man's shoulder width is 1′6″ or 1′8″, but the same man, seated with his elbows propped comfortably on a table, requires 2′3″ of horizontal clearance, three feet clear from his seat to the top of his head, and at least two feet over the tabletop, not counting anything that may protrude downward from the overhead.

Aside from the human requirements, there are others imposed by the nature of cooking and eating utensils. The standard dinner plate is ten inches across, and really requires at least an inch more clearance all around, if accidents are to be avoided. Add to this another eight to twelve inches in the middle of the table for serving plates, bottles, glasses and the like, and in no time you have a table three feet across. It is no accident that the place settings on demonstration boats very seldom show a complete dish-and-utensil setup for four people.

If when examining either dinettes or standard saloon tables you find dimensions of 2′6″ wide by 15″ deep per person, you will have a generous expanse indeed. And of course you can get by with a good deal less—most people do. On summer nights, which is after all when you're likely to be eating dinner afloat, the preferred dining area is the cockpit, as it's probably far too hot and stuffy below. Space topside is a good deal easier to come by, but bear in mind that there will be times when you simply have to eat under cover, and the boat's main cabin should be capable of accommodating the entire crew around the dining table.

In his well-thought-out little *Boat Data Book,* British designer Ian Nicolson

Dinette table in Westsail 28. Note shock-cord retainers on shelves.

suggests that a minimum-size dinette surface for four is 3′2½″ by 2′5½″, with the seats facing each other along the long side. The same author also suggests that a comfortable dinette surface for five would be 2′9½″ by 4′½″, allowing for two seats along each long side, and the fifth at one end.

If you already own a boat with a dinette table that's too small, there are several things you can do about it. Perhaps the most obvious is to add a leaf to the end, if it's a thwartships table, or to one of the long sides if the table's main axis is fore and aft. It is not simply a case of hinging the additional space onto the edge, as you must engineer the addition so as not to impair the table's ability to function as a berth filler.

Say you have a fore-and-aft dinette, where the table fills the empty space in

Fold-down table in Leigh 30 fits into box on bulkhead. Note lack of fiddles.

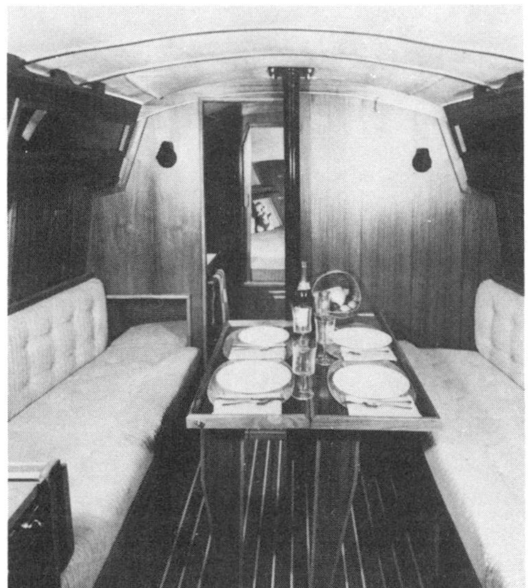

Similar setup on Mariner 28.

a U-shaped settee. It's obvious where the leaf must go, and its width should not be more than the distance from the table to the floorboards when the tabletop is in its fully lowered position, making the double berth.

In most cases, this will still give you an extra 1′6″ of width, as that's the optimum height off the deck for a seat, and eighteen inches will probably solve your problem. If you don't care to hinge the addition, you can build it to slide into fixed supports under the table. Whatever you decide, however, it will pay in the long run to make the construction about twice as hefty as you think the situation requires.

Another thing to be wary of, when buying or adding to a dinette, is blocking the cook's access to the table. There are a number of clever dinette arrangements that, when fully opened, make it impossible for another person to be added to the festivities without dropping a leaf to allow him or her to go by. Here again, it will help to pantomime the various stages of meal preparation and serving to see if you (or the builder) have overlooked something.

Nearly all nautical tables, except on the cheapest boats, have some kind of fiddle around the edge. In all honesty, most of these little rails are symbolic gestures, capable perhaps of keeping a fork or spoon in place, but hardly a match for sliding dishes and cups. Many traditionalist writers bewail the shortcomings of today's rails compared with those of yesteryear, but in truth the functions are considerably different.

As noted earlier, the fiddles around the edges of a dinette table on a small cruising auxiliary exist primarily to keep the mattress cushions from sliding off when the table is lowered to form a bed. They have very little to do with keeping crockery in place when dining under way in a Force 9 gale. For one thing, if you're lucky enough to have anything at all to eat under such conditions, you'll probably be eating it out of a mug or a deep bowl (a far more important utensil than a plate in blue-water boats), which you'll be holding in your lap. For another, most experienced sailors rely on hot drinks and iron rations—candy or fruit bars, cookies, and trail food—when it's really rough. The small cruiser of today is designed and engineered for eating and sleeping at anchor, because boatbuilders know that's what happens afloat.

On the other hand, you may be a true blue-water cruising person, with the realistic intention of making extended offshore passages (and a pocketbook that requires you to settle for a stock boat). If that's the case, you will probably find yourself making some changes in the layout. My only suggestion is that you make them one at a time, after careful thought, and only when a definite need has proven itself.

Aside from the standard dinette, there are increasing numbers of foldaway tables seen aboard today's small cruisers. These are becoming more popular aboard boats where a table exists only for eating—as opposed to cruisers with young families, where the dinette table is an important play center during nearly all daylight hours, or other craft where the table serves of necessity as the navigation center.

If you use the saloon table only for eating, it stands to reason that you need its presence only three times a day, if that. The remaining eighteen-plus hours it can best be folded up against a bulkhead out of the way, making the cabin far roomier and easier to get around in—not to mention a good deal safer, both for the crew and the table.

The number of different folding table conformations is limited only by the ingenuity of naval architects. While there are some widely accepted standards, anyone who's been around a boat can testify that a table can fold up and disappear into damn near anything. There are tables that hinge out of locker doors, both open and closed, tables that recess down into the cabin sole, tables that are hoisted up against the overhead. But the most common general style is the table that folds up flat against the main thwartships bulkhead just forward of the eating area. Typically, this table has a single broad leg, often with its foot keyed into a hole in the deck. Having first opened downward, it can then flip its top sideways, doubling its width. Sometimes there is an extra leg to support this additional leaf, sometimes it is merely done with sliding supports.

There are two things to look out for in any folding table. First, it must be solid and substantial when it's opened out. A table you have to worry about during the meal is no fun at all, nor is one that is so complex you have to tighten up its various components every week. "Solid" does not, however, mean that a folding table should be capable of taking the flung weight of a human being, because practically none of them can do it more than once. Thus, a fact of life with folding tables is that they are not supports, and one of the ship's standard procedures entails folding the table up against the bulkhead when getting under way, and immediately after each meal.

The second point to be wary of is the folding process. You should be able to open and fold up the table with one hand (because sometimes you'll need the other to hold on). Any necessary hardware must be sturdy and well attached. It is particularly important that the table, once opened or folded, not collapse from the desired position, just as it's vital that there be only one proper way to fold or open it.

The alternative to a folding table is one that's fixed, in that while part of it may fold up, the basic unit remains in place all the time. In general, fixed saloon tables are drop-leaf style, sometimes with one leaf, sometimes with two. The standard table's center section is about six inches across, often with one or more compartments recessed into its top, for condiments, napkins, or even small bottles. This is a feature that's useful far out of proportion to its cost, especially in small boats where there are otherwise few stowage spots for such small items.

A two-leaf table is most often seen in boats where there are paired settee berths facing each other across the saloon. The table itself is normally on the boat's centerline, while the fore-and-aft walkway is slightly offset, usually to starboard. The result is a starboard settee that has to be extended to be of use when eating, with a resultant lack of back support, but by contrast the table itself will probably be considerably larger than its dinette counterpart in the same size yacht, and better able to accommodate a full meal for four or even six.

Since a fixed table is inevitably in for more rough treatment than a dinette, its construction requirements are fairly stringent, even in a boat that will seldom venture offshore. The most frequent hazard for fixed tables is their use as a support by crewmembers moving fore and aft under way, when the boat is heeled. It may seem that any one crewmember putting a fraction of his or her weight on the table while going past won't make much difference, but in cumulative terms, the stress is quite something. Add to it the occasional severe blow when someone loses his footing and caroms into the table, or is even hurled from a settee or pilot berth fully into the table's folded-down leaf. This kind of treatment can easily uproot or destroy a poorly made table, and very few builders seem to know or care.

Here are some things to look for in a proper fixed saloon table. First, its frame must be sturdy enough to withstand the full weight of a 180- or 200-pound man bouncing off it. This means that the essential fore-and-aft segment must be a husky piece of timber, or it must be stoutly braced. Second, the vertical members holding the table in place are equally important, if not more so. In a small boat, the forward end of the table can be firmly through-bolted to the thwartships bulkhead, or strapped around a keel-stepped mast, or made fast to a solid grab pole running from the overhead to the deck or through it to a floor—a solid cross-member under the floorboards. The after support will almost necessarily be of this last type, as the table's aft end will nearly always be in the middle of the main cabin, with no convenient brace available as part of the boat's natural structure.

This may sound like a lot of fuss and bother, and if it means rebuilding your boat's table it probably is, but it will be worth it on several counts. To begin with, you'll be free of the exasperating necessity for repairing (and repairing and repairing) a table that was inadequately engineered in the first place. You will have one additional brace to protect crewmembers moving about below-decks in heavy weather, as well as at least one additional and centrally located grab pole. Finally, if your boat has extension berths flanking the table, a secure installation will often serve as a first-rate bunkboard for the windward side settee berth.

Navigation area

Until about a decade ago, smaller American cruising yachts, and some middle-size ones, too, had no formal nav station. European designs, on the other hand, nearly always specified a regular navigation table in 30-footers, and sometimes in smaller vessels. Now, Americans have caught up with the foreigners in providing space for the small-yacht navigators, although it's an open question whether the average cruising skipper really knows what to do with the nav space he's been presented with. There seem to me to be three reasons why American yachts now have navigator's spaces: First, the boats are generally bigger, and in the 30-foot size there's just about enough extra room to drop in a two-foot-deep fore-and-aft surface; second, there are growing numbers of skippers who really want such an area; and third, the galloping fad for electronic navigation instruments has created a corresponding need for someplace to put all those whirring, clicking, flashing gadgets.

Standard chart table on O'Day 30, with seat formed by head end of quarterberth. Note lack of leg room.

I'm a navigation nut by inclination, and while most of the cruising I do hardly requires anything as dignified as a formal nav station, it certainly makes life easier when the chart isn't always getting involved with the dinner. I suspect, furthermore, that the same can be said for most owners of cruising boats in the 27-to-30-foot range. Below that size, space begins to cramp the possibilities again, although one can still rig up quite workable alternatives, as we shall see.

It may be best to begin by examining the ideal navigation layout, created as if the boat's interior had no other purpose save to please the chart-and-dividers wielder. To begin with, the nav station really ought to be as near the cockpit as possible, so the navigator can communicate with the helmsman and can bob out to take a quick compass bearing. In a small cruiser, this means adjacent to the companionway, which is usually a good place, although there are a couple of inherent drawbacks. One of the two-edged aspects is the fact that the companion hatch affords good ventilation, a necessity for many people when faced with the need for reading lots of small numbers while the boat is leaping about. At the same time, however, the open hatch can be a sluiceway, drenching the chart area (as well as the neighboring quarterberth, if any). There is, to my knowledge, no certain way to shield the navigator from spray and rain while preserving his supply of fresh air. In some boats there are rigid or flexible transparent shields between the chart table and the companionway, and the latter, at least, may be a possibility in this size boat, perhaps rigged to roll up like the plastic window in a cockpit dodger.

As for the chart table itself, the centerpiece of the nav station, there are a number of possibilities, some mutually exclusive. Begin with the matter of orientation and, since it's immediately related, tilt: The majority of navigation stations are built around a rectangular surface that faces forward and has a slight tilt upward from aft. The navigator is intended to sit, nearly always on the head end of a quarterberth, while passing his positional miracles. This is all very well, if that's what you want, but it's not necessary. From the viewpoint of navigational efficiency, it probably makes somewhat more sense to have the table facing aft, as the navigator then has a clear view of the cockpit without turning around. This orientation is available on a few small yachts and a fair number of large ones, but if a fixed nav table does face aft, then the bulkhead abaft it is a dead end, and one must forgo the possibility of a quarterberth. (But this presents us with at least one deep cockpit locker). The realities of compromise in small cruisers dictate that this extra berth is worth the small sacrifice in navigational efficiency for most people.

It's also quite possible to have a chart table whose long side runs fore and aft, designed to be used by a navigator standing in the center of the yacht, rather than one sitting down. Only one small boat I know of, the Seafarer 30, has this setup, in which the chart table surface is also the top of the icebox, which is another question entirely. In the kind of hip-shooting navigation characteristic of small cruisers, it seems to me that having a chart table that's equally accessible to a person sitting or standing is a definite asset. There are lots of navigational tasks that don't require being seated, and if the boat is severely heeled with the nav table on the high side, it may be quite a job simply to stay in the seat (although some seats are dished to hold the navigator's tail horizontal no matter what).

What's the ideal size for a chart table's surface? I once chartered a 40-foot yawl that had a three-by-four-*foot* chart table. It was absolutely great to be able to lay out every chart full size—and stow them, free of fold-marks, in the drawer below. But one had to stand up at this table, which itself had to be fairly low, in order for the navigator to reach its farthest corners. There is such a thing as a chart table that's bigger than necessary, and this one nearly achieved that status.

A too large table will, however, be the least of your problems in a small cruiser. The trick will be to get one that's big enough to bother with. In most larger cruising yachts, the optimum size for a chart table top is said to be 24" ×36", not quite large enough to take a standard chart unfolded. American charts are not standardized as to size, but they tend to run in the neighborhood of 33"×42". A standard chart folded in half, then, is about 21"×33", and one may easily subtract three inches of margin from the latter figure. British Admiralty charts are 41"×28½" and, folded once to 20½"×28½", they fit nicely into same size bracket. The increasingly popular chart books are considerably smaller, from about 20"×15" to about 24"×18".

If you can get a 24"×30" surface, you're doing extremely well, and a 20" ×30" table is not bad at all for the kind of navigation most cruisers practice. Bear in mind that the standard coastal chart, with its 1:80,000 scale, in the United States or 1:50,000 in Europe, covers about thirty by forty-five miles, so you're not likely to be faced with the necessity for folding and refolding it at hourly intervals. In fact, you may well find that you use one-half of a single coastal chart more than 50 percent of the time. What of the surface itself? You want something hard enough to resist casual stabbing by divider points, but if you use a chart table seriously, you may well want a surface into which you can stick drawing pins, to hold a chart in place in extreme conditions. The choices that are most common are among formica, plywood, and teak, and my own preference would be the ply surface. There's another possibility, if your chart table has an unattractive surface, and that's to laminate a chart on top of it. Clearly, this will be most satisfactory if there's one chart you frequently employ, and if it doesn't require massive updating every year, but many people find that a polyurethaned or varnished-on chart is a handy reference that cannot blow away; it should be covered in clear acrylic, which can be used to write on.

It's the done thing for boatbuilders to speak of a chart drawer in their nav stations, but very few smaller boats have a formal drawer for chart stowage, nor is it particularly useful in the limited area of this size boat. Far handier and more common is the tray beneath the plotting surface: The tabletop is hinged and lifts up, and the space beneath contains the ready-use charts and perhaps the instruments—pencils, erasers, dividers, plotter. The stowage space doesn't need to be deep—according to Ian Nicolson, twenty-five charts folded in half make a stack half an inch high—but it will be convenient if you can drop a big, fat volume, such as the *Light List,* into the space and still close the top. Speaking of the hinge, it should be near but not at the edge of the table's surface, so that you don't have to clear everything off the top before opening it. Obviously, even the best installed hinge will make a rough spot in the table's surface. A properly fitted hinge makes a very narrow one, and you can usually work right over it if you're using a double-folded chart.

At the forward (in relation to the navigator) end of the ideal table is a semibulkhead on which one may mount electronic instruments or their repeaters (when the original dials are in the cockpit). You need a vertical surface at least six inches high, with, again ideally, three or four inches of dead space behind the wood, to take the backs of the dials and the wiring. If your table is two feet wide, you can get four or five standard dials on this surface, with a fiddled shelf for navigation tools on top of it.

Outboard of the navigator's table will be a couple of shelves or possibly a locker. This is the spot for your boat's VHF radio, the Loran-C, and the RDF or ADF (I said this was an ideal rig, didn't I?). A locker is a bit better than a shelf, if only because the electronics can be stowed away from prying eyes and fingers, although a serious electronics thief can pretty well determine your boat's equipment by glancing up at her antennas. You'll also want space for a few well-chosen books. Unfortunately, navigation volumes are nothing if not ponderous. *Reed's* is 5¾" × 8½", and the big references like the *Light List* and the *Tide* and *Tidal Current Tables* and many pilotage books are about eight inches deep by just over ten inches high; the *Waterway Guide* series are even larger. If you have the space, that's fine, but there are numerous shortcuts in terms of reference books that will allow you to save a lot of space and still have the vital information at your fingertips.

This same area is a logical location for your boat's main power panel, no big thing on a small cruiser, but still a piece of equipment that should be at once visible and accessible. In terms of light, you will want a general overhead lamp, and if you do any amount of night piloting, a red-lit navigator's lamp on a flexible neck about a foot long.

If you have a fixed seat, it should be about a foot below the table's surface, but not less than eighteen inches off the deck. It will be mildly surprising if you have adequate room for your legs and feet, as many designers seem to envision their customers chopped off at the knees. If you plan to work while seated facing forward or aft, you should have some form of brace to hold you in place when the nav station is on the high side of a well-heeled boat. It is remarkably tiring to have to hold on with fingers and toes while trying to do something as finicky and demanding as serious piloting. That's one reason I prefer to stand at the chart table, as it is relatively easier to brace myself upright than while sitting.

Having in a manner of speaking spoiled the reader by describing the ideal, it's now necessary to come back to earth and suggest realistic alternatives when the ideal is absent. In older yachts, the icebox top was traditionally the chart table surface as well, and charts were often stored in a roll ranging from the overhead. But the basic principle of storing charts is fold, don't roll; they can often be stowed under a settee or berth cushion. It seemed then that the average icebox top was a very bad chart surface, and my opinion has not greatly changed. In most small cruisers, it is likely to be the cook's most accessible

Slide-down chart table on Seidelmann 299. Table can be slightly tilted for chart use or level, to make extra counter space for galley.

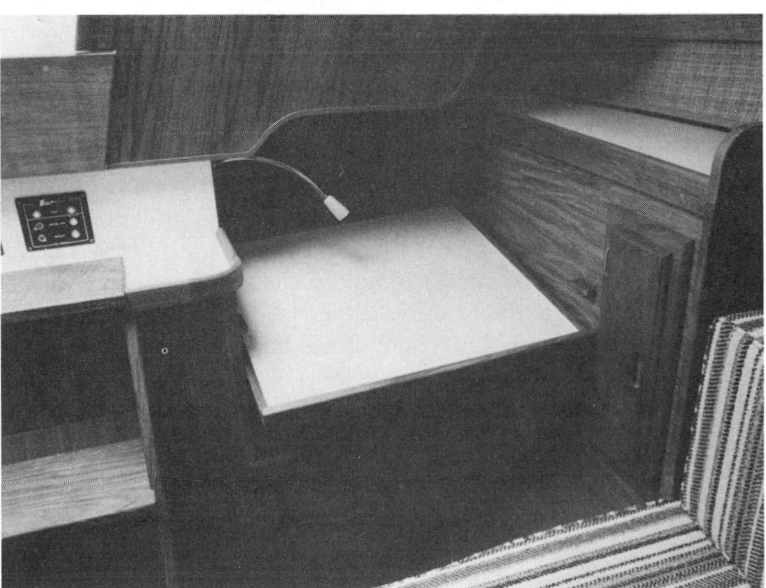

work surface, and the icebox itself is the one enclosure on the boat that's subject to investigation at all hours of the day and night. Moreover, many iceboxes have a recessed finger catch in the top that's cunningly located to be athwart whatever course line you're trying to draw. Your first news of this recess is the soft, rending *pop* as your pencil point goes through the chart.

But if you have no choice in the matter, then the icebox top it must be, and you'll just have to be careful. Considerably better in many cases is the dinette or saloon table. The former is often more useful since it doesn't have to be folded away to clear a passage fore and aft in the boat, but either will do as long as they have a decent light source overhead. If you do have to do after-dark plotting under way, you'll want a portable light with a red-tinted bulb, to avoid waking the crew off watch when you come below to make a log entry or advance a line of position. Obviously, in cases where you're using either the table or the icebox surface, you'll want to make sure the edges are fiddled, and you'll also want to set apart a convenient locker or drawer for navigation tools. The electronics, if any, will have to be spotted where convenience dictates, most likely on the inside of the cabin's aft bulkhead or on the after side of the bulkhead between saloon and head or hanging locker. Your navigation books can go in the locker or in a small bookshelf on a bulkhead.

If this alternative isn't suitable, you may want to rig a folding chart table. A number of small cruisers now come with this setup as standard, and it is usually arranged to fit, when folded, in the space above or outboard of the quarterberth. Opened for use, the table's surface occupies the space at the head end of the quarterberth, which means that it is difficult or impossible for someone to sleep in that berth while the navigator is working. Another good point of this location for a folding chart table is that there's usually a fair amount of space alongside it for navigation tools and books, and of course the location is close to the cockpit. And as a final asset, a nav table in this area is likely also to be near enough to the galley so that the cook can use it as a work surface when a serious meal is in preparation.

The very smallest boats, having neither table nor work surface down below, will have to create some makeshift. For a couple of years, the navigation table in my 17-foot catboat was a piece of quarter-inch marine plywood, with all sharp edges carefully rounded and smoothed, and sealed with four coats of varnish. This board lived inside a heavy transparent vinyl chart case which it exactly fitted. Not only did it serve as a lap nav center, but when I moved on to a larger boat, I kept my little chart board as a cockpit reference and work surface. The case was thick enough to hold the charts I needed, with the one being used on one side of the board and the rest carefully folded and stuffed on the other. When the vinyl inevitably tore, it was easily replaced and the whole rig was good as new again.

X

Engines for the Small Cruising Yacht

Introduction

In order to approach your auxiliary engine in a sensible way, you must first consider carefully what you expect it to do, what role in your boat's existence it will play. At first glance, of course, the term "auxiliary" seems self-defining: We're talking about a secondary propulsion device, that's all.

But is it? On virtually all inboard-powered cruisers, and on many outboard-equipped boats, the engine not only drives the boat but also supplies power to the electrical system and to the various electrically powered or triggered devices hooked into the batteries. In addition, the relative auxiliariness of the engine is defined differently by individual sailors and varying sailing conditions, not to mention by the essential design of boats themselves. One engine may never be needed for more arduous duty than put-putting the last quarter mile up a windless creek; another may be required to bring a beefy ketch home on time for Sunday supper, after the wind has died. Another may have to work the family yacht regularly against wind and tide because the skipper dislikes beating. Each of these power plants may legitimately be defined as auxiliary, in that it takes second place (if only in the owner's heart) to the sails, but the parameters in the three cases are quite different.

Let us begin, then, with a heretical question: Do you need an auxiliary engine in the first place? This isn't intended as an attempt at conversion, because only the reader can legitimately answer yes or no. The irrefutable response is simply, "I need an engine because I want one." But if you haven't arrived at that certainty yet, let me suggest the query. If nothing else, answering it will better define why you want an orthodox (or not-so-orthodox) power plant.

The best literary argument I know in support of the engineless cruising yacht is made by L. Francis Herreshoff in his classic book *The Compleat Cruiser.* Only a fool would try to paraphrase L. Francis's muscular and contentious prose, and in any case, every cruising sailor ought to read and own this splendidly autocratic volume, both to benefit from the author's wisdom and to come to grips with his opinions. L. Francis posited his 28-foot *Rozinante* as a perfect boat for cruising without internal combustion: A lean, lightweight canoe ketch, she could be pushed along fairly easily by one man facing forward and working a couple of sweeps.

One may hold that today's boats are too beamy for this sort of thing, that all marinas and most anchorages are too crowded for primitive exhibitionism, that most sailors' lives are too closely scheduled to allow for being becalmed five miles from home. The best I can give you is a definite *maybe* for the last statement. The first two can easily be disproved by those disposed to try. C. W. Paine's 26-foot fiberglass Frances, a double-ended sloop or cutter (see Chapter III), has been equipped by one of her owners with a pair of twelve-foot ash sweeps fitted to thole pins at the forward end of the cockpit. The skipper can get this full-keel, 6,800-pound vessel up to 2 knots in a calm by sheer Swedish steam, despite her eight-foot beam. Once the breeze gets above 3 or 4 knots, the Frances can step out quite nimbly under sail. Her electrical needs are supplied by solar cells on the raised deck. It can be done, and perhaps more easily than one might think.

The second argument, with its appeal to laziness sugarcoated by an aura of responsibility, is contradicted by the experience of Steve Colgate's Offshore Sailing School, based at South Seas Plantation resort on Captiva Island, Florida. The school's fleet of Solings, each nearly twenty-seven feet overall, is sailed into and out of the resort's crowded marina, through a dog-leg channel with very tricky winds, by students at all levels of accomplishment. There's a certain amount of jumpiness, a few close calls, but it's done day after day, all year round—and it makes for more accomplished sailors. Obviously, there is a size limit to the sailing that can be done in close quarters, and the boats involved must be responsive and their crews skillful. Still, it is possible, and it's done every day.

The only judgmental remark I'd throw in at this point is that any skipper worthy of the title should be able to bring his boat into her slip without an engine, and extricate her as well. Maybe not under sail, but without damage and with a worked-out, well-rehearsed plan.

When it comes to engines, American boats are considerably overpowered by the standards of England and Europe. The 30-foot, 6,700-pound French Arpège sloop, for example, was offered with a choice of 7-hp. diesel or 10-hp. gasoline inboard in the same year that the popular S&S-designed Yankee 28, displacing 6,500 pounds, came with a 30-hp. Atomic-4 as standard. That was in 1973. Nowadays, things have evened out, partly as European boats have acquired larger engines in search of the lucrative American market, and partly as the small diesel has largely replaced the workhorse Atomic-4.

In the following pages, we'll examine the three nominal choices for a small sailing cruiser's auxiliary engine. In only a few cases will all three choices be equally viable; in many, there won't—initially, anyway—be any choice at all. Even so, I think it's useful for the owner or prospective buyer to have some idea of the possibilities, if only for repowering at a later date.

Gasoline inboard engines

Only a few years ago, the inboard gasoline engine was extremely common as standard equipment aboard sailing cruisers in the 27- to 30-foot range. Now it has all but disappeared, and in the few cases where it still lingers, the presumption is that it's a come-on to make possible a lower sailaway price, although the builder fully expects to sell most buyers the optional diesel at a higher ticket. There are, however, a great many secondhand yachts, in service and on the market, with inboard gasoline engines that serve them more or less well, so the gas engine is still a factor in the marketplace. What has an inboard gasoline engine got going for it?

Several things. First is initial cost. Engine manufacturers hate like poison to give prices, and there would not be a great deal of point in printing them in a book, since they'd be superseded two or three times before publication. But figure that a gasoline inboard of a given horsepower will cost about three-fifths to two-thirds what a diesel of the same nominal horsepower will run (there is also a question of the relative propulsive force of gasoline and diesel engines of the "same" horsepower, discussed below). Once installed, the running costs for an auxiliary engine, where only small amounts of fuel are involved, will be about the same.

The second asset is familiarity. To people of my generation, at all events, the small gasoline inboard is reasonably comprehensible. It is far simpler than a car engine, yet essentially similar, and most of us are familiar with its basic elements and what they do. The diesel's unfamiliarity is, I suspect, at least partly a factor of its simplicity: Seeing no familiar spark plugs, our minds tell us that the diesel has something wrong with it, something necessary that's missing, and we brood about it. This may not be a rational reaction, but it happens just the same.

The third asset, so far, is the relatively greater availability of gasoline over diesel. In my part of the boating world, anyway, there seem to be approximately two waterfront gas stations for every one that also offers diesel. The ratio is even more one-sided on land, a factor that will be more important to outboard operators than inboard owners.

Fourth, a small inboard gasoline engine runs more smoothly and quietly than an equivalent diesel. Confronting these assets are some rather more impressive liabilities. For most people the main drawback is the danger of explosion. While it is technically possible to lower diesel's flashpoint into the danger area, for the most part diesel oil is relatively inert, and certainly is many times safer than gasoline. It's easy to make too big a thing of this: I have owned gasoline-powered boats for over twenty years, and the only fire I've ever had aboard was from an alcohol stove. Put it even more strongly: None of the gasoline-engine boats with which I'm personally acquainted has ever had a fire or explosion from its propulsion fuel. The hazard is real, but the incidence is low.

At the same time, this danger can easily magnify the otherwise routine difficulties all of us encounter sooner or later. As an example, I remember the day the float pin on my Atomic-4's carburetor stuck and flooded the bilge with a pint or so of gasoline before I could rectify matters. A very slow-moving half hour ensued, while we emulsified the gasoline with detergent and aired out every corner of the boat's interior. By contrast, when a full diesel fuel filter escaped my hand and spilled its contents, it was a damned irritating mess to clean up, and the smell lingered, but there was no danger involved.

An important side effect of gasoline power is the negative resale value it imposes on an otherwise adequate boat. Not only are gasoline engines more hazardous, but they are also far less long-lived than diesel, and the buyer of your boat, if he's on the ball, is aware that he will possibly have to repower her in the foreseeable future. (The same fact turned around can work to your negotiating advantage if you are buying a gas-powered yacht: You can approach the bargaining table with the premise that the existing engine is virtually worthless, because it is.)

Finally, the gasoline engine's other major drawback in the marine environment is its electrical system. Ashore, an automobile's distributor, points, and spark plugs are relatively trouble-free, but in the damp and filthy cave that's the average small yacht bilge, the electrical system lives a miserable life. Its only recourse is to snap back occasionally by refusing to pass on the requisite spark, and most of the maintenance connected with a small inboard involves keeping the terminals and wires dry and clean.

When discussing the models of gasoline engine available today, there's really only one that matters. For the past decade at least, the Universal Atomic-4 has been *the* small inboard auxiliary for the United States. A marine version of a small tractor engine, the Atomic-4 has a faithful public who love it (I am one), and an equally rabid group—somewhat smaller—who can say nothing good about it. As the name implies, it's a four-cylinder unit, and it develops a maximum 30 hp. at 3,500 rpm. (Actually, the shaft speed is usually half that, as the standard sailboat hookup for the engine is a 2:1 reduction gear.)

As a rule the engine turns a two-bladed solid prop and it weighs somewhat more than three hundred pounds, exclusive of battery and fuel tank. Its great strength is its familiarity: There is probably not a marine mechanic from one end of North America to the other who has not put in hours working on Atomic-4s, and the parts and service are ubiquitous. For some time it was virtually the only marine gasoline engine around, and as a result it was installed in many boats that were far too small to require its push, and in a few that really wanted something larger.

In my own experience with the engine—some five and a half years—I found it an ample power plant for my 10,000-pound Bermuda 30. It would get the boat up to nominal hull speed or even a bit beyond at about two-thirds throttle in reasonably calm waters, and would supply the additional punch to get her home in the teeth of nearly any combination of wind and sea. Very likely the same boat could have functioned quite well with an engine half the size, but there were none with the Atomic-4's reputation available, and when it really came on to blow, especially from windward, the Bermuda 30 needed a big engine to work her way through the seas without excessive leeway.

Other gasoline engines are still available, especially in foreign-built boats, but it seems highly unlikely at this juncture that any new models will appear. For one thing, the U.S. Coast Guard has so tightened its rules on the construction and installation of gasoline-powered engines that most manufacturers are quietly abandoning them, when customer demand hasn't already pushed them in that direction anyway. The existing models you may encounter, usually in secondhand vessels, include the Atomic-2, a 10-hp., two-cylinder younger brother of the Atomic-4; the Watermota 3 or 7, British engines of one cylinder each; the 7.5-hp. Volvo Penta MB7A, which often is coupled to an S drive (see below under Outboards); and the Baldwin 6 and 15 hp. units, also involved in S-drives.

In used boats, you may hit such extinct engines as the 6-hp. Vire, the 22-hp. Palmer M-60, the 27-hp. Palmer P-60, the 10-hp. Albin Combi, or even more exotic brands. These were good engines in their day, but if your boat has such a unit, you'd do well to think about replacing it, and probably with a diesel.

Diesel inboards

What about the diesel inboard engine? To a certain extent its assets and liabilities are the opposites of the gasoline engine's attributes. The most important selling point for diesels is of course safety. Except in certain rare instances, where extremely low temperatures require winterizing diesel by diluting it with gasoline—a problem that's not likely to occur in the yachting environment—diesel is *the* safe fuel.

The diesel engine is also a very simple and rugged device, compared to gasoline power plants. There are two reasons for this. First, the principle of the diesel engine is much simpler than that of the gasoline mill. While both produce power by igniting a mixture of fuel and air, the former requires a

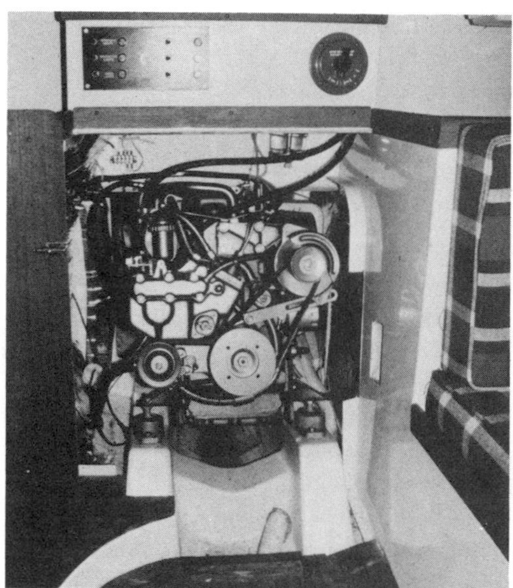

Small diesel installations under galley counter provide good access to fuel lines.

complicated and—in the marine environment—tricky electrical system to produce a timed spark at exactly the proper instant. The diesel, by contrast, superheats air in its cylinders by simple compression, and the air temperature alone ignites injected oil fuel, which in turn produces the combustion power. Aside from an electric motor to pump the fuel and to start the engine, no electrical system is required, hence the engine's simplicity. Its ruggedness derives from the construction necessary to produce the very high compression in the cylinders (16 or 20:1, as compared to 8:1 for a gasoline engine). Most small marine diesels originate as industrial power plants that are designed to run for long hours at a time. With proper maintenance, a diesel engine may well last the life of the boat.

One sales point for the diesel engine has been its operating economy relative to a gasoline engine. This was until recently a rather small element in the overall picture where sailing auxiliaries are concerned, as the number of engine hours involved isn't large. Recently, however, diesel fuel is often more expensive than gasoline, and while a diesel engine of comparable power will use less fuel than will a gasoline inboard (and far less than an outboard), it still shouldn't amount to enough to make a real difference in anything under about a decade's use.

Rather more to the point in these fuel-short days is the fact that diesel engines ingest what is essentially domestic heating oil, the same stuff employed by an oil-powered furnace. There are additives involved, and it's a good idea to have not less than two filters between the tank and the engine, but if fuel is short in your area, you can run the engine on heating oil. More to the point, the price of heating oil will run considerably under that of marine diesel, although your marina operator will probably eviscerate you if he catches you bringing in your own fuel rather than patronizing his pumps.

In economic terms, the diesel's primary assets are the increase in resale value that a diesel installation provides, and the decrease in insurance costs. The former is almost certainly more important, and it may even be the difference between sale and no sale, no matter how the gasoline-powered boat's owner adjusts his price downward. No one but a bargain hunter is really interested in buying a boat and then wrestling with a messy, expensive repowering job.

The diesel's negative aspects are rather less important. First and most apparent is the question of the diesel's higher first cost, mentioned above. That's less and less often a functional matter in a new-boat purchase because diesel power is usually standard these days, if a boat has an inboard engine at all. If the option does exist, you are almost certainly better off choosing diesel over inboard gasoline power, and the only time an outboard is a better choice than an inboard diesel is if you personally have a strong preference for outboards (or cost is that important), *and* you have the most powerful intention of holding the boat for a long, long time.

Many owners and quite a few mechanics are still unfamiliar with diesels, and as a result keeping one properly maintained can be a problem. The small diesel is, however, not a difficult engine to comprehend, especially for the person unhampered by long familiarity with gasoline engines. In my own experience, the chief difficulty has been getting adequate manufacturers' literature—up-to-date manuals and the like—written for the American owner, as so many diesels are of foreign origin. This situation is clearing up as diesels become more common, and there are several good books for the novice (see Bibliography) that can guide one over the rough spots. Since a diesel's fuel system is the nearly certain culprit in any problem, and since all diesel fuel systems are the same in their essentials, it's not hard to pick up the necessary information for day-to-day maintenance and emergency repair, although some of the more elaborate cyclical maintenance chores are probably best left to an expert.

All small engines, both gasoline and diesel, are noisy and prone to vibration out of all proportion to their size. But there is no question in my mind that diesels of one and two cylinders are far noisier, far more likely to rattle the whole boat, than are similar-size gasoline engines. In addition, I am one of those people who find the smell of diesel oil peculiarly repellent; others can handle diesel but are made nauseated by gasoline. The rhythmic *thump-thump-thump* of a small diesel is something one can probably get used to in time. But if the engine vibrates badly, it's as well to do something about it, as this can be bad for the power plant itself and even for the boat. Usually it's a question of proper alignment of the engine on its bed, and proper tuning in operation, but a one- or two-cylinder engine is basically unbalanced so is bound to run a little rough.

As the Mercedes people have pointed out in their advertising, there's no reason why a well-engineered fuel system should smell of diesel. Just the same, it takes a very small amount of fuel to make a really dreadful smell in the bilges, one that will persist far longer than gasoline. Great care is necessary when installing the system, and the owner must supply equal skill when changing filters or bleeding the fuel line. If any fuel spills, clean the bilge and run the blower until the smell is really gone.

(One may, parenthetically, ask why a diesel engine should have a blower, since its fumes are nonexplosive. For two reasons: First, a blower can exhaust smells as well as fumes, and second, a blower can help cool a diesel engine compartment after the engine has been running for some time. Because of the mass of metal involved, a hot diesel can raise the temperature of a surprisingly large cabin, especially in summer.)

In the last few years, the number of small diesels available has proliferated beyond all expectation. It would take too much space to itemize all the individual models available today, and such a list would soon be out of date anyway. The reader thinking of installing diesel power can get an up-to-date list from an annual directory such as *Boat Owners Buyers Guide.* The large reliable companies today—and probably for the foreseeable future—include BMW (7 and 12 hp.), Farymann (7.2, 9, and 12 hp.), Petter (6 and 12 hp.), Renault (7, 11, and 15.5 hp.), Sabb (10 and 18 hp.), Universal (the maker of the Atomic-4: 11 and 16 hp.), Volvo Penta (7.5 and 13 hp.), Watermota (7 and 12 hp.), Westerbeke (7 hp.), and Yanmar (8, 12, and 15 hp.)

Obviously, there are many other firms making larger diesels—I have taken an arbitrary upper size limit of 18 hp. as the maximum for boats of the size we're discussing. The ones listed here offer a good range of power in various sizes. As a glance at the list will confirm, the small auxiliary diesels really fall quite easily into two groups. First is the minimal engine of six to nine hp., in each case a single-cylinder unit weighing from 135 pounds for the Watermota and small Faryman to about 250 pounds for the Yanmar 8-hp. model.

Engines from 10 to 18 hp. may have one cylinder or two, and their weights run from 240 pounds for the BMW and Yanmar 12s to 419 pounds for the Sabb 18, about 100 pounds more than the Atomic-4, which it generally equals in usable power. The 10-hp. Atomic-2 gas inboard weighs 175 pounds, and the smallest gasoline inboard engine currently on the mass market, the Volvo MB2A, is only 64. In these smaller engines, the weight factors are nearly even between gasoline and diesel, and except where absolute weight is a key factor, the differences are of no substantial importance.

Outboard power

Among small cruiser owners, outboard power is a sort of poor relation. An inboard—any inboard—often seems to make the boat that contains it a more serious proposition than the same craft powered with an outboard. And yet

Transom-mounted outboard bracket for electric-start motor. With engine in running position, pull cord would be screened by transom.

there is a great deal to be said for outboard powerplants, especially associated with small boats up to, say, twenty-seven feet or so. Multihulls are even more suited to outboard power because of their relatively light weight and their sensitivity to loads. A small catamaran cruiser, in addition, is ideally shaped to swing an outboard between its hulls, and until one gets up to larger trimarans and cats, inboard power is more a problem than an asset.

In small monohull cruising auxiliaries, however, we can adduce at least six assets for the long-shaft outboard ranging from 3 to 15 hp. Long-shaft engines, by the way, are slightly heavier than standard units and cost a bit more. In return they allow for the fact that sailing boats, unlike runabouts, do not have

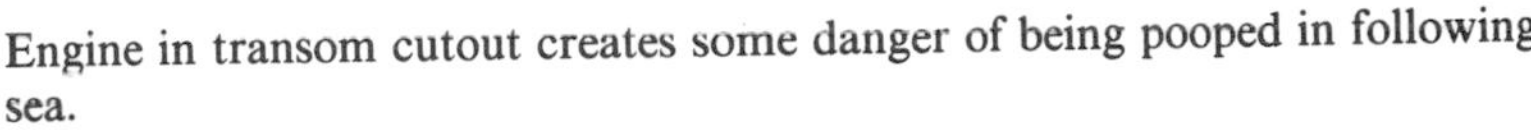
Engine in transom cutout creates some danger of being pooped in following sea.

OMC sail drive installation is essentially an outboard mounted in the hull. Note remote fuel tank aft.

cutaway transoms. The longer shaft makes a difference of five to seven inches length—fifteen to twenty or twenty-two inches. All but the very smallest sailing boats require long shafts for adequate performance.

The first point to the outboard's advantage is price. Simply looking at engine prices alone does not give an accurate picture, as inboards are priced without accessories (such as fuel tanks) or installation charges, whereas the outboard carries its essential accessories with it, and has (at least in this size range) no installation problem. True, there are optional extras in some outboards—typical charges beyond base price are for long shaft, exterior fuel tank of three or six gallons when the engine has an integral tank, battery for electric-start models, and in some cases for an alternator (sometimes referred to as a rectifier) that helps keep the boat's battery charged. But inboards, too, have their extras—instrument panels, batteries, and other incidentals.

Under-hull unit is merely an outboard lower unit bedded to bottom of hull.

A fair comparison is between what the manufacturer charges to equip a boat with an inboard and the price of an outboard suitable to drive the same boat. The prices used here were accurate at the end of 1979, but it seems likely that the proportions of the differences between inboard and outboard will remain the same, while the actual dollar figures are of course obsolete before this book is printed. The Lancer 29 Mk III is a medium-light-displacement (7,800 lb.) sloop derived from the C&C-designed Lancer 30. She comes with a low base price and a long list of options that allows the purchaser to choose among a staggering variety of equipment items and installations, and also to compare the real costs of just about any choice.

The Lancer 29 is offered by the builder with a selection of no less than three diesel engines, the OMC Sail Drive, or an outboard. Let the 8-hp. Yanmar diesel represent the benchmark engine for the boat, at a current U.S. price, installed, of $4,400. One may also have a 12-hp. Yanmar, at an increase of about 5 percent, or the 15-hp., two-cylinder Yanmar for 13 percent more than the eight. A 15-hp. OMC Sail Drive, also installed, is only 70 percent of the price of the smallest Yanmar, while a 15-hp. Mariner outboard, which requires no installation, is only 30 percent of the cost of the small diesel, including the outboard's long shaft and electric-start unit. A 9.9-hp. Suzuki, probably a bit smaller than most people would want in this application, is only 20 percent of the smallest Yanmar. Both the outboards have portable six-gallon fuel tanks, forward-neutral-reverse gear shifts and alternators as standard. An outboard well is a necessary but low price extra, and one may also have a twenty-four-gallon fuel tank for the outboard as an option (it is standard with the inboard). My own inclination would be to buy a second six-gallon portable tank, which costs about one-eighth as much as an inboard tank, but the amount of powering you do and the accessibility of fuel will be factors in your choice.

What about operating costs? Considering the number of running hours the average sailboat auxiliary clocks, it seems doubtful that there are any differences worth adding up between any of the engines noted here.

A second asset of the outboard is size, both in terms of space consumed by it and its accessories and weight. The latter is easier to measure. A 15-hp. Johnson or Evinrude is 82 pounds, with long shaft and electric start, the extra shaft and the electric starting unit each representing 5 pounds on top of the engine's basic weight of 72 pounds. The Suzuki weighs almost exactly the same amount, 83 pounds, without electric starting or long shaft. The portable fuel tanks weigh at most 5 pounds each when empty, and really don't count. By contrast, the Yanmar 8-hp. diesel is 250 pounds, the 12 is 301 and the 15 is 320 pounds. The OMC unit, being essentially an outboard, weighs about the same as a standard unit.

It would be overstating the case to say that two or even three hundred pounds—especially when located below the waterline—is a critical weight for a 29-foot cruising sailboat displacing nearly four tons. Nevertheless, it's a couple of hundred extra pounds that could be used to carry something else, or simply to make the boat that much nimbler. In terms of size, the inboard frequently seems larger because it takes up more otherwise usable space in most boats than does an outboard. When an outboard is mounted in a well, however, this is no longer the case, as the space lost is lazarette area, one of the more useful stowage locations in the small cruising yacht.

Another asset of the modern outboard is its sophistication. Many sailors tend to take this for granted, but I began boating in the Cro-Magnon past, when any boatman would carry two outboards on a voyage, one on the transom as he set out, and one under a tarp forward, to guarantee his return. Nowadays, outboards are among our most reliable citizens, engineered to a point where they require an absolute minimum of periodic maintenance in return for a startling amount of dependable power. Several manufacturers are now producing engines aimed specifically at the sailing market, as we shall see below, and now that electric starting, the battery-charging alternator and the gearshift are taken for granted on relatively small units, the outboard is probably some distance ahead of its inboard cousins in terms of power efficiency.

Fourth on my list is the outboard's portability. This is relative, to be sure: I have carried a 15-hp. outboard down a long pier, and would not care to do it every day. At the same time, a 5-hp. model, suitable for a small, nimble weekender, is no great load. But what is far more important than whether one will regularly cart the engine around is the fact that if you need to remove the thing, you can do it by loosening a pair of clamps, which is considerably more than you can say for any inboard. This attribute, in fact, leads into my fifth asset, which is the outboard's capacity, in certain situations, for a double life. If you are willing to have a slightly underpowered cruiser and a correspondingly overengined dink, you can often use the same small motor for both, thus greatly extending the usefulness of the tender without any increase in cost, beyond the small amount for fuel. True, this asset will be restricted to cruisers that can use an outboard in the 3- to 6-hp. range, but it is still a plus point for the portable engine.

Finally, a sailing yacht sails best when it immerses as little of itself in the water as possible. Any suitable inboard yet offered requires that a propeller and shaft trail through the water even when it's not being used. In nearly all cases, outboard installations on sailing boats allow for the engine to be fully retracted from the water when under sail. (I would add here that it will be worth attempting to modify any outboard well that requires even part of the lower unit to drag under sail.)

Outboard drawbacks

All this makes a strong case for the small outboard. Are there not some counterbalancing liabilities? Of course, and the alert reader will have spotted several already, if only because they are the flip sides of the outboard's assets.

We have, for instance, talked about the asset of portability, and it is an attribute which increasing numbers of thieves value as much as you do. Fortunately, an outboard may be padlocked to its transom or stowed below (preferably locked to a structural member of the boat) or best of all, taken home. But this is annoying, and one must live with the fact that an outboard is not too difficult to steal.

We've also mentioned an outboard's low weight. At the same time, it's only fair to point out that eighty-odd pounds cantilevered off the transom imposes quite a disproportionate weight load on the after end of the boat, to the point that nearly all outboard-powered racers remove the outboard and strike it below when sailing for performance. Too, an inboard's load, placed low and more or less amidships, can well help to make up the ballast in a lightweight boat.

Although many of today's outboards do come with generators or alternators, and these units are indeed helpful, they are on the small side when it comes to providing useful electrical power. The Suzuki 9.9, for instance, has an alternator that develops 80 watts, about enough power to light a medium-size lamp in your home. It may be easier to think about if we exchange terms here: There are three common terms involved in the basics of electrical power, *watts, volts* and *amps.* The Suzuki delivers its 80 watts at 12 volts, and to find its amperage, the usual term in which alternator power is measured, one simply divides wattage by voltage, and in this case comes up with 6.6 amps, not a terribly impressive figure. The Johnson or Evinrude alternator is no great shakes either, turning out 5 amps (or, if you prefer, 60 watts).

An inboard engine will have a 35- or 40-amp alternator almost as a matter of course, providing over 400 watts of electrical power. The outboard's alternator is strictly an auxiliary, intended to provide enough power to light the boat's running or cabin lights, while an inboard can supply power for radio transceivers and other medium-duty equipment.

In transom-hung outboards, there is also the question of vulnerability. This can be especially important to people who keep their boat moored stern-to in slips: A slight miscalculation in the length of one's lines can cause significant damage to the protruding engine, which can also grab lines and get itself crushed against other boats. The inboard has its own areas of likely damage, such as an unprotected prop shaft, but in an outboard the whole engine is exposed.

The most obvious liability of the outboard as compared with the diesel inboard is perhaps the fire hazard of the former. Not that fire is particularly associated with outboards, but it is a danger in all gasoline engines. I feel that outboards are considerably less of a fire hazard than are gasoline inboards, and that the danger, such as it is, can easily be kept within acceptable limits of risk by ordinary care.

Finally, there is the factor of propulsive efficiency. However much they may be altered, nearly all outboards (with the salient exception of the British

Seagull) start off as high-speed power plants aimed at pushing relatively light loads. This is reflected in their high rpm. counts, in their gearing and in their relatively small propellers. Inboards, both gasoline and diesel, turn more slowly even before being geared down, and can swing a prop better suited to pushing displacement hulls at displacement speeds. This is a valid argument, but it seems to me that the payoff is in the long rather than the short term. That is, I suspect that even a well-built outboard will have a somewhat shortened and less effective life as a power plant for the small cruiser, while an equally good inboard, especially a diesel, may outlast the boat itself. For most of us, however, this long-range asset may not outbalance the initial economy and the other advantages of the outboard. The chances are that if you buy a new or nearly new outboard, it will still be hale and hearty by the time you dispose of the boat to which it's attached. A bill may eventually come due, but you will have passed it on. On the other hand, if you're the kind of sailor who uses an auxiliary engine little if at all, then the outboard has an even stronger case: No engine does well when it lies about in a wet climate without being used, but an outboard is designed to survive this kind of disuse better than an inboard.

Before looking at the models available, let's briefly examine the extras that may be useful or necessary when considering an outboard as power for the auxiliary cruiser. There are relatively few.

We've mentioned the need for a long-shaft model and the desirability of current-producing capability via an engine-driven alternator. Gears are not usually an option—small engines are either fixed-forward units or have a forward/neutral shift; mid-size engines have forward/neutral/reverse. Unlike a diesel, an electric-start outboard imposes relatively little strain on the ship's battery. My 9.9-hp. Johnson electric-start worked quite happily off a motorcycle battery and kept it charged, too. Electric-start is an extra-cost option in the size motor we're discussing, generally available in 15-hp. and in some 9.9-hp. models.

Many outboard runabouts carry installed tanks of 20 gallons or more to allow for extended runs without resorting to a multitude of six-gallon plug-in tanks. This kind of extra is not really pertinent to the sailboat skipper, who may have use for a pair of six-gallon tanks, but who will probably have little or no need for anything more. Generally speaking, one is wise to carry as little gasoline aboard as one can get away with, and if your engine use is predictably low, you may find that a small motor with an integral tank—usually a couple of quarts' or liters' capacity—is adequate. In this case, however, a backup tank (one designed for petroleum products) is worth considering.

Whether one has an inboard or outboard, a plastic funnel with a built-in filter is an excellent investment. Get one that's oversize enough to cope with sudden bursts from a gas-pump hose and clean it from time to time. You'll be surprised, I think, at the amount of debris—grit, paint chips, water droplets—passed on by the average gas or even diesel pump.

The installation of an outboard can be a tricky thing. If the engine is attached to the boat's transom, the builder usually supplies (sometimes as an extra-cost option) a fixed or flip-up bracket. The latter, which allows the outboard to be lifted up several inches before being tilted, is definitely preferable. If you choose to do your own installation, remember that there are heavy loads involved, and that through-bolting according to the bracket manufacturer's instructions is genuinely necessary, as is precise vertical positioning on the boat's transom. A couple of inches too high, and the engine's prop will spin in aerated water, depriving you of much of the drive you've paid for.

In the lowered position, an outboard's working controls—throttle, gear shift, choke, and ignition switch—may be very hard to reach from the helm. Some outboards have at least the throttle and kill switch incorporated into the steering-handle tip, while others offer as an extra-cost option the mounting of these controls on the engine's top. If your outboard is going to be exceptionally difficult to get at, you will probably want both electric-start and remote controls, which are available from the outboard's builder. These may be a single-lever control that incorporates both throttle and gear shift or a double-lever unit. There seems to me little or nothing to be gained from the two-lever style, as it merely offers one additional part to get wrapped with the mainsheet or to jab you in the calf. The same comments that apply to inboard engine controls are equally valid for outboards' throttle-gearshift units. Make sure they are securely fastened, properly adjusted, and that there are no unfair curves between the engine attachment and the control plate. While there is no really good place to mount these controls, the inside of the cockpit, fairly high up, is as good or bad a spot as any. You should keep the actual gearing of the controls from being soaked (they're rustproof, but repeated wetting washes away the lubricant), and it's a good idea if you can work the throttle and gearshift without having to bend so low you can't see over the deckhouse. By the same token, the higher on the cockpit seat side you place the controls, the more they'll interfere with sitting.

If you have electric start, you may want to invest in a voltmeter, which is not the same as an ammeter. A voltmeter, sometimes known as a battery condition meter, usually reads from 8 to 18 volts. It indicates the state of charge of your boat's battery at any given moment and will also indicate the level of alternator voltage. An ammeter is also useful, but not normally a necessity on outboard-powered boats, especially if you have a voltmeter. It indicates what the battery is doing—charging, discharging, or neutral—at a given moment. Used with the voltmeter, it can provide lots of useful information about the electrical system, assuming that your boat is sophisticated enough to warrant that level of monitoring. A new instrument offered with Johnson and Evinrude engines of 9.9 and 15 hp. is a water-pressure gauge for the cooling system. Since outboards are prone to picking up plastic bags that can shut off the water intake, this could be a useful gauge—but only if you are the sort of person who scans gauges as he drives along.

A useful accessory for remote fuel tanks is an anchor kit, which consists of chocks to hold the tank in place and prevent abrasion that leads to rust outs. The addition of a webbing strap and buckle can make the tank really fixed in place—a need apparent to sailors but not, as yet, to outboard builders.

Finally, although it comes under the heading of spare parts, it doesn't hurt to carry a replacement connector for hooking the fuel line to tank or engine, a replacement primer bulb for the fuel line itself, a spare shear pin for the propeller, and spark plug(s) for the engine.

Now that the Japanese have invaded the outboard market, there has been a dramatic broadening in the types and styles available. In the 15-hp. and under group, there's an exceptionally wide choice, and you can see nearly all of them at any boat show. My own feeling about outboards is that one should go with a national or international company and avoid the small firms that still linger on the outskirts of the field. Some of these low-volume companies make very good engines, but in terms of service and parts availability, not to mention resale (as an accessory of the boat), you're nearly always better off with a name brand.

The following chart contains engines from manufacturers that have been around for a while and will presumably linger for some time to come. I've indicated special features that seem to me of exceptional interest, but since motors are reengineered from time to time, one should check with manufacturers to make sure that a desired feature is still offered, or that something even better isn't available.

Outboard Motor Chart

SMALL MOTORS: 3.5–6 hp. (All are water-cooled except Mariner; all are long-shaft models; F/N=forward plus neutral gears, R=reverse gear)

Chrysler

"Economate" 3.5 hp., 1 cyl, .5 gal. integral fuel tank. (Derated "no frills" version of Chrysler 4 described below.)

4 hp. 5,250 rpm. @ 2:1 reduction. 1 cyl., 38 lb., .5 gal. tank, F/N shift, 60 w. opt. alternator.

"Sailor" 150, 6 hp. 4,750 rpm. @ 3:1 reduction, 2 cyl., 62 lb., 6 gal. remote tank, F/N/R, 60 w. std. alternator, remote controls.

Evinrude/Johnson

4 hp. 4,500 rpm. @ 2:1 reduction, 2 cyl., 39 lb., .2 gal. tank (remote opt.), top-mount controls opt.

4.5 hp. 5,000 rpm. @ 2.2:1 reduction, 2 cyl., 54 lb., .5 gal. tank (remote opt.) F/N/R, 60 w. opt. alternator.

Mariner

3.5 hp. 5,000 rpm. @ 1.65:1 reduction, 1 cyl., air-cooled, 35 lb., .66 gal. tank, F/N, 15 w. opt. alternator.

5 hp. 5500 rpm. @ 1.9:1 reduction, 1 cyl. air-cooled, 52 lb., 3.15 gal. remote tank, F/N/R, 40 w. opt. alternator.

Mercury
3.6 hp. 5,000 rpm. @ 2:1 reduction, 1 cyl., 36 lb., .5 gal tank.
4 hp. 4,700 rpm. @ 2:1 reduction, 2 cyl., 36 lb., .25 gal. tank, F/N.
4.5 hp. 5,500 rpm. @ 2:1 reduction, 1 cyl., 53 lb., 3 gal. remote tank, F/N/R.

Seagull
"Silver Century" 4 hp. 4,000 rpm. @ 2.5:1 reduction, 1 cyl., 44 lb., 1.25 gal. tank, F/N, 50 w. opt. alternator.
"110" 5 hp. 4,000 rpm. @ 3.1:1 reduction, 1 cyl., 52 lb., 1.25 gal. tank, F/N/R, 50 w. opt. alternator.

Suzuki
3.5 hp. 4,800 rpm. @ 2:1 reduction, 1 cyl., 42 lb., .4 gal. tank (remote opt.), F/N, 30 w. opt. alternator.
5 hp. 5,800 rpm. @ 2:1 reduction, 2 cyl., 47 lb., 4 gal. remote tank, F/N/R, 80 w. opt. alternator.

MEDIUM ENGINES: 7.5–9.9 hp. (All models 2 cylinders, F/N/R shift, remote tank capacity as noted)

Chrysler
7.5 hp. 4,750 rpm. @ 2:1 reduction, 55 lb., 3.25 gal. tank.
"Sailor 250" 9.9 hp. 4,750 rpm. @ 3:1 reduction, 79 lb., electric start, 6 gal. tank, 60 w. alternator, remote controls.

Evinrude/Johnson
7.5 hp. 5,000 rpm. @ 2.2:1 reduction, 59 lb., 3 gal. tank, 60 w. alternator.
"Sailmaster" 9.9 hp. 5,000 rpm. @ 2.4:1 reduction, 82 lb., electric start opt., 6 gal. tank, 60 w. alternator, remote or top controls opt.

Mariner
8 hp. 5,500 rpm. @ 2:1 reduction, 59 lb., 3.15 gal. tank, 80 w. alternator opt., remote controls opt.
9.9 hp. 5,500 rpm. @ 2:1 reduction, 77 lb., 6.3 gal. tank, 80 w. alternator, remote controls opt.

Mercury
7.5 hp. 5,500 rpm. @ 2:1 reduction, 71 lb., opt. electric start, 3 gal. tank, alternator opt., remote controls opt.
9.8 hp. 5,500 rpm. @ 2:1 reduction, 71 lb., elec. start opt., 3 gal. tank, alternator opt., remote controls opt.

Suzuki
8 hp. 5,800 rpm. @ 2:1 reduction, 62 lb., 4 gal. tank, 80 w. alternator opt., remote controls opt.
9.9 hp., 5,800 rpm. @ 2:1 reduction, 83 lb., 6 gal. tank, 80 w. alternator, remote controls opt.

LARGE ENGINES: 15–16 hp. (All with F/N/R, 6-gal. tank except as noted)

Chrysler
15 hp. 5,100 rpm. @ 1.6:1 reduction, 60 lb., remote controls opt.

Evinrude/Johnson
15 hp. 6,000 rpm. @ 2.4:1 reduction, 82 lb., elec. start opt., 60 w. alternator opt. (std. with elec. start), remote or top controls opt.

Mariner
15 hp. 5,500 rpm. @ 2:1 reduction, 77 lb., elec. start opt., 80 w. alternator, 6.3 gal. tank, remote controls opt.

Suzuki
16 hp. 5,800 rpm. @ 2:1 reduction, 83 lb., 80 w. alternator opt.

A note on the builders may be in order. Chrysler is of course a subsidiary of the car maker. Their new (1980) "Economate" is a stripped-down version of their standard, single-cylinder 4-hp. model, lacking the latter model's forward/neutral shift, the lower half of the engine cover and the alternator option. It's planned to come in considerably lower than other three-and-a-halfs. The 6-hp. "Sailor 150" and 9.9 "Sailor 250" are, as the names suggest, specifically designed to power displacement hulls. Note the relatively low rpm. and gearing in each case, as well as the provision for remote controls.

Evinrude and Johnson are, as noted above, elements of OMC. The 4.5, the 9.9 "Sailmaster" and the 15 are geared down for sailboat power.

Mariners are built in Japan, but are distributed in the United States by Brunswick, which is also the parent company of Mercury. Note that the two small Mariners are air-cooled, which suggests that they would do better on a transom than in a well.

Mercury has never gone after the sailboat market, but their engines are well designed and serve adequately on other displacement hulls.

British Seagull is of course the sailboat outboard par excellence, loved or hated by everyone who's ever encountered one. They have recently leaped head-first into the twentieth century by introducing recoil (self-rewinding) starter cords, gear shifts, and optional alternators on their engines. Note the relatively low speeds and gear ratios, as well as the four-blade props. For some reason Seagull has not yet decided that covers would be an asset in keeping the engines dry, although they are well waterproofed otherwise.

Suzuki is the same Japanese firm that makes the well-known motorcycles. Their engines have a good track record in international use and have recently appeared on the American market.

XI

Trailering

Until fairly recently, trailering definitely appeared to be the wave of the future for small boats of all kinds, including small sailing cruisers. Now, however, matters have changed and the future isn't nearly as easy to visualize. What's happened to change the picture? Let's begin by examining how a positive climate for trailering came to be.

For some time, especially in the West, the shortage of marina slip space has been becoming more and more acute. Old-time boatyards have been closing down to be replaced by apartments and waterfront office buildings, and the marinas that remained have catered as much as possible to the big-ticket boats of considerable size and complexity. At the same time, the proliferation of small outboard-powered fishing boats has resulted in the growth of more and more launching ramps and associated parking areas, in parts of the country where permanent berthing facilities are scarce or unnecessary, or where owners prefer to keep their craft at home in the driveway.

Large, powerful family cars and sophisticated trailers made it possible to pull the typical sixteen-foot outboard boat all over the place. The vogue for noncommercial pickup trucks and four-wheel drive utility vehicles, with their greater pulling power, extended the length and weight of the boats that could be trailered to well over twenty-one feet, and brought the outboard cruiser into new popularity. Riding on that wave of enthusiasm, the trailerable sailboat flourished and grew, both in numbers and in absolute size.

In many respects, the sailing cruiser was even better suited to trailering than was the center-console fishing machine. For one thing, sailing boats are so slow in terms of covering ground that in ten hours' serious sailing, one could expect to cover a mere forty miles—just about what one would average in a single hour on the highway. With a trailer, the cruising skipper need not throw away the first day of a vacation or long weekend just reaching unexplored waters: Now he could saddle up and roll his rig a couple of hundred miles in a morning and begin his cruise in an area hitherto untouched by him.

There seemed, in fact, to be no limit to the grounds of a trailer-sailer, and where the travels of an early trailerboat skipper, such as *Yachting* magazine's Bill Robinson in his 24-foot Amphibicon, seemed like genuine pioneering, now it was simply a blueprint for others to follow.

Then, of course, there came the end of the era of unlimited cheap gasoline. While no one would venture a prediction as to the availability of auto fuel in the foreseeable future, all bets are that it will be scarcer rather than more plentiful, and more costly rather than less. Just as sailboats have never looked better, automobiles have never looked less practical for long-haul vacationing.

At the same time, beginning with 1980 models, the pulling capacity of a full-size passenger car will drop to about four thousand pounds, and as a result the heavier rigs—which include many trailerable cruising sailboats—will require specialized towing vehicles, or else heavily beefed-up sedans. And while the pickups and four-wheel drive vehicles certainly have greater pulling power, they're not noted for their economical fuel consumption.

Finally, it seems reasonable to assume that the marina shortage will become more acute, if anything, and the small cruiser will be squeezed hard by the shortage of slips.

It sounds like an unredeemedly bleak picture, but all this fails to take into account the ingenuity of most boating people. While a lot of trailerable cruisers will probably wind up riding at moorings in hitherto disused corners, the trailer itself is definitely here to stay. We will see it, I suspect, most commonly in three aspects. First, and perhaps least functionally, the trailer is a splendid off-season cradle—the only cradle that can carry its contents to and from the water. I used to own a 17-foot cruising catboat that spent its summers at anchor. After the first winter storage bill, I invested in a trailer that was too light to handle the boat on the highway, but quite adequate to support it at rest. My home was five miles or so from the water, and a friend's Jeep provided the towing power. In exchange for a very sweaty half hour early on a Sunday morning (before the police were up and about), we made the twice yearly hegira. All winter the boat was just outside my back door, available for projects or just to stroke from time to time. In two winters I'd completely amortized the trailer cost by eliminating storage bills, and the ancillary yard fees I didn't have to pay were so much gravy.

Another increasingly popular system of boating is dry-sailing, where a vessel spends the week in a cradle—or on a trailer—to be launched for the weekend or just an afternoon, and then returned to the trailer for the next five days, stored handily in a boatyard's or yacht club's parking lot. Not only does this make for a very efficient use of ground space—something that most shoreside facilities are notoriously poor about—but with the increased use of forklifts and crane launchers, boats with quite deep underbodies have now become eligible for dry-sailing, and trailers have been developed to handle them ashore. If you can trailer an Etchells 22 or a Star (and you can), there is virtually no keel form that's out of the question.

Dry-sailing is expanding everywhere, and the exact patterns of its future are not yet clear. At the moment, rigging the average trailer-sailer takes about half an hour, which means that the stack storage used for small powerboats is still somewhat difficult. But that, too, may change. Cut the rigging time to ten or fifteen minutes—which is entirely possible—and there's no reason you couldn't stack sailboats four or five high, in huge, roofed racks, picking them out and launching them with the aid of forklift trucks or even overhead-rail lifts. Just you wait.

In the meantime, however, local trailering will continue to be popular. By local, I don't mean to suggest any particular distance, but rather any short haul that doesn't involve high-speed freeway or motorway travel. And long-distance trailering won't die out either. Rather, I'd expect that its growth will slow and then stop. For the present, there are too many people who've built up a pattern of driving twenty-five miles or more to launch their boats. My only suggestion to readers of this book is that you attempt not to drop into that habit if another type of cruising is possible. Short-haul trailering is fine, as is dry-sailing based on a trailer, but the over-the-highway vehicle doesn't appear to me to have a very bright future.

The three-part combination: boat/trailer/tow vehicle

Since this is a book about boats, the boat is the most important part of this equation. Many sailing cruisers are advertised by their builders as being trailerable, and most are legitimately so. In examining the manufacturers' claims, however, it will help to go armed with your own knowledge, as there are absolute limits to trailability, as well as relative, practicable parameters within which most people will want to operate.

There is no practical length limit to the trailerable boat. At least one builder offers a 30-footer that is legally roadworthy, and there are trailers available to take the boat. But she is, in my opinion, something of a freak, a vessel in which many other things have been sacrificed in order to claim this single virtue. Yacht design being an art of compromise, the longest commonly seen trailerable is 25 or 26 feet. In some parts of the United States, there is a legal limit to the overall combined length of two vehicle and tow, and fifty feet is not an uncommon figure (ask police in your area), but unless you have an extraordinary tow vehicle, the length limit should pose no problems.

Beam, as many readers will already be aware, is the true limiting factor in trailering, and the design revolution that has produced ever beamier sailing boats, in relation to their length, has correspondingly reduced the number of

25- and 26-footers that can legally be trailered. The commonly accepted outside beam limit for no-hassle trailering is eight feet, both in this country and abroad. Do not, by the way, worry about the trailer exceeding this width; if there is a problem, it will lie with the boat. As the designs in Chapter III suggest, today's eight-foot beam is found on rather shorter boats than it was twenty years ago. A 26- or 27-footer only eight feet wide looks quite unusual in a modern fleet, and 24 feet is a more likely upper limit at which to expect a maximum trailerable beam.

In many areas, it's possible to trailer a vessel up to ten feet wide with a special permit and a "Wide Load" sign, but no other real problems. Do not, however, let a boat salesman convince you of the trailability of any boat with a beam over eight feet until you've checked matters with the appropriate authorities. And beyond ten feet in beam, you become a parade, with flashing lights and warning vehicles and endless trouble. The difficulty is likely to come with boats that, because of a designer's or builder's carelessness, or a salesperson's enthusiasm, are billed as being trailerable while they are in fact 8′6″ or even nine feet wide. Chances are, in many areas, that you'll never get caught pulling a marginally overwidth boat—but is it worth the gamble? Not to me.

Among the boats with legally trailerable beams, the next question to answer is whether the hull shape lends itself to this activity. To a considerable extent it will depend not on whether you can find a trailer to take the boat (someone with a welding torch can always make a cradle to fit anything) but how you plan to launch and recover it. If you're able to plan realistically on using a crane or forklift to remove the boat, deposit her in the water, and recover her, then any hull shape will do equally well.

But if you plan to slide her off a dry or semisubmerged trailer, parked on a launching ramp or, in some places, a dirt slope, then the problems become more pressing. The ideal shape for a trailer is probably a nearly flat bottom, with no protrusions that can't be retracted, and just enough V to the hull to give it directional support when sliding on and off. There are sailboat hulls like this, quite a lot of them, and most are indeed designed with trailering in mind. (It's worth noting that designers will frequently have a particular trailer worked into a boat's specification; if the salesperson isn't aware of what trailer will suit the boat, get in touch with the builder or designer.) As one can imagine, however, in order to have a protrusion-free bottom, things like rudders, propellers, and daggerboards or centerboards have to go someplace. Most rudders on such hulls are transom-hung, with quick-release pintle and gudgeon systems. A few retract into the cockpit.

Likewise, a boat like this is more than likely to be outboard-powered. If someone has put an inboard or sail drive into her, it may create a number of serious trailering complications, and you would do well to see if solutions exist, rather than taking anyone's word for it that the difficulties have been handled. Daggerboards, centerboards, and retractable keels that pull fully into the hull will almost inevitably affect the accommodation in one way or another, usually by introducing a certain amount of trunk into the after end of the cabin. This

Keel-centerboard Ericson 25 has hull designed to be trailered.

protrusion reaches its most visible degree in the centerboard trunk of a classic catboat, where it will probably dominate the cabin, splitting it along the centerline. In other boats, the hump may be virtually invisible, cosmetically concealed by carpeting or by fitting it into a table or the side of a seat. While this may work for you, it's been my experience that the almost invisible hump in the floorboards is far more annoying than the easily discernible centerboard trunk you can make allowances for.

Thanks to the wide variety of roller and bunk combinations in today's trailers, a number of bottom configurations can be slid on and off a trailer without too much problem. Three fairly popular forms are the stub keel with no centerboard, the keel centerboard, and the swing keel that leaves a small amount of itself protruding. From the point of view of trailering, these three are essentially the same shape. Except for the latter, they also have no effect on the accommodation or very little, being almost entirely hidden beneath the floorboards. As long as the hull and keel or board are supported properly, these hulls can fit a trailer with no problems of launch or recovery. Virtually the only difficulty can come if there is not a cross-member on the trailer directly beneath

Attaching line from winch to bow eye. When boat rides up into cradle, eye will be well above winch.

a centerboard, daggerboard, lifting or swing keel, so that if the board's pennant lets go there's some support other than the road below.

The full-keel boat is not—saving the presence of a crane or forklift—a practical hull for everyday trailering. Even if the trailer is fully immersible, without the possibility of water damage to brakes, lights, or bearings, you will probably have problems with the towing vehicle, and this class of conveyance cannot be waterproofed. There are salespeople who'll try to tell you that a full-keel boat is easily launchable from a standard trailer. Invite them to demonstrate it—and then to recover the boat afterwards.

Even if a boat is designed to be trailered, there are some special aspects of trailering the designer or builder may have overlooked. Here are things to consider, none of them crippling in their absence:

First, look for attachment points by which to make the boat fast to the trailer. Typically, these begin with a solidly built eye on the stem, somewhat below the sheer. This eye should be hefty enough to take virtually the whole weight of the boat, because it may have to do so, not once but again and again as you winch your vessel back onto her cradle. The eye will also have to take fore and aft the shocks as you start off, and the vertical bumps of off-the-highway driving. It should be high enough so that there's a slight downward lead to the attachment point on the trailer's winch pillar (see below) and should have a large enough diameter to accept not only the winch-wire's snap hook but also additional bow tie-downs to the trailer frame.

The boat's stern will usually be strapped down to the trailer by webbing belts, but you will also want to be sure that the hull has strong attachments —quarter cleats or the like—for spring lines to keep her from sagging back as you accelerate, and a bow cleat for another pair of springs that will keep her from continuing to whiz forward when you brake. These are the normal hardware items one would expect in a small cruiser, but the important matter

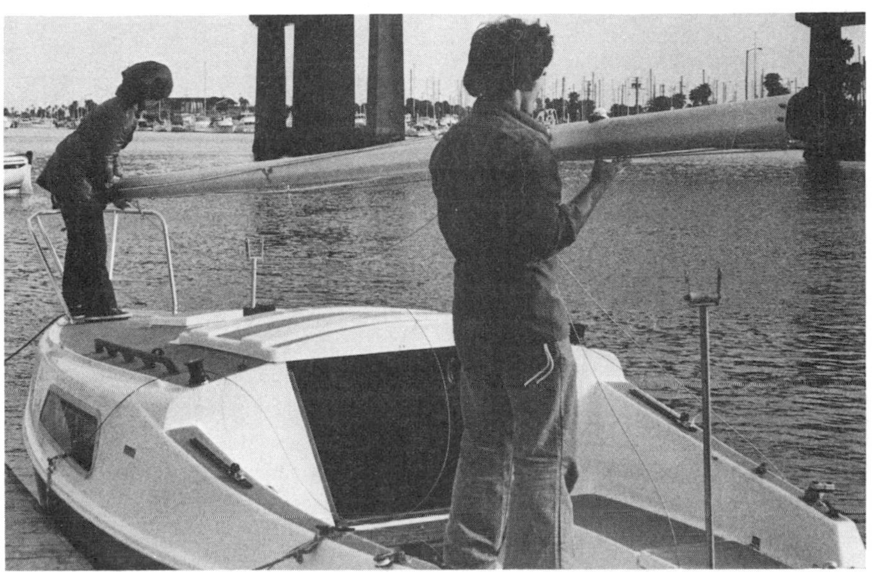

For trailering, mast fits into two removable fork supports fore and aft.

here is that they should be so positioned that lines can lead from cleat to frame without sawing unduly into the hull. (Among the trailer skipper's most valuable extras is a collection of six-inch or one-foot squares of dead carpet, for padding vulnerable edges of the boat.)

The mast will almost certainly pose some interesting stowage problems on the trailer, especially if your boat has one of today's extratall rigs. You will probably want a red flag—a protest flag, International Code "B," is perfect—for the overhanging tip, but more importantly you'll want support at two or three points, when the mast lies along the length of the boat. Three logical spots for supports are at the bow, the mast step, and the transom, and many builders of trailerable boats offer a mast support rig as an optional extra. At

Tripod support for mast is lashed to bow cleats and tack fitting.

least take a look at it before you decide that you can do better for less money.

Finally, you will probably want some kind of wrapping to keep highway grit, dust, and water out of the masthead fitting and the halyard winches (assuming your winches are mast-mounted), as well as caps or covers for the cockpit or deck-mounted winches. It's amazing how much abrasive grime can accumulate on a boat in even a short haul, and if the weather is either very dry or very wet, the potential damage doubles. Cover through-hull openings with adhesive tape.

The next element in our trio is the towing vehicle. Unless you're very involved in trailering, or in camping, chances are that you'll begin by considering the virtues of the family car. Formidable as most modern family cars appear, they were not intended by their makers to be tow trucks. Most cars are engineered to haul their own payload and little else, and a good rule of thumb is not to expect a passenger vehicle to pull more than its own curb weight. While nearly any vehicle can slowly pull a huge load on a dead flat surface (assuming the load's trailer is well engineered), the problems come with such commonplace obstacles as hills, passing situations, turns, and highway entrances and exits. Transmissions and cooling systems, brakes and suspensions—all of these essential elements are inadequate in a standard automobile for heavy-duty trailering at highway speeds.

At the same time, car manufacturers are aware of the trailer market and offer options and kits to add muscle where it's needed. The best way to determine what that requirement may be is first to work out the approximate weight of the combined load of car and trailer. If you haven't yet purchased either boat or trailer, you'll have to guess, but you can probably arrive at some reasonably accurate high and low limits. Let's look, for example, at three standard trailers, all tandem-axle models, designed for common size ranges of boat. The first model is intended to haul vessels from 18 to 21 feet in length, with a gross weight of 4,000 pounds for trailer and tow, of which the trailer itself is about 1,000 pounds. The second is designed to accommodate boats from 21 to 24 feet overall, with a gross trailed weight (GTW) of about 5,000 pounds, and a trailer weight of 1,400. The third trailer itself weighs 1,500 pounds, and will handle a GTW of 6,500 pounds, or a boat from 23 to 26 feet long. Remember that gross trailed weight includes both boat and trailer.

Another equally well known manufacturer offers a single-axle trailer for boats up to 21 feet and gross trailed weights of 5,000 pounds; a tandem-axle unit for boats to 30 feet, with a gross weight of 10,000 pounds; and even a tri-axle rig for boats up to 40 feet, and GTWs of 15,000 pounds.

So you can approximate the gross trailer weight; put it aside and try to calculate the payload of the towing vehicle. This includes fuel, passengers, extra cruising gear, food spare parts, tools—not only the paraphernalia of driving but also that of cruising. Add that weight to the GTW; it should not, for the average sedan, be more than the curb weight of the car itself. And the total of all three weights should not be more than about 4,000 pounds.

These are just rules of thumb, ways of discovering how near (or how far over) the limits you're likely to be. Now go to your car dealer with your slips full of figures and ask what is the rated load—car payload plus tow—of your vehicle. He may well not know, in which case you will have to get in touch with the factory. However you accomplish it, work your way through to someone who knows trailering and who's familiar with your car, and lay the problem in his or her lap.

What are the possible alterations to a standard car? Quite a few. You may be able to install heavy-duty springs and shocks, especially in the rear end, and especially if you plan to use a weight-carrying hitch (see below). These will prevent your car's rear end from sagging and bottoming out under the influence of a heavy load (and remember, you'll almost certainly have a trunkful of stuff as well as the trailer on behind).

Although it will be little consolation if you already own the car you plan to use as a tow vehicle, it should probably have under its hood the largest engine offered for its style. To keep from overheating, ask about the possibility of installing a heavy-duty radiator, perhaps one with a coolant spray and recovery system to help keep the vehicle temperature down. A separate transmission cooler, and a dashboard gauge to monitor this piece of equipment, may also be a good idea, as the strain of towing frequently exacts a toll from the transmission.

It's also extremely important to make sure the rig will stop when you want it to. We'll deal with trailer brakes in the appropriate place, but for the moment let's consider the ones on your car, which can be beefed up by the addition of heavy-duty brake linings and oversize wheels and tires.

Finally, you'll need proper attachment points for the trailer's light harness and possibly for its brake system, not to mention the all-important hitch itself. The hitch, of course, is the attachment on your tow vehicle to which you make fast the trailer. There are essentially two kinds, the first being one of several types of *weight-carrying* hitch. As the name implies, this device takes the weight of the trailer tongue, which should be (as we shall see shortly) 10 to 15 percent of the weight of trailer and load.

On occasion, people renting lightweight trailers for furniture moving get from the renting agency a so-called *bumper* hitch, which fastens directly and solely to the towing vehicle's rear bumper. This is adequate for small trailers and very light loads, but not for anything so considerable as a cruising sailboat. In some areas, bumper hitches are illegal per se, and they should not be considered eligible for the work we're discussing.

If you have a light truck you'll use for towing, it may have a *step-bumper* hitch, which isn't at all the same thing as a bumper hitch, and which can be classified with other weight-carrying hitches, of which the most popular for small-boat towing is the *frame* hitch. Although attached to the tow vehicle's bumper, this device is also bolted to the back end of the car's frame. Properly affixed, it is a reliable hitch for loads—trailer and boat—totaling 3,000 pounds

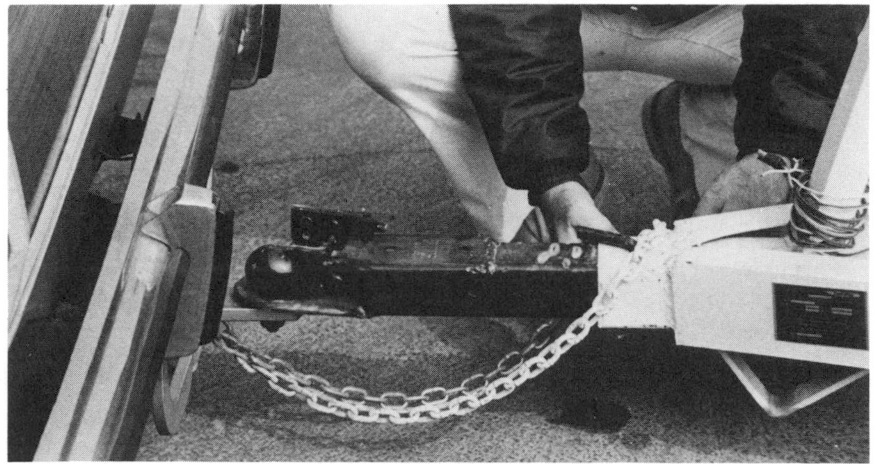

Towing hitch, with safety chains looped under tow bar.

or less (according to the Coast Guard; other authorities give slightly higher weight figures).

As noted above, the frame hitch supports the trailer tongue's static weight, and this, properly balanced, should be between 300 and 450 pounds for a 3,000-pound load. Any less weight on the tongue (for this size load), and the trailer will tend to fishtail, and any more, and the car's rear will drop; with extreme overloading, one may even take appreciable weight off the front wheels, which can result in truly disastrous loss of steering control.

The answer, for heavier loads, is the *weight-distributing* hitch. It too accepts about 15 percent of the trailer's tongue weight, but it distributes the load to all four wheels of the tow vehicle and even passes some of it back to the trailer wheels. Weight-distributing hitches are more complicated and more expensive to install, but they are a definite prerequisite for over-the-road towing of larger boats. If the gross tow weight is over 5,000 pounds, you will be well advised to add another device called an *antisway bar,* which keeps the trailer from swinging back and forth behind the tow vehicle.

The standard hitch terminates in a simple ball fitting, over which the inverted, cuplike socket of the trailer fits and locks. As the accompanying table shows, coupler balls are not all the same size in the United States, although the differences in diameter may not be apparent to the casual eye. One thing to watch is weight classifications of hitch and trailer (the same, in spite of being in Roman and Arabic numerals respectively) and those of couplers, which do not match, although the class numbers are the same. Europeans are more standardized in this respect, and most countries use a 50-mm. ball and socket, even the British.

All this leads up to the trailer itself, the final third of the towing equation. Before discussing trailers in detail, it will be useful to come to grips with the several questions of weight involved. The information largely concerns the

United States, but the principles are pretty sound wherever you are. Still, check with local authorities.

Begin with a couple of acronyms and their definitions: First and most important is gross vehicle weight rating (GVWR). This represents the total designed capacity of the trailer or other vehicle, and includes its own weight plus the maximum weight of the load it is intended to carry. The figure appears prominently on the capacity information label affixed permanently to each trailer, usually on the trailer tongue.

Related to GVWR is gross trailed weight (GTW), which we have seen is the actual weight of trailer and load. Although GVWR indicates maximum permissible load and GTW is (or should be) a real weight, the terms are used almost interchangeably in trailering.

Also seen on the trailer's capacity label is the abbreviation GAWR, which stands for gross axle weight rating, or the maximum weight each axle (one per pair of wheels) is designed to carry. Again, the figure includes the weight of the vehicle plus the weight of its load. On tandem-axle or tri-axle rigs, the combined GAWR must equal or exceed the trailer's GVWR. The proper tires for the maximum rated gross weight are noted alongside the GAWR figures.

In the combined weight table, you see that the static tongue load of a trailer varies somewhat, but should in no case be more than 15 percent of the GTW. In even a light rig for a pocket cruiser, this can come to a couple of hundred pounds, which is why all but the smallest trailers should have a jack-and-caster setup on the trailer tongue. Simply explained, this consists of a small dolly wheel, like a furniture caster only more solid, fixed to the tongue with a built-in jack to allow it to be raised well clear of the ground for towing, or lowered to allow the boat to rest on its trailer in a more or less horizontal position, even when the tow vehicle is detached. Unfortunately, the jack-and-caster is more often than not an optional extra, even on trailers that can obviously not do without one.

All this talk about weights and weight ratings may seem rather pointless. After all, the trailer's weight is known by the builder, and you know (or should) your boat's displacement, so where's the complexity? Well, for one thing, a boat's designed displacement, which is the figure usually quoted in sales literature, has only a theoretical relationship to what the thing actually weighs, fresh off the production line. It may be more, it may be less, but the odds are good that the boat's true weight will be markedly different from what the architect had in mind.

Second, the designer never really comprehends what owners do to boats, and even when you think you've pared the vessel's load down to a bare minimum, you might be surprised at the amount of gear you're carrying aboard. Fresh water weighs eight pounds per U.S. gallon, diesel fuel weighs a little over seven and gasoline is six and a quarter. Storage batteries vary in weight, but they are all very heavy for their size.

And as if this were not enough, at least one trailer authority, who prefers to remain nameless, notes that he has weighed trailers sold to him, only to find

Table of Trailer Weights

Trailer CLASS	Gross Vehicle WEIGHT RATING	Coupler CLASS	Coupler GVWR	Coupler Ball DIAMETER	Shank DIAMETER	Hitch CLASS*	Static Tongue LOAD: % OF GTW	Hitch TYPE
1	to 2,000 lb.	I	1,500 lb.	1 7/8″	3/4″	I	10–15%	Weight-carrying or
2	2,001–3,500	II	3,000 lb.	2″	3/4″	II	10–15%	Weight-carrying to 3,000 lb.; weight-distributing over 3,000 lb.
3	3,501–5,000	III	5,000 lb.	2″	1″	III	15%	
4	5,000–10,000	IV	7,500 lb.	25/16″	1″	IV	15%	
								+antisway
			10,000 lb.	2 5/16″	1 1/4″			

*Note that hitch class relates to trailer, not coupler.

they were up to 20 percent off the manufacturers' listed weight. So it behooves you to allow a margin for safety when buying an over-the-road boat trailer: The Coast Guard suggests that if your estimate of the total weight of boat, load, and trailer is within 15 percent of the upper limit of the trailer's GVWR, you go to a trailer of the next higher size.

How does one go about weighing the various components of his trailer rig? Probably the best and easiest way is to locate a public weighbridge or hunt up (in the Yellow Pages) a local junkyard with a truck scale. Explain to the operator what you have in mind and (if necessary) pay him a couple of bucks for immobilizing his drive-on scale. First, weigh your own car with all the gear you'd normally carry when taking the boat off to a launch site for a cruise. Be generous in your weight estimates. Now weigh the trailer with the boat on it, but not hitched to the car. Next, move the trailer so only the jack-and-caster is on the scale. This will give you the tongue weight of trailer and boat. Go launch the boat, and while she's afloat bring the trailer back for one final check to make sure it weighs more or less what the manufacturer claims. Armed with these weights, you'll know that your rig is within the safety parameters—or that it's not, and that something needs to be added. Trailers are such protean contraptions that you may well find it possible to add an extra axle and/or larger wheels, bringing it up to standard if it's too low, so don't despair too soon.

Depending on the type of hull your trailer is carrying, and on the kinds of launching ramp generally available in your area, you'll have chosen the type of trailer frame that best suits your boat. The simplest is the straight-line, two-wheel unit, with or without jack-and-caster. This will serve adequately for light boats with more or less flat bottoms, launched off average ramps. For deep-hulled boats that will not float easily off an ordinary trailer, it may be necessary to get a controlled-tilt vehicle. This type of trailer "breaks" with a hinge just ahead of the stem roller so that the bow can be jacked up and the boat will slide off the trailer bed.

A more commonly seen version of the same general idea is the automatic-tilt model in which the hinge in the trailer is just forward of the wheels. As the boat is slid off, it overbalances and tilts the stern half of the trailer down, allowing the boat to finish its slide under its own momentum. When loading, the auto-tilt makes bringing the bow on the trailer considerably easier. Because both the controlled-tilt and auto-tilt project the boat off the trailer at an angle to the ramp bed beneath, there must be a drop-off behind the trailer wheels, or at least deep enough water to keep the trailer's stern from touching bottom.

An equally important element in launching is the choice of rollers, bunks, or a combination of the two, to support the boat when she's out of water and to make easier her launch and recover.

As the name suggests, rollers are generally cylindrical supports mounted on small axles and located to support the boat and guide it on and off the trailer. Keel rollers may be slotted or otherwise angled to give the boat some directional orientation, and while there may be several dozen rollers supporting a medium-size trailerable cruiser, it's important that when the boat is fully recovered on its trailer, it be supported at certain key locations—under the turn of the forefoot, at the transom (especially if there's an outboard on it), along the line of the keel, and at the turn of the bilge. Boats with large flat areas of underbody, such as catboats, should have as much closely spaced support as possible under the flat areas.

Rollers are of course most efficient for loading and unloading, but they give minimal support to a structure that is, after all, engineered to be supported evenly at all points of the underbody when at rest. A roller-equipped trailer must be long enough to give its cargo support from one end to the other, and there must be enough rollers to give even support of the entire hull. The rollers themselves must be adjustable to match the individual hull, and the boat cannot be overloaded when on the trailer.

Because of the nature of support given by rollers, it's important to make sure that all heavy weights—such as gear, fuel and water tanks, and batteries—have support directly beneath them when the boat is on the trailer. Make sure that the hull has not been flexed out of its normal shape in its attempt to accommodate itself to the rollers, as this flexing will inevitably lead to delamination of interior bulkheads and even cracking of the hull.

Bunks are one of the generic names for the padded linear supports—often ordinary 2 × 4 timbers—used instead of rollers on some trailers. Also known as *bolsters* and *pads,* bunks provide much better support for most hulls, if (and only if) the bunks themselves are properly curved to take the hull's shape. While they don't of course give the same unvarying amount of support that water does, a good system of bunks can spread the pressures of a trailer-loading situation over wide areas of the hull.

The problem, of course, is that a bunk system by its friction can make launching and recovery a drag, in the most precise and irritating sense of that word. Bottom paint and boot topping can be abraded, and small, protruding fittings can be seriously damaged as the hull is dragged by main force over the bunks. Bunks are ideal when a boat is launched in slings from a derrick, or when the trailer is wholly or nearly submersible, at which point of course recovery of the boat is no problem, although it may be difficult to extract the trailer and towing vehicle.

Because keelboats form such a relatively small fraction of the number of trailered boats, most commercial trailers are designed and engineered with powerboats in mind, specifically the deep-V runabout that has become so overwhelmingly popular in recent years. This is not a shape that's inimical to sailing, given some alteration in the support system, whether it be rollers or bunks. In some cases, a combination of the two may be the answer—rollers to ease the passage of the keel and bunks to support the sides of the boat once she's out of the water. Only if the boat is a full- (or nearly full) keel model will it be necessary to invest in a system of extensions and jacks to support the hull at some height above the keel—see the builders' trailers at any boat show. In this case, you can kiss ordinary trailer launching good-bye, and your boat will

Maneuvering into submerged trailer's supports. Wheel bearings must be drained after immersion.

not really be suited to regular trailering operations unless you can proceed from derrick to derrick.

A vital adjunct to most successful boat recovery is the trailer winch—another indispensable item that still comes on the tab as an optional extra from most trailer builders. In general, a winch is really a necessity for the last third of the boat-recovery operation, when the hull is on the trailer but must be pulled forward until the bow is firmly in the padded V support on the winch column. Both manual and electric winches are available, with the electrics running off the car's 12-volt system. For a reasonably heavy cruiser, an electric winch is a sound investment, and for all cruiser-size boats, one should definitely opt for the slightly more expensive wire rope to replace the standard fiber line on the trailer winch.

If yours is a standard-size American car, chances are that its wheels are considerably larger than those of the trailer it's pulling. What this means is that the trailer's wheels make more turns at higher speed than do those of the car, with a consequent increase in the heat generated by the wheel and its bearings. It's possible, though unlikely, that your trailer may accept the same size wheels as the tow vehicle, in which case you may be able to save on spares. In any case, your trailer must have a spare wheel, which can be locked in place on the trailer tongue. In most cases you will need a special jack for the trailer as well, since the standard car bumper or frame jack has no purchase point on the trailer frame. Probably a good hydraulic jack, with a short length of plank for a base, will be the best, as it can also be used to lift the boat in the trailer when painting around the bunks or rollers.

There are three types of brake system available for today's trailers, and any trailer capable of hauling a cruiser needs brakes. The simplest and cheapest are known as *surge* brakes. These are activated by the trailer's own momentum, when the pulling load of the tow vehicle is removed. Although many trailer sailors find them acceptable, surge brakes are illegal in some areas and are not considered top-of-the-line equipment.

Electrically activated brakes are generally thought of as an improvement over surge brakes, and this is true in highway trailers that are never—or very seldom—immersed in water. As every boatman knows, water and electricity are mortal enemies, and many experienced trailer operators feel that electric brakes on a marine trailer is asking for trouble.

That leaves the final and most costly type of brake, electrically activated hydraulic units. Though not perfect, these brakes are probably the most reliable, working in tandem with the car's own brakes to provide a synchronized stopping pressure for the trailer and its tow. As a final note on brakes, your trailer should have so-called breakaway brakes, which activate automatically if the trailer should ever come loose from the tow vehicle.

To prevent that detachment, every trailer must have a pair of safety chains, steel links that provide a fail-safe connection between the trailer tongue and towing frame. They should be doubled under the tongue to form an X-shaped support, high enough off the road to catch the tongue and carry it so that it cannot dig in and somersault the rig. The chains may be a single unit, but it's safer to have independent chains on either side, with shackles instead of S-hooks for fasteners. The breaking strength of the chain should be equal to the weight of trailer and load.

Trailers of the size we are discussing will need stop lights and turn signals, hooked into the corresponding signal lights of the tow vehicle's electrical system. The wires of the lighting system should be stranded, not single, wire to avoid breaking from continual vibration, and the plug should be secured with waterproof tape when the unit is rigged. Extra rear and side reflectors are a useful addition to the trailer, to pick out for other drivers the general dimesnions of the tow they're overtaking.

Although many trailers' brake and turn lights are advertised as being waterproof, it is asking a great deal for them to continue in that state. By and large, it seems advisable to invest in a detachable lights-and-license rig that can be clamped to the trailer or boat and removed before the rig is launched (or else sited so that it will never be immersed at all).

Nearly all trailers' wheels get immersed to the hubs and over when launching and recovering, and this can be death on the wheel bearings at the ends of the trailer axles. Not only should your spares kit include a complete set of extra wheel bearings, you should also invest in a set of bearing protectors, capping devices that should make the wheel bearings reasonably waterproof under normal conditions.

When buying a trailer, there are a number of good but not vital extras to look for, indicators of a quality unit. Nonskid steps and walkways will be a safety factor when launching and recovering. Look for steps next to the trailer's fenders and a walkway down the centerline under the keel supports. The trailer's frame elements as well as its rollers and bunks should be individually adjustable, and clusters of rollers should be capable of being aligned as a group. Look for conveniently spotted tie-down rings on the frame, as well as fully enclosed wiring and brake lines.

Some trailer manufacturers will offer a special kit to convert a standard trailer to the requirements of sailboat trailering. This rig will involve extension pipes for the hull support bunks, which are precurved, padded 2 × 4s, a mast bracket, extra tie-down points and keel guides.

Trailer operation

Although all the care required in matching boat, trailer and tow vehicle may suggest that trailering in practice is very complex, in fact it is not, especially if you have the proper gear to start with. Thousands of small-boat sailors routinely throw their one-designs on trailers every weekend and think nothing of it. While trailering a cruising yacht is obviously more of an operation, it is intrinsically the same thing on a larger scale.

Much of the work involved in trailering consists of a meticulous predeparture check of gear and vehicles. Begin by checking tires for proper inflation and signs of unusual wear that may indicate off-balance loading or frame adjustment. Check the adjustment points on the trailer frame and tighten up the bolts. Even a small maladjustment on one side of the adjustable trailer frame can throw the whole vehicle out of kilter, as well as imposing severe strains on the boat.

Check the brakes, both on the trailer and the tow vehicle, and at the same time ensure that the brake lights and turn lights on both vehicles are functioning and that the connecting wires are secure. At the same time check the hitch connection, making certain that it's fully seated, and the safety chains.

Next look at the car's radiator and at the transmission cooler, if you have one, to be sure that there's enough coolant in each. At the same time, check engine oil and transmission fluid.

With a wrench check the wheel lugs on tow vehicle and trailer, and adjust the rearview mirrors. Make certain that the tools, spares, and emergency signals are aboard.

Now turn to the boat. Check each of the tie-downs, the spring lines, the bow line and the anti-chafe padding. Make sure the tow and towing vehicle are at the right attitude relative to each other—in more or less a straight line at rest. Check the trailer's wheel bearings to ensure that they're freshly packed with grease and that the bearing savers are attached.

Examine the load in the boat. If your GTW is anywhere near the safety limit, you should be very careful about extra loads, and in any case be sure that gear in the boat is even more securely stowed and wedged in place than when you're afloat. Remember that the rapid bouncing of a highway rig provides far more shocks than the water normally will, and that vibration can loosen fittings insidiously.

Handling a trailer requires rethinking your driving habits, and it may come hard because you'll normally be behind a familiar steering wheel. Practice in handling the empty trailer, especially in close quarters backing and filling, is time well spent. You can, with the aid of a few empty cartons, set up a good obstacle course in a supermarket parking lot on a Sunday.

On the road, however, it's for real. Even if your rig doesn't feel logy, it hasn't got anywhere near the handling qualities or acceleration that the tow vehicle alone possesses. Starting up, be sure to signal your departure from the curb, and take the tow vehicle up through the gears, starting with the lowest to get her rolling. Shift down for corners, even though you normally don't. Unless you have surge brakes, don't brake by shifting down, as you'll only have the trailer riding up your tail.

Passing on a road while pulling a trailer is an operation that requires real advance planning and a genuine need. But once you've determined to go, move out and don't dither. Remember that your total length is now more than twice what it normally is, and check carefully that you're free and past before signaling your return to the slow lane. Courteous drivers may respond to your signal by flashing their headlights to indicate that they understand what you intend and you have the space to accomplish it.

Follow at about twice the normal distance and always leave room for faster vehicles to pass and drop in ahead of you. When you stop, brake down firmly and easily and allow plenty of time and space to lose speed. If you have a weight-carrying hitch, be careful going over bumps, as there'll be a tendency for the back end of the tow vehicle to bottom out.

When you're being passed by large trucks, be watchful for a gust of turbulence as the other vehicle swings by. Grip the wheel hard and concentrate on tracking.

Stop after the first fifteen minutes to check all lashings for shifting or loosening and stop every hour or so to rest, switch drivers if possible, and execute your under-way checklist, as follows: Feel the trailer wheel bearings —they should not be too hot to touch. If they are, open them up and see what's the matter. Check tie-downs all around and put a wrench to the wheel bolts. Give the trailer's adjustment points a check as well, to make sure they're not backing off. Check that the brake and turn indicator lights are still functioning properly.

While under way, you should cultivate the habit of scanning the tow vehicle's gauges to make sure that nothing untoward is beginning. Many skippers who do a lot of towing replace the tow vehicle's idiot lights with old-fashioned dials, so they have a fighting chance of seeing trouble develop before it becomes a full-scale crisis. Be alert for peculiar noises you can't identify or handling quirks that suddenly crop up. Don't be satisfied until you've pinned down the causes of each.

Arriving at the launch site, send someone to scout out the area if it's unfamiliar to you. You can ask whoever's in charge about the degree of ramp slope (if it's not apparent) and how long the ramp is, if the water's too muddy to be sure. Check to see what facilities are available for loading the boat at a finger pier after launching. Make especially sure that there are no overhead electrical wires between the place where you'll set up the rig and the ramp itself. This seems absurdly obvious, but most ramp areas were laid out with outboard runabouts in mind, and quite often it's apparent that no one ever bothered to look over his head. Each year a few sailing skippers are electrocuted because their boats' metal masts hit electrical wires in an otherwise safe launch area.

With the reconaissance out of the way, find a corner in which to rig the boat. One thing that this pause will do, by the way, is allow the wheel bearings to cool. Always check the bearings before launching, and if they have not yet cooled, wait a bit longer. A hot bearing will pull cold water into itself and wash out the grease packing, which can result in a seized bearing once you're under way again.

If you travel with the transom-mounted outboard in its vertical position, raise and lock it before launching. It does not matter a great deal what position you have the engine in under way, although a tilted engine tends to put more fore-and-aft stresses on an unsupported transom than does a lowered motor. If your boat has a hull plug, insert it. If you travel with the centerboard or daggerboard resting on the trailer's keel rollers, now's the time to raise it fully and lash it in place so it doesn't snag when you're launching the boat. If you have a set of removable brake and turn lights, take them off and stow them in the car.

And that leaves the matter of rigging. There are really two ways to raise the mast in a trailerable boat: from forward aft, and from aft forward. Usually the boat's designer will have come to grips with this question and will have engineered the system that's best for the type of boat and rig you have. As a rule, the hinged mast base will only work in one direction, so you know in advance what's going to be right.

You will normally travel with the mast itself already rigged—halyards are reeved, stays and shrouds will have turnbuckles attached, ready to be pinned. (It will pay to have half a dozen spare clevis pins in your tool kit.) Lay the spar out on the ground, remove the covers if any, and check that it's ready to raise. Lift it and position the spar so that the base can be made fast to its hinged fitting. Let's first assume that you're raising the spar from forward to aft. Hook up the upper shrouds and the forward lowers (if you have two sets of lowers; it may be possible to make one set of lowers fast). Presumably you have preadjusted all the stays so that there's a minimum amount of work to be done afterward. In any case, if the mast is stepped on a cabin top, the shrouds will be somewhat slack when the spar is lying down, and will tighten as it is raised to its proper vertical position. If you have trouble visualizing why this should be so, think about the extra height of the cabin top, which is the factor here.

Attach the boom to the mast and make fast the main topping lift, tied off so the boom is vertical, at right angles to the horizontal mast. Run a pair of premeasured lines from the clew end of the boom to the chainplates, to keep the boom from falling over sideways. Now attach the mainsheet to its traveler and to the boom. Using the mainsheet as a handy-billy and the boom as a lever, sowly raise the mast to the vertical. When it's up, make fast the backstay, cast off the boom supporting lines, and you're in business, except for a quick tune—which should merely be a process of setting up the turnbuckles to previously marked positions.

This type of fore-to-aft mast raising requires two or three people, one of whom will have the boring job of holding up the part of the mast that projects over the bow while his companions finish the rigging operation. When the mast-stepping crew knows its stuff, the whole thing shouldn't take more than fifteen minutes.

Raising the mast from aft forward can be a bit harder because one doesn't have the built-on lever of the main boom. Some builders incorporate a socket on the forward side of the mast base, sized to take a spinnaker pole or even a custom-made lever. The raising operation is much the same as the other, only in reverse, with the backstay made fast and the forestay ready to attach. Use the jib halyard to attach to the forward-facing lever and, if necessary, run it back to a cockpit winch for mechanical advantage.

In many small trailer cruisers, no particular mast-raising gear is provided or necessary. The mast, which is lying with its head extended over the transom, is set up with shrouds and backstay made fast. One crewmember climbs carefully into the boat and lifts the masthead, raising it until the second crewmember can get hold either of the forestay or of a rope extension made fast to it. This second alternative is perhaps safer and more effective, as even a strong man will have trouble clasping a thin piece of slippery wire rigging, and should the mast lifter stumble, the wire will certainly pull through the second man's hands, with possibly painful results.

With the boat rigged and as much gear as possible stowed, you're ready to launch. (It is, by the way, very poor ramp manners to rig the boat while on the ramp approach, as a good ramp on a busy weekend is a hive of well-ordered activity.) Swing past the ramp and stop with the whole rig in a straight line, the boat's stern pointing directly down the ramp. Ideally, you should have one person to drive, one person to guide the driver, and a third person to hold one end of the dockline—the other end being secured to the boat.

As you guide the rig slowly backward down the ramp, remember that the steering wheel turns in the opposite direction from normal; some people find it helps to hold the wheel's rim at the bottom. Only slight turns are required: Too much and you will jackknife the rig, which will require you to go forward and straighten out before trying again. Ease the trailer down the ramp until the boat just begins to lift to the water. It would be nice if the trailer's hubs were not immersed, but this will often be unavoidable.

Chock the wheels either with wood triangles or commercially available chocks and set the parking brake, but don't turn off the engine. Work the boat easily off the trailer into the water, at which point it's in the hands of the line tender, who'll bring it alongside the finger pier (if any) for final loading while you park the rig.

If you have a large boat, or one that's exceptionally difficult to control on the trailer, you may want to invest in a front hitch. This is simply a towing ball on the front bumper so you can turn the tow vehicle round and nudge the boat into the water while in forward gear.

Recovering a boat is, if anything, somewhat easier than launching, as you will have the winch to pull her into position. Again, before recovery make sure that the rudder is off the transom and the motor is tilted up. Once the boat is unrigged, run through your normal predeparture checklist, with special attention to the trailer wheel bearings, which may have to be repacked before you can get back on the highway. With practice, the whole operation will become routine, but you should never let it become so cut and dried that you eliminate the important periodic checks that will lead to safe trailering.

If the boat is going to sit on the trailer for some time between launches, it will be a good idea to get the load off the trailer wheels. You can chock up the whole trailer frame with a hydraulic jack and cinder blocks, using shingles or thin planks as shims. Make sure that the trailer supports, whether rollers or bunks, still cradle the hull uniformly, but try to tilt the whole rig enough, assuming your boat has a self-draining cockpit, so that the drains will still function. If you cannot do this, or if your boat's cockpit doesn't have drains, then it will have to be covered, as a cockpit full of rainwater is a terrible load for a trailer frame to support.

In the off-season, you can gloat over your friends' boats stored miles from home in expensive yards while yours is on its trailer only seconds from your living room. Trailering is in many cases a bit more work, but in many areas it's the only way to go cruising economically, or at all.

Bibliography

Amateur Yacht Research Society. *Cruising Catamarans.* London: AYRS, 1972.

Baader, Juan (trans. Inge Moore). *The Sailing Yacht.* New York: W.W. Norton, 1979 (revised).

Beiser, Arthur. *The Proper Yacht.* Camden, Me.: International Marine Publishing Co., 1978 (2nd edition).

Benjamin, John J. *Cruising Boats within Your Budget.* New York: Harper & Bros., 1957.

Blanchard, Fessenden L. *The Sailboat Classes of North America.* Garden City, N.Y.: Doubleday & Co., 1968 (revised).

Boat Buyers Guide. New York: Ziff-Davis Publishing Co., annual.

Bolger, Philip C. *Different Boats.* Camden, Me.: International Marine Publishing Co., 1980.

Bolger, Philip C. *Small Boats.* Camden, Me.: International Marine Publishing Co., 1973.

Bottomley, Tom. *The Boatkeeper's Project Book.* New York: Motor Boating & Sailing Books, 1972.

Bowker, R.M., and Budd, S.A. *Make Your Own Sails.* New York: St. Martin's Press, 1959.

Brewer, E.S. *Cruising Designs.* New York: Seven Seas Press, 1976.

Chapelle, Howard I. *Boatbuilding.* New York: W.W. Norton, 1969 (revised).

Chapelle, Howard I. *Yacht Designing and Planning.* New York: W.W. Norton, 1971.

Chapman, Charles F., et al. *Piloting, Seamanship and Small Boat Handling.* New York: Motor Boating & Sailing Books (various editions).

Choy, Rudy. *Catamarans Offshore.* New York: Macmillan, 1970.

Clarke, D.H. *Trimarans.* London: Adlard Coles, Ltd., 1969.

Colvin, Thomas E. *Coastwise and Offshore Cruising Wrinkles.* New York: Seven Seas Press, 1972.

Cotter, Edward F. *Multihull Sailboats.* New York: Crown Publishers, 1966.

Dawson, Christopher. *The Rig.* London: George Newnes, Ltd., 1967.

Desoutter, Denny M. *Small Boat Cruising.* London: Faber & Faber, 1972.

Doherty, J.S. (ed.) *17 Designs from the Board of John G. Hanna.* New York: Seven Seas Press, 1971.

Duffett, John. *Modern Marine Maintenance.* New York: Motor Boating & Sailing Books, 1973.

Edmunds, Arthur. *Fiberglass Boat Survey Manual.* Clinton Corners, N.Y.: John de Graff, 1979.

Gilles, Daniel, and Malinovsky, Michel. *Go Cruising.* St. Albans, England: Adlard Coles, Ltd., 1978.

Gillmer, Thomas C. *Cruising Designs from the Board of Thomas C. Gillmer.* New York: Seven Seas Press, 1972.

Hamilton, Donald. *Cruises with* Kathleen. New York: David McKay Co., 1980.

Henderson, Richard. *Choice Yacht Designs.* Camden, Me.: International Marine Publishing Co., 1979.

Henderson, Richard. *The Cruiser's Compendium.* Chicago: Henry Regnery Co., 1973.

Henderson, Richard. *The Racing-Cruiser.* Chicago: Reilly & Lee, 1970.

Henderson, Richard. *Sea Sense.* Camden, Me.: International Marine Publishing Co., 1972.

Henderson, Richard. *Singlehanded Sailing.* Camden, Me.: International Marine Publishing Co., 1976.

Herreshoff, L. Francis. *The Compleat Cruiser.* New York: Sheridan House, 1956.

Herreshoff, L. Francis. *Sensible Cruising Designs.* Camden, Me.: International Marine Publishing Co., 1973.

Hiscock, Eric C. *Come Aboard.* Oxford: Oxford University Press, 1978.

Hiscock, Eric C. *Cruising Under Sail.* Oxford: Oxford University Press, 1965.

Hiscock, Eric C. *Voyaging Under Sail.* Oxford: Oxford University Press, 1959.

Howard-Williams, Jeremy. *Sails.* Tuckahoe, N.Y.: John de Graff, 1971.

Illingworth, John. *Offshore.* London: Adlard Coles Ltd., 1953.

Johnson, Peter. *Ocean Racing & Offshore Yachts.* New York: Dodd, Mead Co., 1970.

Johnson, Peter (ed.) *Offshore Manual International.* New York: Dodd, Mead Co., 1977.

Kinney, Francis. *Skene's Elements of Yacht Design.* New York: Dodd, Mead Co., 1973 (8th edition).

Lane, Carl D. *The Boatman's Manual.* New York: W.W. Norton, 1979 (revised).

Leather, John. *Gaff Rig.* London: Adlard Coles Ltd., 1970.

Letcher, John S. Jr. *Self-steering for Sailing Craft.* Camden, Me.: International Marine Publishing Co., 1974.

Lipe, Bob and Karen. *Boat Canvas.* New York: Seven Seas Press, 1978.

Marchaj, C.A. *Aero-Hydrodynamics of Sailing.* New York: Dodd, Mead Co., 1979.

Marchaj, C.A. *Sailing Theory and Practice.* New York: Dodd, Mead Co., 1964.

Marshall, Roger. *Designed to Win.* New York: W.W. Norton, 1981.

Marshall, Roger. *Race to Win.* New York: W.W. Norton, 1980.

Mason, Al. *29 Designs from the Board of Al Mason.* New York: Seven Seas Press, 1972.

Maté, Ferenc. *The Finely Fitted Yacht.* New York: W.W. Norton (dist.), 1979.

Miller, Conrad. *Engines for Sailboats.* New York: Ziff-Davis Publishing Co., 1978.

Miller, Conrad. *Your Boat's Electrical System.* New York: Motor Boating & Sailing Books, 1973.

Nicolson, Ian. *Boat Data Book.* New York: Ziff-Davis Publishing Co., 1978.

Nicolson, Ian. *Surveying Small Craft.* Camden, Me.: International Marine Publishing Co., 1974.

Pardey, Lin and Larry. *Cruising in* Seraffyn. New York: Seven Seas Press, 1976.

Phillips-Birt, Douglas. *Sailing Yacht Design.* London: Adlard Coles, Ltd., 1966.

Robinson, Bill. *Cruising: The Boats and the Places.* New York: W.W. Norton, 1981.

Robinson, Bill (ed.) *The Science of Sailing.* New York: Charles Scribner's Sons, 1961.

Ross, Wallace. *Sail Power.* New York: Alfred A. Knopf, 1974.

Roth, Hal. *After 50,000 Miles.* New York: W.W. Norton, 1977.

Rules for Building and Classifying Reinforced Fiberglass Vessels. New York: American Bureau of Shipping, 1978.

Safety Standards for Small Craft. New York: American Boat & Yacht Council, periodically updated.

Sailboat & Equipment Directory. Boston: United Marine Publishing Co., annual.

Scott, Robert J. *Fiberglass Boat Design and Construction.* Tuckahoe, N.Y.: John de Graff, 1973.

Sleightholme, J.D. *Cruising.* London: Adlard Coles, Ltd., 1979.

Sleightholme, J.D. *Fitting Out.* London: Adlard Coles, Ltd., 1977.

Smith, Hervey Garrett. *The Arts of the Sailor.* New York: Funk & Wagnalls, 1968.

Street, Donald. *The Ocean Sailing Yacht.* New York: W.W. Norton, 1973 (vol. 1), 1978 (vol. 2).

Taylor, Roger. *Good Boats.* Camden, Me.: International Marine Publishing Co., 1977.

Toghill, Jeff. *The Boat Owner's Maintenance Manual.* Tuckahoe, N.Y.: John de Graff, 1973.

Warren, Nigel. *The Outboard Book.* New York: Motor Boating & Sailing Books, 1978.

Wiley, Jack. *Fiberglass Kit Boats.* Camden, Me.: International Marine Publishing Co., 1973.

Wiley, Jack. *Modifying Fiberglass Boats.* Camden, Me.: International Marine Publishing Co., 1975.

Zadig, Ernest A. *The Boatman's Guide to Modern Marine Materials.* New York: Motor Boating & Sailing Books, 1974.

Index